There was no other way to describe it. The man glowed . . .

Zoe raised the binoculars to her eyes and gazed out to the newly arriving guests. A man came into focus. *Good*, Zoe thought, *now let's get a look at him.* Her heart beat a little faster.

Suddenly, inexplicably, an unfamiliar dryness cottoned Zoe's mouth. The man's cocky posture made her think of the pirates who'd hidden their plunder in the island's bays two hundred years before.

She commanded her hands to take the binoculars away from her eyes. But then the man took off his ball cap. And when he lifted his strong-angled face toward the sky, as if he'd missed it, something weird happened.

He harnessed the sunlight.

Avon Books are available at special quantity discounts for bulk purchases for sales promotions, premiums, fund raising or educational use. Special books, or book excerpts, can also be created to fit specific needs.

For information, please call or write:
Special Markets Department, HarperCollins Publishers, Inc., 10 East 53rd Street, New York, NY 10022-5299.
Telephone: (212) 207-7528. Fax: (212) 207-7222.

CHRISTIE RIDGWAY

Wish You Were Here

AVON BOOKS ◆ NEW YORK

This is a work of fiction. Names, characters, places, and incidents either are the product of the author's imagination or are used fictitiously. Any resemblance to actual events, locales, organizations, or persons, living or dead, is entirely coincidental and beyond the intent of either the author or the publisher.

AVON BOOKS, INC.
An Imprint of HarperCollins*Publishers*
10 East 53rd Street
New York, New York 10022-5299

Copyright © 2000 by Christie Ridgway
Inside cover author photo by Christie Ridgway
Published by arrangement with the author
Library of Congress Catalog Card Number: 99-95333
ISBN: 0-380-81255-X
www.harpercollins.com

All rights reserved, which includes the right to reproduce this book or portions thereof in any form whatsoever except as provided by the U.S. Copyright Law. For information address Avon Books, Inc.

First Avon Books Printing: February 2000

AVON TRADEMARK REG. U.S. PAT. OFF. AND IN OTHER COUNTRIES, MARCA REGISTRADA, HECHO EN U.S.A.

Printed in the U.S.A.

WCD   10 9 8 7 6 5 4 3 2 1

If you purchased this book without a cover, you should be aware that this book is stolen property. It was reported as "unsold and destroyed" to the publisher, and neither the author nor the publisher has received any payment for this "stripped book."

For you, Mom.

MILLENNIUM MAN FALLS OFF THE FACE OF THE EARTH!

NASA golden boy, Astronaut Yeager Gates (Commander, USN) was a last-minute no-show on both Jay Leno and David Letterman this week, leading to wild speculation about his condition following a car accident last month.

Officials at NASA scrambled to reassure a worried and adoring American public that Gates, pilot *extraordinaire* and all-around daredevil, will make a full recovery. It's certainly hard to believe that a man who has flown faster than the speed of sound, who has rocketed miles above the earth on the space shuttle, and who is designated to pilot the Millennium program's lunar module next month could be felled by a sweet little grandma on her way to play bingo, but that seems to be the case.

Houston resident Irma Swenson, 78, says she feels terrible about turning her Buick into the path of Gates's Harley Davidson. "I know it's all my fault," she fretted. "But I was late and I had a lucky feeling about B-4."

Gates, often in the company of some of the world's most beautiful women, hasn't been seen in public since a week before the accident, when he accompanied 22-year-old actress Shanna Reynolds to the premiere of her new movie, *Nymphet*. According to sources, Gates left the hospital ten days ago but hasn't made any public appearances since. The brunette and curvaceous Reynolds said, "I sent him a huge teddy bear and like a gallon of chocolate kisses. I just want to know he's okay."

She's not the only one. NASA reports letters and

gifts continue to pour in from around the country and around the world. No doubt why—Gates, dubbed by Leno "Captain America," is the hippest and handsomest of NASA's new breed of astronauts. The icon of America's latest space program, Millennium, he's been a regular on press junkets to fan the flames of enthusiasm for the first mission to the moon in over thirty years.

Rumors are rife that another astronaut will replace Gates on the Millennium I crew, scheduled for lift-off in just weeks, but can another take Gates's place in America's heart?

Don't forget *Celeb!* is always seeking tips. If you spot Commander Yeager Gates or any other celebrity, we want to know! Call us at 1-900-555-0155. (99¢ per minute, average call 5 minutes.)

1

Someone was breathing on Yeager Gates's right arm. The exhalations, cherry-lollipop-sweet, fanned against him in time with the surges of the ferryboat that chugged through the Pacific Ocean toward Abrigo Island. Seated on the aisle, but trapped between his buddy Deke Nielsen and the Breather, Yeager tamped down his irritation, squeezed his eyes shut behind his dark glasses, and pretended to be asleep.

With each choppy bounce of the boat along the waves, cool wind puffed through an open window against his cheek. He could hear the buzz of conversation from the few other passengers, feel the thrum of the ferry's engines against the soles of his running shoes, and smell the sharp tang of saltwater—as well as the sticky aroma of each gust of the Breather's breath.

One row of seats behind him, a woman started speaking excitedly. "There it is! I think I see the island!"

The breathing stopped as small footsteps

scurried away, and the sense of being scrutinized disappeared too. Relieved, Yeager tugged his cap down farther on his head and slumped deeper against the cushioned seat, stretching out his stiff leg before him.

He released a slow sigh. The whole point of this escape from Houston's space community was to avoid prying eyes, even those so obviously child-sized. Screw the hospital's pen-clickers, who claimed withdrawal and avoidance were classic signs of the first stages of grief. He'd be damned if he'd cry about anything. He just plain needed to get away, so he could focus on the healing that would get his life back on track.

The woman behind him was speaking again. "The island's right there. Rising out of the mist. See? The green cliffs, the sandy beach, palm trees." Her voice hushed. "It looks . . . enchanted."

Other voices in the ferry's cabin rose in matching and unignorable excitement, and uneasiness ran down Yeager's spine. When Deke had offered to take him along on the trip, he'd only said Abrigo was the southernmost of the Channel Islands off California's coast. He'd said it was a good place for a man to go underground. But he'd said nothing to warrant the other passengers' eager anticipation.

He'd said nothing about *enchanted*.

Yeager elbowed his friend. "You promised anonymous, Deke. Enchanted doesn't sound like anonymous."

He felt the other man's shrug. "Relax. It's just an illusion. Happens on foggy mornings.

The island suddenly pops up from the haze on the horizon."

The woman behind them was exclaiming again in wonder. "One moment it was misty, and the next it just . . . appeared."

A second voice joined in. "This is my third visit, and it still amazes me. So lush and green against the deep blue ocean. Two hours by ferry, and it's like arriving on another world."

Deke's shoulder nudged Yeager. "See? Just what you wanted, right? A break from reality."

A break from reality. He needed one for damn sure, he thought, thumbing his dark glasses more firmly against his face. A break to get his life together. A break to understand why, though last year he'd hugged fifteen stories of rocket fuel as it shot him into space, he couldn't think past tomorrow without his hands shaking.

He sucked in a gulp of ocean air while deep, deep in his belly a desperate but unnameable emotion rumbled. He didn't want to believe his life would never be the same. Could never be the same.

"You all right?" Deke asked.

"Why shouldn't I be?"

Deke's voice sounded doubtful. "Sure?"

It wasn't so hard to grin. "A-OK."

"Then let me tell you what's ahead. The ferry will take us to the harbor directly adjacent to the village of Haven. Houses, including the one where we'll stay, are mostly on the hillsides surrounding the town."

Yeager's right leg cramped in tension. Village. Houses. "That sounds like a lot of people, Deke," he grumbled. More curious glances. Pity, even.

"I said it was isolated, not deserted," Deke defended himself. "Sure, people live there. Sure, people visit. But most tourists go to Catalina Island. Abrigo is only known because—"

From behind them a little kid's squeaky voice piped up: "It's magic?"

Obviously just as unused to children as Yeager, Deke merely grunted a startled reply.

But the kid's goofy question eased some of Yeager's edginess, and he forced himself to relax, massaging the stiff muscles of his right thigh. Magic, he thought, half amused by the idea. Enchantment. Gee, maybe he could convince the magic island's requisite witch to lift the evil spell he was under.

"Jesus. Magic," Deke muttered under his breath, sounding disgusted. "Do I look like the kind of man who believes in magic? What am I supposed to say to that?"

"You're supposed to say you're not wrong about the island," Yeager replied. An island! His amusement evaporated as tension once again clawed at his leg. A little dab of rock bounded by ocean. Shit. Along with everything else, he'd turn claustrophobic for sure. "You said it's been twenty years since you set foot on the place."

"Believe me," Deke answered. "On Abrigo, twenty years might as well be twenty minutes. Very little changes."

On the ferryboat very little changed too, Yeager suddenly realized.

The Breather was back. Air, smelling sticky and cherry, soughed rhythmically against the sleeve of Yeager's shirt.

He played dead.

But the Breather crowded closer, even as Yeager made himself morgue-still. "I know you," the Breather's squeaky voice said.

The new skin on Yeager's cheek twitched. Know him? *I don't think so.* Unless the kid thought he'd found Frankenstein or some gruesome action figure with torn muscles and a fresh facial scar come to life.

"I seen you on *Sesame Street.*"

Yeager's gut tightened, but he didn't move a finger. Was it possible that the kid had really recognized him? Yeah, six months ago, when his world was still spinning in the right direction, he'd explained to Big Bird that the Man in the Moon was just for fun and the moon was made of rock and dust and not green cheese.

The Breather moved closer still, his cherry breath against Yeager's cheek. A piece of paper and a crayon were shoved into Yeager's hands. Reflexively, he grabbed them.

So much for playing dead.

"Write your name, astro-man!" the Breather commanded.

Astro-man. Yeager thought about denying it. Even took a breath in preparation.

But from the day of his birth, the day his just-widowed air force pilot father wrote "Yeager"—after test pilot Chuck Yeager—on his birth certificate, he'd been raised to fly. Though he and his dad formed more of a two-man air squadron than a family, the nomadic life of an air force brat had suited him as much as controlling a joystick had later satisfied his soul. And the only real order of his father's he'd ever rebelled against was when Yeager chose to become a navy jet jockey instead of an air force one.

A jet jockey. That was who Yeager was. A man who needed nothing more than a place to sleep and a training schedule that included plenty of hours in the air. A flyer, an astronaut.

All right, an astro-man. But Yeager shook his head. Despite the fact that he'd been made, he didn't owe anything to a cherry-breathing, privacy-busting little kid.

The boat bucked forward, and the Breather steadied himself with a hand on Yeager's arm, then spoke again. "You sunged that song. I liked it."

Yeager groaned, bitterness bubbling to the surface. What he'd done for his country! Somehow those Sesame folks had persuaded him to lend his lousy baritone to a duet with that gawky yellow bird. The words hadn't left his brain for weeks, something about every body and every bird needing a place to nest.

"I hate that song," he muttered.

"Huh?"

Yeager opened his mouth to repeat the statement. Louder this time. But then he pictured the Breather standing beside him. He remembered Big Bird's cocked and feathery head. Elmo's bug eyes and rounded orange nose quivering with interest. The passel of Sesame kids who'd looked up at him with stars—and moons—in their eyes.

Sucker.

With a resigned sigh, he flattened the paper against his aching thigh.

Beside him, Deke chuckled. "I've been hearing rumors since the accident. Disappointed women claiming you've turned from playboy to Boy Scout. Now I believe 'em."

Yeager ignored him. He particularly ignored the crack about the disappointed women and turning Boy Scout. He'd deal with that problem later. With reluctant fingers he started scrawling.

Only his first name. Even if the Breather showed it to mommy and daddy, what would "Yeager" mean to them?

No reason to think they'd connect it to Yeager Gates. To the Yeager Gates who had once explored the universe but who now couldn't cross the street on his own.

Especially "Yeager" on a scrap of paper, in crayon, written by a seclusion-seeking man with a recent head injury who was broken, scarred, and—though only temporarily—completely blind.

Just as in fabled Camelot, where King Arthur decreed idyllic weather, the fog didn't dare linger on Abrigo Island. Zoe Cash smiled at her fanciful thought, but still found herself drawn outside her kitchen to the now bright morning.

Light always entranced her. Particularly all
the different kinds of it on her island—the cool
moonlight, the fiery tongues of a beach bonfire, the sparkle of morning sunlight caught in
the last drops of mist on the herbs in her garden.

Even with dozens of things to do today, she
abandoned her mental list to stroll in dreamy
contentment down the path that separated her
home, Haven House, from the cottages used
by the guests at her and her younger sister
Lyssa's bed-and-breakfast. At the garden of
herbs tiered against the hillside, she stopped
to sit on a low wall, stretched her bare legs in
the sunshine, and inhaled a deep breath of
their mingled scents.

Mmm. Warmth and health. She idly plucked
some leaves of a nearby herb and rubbed them
between her fingers. Rosemary for remem-
brance. Then, stretching high, she reached toward an aloe vera plant. Her sister, sometimes
endearingly New Age, insisted Zoe daily treat
a recent and nasty grease burn on her forearm
with the stuff. But catching a glimpse of the
wound, Zoe lowered her arm. It was nearly
healed!

She leaned against the warm earth behind
her. No surprise there, really. Smiling, she let
her eyes drift shut. The island was a healing
place. It had always taken care of her and
Lyssa.

Bong. Bong. Bong. The chimes of Abrigo
Methodist Church rang on the hour from
8 A.M. to 5 P.M. and roused Zoe from her
drowsiness.

Bong. Bong. Bong. She opened her eyes a slit. Soon she would have to get moving. She had a meeting today and new guests arriving. *Bong. Bong. Bong.* Only an hour until—

Bong.

Not an hour! *Now.*

Scolding herself for losing track of the time, Zoe popped up and ran to the house and then through the kitchen to the back hall. A quick right, then she dashed up the stairs of Haven House to the white-railed widow's walk overlooking Abrigo Island's Haven Bay. Braking beside a cushioned patio chair, she slapped her hand against her forehead and spun a quick about-face. "The binoculars," she muttered.

Back down the honey-toned hardwood steps, past the second-floor bedrooms belonging to her and Lyssa, to the first floor. Past tiled kitchen counters with their neat rows of heavy pottery canisters. The only thing on the gleaming dining table was a rustic wooden bowl piled with peaches and Santa Rosa plums. In the living room, a vase of tall and ruffly yellow gladioli, fluffy chintz pillows, and the smell of lemon furniture polish.

But no binoculars anywhere.

"Lyssa!" Zoe yelled. "Lyssa! Have you seen the binoculars?"

Zoe's sister, Lyssa, materialized on the stair landing. Ever since she was a little kid, she'd had this near telepathic ability of being where you wanted her the instant you wanted her there. Her hair was turbanned in a towel, and clad in a thick white bathrobe, she looked rosy and relaxed. The picture of health.

Zoe couldn't help smiling. "You must be feeling well."

Lyssa didn't bother answering. "What are you looking for?"

"The binoculars." Zoe wiggled her eyebrows Groucho-style. "Our new guests are due in on the *Molly Rose*. It docks in a few minutes."

"Then you'll see them person to person in just a few more than that," Lyssa said, ever reasonable.

"Not me. I'm due at a Firetail Festival meeting. I'll need you to check them in, 'kay?" Zoe whirled around and made for the antique armoire in the entryway. "Where did I put the darn things? I thought I had my hands on them this morning."

"You definitely did."

"Hmm?" Zoe paused.

Lyssa was smiling as she plucked at the lapels of her robe. "Right here, Zoe."

Zoe blinked, then looked down. Oops. The compact binoculars hung by their black cord around her neck. "Sheesh!" She took off again up the stairs, touching the reassuring solidity of Lyssa's shoulder as she breezed by. "Thanks."

Back on the widow's walk, Zoe swept the binoculars across the horseshoe-shaped bay. From Haven House's hilly vantage point at one end of the horseshoe, she could see the *Molly Rose* chugging slowly past an anchored armada of pleasure boats toward the ferry landing at the small Haven marina. With a little sigh, she dropped into one of the patio chairs and propped her bare feet on the railing, which was warmed by the early June sun. Deep pink geranium blossoms overflowing the attached flower boxes tickled her toes.

With the *Molly Rose* not yet ready to dock, Zoe lifted the binoculars again to inspect the town of Haven itself. Various-styled houses—Mediterranean villas, clapboard cottages, over-windowed contemporaries—ringed the hillsides above the more level streets of downtown Haven. On Crest Street, on the hill opposite to Haven House, it looked like the Dobeys were getting ready to repaint their blue and white Cape Cod cottage. The garage door was already a deep green. Though the new color was a pretty contrast to the scarlet bougainvillea tumbling over their bank, Zoe wished they'd stick with blue and white. She liked Haven to stay exactly as it was.

She let the binoculars drift down the steep green hillsides to the village itself. Early on Saturday morning, traffic was light. By noon, gas-powered golf carts—the only transportation for tourists besides bikes and taxis—would tootle along the main shopping streets.

Zoe smiled with satisfaction, noticing the bright blue, silver, and crimson Firetail Festival flags hanging from the ornate poles along beachside Del Playa Avenue. Herb Dawson, the chairman of the committee, must have had them hung first thing this morning. The flags—a blue background for the Pacific Ocean, with the silver and red sardine shapes of the firetail

fish—went up every year for the several
weeks preceding the festival itself. They her-
alded the return of the island's talisman and
stayed up until the autumnal equinox, when
the fish left their spawning grounds off
Abrigo.

Haven townspeople, even a few on the festival committee, had made noises about leaving the flags down this year. With marine
biologists questioning the return of the firetail
fish for its annual visit to Abrigo's beaches,
some—many, Zoe admitted to herself—had
wanted to cancel the festival itself. But Zoe
had prevailed.

The firetail would return. They must.

She couldn't even think what would happen
if they didn't. Nothing must change on
Abrigo.

Zoe retrained her binoculars on the ferry
and smiled, imagining her guests aboard the
Molly Rose and their initial glimpse of the island. When she was ten, she'd seen it just that
way for the first time herself, from the upper
deck of a ferryboat. Apprehensive about yet
another move—another bed, another school,
another set of new kid jitters—she'd made the
passage from the mainland straining her eyes
for a look at Abrigo.

At first, when a dark cloud had appeared
on the horizon, her heart had stuttered, and
she'd dug her nails in her palms, terrified by
what seemed to be a bad omen. But then
slowly the cloud dissolved, and behind it, becoming clearer and clearer, materialized the
green cliffs of Abrigo.

It was almost as if she'd wished it there, a piece of green permanence in the fluid blue ocean. And though she'd never been to church she'd prayed. Gripping the ferryboat's railings, she'd prayed to a god with a face as permanent and unchanging as one on Mount Rushmore that she'd get to stay forever on her piece of conjured-up magic.

"Well?" Lyssa strolled onto the widow's walk, now wearing a short-sleeved cotton knit sundress. "Have you glimpsed our new guests?"

Zoe looked over her shoulder, squinting as the sun gleamed against the yellow-blond of her sister's drying hair. It was long again, past her shoulders. Zoe touched the ends of her own layered mass. Hers just didn't seem to go anywhere.

The breeze plastered Lyssa's dress against her body, and Zoe allowed herself a small sigh. While it was wonderful that her sister had regained her lost weight, Zoe still couldn't suppress the small regret that she herself remained as scrawny as ever. Though they had the same blond coloring, Lyssa's voluptuous curves and sleek fall of hair didn't bear an iota of resemblance to her own scrappy physique and cap of short waves.

But the feeling was petty and their differences long ago accepted. "I'm still waiting for the boat to dock," she said to her sister. "Have you seen my sunglasses?"

Lyssa sighed and patted the top of her head.

"Oh." Zoe put her hand up and slid her sunglasses down to cover her eyes. She redirected the binoculars toward Haven's small harbor and couldn't suppress a small bounce of anticipation. "Two men, Lyssa. I can do great things with two."

Her sister sighed. "Do you really think you should get your hopes up, Zoe?"

"You know I'm an optimist. And I get to have them for weeks!"

Lyssa sat down in the chair beside Zoe's. The breeze caught her long hair and lifted it off her shoulders. "I understand you have a reputation to consider, but I'm wondering—"

"Don't say it." Zoe lowered the binoculars and frowned at her sister. "You're the one who is always feeling stuff. Knowing things. Seeing signs and portents, you say. Well, this time *I've* got a feeling."

Tiny lines appeared between Lyssa's brows. "Zoe—"

"The matchmaker of Abrigo Island is back," she insisted. "I've already pegged the women for these guys. Susan and Elisabeth."

Lyssa groaned. "Susan hasn't even been divorced two months—"

"What's that got to do with it?"

"—from the last guy you set her up with."

Zoe turned back to viewing the harbor. "I'm certain she doesn't hold a grudge."

Lyssa touched her forearm. "Of course she doesn't. Nobody blames you, honestly. It's just that your matchmaking hasn't been . . ."

"Go ahead. Say it. Hasn't been one hundred percent successful."

"Zoe! *Nobody* you've ever set up has made it through an entire year of marriage!"

"I got them to the altar, didn't I?"

Lyssa mumbled something.

"What was that?"

"Maybe you shouldn't interfere."

Zoe refused to consider it. "Why else would I live in a small, isolated place if not to interfere? I want people to be happy. Susan and Elisabeth want to be happy. I've already told them these men would be perfect for them."

Lyssa sighed again. "Maybe you could start watching soap operas, like normal people."

Zoe flashed her a grin. "I don't like to watch soap operas. I like to create them."

Lyssa's gaze fixed itself on Zoe's face. "Make a match for yourself, then," she said.

Zoe's grin didn't fade. "Yeah, right." For starters, who would she fix herself up with? She'd grown up beside the few eligible men living on the island and considered them practically brothers. As for getting involved with a temporary visitor, why would she stand in line for heartbreak? She loved the island and had no plans to leave it. "Anyway, we're not talking about me. We're talking about our soon to arrive guests."

Lyssa shook her head. "How do you even know these men are single?"

Zoe snapped her fingers. "The old 'and will your wife be accompanying you?' gambit."

"Oh, Zoe."

"Oh, Lyssa. Don't you want to see people happy?"

"I want to see *you* happy," Lyssa said fervently.

Surprised, Zoe lowered the binoculars

again. She stared at her twenty-three-year-old sister, blond, blue-eyed, healthy. "I have you for company. I have the wonderful island where we grew up. We have this great business. What more could I want?" At one time it was more than she'd dare hope for.

Lyssa was distracted by an oversized blue-black bird that landed on the railing beside her. "Raven," she said.

Lyssa had a thing for the species, which was sacred to the Native American people who had once lived on the island. To Zoe the birds looked beady-eyed and more than a little mean.

This one was training its eerie stare on her. Zoe tried staring back but had to break her gaze. She would have shooed it away if Lyssa hadn't been so partial to the spindly-legged things.

A second bird circled above them, something shiny in its beak. The something dropped into Lyssa's lap just before the bird settled beside the first one. Zoe peered at a gold key glinting against her sister's cotton dress.

"Two," Lyssa said faintly. "Two ravens."

Two! Reminded of her quarry, Zoe grabbed up the binoculars, hoping it wasn't too late. She wanted to get a good look at Haven House's new guests before leaving for the meeting. That way, while committee members yammered on about parking enforcement and parade permits, her subconscious could do its matchmaking stuff, like figuring out which man would be best for Susan, which for Elisabeth.

Of course, Lyssa might have a point about getting her hopes too high. Maybe she shouldn't be so rigid about which women she'd make happy. But she'd match up some lucky ladies with these men, no doubt about it. She had a reputation to protect.

She thought briefly of her six previous failures.

Make that a reputation to recoup.

She'd been waiting for Lyssa to ramble through her usual spiel about Zoe matchmaking because it was romance without the risk, but thankfully she'd desisted this time. They didn't need to go over it again. Given her history over the last few years, Zoe would have been an idiot to willingly serve up her heart. Matchmaking was much safer.

The *Molly Rose* pulled smoothly into its slip as freckle-faced TerriJean from T.J.'s Cartopia jogged to the boat, ready to offer a golf cart shuttle to the new arrivals.

Where were they? A little zing of excitement bubbled through Zoe's bloodstream. The cabin door was flung open. Zoe fiddled with the focus dial to sharpen her view. A man stepped out.

Wide-shouldered and hard-looking, he was fortyish, with close-cropped dark blond hair. *Wonderful*, she thought, ticking one concern off her mental list. Handsome and perfectly eligible.

He stepped aside for a shadow emerging from behind him. *Good*, Zoe thought, *now let's see the other one.* Her heart beat a little faster.

The shadow became a man.

A tall man, younger than the first, probably in his early thirties. Suddenly, inexplicably, an unfamiliar dryness cottoned Zoe's mouth. Maybe it was the mysterious dark glasses he wore. Maybe it was because, as he widened his stance against the mild pitch of the boat's deck, his cocky posture made her think of the pirates who'd hidden their plunder in the island's bays two hundred years before.

Then an ominous chill waved over Zoe's body. She squirmed in her seat, a strange anxiety settling on her. Maybe she needed to get to that important meeting right now.

Not even stopping to examine her sudden and instinctive urgency or why she still couldn't swallow, she commanded her hands to bring the binoculars away from her eyes.

But then the man took off his ball cap. And when he lifted his strong-angled face toward the sky, as if he'd missed it, something weird happened. Very weird.

He harnessed the sunlight.

Snared in the dual lenses of his dark glasses, the sun blazed from his face. Yet it was still reflected off the water too, washing up and over his muscled body and tanned skin, tangling in the golden-brown disorder of his hair.

Zoe held onto the binoculars for dear life, dazzled.

There was no other way to describe it. The man glowed.

Pirate, shmirate.

In her first year at Abrigo Elementary School

they'd studied Greek mythology. The textbook had included an illustration of Apollo driving his golden chariot across the sky. That's who this man reminded her of, the god of the sun, exuding heat and light and undeniable charisma. A being who controlled one of the very forces of the universe.

He shifted, his face turning directly toward Zoe, and she automatically sharpened the binocular's focus. *Whoa.* There was something on that arresting face she'd missed at first—a fresh scar, which ran from the edge of his sunglasses down his lean cheek. So the dazzling man wasn't the perfect Apollo after all.

Either that, or he'd taken one mighty and brutal fall from the sky.

In the breeze his hair fluttered. Her heart did too.

Zoe shrugged away the odd sensation and clamped down on her imagination. Whether he was scarred or not, whether she'd responded so strangely or not, there were still Susan and Elisabeth, she reminded herself firmly. Lucky women. Zoe was glad she'd already spilled her plans to them. She bit her lip, thinking quickly.

The older man—the one who turned so solicitously toward his friend—for Susan. The younger man—

Zoe's heart slid to the frayed hem of her cutoffs.

The younger man sidled closer to his friend. His so solicitous friend. His too solicitous friend, who, as she watched, drew the golden

man's arm through his as they walked slowly
down the deck.

Her shoulders slumped, and she dropped
the binoculars in disappointment. They
bounced against her almost nonexistent
breasts with the uncomfortable weight of an
albatross.

Oh, no. Poor Susan. Poor Elisabeth.

Poor me.

Hope rebounded for an instant. Maybe . . .

God, no.

Face it, even if she had six *successes* beneath
her belt, this was beyond her matchmaking
powers. Because she had the distinct impression that the two single men she had planned
to hook up with Susan and Elisabeth, the two
single men who were to turn around her tar-
nished reputation as someone who could
make love happen, weren't interested in
women at all.

When Zoe returned from another frustrating Firetail
Festival meeting, Lyssa was nowhere to be
found. Just as Zoe was deciding what to do
with herself, from the street outside came a
distinctive and familiar squeal of brakes.
Aware of what the sound denoted, she has-
tened to open the front door.

"Hey, there, Zoe!" Pony-tailed Gunther, in
pith helmet and Postmaster-issued shorts,
wrestled an armful of mail up the porch steps.
Abrigo didn't provide door-to-door mail delivery, but on Mondays and Saturdays Gunther liked to don his preretirement duds and
play postman, saving his immediate neighbors

the necessity of a trip to their post office box. Gunther held out a thick stack of envelopes and a largish box. Puzzled, Zoe frowned. She couldn't remember making any recent mail orders.

"For us?" she asked.

"Must be for a guest," Gunther confirmed, then tripped on the second-to-the-last step, so that Zoe caught the package on the fly.

"Y. Gates," she read off the brown wrapping.

Y. Gates. The older man or the one that . . . glowed? A little shiver slipped down her spine. She pursed her lips and ignored the tickle, instead thanking Gunther and bidding him a quick good-bye before carrying the package and the rest of their mail into the crowded alcove office off the kitchen. There she noted the keys for Ambrosia Cottage and Basil Cottage were gone. Obviously Lyssa had checked in the two men.

Zoe paused for a moment. *Two* cottages for the couple? She hadn't thought a thing about it when the reservations were made.

The bed-and-breakfast consisted of their two-story, white-on-white Victorian house with overstuffed flowerboxes and six similarly styled cottages sitting on the hillside path behind it. Both Ambrosia and Basil had a spacious bedroom and bathroom, a tiny kitchen, and an ocean-view railed patio.

Just this morning Zoe had inspected the mens' assigned cottages. Plumping a deep feather pillow here and placing a welcome basket of oranges and fresh-baked sugar cookies there, she'd imagined the unattached males and just how she'd go about attaching them to two of the single women on the island.

Vacationers were a funny folk. Relaxed, open to new experiences, and often burned out in their normal lives, it took just a word and a nudge to set them on the path to romance.

Sometimes people connected with another guest, occasionally with an Abrigo local. In any case, after six of her nudgees married, Zoe had garnered quite a reputation.

Which lately, with the announcement of the sixth separation, had embarrassingly unraveled.

That's why, no matter how unreasonable, it was hard for a matchmaker like herself not to feel dismayed at the unavailability of Mr. Y. Gates and his pal.

Well, Haven House prided itself on friendliness and service. The least she could do was deliver his mail promptly. She could even mention that they needn't pay for a second king-sized bed when only one would do.

2

A warm, herb-scented breeze blew across Yeager's face. Thirty paces from the front door of his cottage, at the twelve o'clock position, was a sliding glass door that led to a wood-railed patio. He'd stubbed his toe on one leg of a glass-topped table and then jammed a splinter of railing into his thumb before finding the lounge chair he sat in now.

He sucked the blood from the wound in his finger. It served him right for booting out Deke before getting the other man's assistance to fully explore the perimeter of this latest cage. But with nothing to see and nothing to do with himself, the cottage was essentially no different from the ten-by-ten hospital room or the slightly larger confines of his Houston condo.

A man used to constant activity, he couldn't seem to get the hang of just sitting. For God's sake, even sitting had always meant doing. Ensconced in the pilot's seat, cradled in the cockpit of a plane, he felt confident and in control. But dressed in civvies and bat-blind, the only thing he had confidence in now was the uncertainty of his vision . . . and his future.

Gritting his teeth, he mentally sidestepped the sickening feeling and lifted his face to the sky, letting the sun's heat wash over him. He was supposed to keep his healing skin protected, but the scar was nothing to him. He had bigger problems than that—hell, he could be standing in front of a mirror and not even see the damn thing—and the warmth felt too good.

On a day just like this one, he'd taken the controls of a plane on his first solo flight. Smoothly lifting off into the still, hot air, the sky had unrolled before him like a vast blue carpet. He'd walked out into it as if he belonged there. And felt as if he'd found home.

In the hospital, the pen-clickers had assured him he'd fly again. When his eyesight returned, he'd pass the FAA's vision test just like before, no problem. But they'd also stated that the compromise to his health and the risk of re-injury gave him the swift boot out of any military flight program. Including NASA.

Especially NASA.

For the hundredth time, Yeager tried to wrap his mind around the notion. It wouldn't sink in. He was just too numb.

Maybe it was the numbness that explained the Boy Scout thing Deke had alluded to on the ferry. Not that there was anything physically wrong with *that* part of Yeager's anatomy, and not that he was ready to admit it aloud, but the accident had affected something besides his vision.

Since the day he'd come to in the scratchy-sheeted hospital bed, at last not drugged-up enough to mask the fact that he couldn't see, he'd discovered another disquieting truth.

His sexual urges were as absent as his ability to distinguish light from dark. So in addition to waiting for his eyesight to return, he had to wait for his hormones to report back to work too.

Not that he hadn't tried to hurry the process along. Women had been invited to his hospital room and then his Houston condo—admittedly only the few he could trust to keep their mouth shut about his condition. Each one, he knew, was beautiful and certainly skilled enough to bring a dead man back to life.

But he was deader than dead.

He needed a distraction. He needed a purpose. He needed something to effing *do*.

As if he'd yelled the thought aloud, a knock sounded on the front door.

"Mr. Gates?"

At the sound of the strange voice, his gut pitched. Dammit. Had the press found him here already? That was another beast he'd hoped to dodge by retreating to the island. Since the night he'd entered the hospital, they'd been after him. Staked out in the waiting room, cell phones ready to call in a story or a camera crew, reporters had begged any and all visitors on his list to pass along their interview requests.

But he couldn't face the media. He didn't want to answer questions about fumbling about in the dark or losing the most coveted seat in NASA's recent history.

Another knock rattled the door, but Yeager stayed where he was. Maybe if he didn't answer, the intruder would go away.

"Mr. Gates?"

He hesitated. In his long and recently unpleasant experience, anybody looking for a story thought they had the right to call him Yeager. "Who's there?" he called out cautiously.

"Zoe Cash." Even through the door, her voice had a subtly husky quality he wouldn't have noticed when he could see. "I run Haven House."

The other one, the one who had given them the keys, called herself Lyssa Cash. Sisters. By their voices, in their twenties.

"Let yourself in!" he called again, remembering his sore toe. He needed a little more practice in the cottage before he went rushing around.

A click and a spurt of air signaled the opening door. "A package was delivered for you," she said. "Where would you like me to put it?"

Another puff of air moved past him. It crackled with female energy and smelled distinctive and sweet. He detected shampoo and powder. Woman air.

He turned his head toward it, toward her, the fragrance tantalizing.

His mood—for the first time in months—surprisingly lightened.

"Excuse me?" he said, hoping to lure her a little closer.

"A package," she repeated. "The mailman delivered one for you today."

Mail? "Who from?"

Her voice drew nearer and so did her scent. "No return address, but it's postmarked Houston. Do you know someone there?"

Yeah, he thought, his black mood returning. And he hoped the guys at the Space Center had chipped in for a kegger, because being drunk might be the easiest way to spend the next few weeks. Maybe the rest of his life.

She came even nearer. That good scent came nearer too, and Yeager surprised himself again by his acute awareness of it. "Can you bring the package this way?" he asked.

He sensed her movement. The herb-scented breeze brushed across him again, momentarily driving away her unique smell. But then she was close. So close that the air beside him warmed. It seemed to expand around him like a bubble, filling with her fragrance, cocooning him in Woman.

Suddenly, unexpectedly, but like any real man, he got a hard-on.

Startled, he froze. Afraid to upset whatever delicate combination that had restored this bit of normality to his life, he took careful, slow, breaths.

The pull in his groin made the healing muscles in his thigh ache. But Yeager welcomed it, breathing through the twinging pain. In, out. Her soft scent entered his lungs and he went even harder.

Just barely, he resisted the urge to punch his fist in the air and shout *whoop-whoop-whoop*! Instead, he slowly turned his head and smiled in her direction.

Reduced to four senses, he found his hearing was more acute. He picked up her little gasp.

Yeager remained still. He wanted this sensation to linger—he wanted her to linger—and he wasn't sure the best way to go about it. He needed to be friendly, charming even, and his male-to-female skills were so rusty, and his arousal so sudden and so fierce, he wasn't sure he wouldn't scare her when he tried them out.

Afraid of startling her, he spoke softly. "Hi, there."

Damn. She drew back, despite his gentleness, her scent receding a bit as she moved. "Nice to meet you, Mr. Gates," she said, husky but brisk.

"Yeager. Call me Yeager," he said, aware he was still smiling. *Call me forever in your debt, honey. I haven't lost it all!*

"I'll leave your mail right here." Something heavy thumped to the table beside him. Her shoes scuffed against the cement patio as she scurried back a few steps.

No. No. Don't! Yeager straightened a bit, guessing she didn't know he was blind. He guessed she probably thought him some kind of oaf too, a man who wouldn't stand and help a woman with a weighty package. So much for charming her.

"I'll be going, then," she said.

"Wait!" He couldn't lose her scented pres-

ence so soon. Or the good ache of arousal—
especially the arousal. "Could you open it for
me?" He held up his bleeding thumb. Yeah,
he could tell her about his real injury, but he
hated curiosity and pity even more.

"Oh."

Lifting his face in her direction, he tried
smiling her way again.

"Oh. Okay." She shuffled a bit closer. "I
wanted to mention something to you anyway."

He listened to the sound of her opening his
package, imagining slim woman fingers
plucking, stroking, sliding. His head drifted
back against the lounge chair. For the first time
since the accident, the salty-sweet anticipation
of sex coursed through him.

"So where's your, uh, friend?" she said.

"Hmm?" Yeager waded out of his warm
reverie.

"Your friend." There was a funny note to
her voice. "The man you came with."

Annoyance pricked him like another splinter. "Deke? You've met Deke?"

He sensed movement, but she didn't say
anything. *Great*, he thought. He had no idea
whether she'd nodded or shaken her head.
"Deke had an appointment with an attorney,"
he said. "We're here because he inherited
some property."

That stilled her. Her voice registered surprise. "Property? I just assumed you two were
here for . . . pleasure."

Two men on a long pleasure trip? Yeager
frowned. An odd assumption. "Nope. An un-

cle left him some old place on the island."

"Well," Zoe said. He detected the pop of mailing tape and the papery rattle of Styrofoam popcorn. "Shrink wrap, but we're getting somewhere."

He smiled and let his mind drift to her hands again. The tantalizing scratch of feminine nails and the small, soft pads of a woman's fingertips. Just imagining them was making him feel a whole lot better.

"Mr. Gates, about your Deke."

Deke who? he thought absently, then refocused his attention and cleared his throat. "Deke? Now what could you have to say about him?"

"That it's fine here. That the town of Haven, that everyone on Abrigo Island . . . Well, we may be small, but we're very much live and let live."

Live and let live? As he tried to figure that one out, the crackling feather weight of shrink-wrap plastic floated against his thigh, then his foot, on its way to the ground. "What's in the package?" he asked.

Her voice was puzzled. "Some kind of plastic thingie. It's all folded up."

He frowned. "Strange." He frowned deeper. "And what do you mean about live and let live?"

"I mean—" She broke off and began mumbling to herself. "I think it inflates or something. I feel a valve around here."

Yeager couldn't help but think of her hands again, searching for a valve. In a burst of near giddiness, he couldn't help but think of her hands searching for *his* valve. He smiled once more.

Suddenly she was speaking again, her words rushing out. "I mean to say that you and your, um, significant other, Deke, don't have to pretend around here!"

Behind his sunglasses, Yeager blinked. Significant other? He blinked again. *Significant other?*

To cap off that stunner, a *burst* and *whoosh* assaulted his ears.

A shriek rent the air.

A woman fell into his lap.

He accepted Zoe's unexpected descent with the barest of *whoofs*.

For several moments, the woman in his arms didn't move, giving Yeager a much needed opportunity to assimilate the entire event. And now that his brain was catching up with the conversation—you and your significant other Deke!—he wasn't sure who had screamed first, his ego or her.

Zoe suspected her eyes were as wide open as her mouth. Through that particular feature she drew in a desperate breath, the air having been shocked from her lungs when Yeager Gates's package had self-inflated and knocked her into his arms.

Her own arms were wrapped around the package, which she suddenly realized was a full-sized naked rubber woman.

What?

Shocked once again, she jumped from the heat and hardness of her guest's lap. The doll, still in her arms, emitted a delighted squeal, and Zoe batted the thing away.

"Oh, my God." Still not able to make sense of it all, Zoe hightailed it for the door. "Excuse me."

"Wait!" Yeager's voice rose. "Don't leave! What's the matter?"

Seductive smiles, lap landings, and plastic playmates, for a start. But she couldn't face him. Not the man who'd glowed like a god this morning and who just seconds before had burned like a furnace beneath her thighs. Her hand slipped nervously on the brass doorknob and then gained traction. With a dorky "Have a nice day!" she escaped from the cottage and darted down the path to Haven House's back door.

Safe in the kitchen, she slammed the French door behind her and leaned back against it, breathing hard. Lyssa, teapot raised to fill her cup, stared at her.

"What's the matter?" Lyssa asked.

Zoe tried to figure it out. "I brought a package to Yeager Gates's cottage. He invited me in." And then he'd turned her way. Looking like a movie star in his dark glasses, he'd grinned at her and she'd melted like Doris Day under the heat of Rock Hudson's smile.

"And so?" Lyssa prompted.

"Then he asked me to open the package." Her mind flashed back to the moment. Yeager's jaw dropping the instant before the package exploded and she landed in his arms.

His hard arms. His wide chest. That heat from his thighs.

Funny. The Rock Hudson comparison didn't seem quite right.

The house phone rang and Zoe automatically reached for it. "Can I help you?" she asked.

"What the hell was that?"

Yeager. Zoe swallowed, her cheeks already starting to burn again. How had she ended up cuddled against his chest? "Was what?"

"My package. That *thing*."

"W-what do you mean?"

"Listen, Zoe, I can't find the thing, but I know it makes noise."

"It squeals." With the high pitch and delighted tone most women reserved for hot fudge sundaes—though Zoe didn't think that's what the rubber doll was supposed to be pretending to be so happy about.

"Well, it's not squealing any more. What the hell was it?"

She frowned. Nothing was adding up here. "Just a second."

With her free hand, she pulled open the kitchen door and, carrying the cordless phone, trotted down a path, encroaching tendrils from the bushes of orange and gold lantana brushing against her calves. From a lower point of the property she had a view of the back porch of Yeager's cottage. She could even see him, dark glasses intact, sun glinting off his dark gold hair again, the long white cord of his phone stretched across the patio. "Uh, Yeager."

"Yeah?" He sounded impatient and not a little miffed.

"She kind of fell over the railing. If you reach your right hand out, you'll make contact with her foot."

"She? What? Her foot?" But even as he asked the questions, he found the rubber appendage and pulled the inflated dummy over the railing. It floundered on top of the patio table, its head dangling over the edge.

Yeager wore dark glasses.

He had blindly groped for the doll's foot.

Zoe suddenly put the pieces of the puzzle together.

And Zoe suddenly felt as ditzy as the doll looked. "There you go," she said, mortification washing over her.

The man couldn't see! That's why he'd walked off the ferry arm in arm with his friend. It also explained why he'd asked her to stick around and open his package. And when he'd sent that dazzling, let-me-have-you smile her way, he hadn't even seen her face! "Call if you need anything else," she said brightly.

"No! Wait!" From where she stood on the path below she saw his hand still touching the dummy's naked foot. "What the hell is this thing?" he asked.

Zoe didn't answer, deciding instead to move away. But then her last glance caught on the sight of his long thumb slowly brushing over the dummy's rubber instep.

"Zoe?" His thumb stroked down.

Her cheeks burned, but this time not from embarrassment. She stared at his moving hand, frozen by the sight of the wandering thumb. *Go*, she told herself, *back to the kitchen. Hang up the phone. Turn away!*

Her leg muscles bunched in obedience, but then his long fingers wrapped themselves around the doll's shapely ankle to slide up the line of her shin. Zoe's muscles loosened, melted even, and the corresponding skin of her leg prickled. *Silly reaction*! She wanted to rub the sensation away but found herself too mesmerized to move.

His palm cupped her knee—Inflatable Girl's knee—and Zoe's stomach quivered as his fingers edged upward over the rubber thigh. But he skirted the center line, instead slowly tracing the doll's hip and ridiculously tiny Barbie-doll waist.

Okay, now she really should retreat. But not a bit of her responded to the admittedly weak-willed command. Her eyes stayed glued to the masculine fingers running along the feminine shape.

Zoe licked her lips and tamped down a brief surge of guilt. Was it really voyeurism if one of them was vinyl?

His hand was tanned and big, so very male, against the pale rubber dummy. His fingers stroked upward, and the flesh covering Zoe's own ribcage shuddered. She touched herself there, palming the skin as if she could calm her responses.

But her movements stilled and her tongue stuck to the roof of her mouth as Yeager's hand crept upward. Heat washed down her body as his big palm discovered, then covered the double-D ampleness of Inflatable Girl's breast.

"Aah," he said into the phone.

Another wash of heat burned through Zoe. Her nipples hardened.

"You still there?" he asked.

She didn't know if she was. She didn't know who she was. The twenty-seven-year-old Zoe Cash she knew wouldn't spy on a man touching a woman—even an inflatable woman! She wouldn't feel his touch down to her bones . . . and beyond.

It wasn't that she was a prude, as far as she knew. It was just that after very, *very* few and limited high school and college romantic experiences, her life had been rocked by tragedies that took precedence over romance. And it was only three years ago, after Zoe had made a dozen bargains with God, that she and Lyssa had been able to return to Abrigo Island. With Lyssa and their business to nurture, she hadn't felt the need for anyone or anything else.

Especially not the need for this kind of unpredictable, combustible feeling.

"Zoe?" Yeager said.

She swallowed. "Is there, uh, something you wanted to tell me?"

"Besides the fact that I import inflatable dolls?" There was an uneasy laugh in his voice. "I find I need to clear up a little something else, though."

Finally, she found herself backing away toward the kitchen. Nothing was as it should be. Matchmaking, men, her own responses.

Safer to go back to two days ago, to two hours ago even. "Really, I'm sure whatever it is it's none of my business."

"Well, I'm sure it's not too enlightened of me, but I want you to know something."

Watching his large hand resting so casually on the plastic doll, Zoe thought she knew plenty.

But Yeager kept talking. "While I can't see," he said. "I'm delighted to say I *can* have sex."

Zoe squelched the childish urge to hold her hands over her ears. The personal life of a man like him couldn't matter to a woman like her.

"And Dolly here," Yeager continued, "is much closer to my taste than Deke."

Zoe watched her sister clap her hands over her mouth in an ineffectual attempt to stifle her laughter. She frowned at Lyssa, then bent to take a baking sheet of cheese straws out of the oven. "I don't think you're fathoming the depth of my embarrassment here." She'd been trying to explain exactly how she'd made the mistaken assumption about their new guests' sexuality.

Lyssa moved her hands to the pockets of her blue gingham apron and pursed her lips, as if still holding back a smile. "Sorry. It's just that I've met both men, you see. And to think . . ." A giggle escaped.

Zoe let go of her own reluctant smile. She hadn't intended to tell the story on herself, but as they bustled about the kitchen taking care of their daily baking, Lyssa seemed too quiet. Zoe, ever vigilant on her sister's behalf, had decided to entertain her with a recounting of the escapade with the dummy.

But she'd told Lyssa only half the story, climaxing with Zoe and the doll fighting for parking space in Yeager's lap. Water torture wouldn't get her to confess what had happened next. She'd go to her grave with the secret sensations his hands could bring. Hands stroking someone—something else.

With a spatula she lifted each delicate and cheesy pastry twist to the cooling rack.

"So tell me about the other one," Zoe said. "Deke. Anything special about him I should know? There's still room in my mouth for another foot."

From the corner of her eye, Zoe noticed that Lyssa stilled. "Special? I don't know...." Then Lyssa busied herself putting utensils in the dishwasher.

Zoe remembered focusing on the other man through the binoculars. Somewhat shorter than Yeager and older. Fortyish, with a little gray mixed in with his blond hair. "Yeager said he'd inherited some property on the island. Heard anything about that?"

"Property?" Lyssa looked over her shoulder, her blue eyes wide.

"I don't know a thing about it either. Nobody's died lately that I can think of." Zoe opened a cupboard and pulled out another baking sheet.

"No, nobody's died lately," Lyssa agreed. "But perhaps this was just the right time for him—for them to come."

Zoe shrugged. "I guess. You know what these guys do for a living?"

Lyssa turned completely around. "You don't?"

Zoe blinked. "Should I?"

"Yeager Gates? That name doesn't ring any bells?"

Zoe shook her head. "Should it?"

A sigh escaped Lyssa. "Really, Zoe. You have to read something besides the weekly *Island Inquirer*. Things are happening in the world."

"Not in my world," Zoe retorted. "And I like it that way." She ran water over the baking sheet, but then her curiosity got the better of her. "Okay, what gives? He's a presidential candidate?" *One smile and he'd sew up the female vote.*

"He's an astronaut."

"Huh?"

Lyssa shut the dishwasher with a click. "Slated to be the pilot of the expedition to the moon next month."

At Zoe's blank expression, Lyssa sighed again. "In just a few weeks, NASA launches a new phase of the space program, called the Millennium. It's to build the first lunar colony."

An image of the golden and desperately handsome Yeager popped into Zoe's mind. Her heart clenched again. *An astronaut.*

She could see him now, Apollo again, hurtling though the sky on a chariot, controlling rockets instead of the sun. Flying above the earth so high that Abrigo Island was just a speck of eraser dust. And Zoe, a speck on a speck.

The Millennium program.

She swallowed. The Millennium Man.

The knowledge just underscored what she'd already sensed. For goodness sake, she had no business even knowing a man like this, let alone dwelling on his smile, his hands, his touch, or the heat of his body against her backside.

"Oh." Zoe shivered, then blinked, something niggling at her. "And he can do all this blind?"

Lyssa shook her head. "He can't do any of it, Zoe. A couple of months ago he was injured in a motorcycle accident. A car ran into him. It was reported all over the place. *USA Today*, the *Today* show."

Injured. That brutal and mighty fall from the sky. Zoe swallowed hard. "What kind of injuries?"

"It was never said. But De—his friend told me that his head hitting the pavement caused his blindness. Though it's supposed to get better, he won't be piloting the launch."

"Oh," Zoe said again, her heart clenching. She knew about drastic life changes. Not all that long ago fate had scrambled her world too.

She suppressed another shiver, then stiffened her spine. Nothing was going to threaten their peaceful, safe existence on Abrigo Island. Especially not this weird interest she had in Yeager Gates. An Apollo. An astronaut.

Grounded or not, he was still a Millennium Man.

Still trying to regain her equilibrium, that afternoon Zoe found herself in her living room holding the familiar comfort of a dustcloth and Lemon Pledge. She couldn't understand why Yeager Gates wouldn't leave her mind. Good-looking men had visited the island before without having the slightest effect on her.

Her arm poised above a gateleg side table, she sprayed on a thick frosting of furniture polish. Soothed by rubbing in the lemony stuff, she sighed.

Her parents had been killed in a tragic bus accident six years before on one of their rare trips off island. But if Mom and Dad had been alive, certainly they would have pointed out that it was more likely that the pressure of her Firetail Festival responsibilities and not the new guest was making her nervous.

There was no doubt that the firetail nay-sayers had her on edge. And once on edge, it had only taken the unanticipated and unfore-seen nudges of a blind man and bare-naked dummy to disturb her normal equanimity— temporarily.

It just wasn't easy to forget the prediction that the firetail fish wouldn't return. But she couldn't even begin to let her mind go in that direction. Because with the firetail's demise, the island's economy would wither and die too. Haven House and every other business on the island would close, and they'd have to move off island. Away from the magic. Away from the healing.

Away from safety.

Swallowing hard, Zoe clutched her rag and slipped out the back door to shake it free of dust. The air smelled warm and fresh, and she followed her sudden impulse to move closer to the ultra-clear Abrigo waters, her steps taking her down a flagstoned path toward the best view. Below where she stood, a low cliff fell away to the ocean. Fish—sea bass and garibaldi, it was too early in the season for the firetail—moved slowly out of the shadows. Sunlight illuminated the Pacific waters, turning them from gray to greenish blue.

She smiled, cheered by the beautiful sight. The ocean was like a moat for her island home, wrapping itself around all the island's creatures, protecting them, protecting her and Lyssa, keeping them safe from intrusions that might shatter their lives.

Intrusions like Yeager Gates, for example. Lifting her arm, she absentmindedly shook the rag.

Somebody sneezed.

Zoe jumped, automatically swiveling her head up and around in the direction of the sound.

"Good afternoon, Zoe," called Yeager from the shadows of his patio just above her.

Her insides slowly tilted sideways.

Embarrassment would do that to a person, right? After all, the last conversation they'd shared regarded this stranger's sexual preferences.

She swallowed, trying desperately to re-right vital organs. "Afternoon."

"What are you doing?" he asked.

She shrugged, then swallowed, wondering how long politeness dictated she chat. "Admiring my surroundings, I suppose."

"Which part? The rock? The water?"

But Abrigo was so much more than rock and water, and she felt compelled to give him a little history. "This island was a Native American community and a pirate hideaway at one time, I'll have you know. After that, cattle ranches."

"Okay. Rock, water, and cow patties."

Despite her discomfort around him, Zoe had to laugh. "It's been a while since we've had to worry about where we step. My great-grandparents used the land as a ranch, but my parents turned some of the property into a bed-and-breakfast when my sister and I were kids."

"So you're a native islander, then?"

"No. At one time we lived on the mainland. My dad was a salesman." A lousy one. Their family had traveled like nomads as her father moved from one sales position to another, each job and each town a little seedier than the one before. "But once my great-grandparents passed away, Dad and Mom came to the island. Dad was a much better host than he was a salesman."

"Haven House was an instant success?" Yeager asked.

"I don't know about instant, but it didn't take long. Visitors are drawn here for the island's beauty. And once a year to see the special fish that spawn in Abrigo waters. Things really hop then."

He pushed his sunglasses further up his nose. "What's so great about a fish?"

She forgave him his ignorance, because what would an astronaut know about the ocean? "First off, they're beautiful, moonlight silver with frilled, scarlet fans for tails and fins. Second, they spawn here, and only here, and once the bonded pairs have filled their nests, they tend the eggs together. If the nest is threatened, they'll even dance, spinning wildly to distract predators."

Yeager grunted in acknowledgment, and Zoe didn't think he was much impressed. But the firetail's highly unusual behavior had attracted marine biologists and then scuba divers and then other nature lovers who appreciated the uniqueness of the only place in the world they were known to reproduce. But few of the fish had arrived the year before.

The scientists had detected a parasite depleting their number, and that, along with a shift in the Pacific currents caused by the latest El Niño weather pattern, caused the "experts" to predict that last year had been the last year of the firetail.

But Zoe couldn't live with the idea. As a matter of fact, it made her so uncomfortable that she automatically took a step back on the path to Haven House. "I've got to go."

"Do you, Zoe?"

She took another determined step back. "Yes. Wait a minute." Her eyebrows drew together suspiciously. "You knew it was me even before we started talking. How's that?"

For the first time, Yeager moved out of the shadows on the porch and into the sunshine. He slid his hands into the pockets of his jeans and smiled. That sense of heat and light—that dazzle—returned with a vengeance. Deep inside Zoe, something hot and needy sparked to life.

He chuckled, and his voice turned light and teasing. "Wouldn't you like to know?" he said.

Zoe stared at him. He was so broad and tall, and his hair glowed, the sunlight caught in the golden strands. Her gaze traveled down to where his hands were shoved low in his front pockets, drawing her eyes to—

She jerked up her head. Watching him was getting way too habit-forming. At a loss for what to say or do next, she licked her lips and ran a hand through her feathery hair.

"Hot damn," he said inexplicably, a grin breaking over his face. "It's just like before."

At that smile, warmth shot through her bones. She groaned inwardly. It *was* just like before. Stomach-tilting, world-tipping. The man was still affecting her. If she hadn't been a mature woman, she would have stamped a foot in frustration.

"I've got to tell you, Zoe," he said, sounding pleased, "for the first time in a long while I'm feeling much more like myself."

Yet she didn't feel like herself at all! Mature or not, she stamped anyway.

He stilled. "What's that?"

"Nothing," she answered quickly. "I didn't say anything."

He smiled again, obviously still pleased. "The beauty of it is, you don't need to."

She frowned. "What are you talking about?"

"Just something between me and my—a little friend of mine."

Zoe decided she'd spent more than enough time chatting. "I'll leave you to it, then." She took another step back.

His head followed her movement. "Do you have to go so soon?"

"I do," she answered, clutching the dustcloth over her heart. Of course she did. Flowers awaiting arranging. Her great-grandmother's silver coffee service required polishing. As Zoe had stood there, trying to explain her island to the man who so strangely affected her, dust had gathered on shiny surfaces, marring their luster.

Yes, she had to go. Her home needed tending. Her contented way of life needed protecting.

3

After Zoe retreated to the house, Yeager found a chair on the patio again. He sat in it for a couple of hours, growing increasingly bored and then increasingly frustrated by the boredom.

"We need to find a hobby," Yeager said, directing his remark to Dolly, the inflatable woman, whom he'd propped up in the patio chair beside him. She'd been completely quiet since he'd placed her there, and it didn't surprise him. Judging by her contours, she was more tits than talk.

"I'll tell you right now, I'm not going to be able to just sit here day after day." Not when he was used to a full schedule at the Space Center. And he hoped the unfamiliarity of the inactivity also explained why he was starting to converse with plastic bimbos, though for some reason it seemed a step up from talking to himself.

He groaned. "Oh, Dolly, I believe I've hit a new low."

"To balance the abnormal highs of your life, then," Deke said.

Yeager whipped his head toward the sound of the other man's voice. "Jesus, you must walk like a cat."

"Uh-uh."

Yeager could make out the scrape of another patio chair against the pavement.

"I came in while you were talking with your, uh, date," Deke said.

Yeager nodded. "That's right. You haven't had a chance to meet her." He waved his hand between his two companions. "Dolly, Deke. Deke, Dolly."

"I've always considered you resourceful, Yeager, but this . . ."

"Don't credit me. It's from Houston."

"Ah."

Yeager patted Dolly's plastic arm. "Guess they worried we might get lonely."

Deke snorted. "Not me."

"What? Found an interesting woman already?"

Deke snorted again. "Women don't interest me."

"Watch out, buddy," Yeager warned. "I wouldn't say that around here." He knew what Deke meant, though. Badly burned years ago, the older man still appreciated women. But sophisticated women, who played on the same field as Deke. With the same two rules: torrid and temporary.

"What're you talking about?" Deke asked.

Yeager generously gave Deke his laugh for the decade by passing along Zoe's little misconception. "Hey," he finally said to quiet his friend down, "she had the wrong idea about you too."

Deke laughed again. "Yeah, but she hadn't met *me*."

"So you haven't seen her?" What kind of appearance went with Zoe's potent scent? She'd been in his lap so briefly, he'd barely had time to register her small stature and light weight. But the memory quickly washed away his earlier frustration and irritation. "You don't know what she looks like?"

"Nope."

Yeager inhaled the warm and salty island air, hoping to pick up a breath of that particular and unique Zoe scent. What did it matter what she looked like? What mattered was she'd made him feel like a man again.

The thought made him even able to smile in Deke's direction. The other man had recently finished a big project for NASA, and as an independent contractor had scheduled time away to take care of some business on the island that he'd been putting off. Knowing how pressured Yeager was feeling in Houston, Deke had invited Yeager along.

"That can't be a smile." Deke's voice sounded surprised. "What's up with you?"

Yeager shrugged, unwilling to explain what had altered his mood. When he'd been near Zoe—both times—he swore he could feel himself healing with every moment his sexually charged blood rushed through his body.

A moment passed, then Yeager detected movement and heard the thud of Deke's booted feet being propped upon the tabletop.

"Lucky fluke that we came here this week," Deke said, apparently giving up on an explanation for Yeager's good mood. "According to the attorney, part of the roof on my uncle's old house collapsed Thursday."

Another breath of island air washed over Yeager's face, and he settled further into his chair. "Yeah," he agreed absently. "A fluke."

Deke rattled on about his meeting with the lawyer, and Yeager listened with half an ear until his own words suddenly registered. A fluke! God, what if his reaction to Zoe had been just that, some short-lived, crazy fluke? And here he was feeling all optimistic and manly when it was really just another of those cosmic practical jokes pulled on him lately?

He rubbed his hand over his scarred cheek and tried stilling his almost panic by taking a deep breath. God knew he had more important problems than sex, but crazy as it sounded, he just knew it was the first step toward restoring his vision. And from there, the normal course of his life.

The *thwut-thwut-thwut* of a bird's wings passed overhead, and his anxiety refused to dissipate. He needed to be certain his sex drive was back. He needed to get close to her. He needed to smell Zoe one more time and see what happened.

Or didn't happen.

He refused to consider that possibility. This time, when the sexual arousal made another grab for him, he was going to stick by her. She might not like it, but hell, he'd charm the pants off her if he had to.

He nearly laughed at the stupid but too appropriate pun and was astonished at just how easy it was. Just thinking about the woman eased him somehow.

Pushing back his chair, Yeager interrupted Deke's inventory of his inherited home's needed repairs. "Didn't that other one, Lyssa, say they served something down at the house in the late afternoon?"

He could tell that Deke wasn't moving. "I have a couple of six packs in the refrigerator in my cottage." There was unfamiliar tension in Deke's voice. "What they have to offer down there . . . It will be too young and sweet for me."

"Young and sweet?" Yeager stood and dragged his buddy up by the arm. He wasn't going to let Deke stop him from going after Zoe. "What are you talking about? It'll be aged wine and caviar."

And, Yeager hoped, something else just as savory. He'd always been good with women, that was certain. And he was just as sure that a sexual flirtation—or just plain sex, if he could persuade Zoe to participate—was going to make him whole.

At Haven House's "tea time," in the spacious living room, the guests from Rosemary Cottage and Wisteria Cottage were enjoying aperitifs and finger foods. Tidying the kitchen, Zoe began to think she'd shucked the hostessing duties onto Lyssa for nothing. She'd wanted to avoid further contact with Yeager, even though it was she who usually served and chatted with their guests while Lyssa did kitchen duty. The habit had started years ago, when Lyssa was self-conscious about her near baldness, her hair just beginning to grow.

But now it appeared Zoe's precautions were unnecessary. Their two newest guests weren't going to show.

But then other voices suddenly sounded. Lyssa's, soft and sweet, performing introductions. A deeper one, presumably Deke's, then Yeager's, brushing across Zoe's nerves like a swatch of dark cashmere. Her hand squeezed the dishrag, then relaxed.

Kitchen duties needed to be performed, she reminded herself, wiping down the gleaming stove once again. She had a perfectly good reason for hiding—*for staying*—in here.

The countertop closest to the swinging kitchen door was particularly sticky. Zoe rewet her cloth and worked at the white tile diligently, sparing just a quick glance through the crack in the door. If she hunched her shoulders and squinted one eye, she had a reasonable view across the expanse of the dining table into the living room.

Against one custard-colored wall sat Great-Grandma Cash's long walnut sideboard. Lyssa had moved to one end a fluted vase filled with white statice and Shasta daisies and spread over the other a delicate, crocheted piece of Great-Grandma's handwork. Atop this table-cloth sat the wines, goblets, and a large platter of crudités.

One of the guests—they were teachers from Arizona—was refilling her glass there, while others gathered near the matching blue-and-white chintz sofas and the coffee table that held the rest of the hors d'oeuvres.

Yeager stood apart from them and beside the tiled fireplace, wearing soft-looking jeans, a knit shirt, and his dark glasses. Zoe's mouth went dry as Death Valley when he smiled as Lyssa gently touched his arm to direct him to a chair. Zoe could almost feel the hard heat of his forearm herself. His lips curved again, and she wondered how Lyssa could stand to be so close to him. Even from here his smile set her flesh on fire, like the first blast from a hot shower.

Then Lyssa turned toward the kitchen. Zoe jerked back from her peeping stance and retreated to the center butcher block island, working the crick out of her neck as she lined up the regiment of spice jars into perfect soldier rows.

The kitchen door squeaked as it swung open. Lyssa's face looked rosy, almost luminous, and Zoe guessed it was a reaction to Yeager's golden charisma. She shook her head ruefully. No doubt about it, the man had something. "Everything going okay?"

Lyssa bustled toward the refrigerator. "They want microbrewed beers. Deke and Yeager."

From the stand-alone freezer, Zoe grabbed a couple of thick glass beer mugs she had chilling. "You're handling everyone perfectly."

Lyssa shot her a glance. "How do you know?"

Zoe decided against admitting she'd
peeked. "Because you're beautiful and charming, and I'm—"

"Full of it." Lyssa grinned. "I saw your eye-
ball glued to the door crack."

That was the disadvantage of having such a
close relationship with a sister. She knew all
your bad habits.

Lyssa's grin widened. "He's asking for you,
you know."

Zoe's heart flew into her throat. She swallowed it back down. "Yeah?" she said casually. "And what did you say?"

"I said you were busy."

That was the benefit of having such a close
relationship with a sister. She covered for you
when necessary. "You're the best."

With the beers and frosty mugs piled on a
tray, Lyssa pushed against the kitchen door.
"You deserve it."

Zoe returned to that pesky countertop.
Hunch-shouldered and squinty-eyed again,
she could see that with the exception of
Yeager, the arrangement of the people in the
living room had shifted. Everyone was sitting
now, and the only one facing the kitchen door
was Yeager.

Blind Yeager.

Her nasty and heretofore controllable vo-
yeuristic streak showed itself again. If she
crept out of the kitchen, she could sit in the
side chair in the corner of the dining room,
partly obscured by a tall ficus. The only one
who could possibly see her was Yeager.

And he couldn't see.

She didn't bother coming up with a rationale for her behavior. She didn't try explaining to herself why she wanted to be closer to a temporary man she had an unprecedented attraction to. Instead, she quietly exited the kitchen—gritting her teeth at the door's squeak—and dashed across the plush Oriental carpet to sink into her designated peeping-chair.

Between the glossy green leaves of the plant, she watched Yeager. A golden-brown lock of hair fell over his forehead. He impatiently pushed it back, and she stared at his long fingers again, remembering them stroking, smoothing, rubbing. . . . Goose bumps prickling her skin, she jerked her gaze away, forcing her head around to look out the dining room's French doors instead.

The familiar postcard view of tiny Haven Harbor soothed her. A boat, its white sail as fat with wind as a pillow with feathers, smoothly swung toward its home berth. She sighed.

"Gotcha."

Her heartbeat zoomed to rocket speed. Her head jerked up to find Yeager standing right in front of her, pinning her into the corner. "What?"

"I was hoping to find you," he said, another one of those disarming smiles crossing his face.

She popped out of the chair. "I'm busy," she answered, remembering Lyssa's excuse. "I must uh . . . uh . . ." With a quick twist of her hips, she got herself around him.

He turned, following her movement. "Where are you going?"

She headed quickly for the squeaky door. "I've got to do something in the kitchen."

"I'm hard to get rid of," he said, the hint of a smile still on his face. "I've got this thing for your scent, you know. I'm chasing it."

She looked over her shoulder. Indeed, he had moved in her direction. But between him and her was the imposing and painfully solid dining room table, polished to a gleam. "Did you need to speak to me for some reason?"

He shrugged. "I'd like you to get to know me better. I'd like to get to know you better. I'm . . . curious."

She could imagine what about. How she could have been so mixed up about him and his, uh, preferences. How she could have embarrassed herself by landing in his lap. Why just looking at him made her thighs tremble and her heart bobble. If she dodged into the kitchen right this instant, she could probably dodge every one of those issues.

But if he dodged after her, he'd end up with one heck of a table bruise.

She looked at the kitchen door, the dining room table, the half-smiling man unaware of the painful obstacle.

Sighing, she made herself return to him. *Really, Mom*, she said to her mother's mannerly memory, *sometimes being a nice person is the pits*.

Zoe grasped his arm, not thinking about the feel of his skin against her palm, and pulled it through hers. "Come on," she said, not bothering to disguise her grouchiness.

He didn't bother disguising his triumphant smile either, darn him.

Seeing Zoe pop out of hiding had given Lyssa permission to leave the afternoon party and follow the one guest who'd slipped away early. It took only a few minutes to reach the outskirts of the town of Haven. Once the hills became more rugged, the paved streets and houses ended. Then only dirt tracks ran amongst the manzanita and island oak and ironwood trees.

One track was wider than most, wide enough for a car to pass, and Lyssa followed a set of footprints in the thick dust. The trail led over the top of a hill, down through a shallow canyon, then up again.

As Lyssa strode along the steep path, she thrust her hand in the pocket of her cotton sundress, pressing the key she found there against the flesh of her palm as if to make a lifelong impression.

It was after 6 P.M., and on this isolated hillside, with its view of tiny Lover's Cove, the afternoon wind had died. The sun wouldn't set for another hour, plenty of time for her to confront Deke before darkness.

Lyssa knew where to find him, though he'd studiously avoided her and any question she'd directed his way this afternoon. But he'd told the teachers vacationing in Wisteria Cottage that he was here because of the old McCarren house, and she'd seen him head off in that direction the minute he'd finished his beer.

Just before the house came into view, the

track widened, and Lyssa paused to catch her
breath. Her heart pounded, banging as rhythmically as a tribal drumbeat against her breast-
bone. The exercise was nothing to her, but this
meeting with Deke—their first, private meeting—meant everything.

To her right, ravens rustled in a spreading
white lilac surrounded by a guard of prickly
pear cactus. One black bird broke from the
brush and with one of its hoarse croaks rose
skyward, maybe the very raven that had
dropped the key she now held. The intelligent
and curious birds loved shiny things, shells,
beads, and such, but this had been different.
When the key fell into her lap this morning, it
had felt hot to the touch, almost burning.

Zoe would laugh and say it was because of
the warm morning sun, but Lyssa knew it was
something more. When her sister had pulled
off the binoculars and rushed away in a huff,
Lyssa had picked them up herself to train
them on the two men.

And she'd felt that certain heat again—not
from the key, but from the very center of her
heart—when the lenses focused on Deke Nielsen.

Then just a few minutes later, when they'd
met face to face during check-in, she was certain he'd felt that heat instantly too. But he'd
done everything to avoid her touch. His gaze
had cut away instead of meeting hers, and yet
she'd caught him staring when she'd suddenly
turned.

Poor man. She was going to have to make
it clear he didn't stand a chance.

With a last deep breath she resumed her walk, quickly striding up the path. If there was one thing she didn't like, it was wasted time.

The last few years had demanded every ounce of her strength, patience, and optimism. Well, she'd discovered strength begot strength and optimism begot optimism, but she was flat-out empty of patience.

For over five years she'd wondered if she'd ever feel truly alive again. And now that she did, she intended to grab with both hands for the sensation. And for the man who made her feel that way.

The McCarren place sat in a clearing cut into the shrub-covered hillside. Queen Anne style, the house was three lacy yet peeling tiers set on a raised foundation of native stones and shells. At one point it must have been as fanciful and fancy as the wedding cake she'd dreamed of as a little girl, but it had stood empty and neglected for as long as Lyssa could remember.

On the scrubby crabgrass at the bottom of the porch steps she tapped the toes of her sandals to shake the dust from her feet. A breeze tickled the hem of Lyssa's dress and sent a scattering of brown leaves scurrying like mice down the wooden steps.

Shading her eyes against the setting sun, she looked up, searching for a sign of Deke in or about the place.

Behind her, a surly voice spoke. "What are you doing here?"

She jumped, startled by the unabashedly cold welcome. Inhaling a calming breath,

Lyssa paused a moment before turning around.

"I said, what are you doing here?"

Lyssa turned, gulped. Deke all right, wearing jeans and hiking boots and nothing else. Behind him she could see the workshirt he'd been wearing thrown over some encroaching chaparral. He held a pair of shiny shrubloppers in one hand. She tried speaking, but it was hard to think of a sparkling opening salvo with him standing so close. Deke's body was lean and hard, and a faint sheen of sweat glistened on his chest. He shifted, and his muscles did too, bunching then stretching with raw male power. Lyssa's womb clenched, released, clenched, and her legs melted.

"Damn," Deke muttered, reaching for her.

She didn't know why, but she didn't protest as he hauled her to the porch steps. Commanding and certain, his hand felt like heaven clamped around her upper arm.

He pushed her to sit on the steps. "You look like you're about to faint." His fingers wrapped in the strands of her hair and pushed. "Put your head between your knees."

He was crazy if he thought she'd spend their first moments together in such an undignified position. "I'm not going to faint," she protested, slightly offended. She'd never fainted, not even through any of the medical tests or treatments.

He immediately released her hair and stepped back. The loppers were still in one hand, and he looked down at them as if he couldn't remember how or why they were

there. He looked back up. "What are you doing here, little girl?"

Little girl. Lyssa had to hold back a smile.
She'd wondered how he was going to play this
moment. Apparently he was going to start
with the age card. "I'm twenty-three."

He didn't even blink. "So what are you doing here?"

Lyssa hesitated. For all her certainty about
Deke himself, she didn't have much of an idea
of how to go about approaching him. At the
time when most girls had been mastering
male-female relationships, she'd been honing
more basic survival skills. "I thought we could
. . . talk," she said.

Lame.

His expression agreed with her. "I'm too
busy to talk." He turned and started to walk
away.

"You could tell me about yourself."

He didn't pause.

"You could tell me about the house."

Though his feet stopped moving, he kept his
back to her. His shoulders were wide and
tanned, the shoulder blades strongly angled.
That deep, female pulsing started again, making her insides warm and melty.

"The house," he said. "I inherited it from
my great-uncle. I'm here to get it back into
shape."

"And then?"

He shrugged, then turned her way. "I con-
sult for NASA. I'll go back to Houston or the
next place they need me."

She smiled brightly. "Four whole sentences! See, that wasn't so hard."

His eyes narrowed. They were light gray and right now looked icy. "What are you trying to do?"

Lyssa squirmed. *What am I trying to do?* She thought of her life before that fateful day, when she was just seventeen. Before that day had she known the way to go about this? How did a female send out those signals to let a male know she was interested in him? She nervously smoothed her hand through her hair and noticed he followed the movement with his eyes.

Good. He liked her hair. She liked it too, because the long cornsilk-colored mass symbolized health and normality. Without thinking, she wet her lips. That got to him too. He shifted and once again cut his gaze away.

Lyssa decided there was too much distance between them. She stood and took a few steps toward Deke.

He took several steps back.

She took another step forward. He took another step back. Oh, it would've been laughable if it hadn't been such a silly waste of time and energy! "Do we really have to tango?" she said, exasperated.

For a moment she thought he might crack a smile. But then his jaw tightened. "Not if you'll just go back home."

He didn't say them, but the words were there. *Little girl.*

She sighed. She wasn't a child, and a lot more than twenty-three years had gone through this body. Though she didn't look old, Lyssa knew she was wise in the ways of living. She'd beaten leukemia, hadn't she? She'd beaten death.

"Why don't you want me here?" she asked. *Why are you retreating from what we both feel?*

He hefted the loppers and started walking toward the holly that grew up and around the front steps. "I'm forty-three."

"Lyssa," she said. "Say, 'I'm forty-three, *Lyssa*.' " She needed him to say her name. To acknowledge her in that small way.

His eyes went icier still. "I'm forty-three years old. I don't want or need a playmate."

Finally. At least he wasn't pretending any longer that he didn't know what this was about. What they were about.

"I'm not playing," Lyssa said.

He ignored her and turned away to attack the shrubbery. In minutes, long branches started falling against him and around him, and he ignored them too, sweat pouring from his back. On his arms scratches from the holly thorns oozed drops of blood.

Stunned, she stared. "What are you doing?"

More branches fell. From his shoulder blood trailed like an unending tear.

"Stop!" Lyssa couldn't stand seeing him bleed. But he continued working furiously. "I said stop!"

But he hung on, cutting, sweating, dripping blood.

Frustrated, she raised her voice even louder. "Okay, okay! I get it! I'll go."

The loppers dropped to his side. "What a good idea," Deke said calmly.

Great, Lyssa thought, her heart suddenly heavy in her chest. *The man I'm destined to spend the rest of my life with can't stand the sight of me.*

Turning toward the path home, she started walking and shoved her hands in the pockets of her dress. The key. It nestled in her palm, feeling solid and hot. Lyssa smiled, recognizing what it meant. Zoe would say it was merely the transference of Lyssa's own body heat, but she knew different. It meant Deke was hers.

So having him wouldn't be easy. No one ever accused her of being a quitter. Heart buoyant once more, she paused to look over her shoulder.

He was trimming the holly again, though more slowly this time. She stilled. Taking extra care, he was cutting around something.

At the base of the house's steps, a sign emerged from the mass of green as he worked. Then he moved to the opposite side of the steps, cutting carefully there too. Another sign was revealed. The holly must have protected them from the elements, because the black words on the bleached scraps of wood were still quite plain to see: NO WOMEN ALLOWED.

Zoe busied herself around the kitchen, putting away the remains of the afternoon's repast. Thank heavens people liked her cooking. Once she'd led Yeager to the kitchen, only seconds passed before the rest of the party, with the exception of Deke and Lyssa, had moved in to join them.

Glad for the company, she'd refilled wine goblets and the bowl of spinach dip, then bribed the other guests to stay even longer with hot hors d'oeuvres made by broiling basil pesto on top of baguette slices. With the buffer of the others between them, she wasn't the sole recipient of Yeager's devastating charm.

But everyone else was gone now, and she didn't know quite how to handle it—to handle him. She dared a quick peek at him, sprawled in a chair beside her kitchen table, just to see if she could tell what he was thinking. Was he preparing to leave too? Or gearing up to sling another devastating round of charm her way? But a peek was way too brief.

Then she stopped, smiling at herself. How many times would it take her to remember? She could look as long as she wanted, goose! The man couldn't see. Crossing her arms over her chest, she stepped back to study him dispassionately. Wide-set shoulders, strong, tanned neck. That attractive, angularly planed face, with its long scar pointing toward a mouth both finely etched and sensually full.

Dispassion lasted, oh, maybe two seconds. Then her heart started a slow, insistent thud against her chest, and her blood moved slowly too, like honey, inching through her veins. Zoe realized she'd never looked at a man like this, really looked and admired. A trembling weakness invaded her upper thighs, and her stomach seemed to float upward, bumping gently against her heart. Her mouth went dry.

"What?" he said, his head suddenly turning

in her direction. The overhead light glinted in the dark lenses of his glasses.

She jumped, her eyes widening. Caught! But how did he know? "What, what?" she tried.

The corners of his lips turned up. "Why are you looking at me?"

She frowned, shifting uncomfortably on her feet. "Are you sure you can't see? It seems too easy for you to tell where I am and what I'm doing."

His mouth widened into a full smile. Zoe ignored the punch it poked at her still thudding heart. "I told you. I can smell you."

"That might tell you where I am, but how'd you know I was looking at you?"

He shrugged. "You might call this arrogance, but . . ."

Way too easy to see where this was going. "But around you women are always looking?" she asked sarcastically. The best defense was a good offense, she reminded herself, barely resisting the urge to throw a potholder at him.

He had the gall to appear hurt. "No. What I was going to say was that I'm pretty adept at reading people—reading you. You move around all the time unless something puzzles you."

"All this on such a brief acquaintance?"

He shrugged again. "When you can't see, other senses kick in."

She narrowed her eyes suspiciously. "I'm still doubting the blindness thing."

His voice quieted. "Yeah? Well, I keep thinking this is all a long nightmare myself. But the truth is, I was in a motorcycle accident.

When my head bounced off the street, it caused a hemorrhage that's affecting my eyesight. When the blood clears, so will my vision."

Zoe felt bad about the potholder impulse. "But not in time for the first Millennium launch."

He ran a hand slowly through his dark gold hair. "But not in time for the first Millennium launch."

"Maybe the next one, though?" Zoe asked.

His head turned away. "Right."

Still, Zoe's heart contracted painfully. It didn't seem fair that Apollo was even temporarily grounded. Eager to redirect the subject and her dangerously soft heart, she grabbed a plate of leftover cheese straws and plunked them on the kitchen table beside him.

"Something to eat?" she asked brightly. "You didn't have anything before."

He turned toward her again, and his grin returned with that same devastating power. She felt another rise of heat in her belly. It traveled upward, outward, to her thighs and her breasts. Even her fingers and toes tingled.

"Or we can talk," he said. "I'm going to be here on Abrigo for some time." There was a sexual edge to his voice that even inexperienced Zoe couldn't fail to recognize. "I'd like to know more about you. We could get . . . acquainted."

Acquainted? Zoe stepped back, that burr in his voice turning that tingle in her body to an out-and-out fizz. Oh, there was a bad idea. Any more acquainted with him and she just might go into lust overload! For the absolutely wrong kind of man.

"You can eat," she countered, taking a firm hold of herself and the conversation. There would be no getting acqainted. She'd be much safer if he didn't come any closer to knowing her. An emotional distance and his blindness gave her a little cocoon of safety that she liked huddling within, thank you very much.

Reaching out, she pushed the cheese straw plate closer to him, nudging it against his hand, which rested on the table. "Try one of these."

He felt for a twist. "This takes a lot of trust, you know. I don't like to eat in front of other people. Half the time my fork goes in my milk instead of my mashed potatoes."

Trust. She turned away from him to slip the rest of the leftovers into the refrigerator. That was the real deal. How could she trust herself around a man like him? He was an adventurer, an explorer, a man of the world—no, make that a man of the galaxy. Everything she wasn't.

In addition to that, her hair-trigger reaction to him was something she was completely unprepared to handle.

"And I'm always afraid I'm going to feed my ear instead of my mouth," he said.

Despite herself, the image made her laugh. Shaking her head, she looked over at him. He reached for another cheese straw and straightened his leg to push out the chair beside him with his foot.

"C'mon, Zoe. Take a break."

She shouldn't risk it. But then she looked at him again and saw that a little cheesy crumb was trembling on the edge of his lips. Despite herself, she couldn't help but smile. He was charming. Maybe she just needed to get comfortable around him.

With another smile and a shake of her head, she sat down. How hard could it be to handle one guy who needed a second pair of eyes and a napkin? And wasn't meeting the requests of guests the hallmark of a good innkeeper?

"So tell me about yourself, Zoe." He smiled at her, the edge of his seductiveness still blunted by the stubborn cheese straw crumb.

What could she tell him? What would satisfy him but be impersonal enough at the same time? "Shalimar," she said suddenly. He'd wanted to know about her scent, right? She had a bottle of the stuff around somewhere. She smiled back at him, pleased with her oblique answer.

"Ah. Shalimar perfume." It bugged her that he was so casually familiar with a brand of women's fragrance. But he shook his head. "I don't think your scent comes from perfume, though. And anyway, I was thinking about something . . ."

She narrowed her eyes. "Something?"

"I was thinking about something . . . more." He smiled again.

Zoe found herself thinking about that crumb. It was starting to bug her now, focusing way too much of her attention on his mouth. His very male, very sexy mouth. "More what?" she responded absently.

If he'd been a woman friend, she'd have just come right out with it and mentioned the little dab of cheese straw. But he was a man, and one who'd just admitted he was leery about eating in front of others.

"More . . . personal," Yeager said.

If she'd been giving a party, she would have tried catching the eye of the guest and brushing her hand across her own mouth. On reflex, just about anybody would mimic the movement.

Anybody who could see, of course.

Leaning toward him, she attempted a little experiment. Instead of breathing out normally, she tried pursing her lips and blowing in the direction of his lips. The obstinate thing didn't budge.

"More personal," Yeager prompted again.

She narrowed her eyes. By rights, he should look silly with the darn thing pressed against his skin like a . . . like a kiss. She jerked back. *Where did that treacherous thought come from?*

"Come on, Zoe. Give me something to go with the Shalimar," Yeager said. "A description."

That distracted her from the crumb. A description the man wanted. She rolled her eyes. Really, she didn't have to be a femme fatale to know that sometimes men were just too predictable.

She crossed her arms over her chest. This was going to be easy after all. "Tell me something about you first. Something"—just for the heck of it she tried blowing the crumb again,

so the last word came out all puffy and sexy—
"personal."

He smiled, crumb intact, as if pleased by her
flirtatious rejoinder. "You name it."

"What's your fantasy?" she asked. "Long,
long legs?" she continued, taking a guess.
"Long brunette hair, big brown eyes, big . . .
everything else?"

Like a dog at a water dish, he lapped it up.
"Yes, yes, yes . . . yes."

She sat back in her seat. "I look nothing like
that."

He smiled, as if he didn't realize the joke
was on him. "Heck, that's old news."

"It is?"

"Haven't I had you in my lap?"

Oh, she knew that had to come up some
time. She steeled herself for more embarrassment.

"But let me try something here. Something
a guy in rehab taught me."

Surprised he was off the lap incident so
soon, she narrowed her eyes. "What?"

"Give me your hand."

"Why?"

"Not because I want to nibble on your fingers." He looked disgusted. "Come on." He
put out his palm.

Still suspicious, she tentatively placed her
hand in his.

Warm. Hard. Palm abraded palm, just for a
rough-sweet instant, before he turned it over.
His big hand cradled hers, and the fingers of
his other hand started to lightly trace patterns
over her sensitive skin. His fingertips were

rough too, and she grimaced as she fought the shiver shimmying up her arm.

"This guy swore he could 'see' a woman by touching her palm," Yeager said.

Zoe frowned. "This guy had quite a scam going," she grumbled.

His touch trailed her skin with fire. Sparks jumped from nerve ending to nerve ending, hot pulses telegraphing sex . . . sex . . . sex.

Helpless and fighting shivers again, Zoe stared into the lenses of his dark glasses, trying to understand what made her want his touch so much, what made him want to touch her like this. But she only saw her own reflection.

"I think I'm getting a picture here." Yeager raised his face to the ceiling, as if to concentrate better. "Definitely a picture, though it's a little fuzzy."

Suddenly, Zoe noticed his cheese crumb was gone. Her breath fluttered out in a little panic. That crumb was her safety net! The cozy corral that would keep all these peculiar, womanly, dangerous feelings confined!

She tugged at her hand, but he didn't let her loose. "Hold on," he said. "It's coming into focus."

His confident touch skated over the surface of her palm. "Yes," he said. "Quite clear."

Quite clearly she was locked into place. She tried breathing deeply, tried not thinking of his warm fingers and all the heated places where she wished they'd wander.

"A young woman, mid-twenties. Short and slender."

It didn't matter that he'd figured that out, Zoe assured herself quickly. Knowing her age and her build wasn't knowing her. It wasn't anything she cared about keeping from him.

His fingers were still moving, stroking little circles against her skin. The sparks shot across her flesh again.

"Short, curly blond hair and wide blue eyes."

"Hey!"

"Okay, okay, the teachers in the other cottage told me that part." He grinned.

She closed her eyes, refusing to let his smile turn her insides to ooze. Blond and blue-eyed. Who cared? That was a zillion women.

"Bright, sunshiny type of gal." Then his fingertips abruptly stilled. "But you're hiding something."

Zoe's heart froze and threatened to stop her breathing. This wasn't good.

"Something buried so deep you think I'll never find it."

Her fingers chilled. Not good at all.

"But I will, Zoe," he said. "I will."

Then his free hand clapped onto hers. Three of his long fingers pressed against the pulse point at her wrist. Her heart restarted, and her pulse beat wildly against her skin, his words, his touch scaring her, sensitizing her.

This golden man who couldn't see but who had made a lucky guess or who had found some eerie window into her soul sandwiched her, trapped her, holding her within his male heat and hardness.

Heat rushed over her skin, and her breath blew out in a nervous stutter. Because most frightening of all was the fact that she didn't want to get away.

4

The next morning Zoe prepared breakfast for her guests—Belgian waffles, fresh strawberries, just-whipped cream, and slivered pecans—then quickly gathered her sweatshirt and keys for a speedy getaway. Lyssa didn't say a word when Zoe claimed Firetail Festival duties and left the house before the first guest found his way to breakfast.

Anyway, Zoe wasn't fibbing about the festival duties. On her moped, she zoomed to the corner of Del Sol Avenue and Cabrillo Street, where she picked up a thousand bright blue Firetail Festival flyers from the Haven Copy Hut. Next she delivered stacks of them to the busiest shops on Del Playa and Del Sol Avenues, setting them beside the cash registers, so that tourists and community members would have easy access to the schedule for the two-day festival.

The last stack went to the Shear Terror Styling Salon, owned and operated by one of Zoe's closest friends, Marlene. Shear Terror came by its name from the claim Marlene made that islanders were like a primitive people. They had a subconscious fear that lopping their hair meant losing part of their soul. She said everybody just felt better if she flat-out acknowledged it.

As far as Zoe recalled, that soul-losing thing really had something to do with getting one's photograph taken, and Terror was a better name for Dr. Tom's dental clinic, but she'd never debated the point with Marlene. And really, after considering the caterwauling that accompanied little Benny Malone's first haircut, maybe Marlene was right.

As Zoe laid the flyers on the counter, Marlene closed the register's cash drawer with her elbow, said good-bye to her latest customer, then cocked her head to improve her upside down view of the papers.

"The schedule's out already?" she asked.

Zoe collapsed in a basket chair in the shop's small waiting area. "Yup. We're organized better than ever this year." She ran her fingertips idly over the tower of old magazines on the little table beside her. "I'll replenish your supply every few days."

Marlene came around from behind the counter and sat in the chair across from Zoe. "Are you sure you'll need to?" She hesitated a moment. "On Saturday I trimmed the hair of that marine biologist who's been hanging around."

At the mention of the annoying woman, Zoe grimaced. "Maybe you should have trimmed her tongue instead."

"Zoe!"

To avoid Marlene's gaze, Zoe tried pretending an avid interest in the wind chimes hanging outside the shop window. The damp breeze set the metallic chime ornaments ringing—the tiny scissors as they touched the tiny brush, the minuscule comb, glinting in the morning sun, as it brushed against the little blow-dryer.

Zoe sighed. "Was she talking about the firetail again?"

"She still says the fish aren't going to return."

Zoe slid an outdated *People* magazine off the stack and started turning the pages. The firetail had to return. The fish kept Abrigo alive. There were three thousand year-round residents of the island, like Gunther and TerriJean, like Lyssa and Zoe, who needed this bit of magic that was theirs; residents like Marlene, who had escaped an abusive marriage on the mainland to find safety and friendship and family here on Abrigo.

"They'll be back," Zoe said firmly.

Marlene was silent a moment. "Are you—"

"Come on." Zoe didn't look up, instead flipping over another page with her index finger. "Let's talk about something else."

Marlene sighed. "Want to tell me about your new guests, then?"

But suddenly Zoe found she couldn't speak. Her tongue was stuck to the roof of her mouth, and her gaze was stuck on the montage of celebrity photographs on the page in front of her.

Yeager. In a tuxedo, in a flight suit, in a uniform with shiny gold buttons and shiny gold medals. Photos obviously taken before his blindness, because in each one he was looking at the camera with warm brown eyes and smiling, his charisma slicker and glossier than the pages themselves.

She tried to swallow, remembering that same powerful smile directed at her from across her kitchen table. She remembered his fingertips running across her palm, the sweet rush of heat in her blood.

God, she was right to avoid him. So easily he charmed her. So confused he made her. So besotted, just like the women he was with in the three pictures on the pages in front of her.

The captions told it all. One woman was a supermodel with a single unpronounceable name, another was an MTV veejay, while the third was a breast-enhanced, bodice-impaired starlet who was nominated for a best supporting actress Academy award for playing a hooker. Yet even the dazzle of these women couldn't begin to compare with his.

"Your guests?" Marlene prompted again.

Zoe swallowed. "They're . . . he . . ."

Dazzle is what Yeager had done to her last evening. When Deke had come to collect him from the kitchen, Yeager had said good night and given her one more of those let-me-entertain-you smiles. She'd gone to bed, her skin still sparking in reaction.

And gotten up in the morning, unsure exactly how to handle the feeling.

"They're . . . interesting," she told Marlene.

But interesting or not, Zoe had to remember

that the astronaut was completely out of her league. She had to ignore his dangerous charisma, too. Because it was obvious, from the look of the magazine article, the man was practiced in the ways of women. He'd unbury her secrets, indeed! A man with his past—starlets and supermodels!—would make a provocative remark like that to every woman he came across.

And make each one believe him.

Marlene sent her a quizzical glance, and Zoe hastily stood and made an excuse to leave, deliberately clapping the pages of the magazine together so that one smiling image of Yeager slapped against another.

Blast her inexperience! It made her too easy a target for him. But she wouldn't be taken in by him and his charm again. Just as she'd known from the first, he was dangerous to her. She'd steer completely clear of him and advise anyone else she knew to do the same.

Although she'd vowed to avoid her new guest, after lunch it seemed safe enough to Zoe to venture out into Haven House grounds. She needed to gather herbs from her garden in order to prepare more basil pesto this afternoon. While she was at it, she'd also gather mint and parsley for an artichoke and pasta dish she wanted to make for her and Lyssa's dinner that night.

With a basket hooked over her arm, Zoe moved to the gentle slope where her herbs were planted. The tiered garden lay just below the back porch of Basil Cottage—hence its name—but Zoe refused to even glance up in the direction of the patio where she'd first met Yeager.

This part of the property was sheltered from much of the usual afternoon breeze, and Zoe breathed in the mingled smells of sun-heated herbs. A couple of bees buzzed by the lemon verbena, and she pinched off a leaf and rubbed it between her fingers, enjoying the tart aroma.

Pulling off her sweatshirt, she let the sunshine play over her shoulders, bared by her skinny-ribbed tank top. The purple-tufted lavender was in easy reach, and she plucked a few stalks in order to brush on their delicious smell. The soft flowers tickled the skin of her chest as she rubbed them along the neckline of her top. Another woman—one of Yeager's *People* magazine dates, say—might have touched the natural perfume to her cleavage, but Zoe was so flat-chested she wasn't even wearing a bra.

"There you are!"

"We found you!"

Startled by the unexpected voices, Zoe jumped and dropped the lavender. She swung around with a sinking heart, already sure whom she'd find. Yup. Susan and Elisabeth.

Both just thirty, the women worked in one of the island's realty offices. One blond, one brunette, they were like a pair of salt and pepper shakers in their nearly identical black skirts and cream silk blouses.

Zoe curled her fingers in a wave. "What are you ladies up to?"

Susan and Elisabeth made simultaneous eye rolls. "What do you think? When you didn't come to see us, we came to see you. It's time for a full report on our men."

Zoe's heart sank lower, all the way to the toes of her tennies. She'd hoped they'd forgotten about her promise. "Well, uh"—she gestured toward her basket and clippers—"I'm kind of busy right now."

Susan ignored the hint. "You just go ahead. We'll sit right over here until you're done." In seconds she and Elisabeth had seated themselves just a few feet away on the wrought iron loveseat tucked into a wide curve of the garden path.

"Oh. Well. Okay." Zoe resigned herself to the disappointing conversation. She'd just have to tell them the men—Yeager anyway, and it was simpler to include Deke too—were unsuitable. In good conscience, she couldn't fix up either Elisabeth or Susan with a man with a celebrity past and a past of celebrity women. A man like Yeager—an astronaut, temporarily blind or otherwise—would never be content with the boundaries of island life.

As she bent to gather up the fallen lavender stalks, a small movement caught her eye. Directly above the loveseat, at the top of the slope, was Basil Cottage's patio. Zoe's eyes widened. From this vantage point, she could see through the rails. Shoot. There was Yeager lying on his back on the lounge, napping—oh, she hoped he was napping—in the afternoon sun.

Pasting on a bright smile, she straightened. "Ladies. Why don't you follow me into the kitchen." She tried to keep her voice calm and quiet. "I have some fresh sun-brewed tea in the refrigerator."

Please, please, please, please, she wished. *Don't let him wake up before I get Susan and Elisabeth and their talk of the men out of here.*

But Susan and Elisabeth were already shaking their heads.

"No, thanks," said Elisabeth. "If we go inside, you'll get interrupted and we'll never get the scoop on these two new guests of yours."

Susan chimed in. "And I'll end up eating your cookies and won't be able to button my skirt tomorrow."

Zoe sent a swift look up toward the cottage patio. "They're fresh-baked," she said, adding a tempting sing-song to her voice. "White chocolate and almond."

The women groaned instead of budging. "Don't do it to us, Zoe. C'mon. Tell us all about these two great guys who are going to change our lives."

Oh, crud. Had she promised such a stupid thing?

"C'mon, Zoe."

She glanced up at Yeager's patio again. He'd rolled onto his side. Between the wide-spaced rails, she could clearly see his face. He had his sunglasses off, and his eyelashes were dark and thick against his high cheekbones. She *thought* he was asleep.

"You two don't really—"

"Zoe!"

She swallowed, then sighed. Maybe she should just get the conversation out of the way. "Look, I'm sorry to have to say this, but

they've turned out to be a couple of duds."
There. That should send the two women back
to their office.

Instead of getting up to leave, though, Susan
and Elisabeth drooped against the back of the
loveseat.

"What exactly is wrong with them?" Elisabeth asked.

Zoe sent another quick look in Yeager's direction. Should she whisper or make some sort
of sign to let them know that one of the men
might be awake and listening in? But the
downside of that idea was that Susan and Elisabeth would likely take an instinctive look upward, right at the marvelously handsome mug
of Yeager Gates.

Then she'd never get rid of them.

"Yes." There was something bordering on
suspicion on Susan's face. She crossed her
arms over her chest. "Describe them for us."

Zoe thought quickly. "Below average. Two
on a scale of ten."

Susan wasn't buying it. "Be more specific."

Zoe pursed her lips and kept her gaze away
from Yeager's patio. "Well, um, the older one.
He's not so bad. Quiet though." She cleared
her throat. "But you have to wonder about
him anyway. You know, when he's got a
friend like *that*."

She hoped "that" was the most detailed description of Yeager she would need to make.

Elisabeth's brow furrowed. "And what does
'that' mean, exactly?"

Zoe sighed. Okay, so the brunette was
brighter than she looked. "He's . . ." Tall,

golden, handsome. Oh, yeah, and an astronaut. A *wounded* astronaut. With military bearing and more magnetism than could be found at the very core of the earth.

Sure. That'd warn them away from him.

Involuntarily, her gaze moved up. Oh, terrific. Yeager was definitely awake. His sunglasses were on, and he'd propped himself up on one elbow, a faint smile on his face. He'd pulled his shirt off too, and his rugged pecs and rippling abdomen looked as delicious as an apple fritter after a week of fasting. Her nerves started that pulsing telegraph again. Sex . . . sex . . . sex.

Zoe shook herself and crossed her arms over her own meager chest. The darn man was obviously enjoying this. "I'll tell you all about him," she said to the other women. "He's scrawny and balding and"—she was getting a little reckless here—"and has quite a bad body odor problem."

Susan's suspicious expression was back. "And halitosis too, I imagine."

Why not go all the way? Zoe thought. She nodded. "That too."

Instead of appearing disappointed, though, both women stood up, their expressions displeased. "Zoe!" Elisabeth said. "This isn't like you at all."

"Huh?"

Susan shook her head. "TerriJean says that the older one, Deke, is a hunk. She only caught a brief glance of the younger man, but he's definitely not balding or scrawny."

Elisabeth chimed in again. "And I really

don't believe there's any odor problem."

"No?" Zoe tried.

"No." They spoke together. Their faces said they were mad.

With identical irritated strides, the two brushed past her in the direction they'd come. Susan's voice was pitched loudly to aim the parting shot.

"I think you're just trying to keep him for yourself!"

Frozen, Zoe could just stare after them. Then soft, masculine laughter drifted down and rained upon her new embarrassment and still tingling nerves.

"So what about it, Zoe?"

At the sound of Yeager's voice she frantically gathered up her things and hurried off toward the house herself.

Not fast enough to avoid his last teasing comment, however. "Are they right?" he called after her. "*Are* you trying to keep me for yourself?"

Yeager unerringly followed Zoe to Haven House. He'd been working on becoming familiar with his new environment. In his own cottage, the only things he'd tripped over that morning were his running shoes, which he'd stupidly left outside the closet, and his pillow, which he'd tossed off the bed sometime during the night. The sixty-four steps from his place to the back door that led straight into Haven House's kitchen he was confident he'd committed to memory. Lyssa had suggested he use that entrance when coming in for breakfast, because it was the most direct.

He used it now because he suspected he'd find Zoe there.

After last night, he thought she might try avoiding him. But remembering the soft sensation of her hands in his—and his body's reaction—he wasn't going to let her get away with it. Not when she'd been fluttery and so intriguingly silent when accused of saving her for himself.

And of course there was her description of him, scrawny and smelly. And balding! She couldn't possibly expect him to let that go by. No, the opportunity and Zoe herself were just too tempting.

His outstretched fingers touched the kitchen door, and he decided against knocking. Lyssa had told him this morning to walk right in, and with prior warning Zoe might just slip away.

He turned the knob and opened the door. Garlic, onion, other good smells he couldn't identify immediately assaulted him, along with the sizzle of something browning in hot oil.

His mouth instantly went wet, and just to remind him it was way past lunch and he hadn't eaten, his stomach grumbled.

So did Zoe. "What do you want?" she asked.

"What are you making?"

"Potato and vegetable pancakes. If I'm not interrupted now, I'll be serving them this afternoon with a sour cream dip."

He ignored the hint. Potato pancakes and sour cream. After a childhood of motherless meals followed by an adulthood of military food, pouched astronaut fare, or his own—and to be honest he was no better in the kitchen than his father, the brigadier general—Yeager had an obsessive appreciation for home cooking.

Maybe he could postpone the sexual flirtation for a few minutes. He flashed an ingratiating smile. "What would it take to get a taste now?"

She didn't instantly succumb. But then he heard her little sigh and the sound of a plate clapping against the wooden kitchen table. "Oh, all right. Sit down, then."

He found a chair and seated himself. Fingers outstretched, he reached for the plate. They contacted burning-hot pottery and he jerked them back. "Ouch!"

Zoe flew to him in a gratifying rush of scented air. "I'm so sorry! I didn't even think!" She pulled him up by the wrist and dragged him to the sink. "That plate has been in the oven."

The faucet *shooshed* on, and she held his hand beneath the cold spray. The sound of the water reminded him of his excuse for coming to the kitchen, and now that she'd burned him before even one bite of potato pancake, he decided to go ahead and bring it up right away.

"I took a second shower today because of you," he said, trying to keep his voice serious.

She didn't answer.

Of course she'd just been telling stories

about him to her two friends. But it would be interesting to know why she'd done so.

And he liked making her react.

"Brushed my teeth again and used mouthwash too," he said, leaning closer to her, so close that her hair tickled his chin. He inhaled, and the scent of her clean hair and warm skin was so fresh and sweet he could taste it on his tongue. His eyebrows came together. There was another, different note to her fragrance.

She shut off the faucet and moved away from him.

He took another sniff. "You smell different."

"Maybe I need another shower."

He couldn't stop his grin. He liked it when she sassed him back. He'd liked it when she grumped at him last night. With the exception of Deke, since the accident and the blindness everyone had treated him differently. Like an oddity or an object of pity.

He moved toward her. "Let me guess what the scent is."

Her voice came from a different direction this time. "Go sit down and eat your pancakes. The plate's cool now."

He didn't reverse direction, though the mention of pancakes was quite an enticement. Getting close to Zoe was a greater one.

This time he felt her quick movement to elude him. He reached out, his fingers just brushing skin, but she got away.

Pretending defeat, he headed for the kitchen table. Then he smelled her nearby and reached out again, grabbing her.

She squeaked.

His hand was on her arm, and he reeled her close. "I always was good at blindman's bluff."

In his grasp, her arm went limp. "You got me."

He frowned. This wasn't fun. He wanted her sparring with him. Grumbling, resisting, making him work for even a skosh of the sunshine she shone on the other guests.

Frustrated, he pulled her even closer. "So what is that new smell?" As he put his face close to her hair again, she stiffened, and he smiled with satisfaction.

She cleared her throat. "Eau de Onion."

"Nuh-uh." He lowered his head to where the deep-noted scent seemed strongest.

"It's lavender, okay?" She broke from his grasp, and the sound of her steps told him she put the kitchen island between them.

"The color lavender?" he asked, puzzled.

"No. The plant lavender. It has flowers that I . . . rub on my skin sometimes."

That she rubs on her skin sometimes. He could see it in his head. Purple flowers painting scent on Zoe's skin. If that image didn't ignite a sexual healing, he couldn't think what would.

"What's the matter?" she asked anxiously. "Do your fingers hurt?"

She must be in a position to see the expression on his face. "It's not that kind of pain," he said, shifting his weight on his feet.

"What hurts? Your head?" Near to him now, he felt Zoe's touch on his arm.

It caused his blood to send a sizzling message southward. Yeager found and captured her hand. "I told you, it's not that kind of pain," he said softly, hearing the sexual burr in his voice.

Her fingers went cold and trembled. Her breath hitched, a nervous, flighty sound.

Cold and trembling? Nervous and flighty?

Suddenly, the night before came back to him. Holding her hand. Teasing her about her womanly secrets. Her fingers had gone cold then too. A nervous chill.

Not the reaction of a woman used to a free-and-easy flirtation.

To test out the dawning and disquieting theory, he squeezed her fingers. They trembled again. Uneasiness rolled off her in waves.

Like another blow to the head, a realization struck him. She didn't want him flirting with her.

She didn't want him.

Stung by guilt, he abruptly let go of her. If his mental compass was correct, the kitchen table was ninety degrees to the right. With measured steps, he found his way there. Calling himself a selfish jerk, he sat down to his cooled potato pancakes.

Damn! What else could go wrong with his life? Yeah, he wanted to feel aroused by Zoe, relished it in fact. But not if it made her nervous or afraid.

That wasn't the kind of man he was.

With a metallic *ping*, she set something beside his right hand. She cleared her throat. "Fork."

He picked it up and reached out with it to locate the plate. "I'm . . . sorry." The words didn't come easy.

She cleared her throat again. "For what?"

Yeager closed his eyes. God, before the accident nothing was complicated. Space flight gave him the freedom he craved. That sense of limitlessness that was as much a part of his soul as four chambers were a part of his heart. The distraction and companionship of women had been available when he wanted them. Then, he could read a female by the look in her eyes and the language of her body. But with sight taken away—hell, face it, he'd screwed up.

"For what?" she asked again.

"For . . ." He ran his hand over the new scar. "I suppose you're in a serious relationship or at the very least seeing someone. Without my eyesight, I guess I'm mistaking the signals you're sending my way." Or he'd been so damned selfish he hadn't looked for any.

Her breath made that funny hitch again. She wasn't moving. Before, he'd thought Zoe not moving meant Zoe confused or puzzled. Now he wasn't so sure.

"What—" She broke off, and he heard her swallow. "What signals am I sending you?"

He shrugged. "I told you, I must be misinterpreting. You have a boyfriend, right? I can only hope he'll hold back from slugging a blind guy."

She spoke carefully. "Why would my . . . my boyfriend want to slug you?"

He smiled ruefully. "Because I'm flirting

with you, honey. And the part I had wrong
was the part where I thought you were enjoying it." He smiled again. "Do me a favor and
tell me I didn't seem as stupid as I feel."

"You didn't seem stupid at all."

He smiled ruefully. "Now you're just being
nice."

"No," she said softly. He heard her swallow
again. "To be honest, I don't have a boyfriend."

His eyebrows rose, but then he shrugged.
"Okay. So you like to play the field but obviously I'm not one of your favorite positions."

She was silent again.

"Zoe?"

"I'm not exactly sure what you just said, but
I, um, don't play the field either. I'm pretty
much . . . dateless. Manless."

Yeager made himself spear a bite of potato
pancake. Find his mouth. Chew it. The flavor
was ecstasy to his taste buds, but its goodness
couldn't overwhelm his surprise.

"You see, well, I'm busy," Zoe said. "I
haven't found . . . haven't wanted to . . ." Her
voice stalled. "I just haven't."

Yeager froze, second forkful halfway to
mouth. Haven't what? He set down the fork.
"Well." Jesus! What did that "haven't" mean?

"Well," she echoed.

"Well, I'm still sorry I got my wires
crossed." Those cold fingers of hers were
proof that his blindness could make him as
clumsy as a rookie operating the shuttle's ro-
botic arm. "You should have just told me you
weren't interested. Or that I don't affect you."

There was more silence and stillness. Then she mumbled something.

"What?" he asked.

"I really couldn't have said that."

The small-voiced admission shouldn't be such a big deal. But for a moment, just one startling moment, he reexperienced that high-octane sensation of seeing his name on the crew list for his very first shuttle flight. Blood rushed to his groin with the good news.

He let out a slow breath. God, the blindness was really playing games with his mind. So a woman had implied an attraction was mutual. A sweet-smelling, cold-fingered young woman who confused and entertained him. No reason to be so damn pleased.

No sense in immediately doing something about it either.

He picked up his fork again, determined to take things easy. It didn't take a NASA-trained brain to realize Zoe was skittish. He'd have to go slow with her. Tease her some more. Make her grumpy again. Let her get comfortable before he tried to get closer. He could afford to wait.

Especially when he was just as certain as before that Zoe somehow would help him see again.

And lucky for him, Zoe wasn't unwilling.

The chair beside him scraped against the floor, and she sat down. Her light scent floated over him, and he smiled. Not today, not tomorrow, but the next day he'd touch her again. He'd make her breathless, waiting for it, anticipating how he'd find a way to brush his fingers against her skin.

"Yeager?"

"Hmm." She said his name like no one else. Maybe because he'd never seen her with his eyes, he noticed more about her with his other senses. Her voice held a vulnerable hesitation, a sweet warmth, all wrapped up with a slight huskiness that was like a velvet ribbon.

"I don't want you to get the wrong idea."

Oh, he knew his ideas were right now. There had been something different about Zoe from the moment they'd met. She'd stirred something back to life in him, and he would be happy to return the favor. He smiled at her. "What are you talking about, honey?"

"The 'honey' . . ."

He didn't bother looking shamefaced. "It's just a habit. I've never spent much time anywhere—air force brat, you know—but I've been in Houston the longest. The Southern stuff has just rubbed off." He leaned back in his chair, relaxed, satisfied to let things between them simmer for the moment.

"Look, I'm trying to be honest with you," she said.

"And I appreciate it. Let me tell you, when you can't see somebody's face, you lose about half the meaning of what they say. From now on, just give it to me straight, okay, honey?"

"You want it straight?"

"Sure do." He smiled confidently. "Straight from the heart. Honest."

He heard her take a breath. "Well, Yeager. You see—" She broke off and inhaled another big gulp of oxygen. "While I can't say you don't . . . do something for me, I can say I'm not interested. Do you understand the difference?"

Behind his dark glasses Yeager blinked. "Huh?" You would never know he'd earned an advanced degree from a top-flight military academy.

"I'm not interested," she repeated, and then her voice turned bright. "But I'm honest. And I honestly want to fix you up with someone else."

5

"And after she asked if she could fix you up, what did you say?" Deke didn't even have the decency to disguise the laughter in his voice.

Yeager repressed the junior high urge to give his friend the finger. "What do you think I said? I said okay."

Deke hooted. "I can't believe it! A blind date for my man Yeager!" And then, as if his pun was the cleverest of the century, he started laughing even harder.

Yeager ground his teeth together. For Deke, he'd sketched out the bare bones of his conversation with Zoe. His worry that he'd read her signals wrong. Her assurance that he hadn't. Her next request to introduce him to someone else.

"And are you sure she's fixing you up with another *woman*?" Deke's laughter resurfaced. "Remember her first impression of you?"

For all Yeager knew, she was going to fix him up with a billy goat. But he'd go along with it, all sunglasses and smiles, because he'd be damned if he'd show Zoe that he was disappointed.

He'd been so dumbfounded by what she'd said that he'd sat there like a wart on a toad while she babbled on about liking her life just the way it was, about how she was a well-known matchmaker on the island, about how she'd promised him to someone else.

Then he'd accepted her "deep-felt gratitude" for agreeing to the setup. She said he'd win her back a couple of friends.

Funny thing was, he didn't ever remember saying yes.

But, dammit, he'd do it anyway. He had enough problems without tying the return of his vision and his libido to Zoe. They were both a matter of time, not a matter of Zoe.

Some other woman would turn him on. Some other woman, who, though she might not cook as well, wouldn't turn him inside out with her upside down logic. Some other woman who, though she might not smell as erotic, would tremble less at his touch.

Oh, yeah. Zoe had probably done him a favor.

A few nights later Yeager sat on the back patio of his cottage, waiting edgily for Mickey Mouse. The young daughter of a shuttle crew buddy had lent him a special Disney watch after learning of his blindness. At the half hour, Mickey announced the time. On the hour, he added a tinny and not nearly short enough verse of "It's a Small World."

Every time he wore the watch, Yeager worried he might let loose and bare-handedly kill the mouse. It was a fact that astronaut emergency preparedness included jungle training. So, at night, when his resistance was lower and his instincts sharper, he made sure to muffle the watch by balling it in a sock and stuffing it in a sweatshirt sleeve. Only that kept Mickey alive to see another day—that and the memory of little Jenny and his sacred promise to return it to her when he regained his sight.

Most days, though, he kept the watch in the sock and did without knowing the time. It had bothered him back home in Houston, accustomed as he was to a tight schedule, but on Abrigo Island he hadn't thought about it once. He'd de-socked Mickey tonight only because he'd told Zoe he'd go down to the house at 8 P.M.

He took a long breath. The evening air felt so clean it burned coldly as he inhaled. He drew the island's smell into himself, a fragrance part salt, part wet, and part green, like a ripe calm. He listened to the silence, then suddenly realized it wasn't quiet at all. Crickets scrubbed their wings together. Birds cheeped and burped, and there were deep-throated raven *caws*. He'd never before so strongly noticed earth-bound sounds.

Suddenly, from the direction of Haven House, an eardrum-damaging noise burst the tranquility. The raucous cacophony sounded like someone had popped the lid off a can of out-of-tune notes from poorly played musical instruments. Yeager cringed as another chorus of sound shrieked. A filling in one of his molars rattled in protest.

Yeager jumped to his feet. Earlier than the appointed hour or not, those sixty-four steps to the Haven House kitchen had to be made this moment. Because unless he guessed wrong, either Zoe or Lyssa, or both of them, was murdering an accordion. Possibly a saxophone. Considering his frustrated impulses toward Mickey, he thought he might just help.

It was Lyssa he found in the kitchen. Even with the clashing background music playing louder now, he could tell it was Zoe's sister moving about. He smelled steeping tea.

"Hi, Lyssa," he said over another wail of a tortured instrument.

There was a smile in her voice. "Good evening, Yeager. How did you know it was me?"

He shrugged, talking loudly so he could be heard over the noise. "You have a different feeling about you than Zoe. She crackles with energy. You have a different . . ."

"Aura," she supplied. "You're experiencing our distinct auras."

Yeager raised his eyebrows. That's right, technically the island *was* in California. "Well, uh, maybe so." He jerked his head in the direction of the living room. "Somebody in there performing an exorcism?"

Lyssa laughed, just as the discordant notes died down. "Sh," she said. "That's Zoe's pet project."

"And it's the pets that are playing?"

Lyssa giggled again. "No. It's—"

Yeager heard the creak of the swinging kitchen door. Energy suddenly filled the room, and Zoe's distinct scent. "It's the Island Community Band," Zoe said. "And we have a big gig coming up." Her voice sounded grumpy again. "You're here early."

He smiled. "I couldn't wait to meet those women you told me about."

No response from Zoe.

"She's speechless," Lyssa murmured as she brushed by him, sly humor in her voice. "Remarkable."

Yeager smiled again. "Do you want me to come back?"

He could almost feel Zoe's grimace. "Never mind. Maybe if you meet them now, the rest of us can get some work done."

"The rest of us?" he asked.

"This is a meeting of the Firetail Festival committee. Festival weekend is at the end of the month, and we have a lot of work to do."

Yeager nodded gravely. "Especially the Island Community Band."

A stifled giggle came from Lyssa's direction. Zoe just groaned. "Do me a favor and keep that thought to yourself, will you? I'm trying to persuade the committee that the band will be ready to perform in the festival parade."

Personally, Yeager thought the band wouldn't be ready in a decade, let alone a month, but he asked politely, "And what was the piece they were playing as I came down the walk?"

Zoe's voice went disgruntled again. "Depends on who you ask. The accordion, the electric guitar, and the sax thought it was 'Beyond the Reef.' The banjo, piccolo, and tambourine played 'Mr. Bojangles.' "

Yeager managed to swallow his grin. "Well, there you go. Play the same song and the band'll be great."

Zoe sighed. "By the Island Band's standard, that was great."

Yeager turned away, trying not to laugh. But hell, this place was a hundred times more entertaining than he'd ever expected. He'd thought to hole up, licking his wounds, yet instead Zoe had him walking out of that hole and choking back laughter. Each day around her the heaviness hanging over him lightened.

Mentally shaking his head, he turned back to her. "I've got to meet these women you've staked out for me. Any of them band members?"

"No. But all are on the festival committee. Distract them with your dazzle, and I'll push the band approval through."

He felt her take his arm, and he breathed in a sustaining lungful of her scent. "I dazzle, huh?"

The kitchen door creaked as she pulled him through it. "In a rhinestone sort of way."

Once again he couldn't help smiling. "I love it when you sass me."

"Save your sweet talk for the ladies I'm about to introduce you to."

She halted him just on the other side of the kitchen door. Yeager could hear mingled voices and mangled notes coming from the living room. Zoe must have stood on tiptoe, because suddenly her mouth was at the level of his ear. "All three of them are sitting on the couch on your left. Blond Susan and brunette Elisabeth are the ones you overheard me talking with the other afternoon. And just for variety I threw in a redhead—Desirée."

As she drew out the name, the word blew sultry air across his neck and earlobe. He ignored it. "Desirée. That sounds interesting."

Her breath jumped to his cheek as she *humphed* mildly. "No doubt." She tugged on his arm. "We might as well get it over with. By the way, everyone in there knows you want to keep who you are quiet, and the women have been properly warned."

He resisted her forward movement. "Properly warned?"

She sighed. "I'm a matchmaker, Yeager. With a man like you, I promise nothing."

"What do you usually promise?"

"I *hope* for permanence, happily ever after, that sort of thing. A man a woman could spend the rest of her days with. Like I said, with you I gave no guarantee. Zippo."

Zippo? "I've never been a zippo in my life."

"Trust me, *honey*," she said, all sass and saccharine sweetness. "This time you're a zippo."

He lifted his free hand. By some good luck, he found Zoe's face and brushed the back of his knuckles against the smooth curve of her cheek. "Why don't we let Desirée be the judge of that?"

She *humphed* again, louder, and dragged him posthaste into the living room. Swift introductions were performed, and then he found himself on a straight chair beside the couch that held the three contestants.

That was how he thought of them, because that's how they reacted to him—like he was a beauty pageant judge and was scoring them on charm, congeniality, and potential contributions to the world. As the formal part of the meeting broke up and he and the three ladies began chatting, he tried to work up some interest in them. Truly.

Contestant Number 3, Desirée, certainly did her part. She had a sultry, sexy voice and wore an expensive perfume, and quite early in their acquaintance she put her hand on his knee. He registered the touch, trying to imagine her long fingers, a slim arm, frothy red hair, and a model's face. He tried to have a response too, but his pulse rate remained steady and his skin remained cool.

To further frustrate his efforts, he was distracted by Zoe, who from the chair beside his was lobbying passionately for the band, and he could tell it wasn't going well.

"We've always had an island band in the parade," she said. "For thirty years."

An older man's voice answered her. "But Zoe, the Lindstroms moved back to the mainland last year. Old Burt is visiting his daughter for the summer, and Young Burt has a broken wrist and can't play right now. We all know those four have been the core of the Island Community Band for the last decade."

Zoe's agitation rolled off her in waves. "But—"

"Zoe." Another male voice interrupted her.

"I'm still not convinced we shouldn't cut our losses right now and cancel the festival."

She groaned loudly. "William, we've been through this before. All of us on the island depend on visitors one way or another. The tourists depend on the Firetail Festival."

The first voice broke in. "And the festival depends on the *firetail*, Zoe. If we put out the expense for the events and then the fish don't show, won't the visitors feel duped?"

"The firetail are coming back." Zoe's voice was tight and held a strange note, almost of desperation. "Nothing is going to change here ever."

Several more voices jumped into the discussion.

Nothing is going to change here ever? Yeager shifted in his chair and tried to forget Zoe's strangely urgent words by refocusing on the scented and sexy Desirée. But as he heard the worried note enter Zoe's voice again, the details of Desirée's stained glass business just couldn't hold his interest.

"Excuse me," he said, interrupting her. "Could you tell me what the argument is about?"

Desirée sighed, but luckily didn't seem in the least put out. "Our very lives here, when you get right down to it."

"What do you mean?" Yeager asked.

"The firetail fish aren't supposed to return this year. Last year their numbers were down. Now it's something about a change in the Pacific Ocean currents. So what should we do?" She sighed again. "Cancel the festival? But then what if the fish *do* show up? Or hold the festival and then be embarrassed when the firetail don't arrive? And if they are never to return, maybe we should all be packing up."

"What?"

Susan or Elisabeth joined in. "Abrigo will die."

Yeager frowned. "No way."

"We need visitors to survive," Desirée said. "The festival provides most people here with the majority of their income."

"What's Capistrano without the swallows?" Susan added.

"Or McDonalds without the french fries?" Elisabeth chorused.

Desirée made a bit more sense. "Yes, there's year-round tourism, but it's nothing compared to the festival. And without the fish, well, there are plenty of mainland beaches cheaper and easier to get to. For the island experience, Catalina is closer and better known."

Yeager shook his head. "Zoe seems sure the fish will come back."

Desirée's fingers squeezed his knee. "Zoe *wants* them to come back," she said. "As we all know, though, *wanting* something and *getting* it are two entirely different things."

Yeager grimaced. It sounded like Zoe was heading for trouble. Just another reason to be grateful she'd deflected his interest. He was a keep-it-loose, keep-it-light type of guy, so he always took a fly-by on women with too much at stake.

He wished Zoe the best, of course, but he

turned toward Desirée without regrets and
gave her his most engaging smile.

Her hand stayed on his knee, and she
started chatting again. Susan and Elisabeth began asking him about himself, a tactic that
should have worked like a charm. But even
though there was plenty to occupy him, Zoe's
voice kept infiltrating his mind. Sure, he kept
small-talking with the three ladies and kept
smiling, but he shifted in his seat little by little,
edging away from them.

All the while, Zoe continued to defend her
position on the Firetail Festival, her voice tired
and near desperate again. The sound pierced
him, and without thinking, Yeager slid the final inches until his arm brushed against hers,
an uncharacteristic and unspoken offer of
moral support.

With Desirée's hand on his knee, his bicep
pressed against Zoe's, he froze.

Because automatically, his body had reacted, hardening again, just as it should, just
as he'd been waiting for.

But in response to the wrong woman. In response to Zoe.

And despite the fact that he could think of
fourteen and a half reasons to keep away from
her, he knew none of them mattered.

6

Deke couldn't believe the old tree house was still there. The last time he'd been to the island, he hadn't come looking for it. But this evening, after battling through the brush behind his great-uncle's house, he'd found the oak tree, thirty years older than he remembered, its spreading horizontal branches longer and stronger, the higher branches reaching gnarled fingers to the sky.

There'd been a rope swing once as well, now long gone, but the seven scraps of hardwood that he'd nailed to the tree trunk as toeholds were still there. Set into the trunk's lowest fork, the floor of the tree house looked mainly intact too, though some of the railing that had made it more of a tree deck was missing.

After testing his weight against the toeholds, Deke swung himself up to the level of the tree house. Hanging onto a higher branch, he gingerly stepped over the flimsy railing. The floor held. He tried his other foot, more weight. The floor held again.

With a shrug and a whole hell of a lot of confidence in his thirteen-year-old carpentry abilities, he let go of the upper branch and sat, scooting to a favorite spot, where he could lean against a thick, sky-reaching branch and look out over Lover's Cove and the Pacific toward the too distant to glimpse mainland.

Unfamiliar tightness kinked the muscles across his shoulders. He'd worked at the house all day, tearing rotting shingles from the roof and then throwing them down the makeshift chute he'd built that led to the debris bin. It was going to cost him an arm and a leg to have the stuff hauled off island, but that didn't matter. He'd planned on paying for that. He'd planned on paying a laborer to do the grunt work that was knotting his muscles now too.

Damned if he knew why he was killing himself over here every day instead of lounging in the sun drinking beers with Yeager.

Damn, but he did know why.

It was because of her. Lyssa.

The sight of her had hit him like a medicine ball to the belly the moment he'd seen her. All young curves and flowing blond hair, she'd held out the cottage keys and looked squarely into his eyes, smiling. Her full, curving lips had made his pecker go hard and his knees soft.

Afraid he might start stuttering any second, he'd grabbed the keys and made an instant vow to keep clear of her. As much as she was a walking, breathing wet dream, she was just as much his every nightmare. A woman with more than temporary on her mind.

A young, innocent woman. Her visit to the house had proved that. She'd actually thought it safe to approach him!

Below his perch, a small, sleek yacht chugged across the bay of Lover's Cove. Likely it would sail right around Breakers Point, heading back to a mooring in Haven Bay before dark. He should head back himself. But every evening he put off as long as he could his return to Haven House.

And he knew why he did that too.

It was because of her. Lyssa.

Then, as if just thinking of her had willed her presence, Deke saw her.

From here he had a quarter-mile view of the narrow dirt road that led over the hill and then to the house. Lyssa trudged up the steepness steadily, the long skirt of her yellow dress swirling around her calves. She stopped, look-ing in his direction, and instinctively he backed against his supporting branch. The evening breeze picked up her long blond hair and billowed the skirt of her dress, and against the green weeds and the blue ocean backdrop she was a candleflame of color.

His fingernails dug against the new calluses on his palms. Christ! Candleflames! He should be thinking of caution signs or yellow warning lights.

He tried to look away but found his gaze drawn back to her, to the colors surrounding her, which blended like an Impressionist painting. Lyssa belonged there, and maybe it was because she seemed so much a part of the beauty of the island—a place where he'd been

his most happy and most miserable—that he
found himself so fascinated by her.

Or maybe he was having a midlife crisis.

She was moving again, continuing toward
the house. Deke plastered his back to the tree.
When she didn't find him, she'd go away and
leave him in peace. That was the very best
cure for an old-fashioned case of lust.

But God, she must be part bloodhound. In
minutes she reached the house and walked
without hesitation around to the back and in
the direction of his tree.

He could hear her rustling through the same
scrub that he had, and he closed his eyes
against the image of her coming to him. Too
tempting. Too easy to call out and then let her
enter his private place.

"Deke?"

He stifled his groan. Her soft, young voice
was coming from the foot of his tree. He refused to open his eyes. If he didn't look at her,
maybe she'd go away.

"Is there something I should know before I
come up there?"

That I don't trust myself around you.

"Will these little steps hold my weight?" she
asked.

He opened his eyes to grasp at the chance
given him. "No!" Staring down at her, he
found himself mesmerized by her eyes. They
were wide-set and crystal blue and so trusting
they made his chest hurt. "No," he said again,
lying through his teeth. "You can't come up."

She must have thought he meant to add
"that way," because before he could protest

again, she went on tiptoe to grasp one of the lower branches. Then she started swinging her legs. Her long dress fluttered up toward her thighs, nearly giving him a heart attack.

She was panting, too.

He was frozen, watching her with horrified fascination.

She was still unsuccessfully swinging and panting. Her face was getting red.

Finally, she broke the exertion-filled silence. "I—think—I need—help."

Shaking his head, Deke held back his smile and his desire. Parts of him would like nothing better than to reach out and pull her up to him. "Go ahead and drop," he said. "The toeholds are safe, but I'm coming down."

He'd barely gotten the words out before she'd gone ahead and used the toeholds to scramble up beside him. She sank onto the dirty planking between him and the stairs, her full skirt opening around her like a flower, its petals wide enough to nearly reach his work boots.

He frowned at her. "I said I was coming down."

She shook her head, little tendrils of hair curling about her still pink cheeks. "I like it up here."

He looked at her sharply. "You already knew about the tree house?"

"Zoe and I found it when we were girls. I haven't been here in years, though." She looked about her as if the seven-by-four-foot house might have been remodeled during the intervening time. "How do you know about it?"

"I built it. When I was thirteen."

That surprised her. Her blue eyes widened, and he tried not to fall into them. "You lived on the island?" she asked.

"A few summers when I was a boy."

She seemed to think about that. He thought about the first time he'd seen her. Like now, he'd been struck by an intense, burning impulse, and the heat made him nervous. The heat made him distrust being alone with her.

"It's time for you to go back," he said abruptly. "It's getting dark."

"You'll take care of me," she said absently.

He dug his nails into his palms again. How dare she! It pissed him off that she thought she could count on him.

He tried to imagine himself letting her set off alone in the night.

It *really* pissed him off that she was right.

He nursed the anger, letting the feeling override the tension that came with being so close to her. He let his angry eyes run over the young, curving line of her cheek, the almost-stubborn tilt of her chin, to her slender neck, and her not so-slender—

Christ. He had to get out of here. All this crap about heat and burning impulses was just some over-the-counter lust for a pretty young thing. He should be ashamed of himself.

"I'm leaving," he said.

Instead of answering, she edged toward one of the other thick branches growing close to the deck's railing. Her skirt trailed across his feet, and he felt cotton caress leather like it was a skin-to-skin touch. His chest tightened again. *Shit*. Maybe he *was* going to have a heart attack.

Kneeling, she reached up and her small fingertips traced over the branch's bark. "DN. Those are the initials carved here. I found them years ago. Those aren't yours, are they? Deke Nielsen?"

Her blond hair rippled down her back like an angel's. "Yeah," he said gruffly. "I guess they are."

She sat back on her heels abruptly and looked at him, the pink color quickly draining from her face. "I—"

"What?" He scrambled toward her, worried that she might be fainting again and would topple out of the tree house. "For God's sake, what's wrong?"

She pointed to the branch again, her finger quivering. "I put my initials up there too. LC."

He wasn't going to let himself touch her. Even though up this close her skin was fine-grained and smooth and her lips looked like something he just had to kiss. He inched back from her. Lust could make a man very stupid.

She swallowed, and he made himself look away from the vulnerable chords of her neck. "I think I knew," she said. "Even then."

"Knew what?"

"Us," she said simply.

Damn her. There she went again. "Listen, little girl," he said, getting impatient. "There is no 'us.' There won't be an 'us.' I don't know about you, but I can assure you I've lived through a case of the hots a hundred times."

"Deke—"

"Just listen to me. We don't have to do anything about it. We're not going to do anything about it. Lust comes, it goes, it means goddamn nothing."

She looked a little impatient herself. But not disappointed or cowed or even the least bit hurt. "Would you just look at this," she said, pointing again to the tree. "When I was thirteen years old, I put my initials up there too. And being an imaginative and romantic thirteen, I added a little embellishment."

With a gusty sigh, Deke indulged her by squinting up at the tree. He had to move closer to her to see what she'd indicated, and he ignored the warm, sweet heat coming off her body.

Then he forgot about the heat.

He forgot to breathe too.

Because he saw it quite clearly. His thirty-year-old initials, "DN," slashed inelegantly into the bark. Below it, Lyssa's "LC." And between them a plus sign.

And around them a heart.

"See." He heard Lyssa's voice as if it whispered out of the center of his chest. "I knew it then too."

After the Firetail Festival meeting, Zoe scurried around the living room, collecting discarded napkins and coffee cups and edging furniture back into its proper position. She was doing it by herself because Lyssa had disappeared somewhere and because the man comfortably and apparently firmly ensconced on her love-seat wasn't much good at finding things when they were out of place.

Yes, Yeager. Not only was he blind, but he'd developed an annoying habit of sticking around when everyone else had gone away.

Wasn't this whole evening about getting rid of him? Out of her hair, out of her imagination, and at the very least, out of her living room!

She squeezed a cocktail napkin into a paper pebble and tried not looking at Yeager's sinewy and tanned hands, open and relaxed against his denim-covered thighs. His fingers were long and strong-looking, and when his knuckles had brushed her cheek earlier in the evening, goose bumps had burst over her skin like freckles under full sun.

She realized she was staring at him again.

But what else was new? All night she'd been too aware of him. Of his occasional laughter, the warmth of his body when he'd been sitting beside her, the very male note in his voice when he chatted with the other women after the meeting ended.

That wouldn't have been so bad if listening to his casual banter hadn't reminded her of what he'd confessed to her a few days before. He'd been flirting with her.

And while that wasn't such a mind-blowing revelation—she'd known he was flirting—he'd also suggested, sort of implied, that there was an attraction that wasn't just automatic.

Another unladylike wash of heat rushed over her skin. *Argh.* Unautomatic attraction or not, three days ago she'd been smart enough to deflect all that roguish charm. She wasn't interested. She'd told him that.

Only someone had dropped the ball when passing on that message to the newly awakened woman inside her island innkeeper's body.

It was time to get rid of him, she decided firmly. "You must be very tired," she said, trying to sound cool and nurselike. "Do you need any help finding the door?"

He didn't budge. "Oh, yeah. It's exhausting to sit on my ass all day and stare at nothing. No, I think I'll just keep you company a while longer." His long legs stretched farther, and he crossed his ankles as if to really settle in. "Is there anything for me to eat?"

Of course he wouldn't take the hint. Emitting a little grunt of frustration, Zoe stomped closer to hand him a plate of leftover cookies, then continued picking up the room. Maybe she should blame herself. Maybe she should have selected some other women for him to meet. Wasn't a one of them savvy enough to have taken the guy home, or at least out for a drink?

Just as she'd requested, he'd dazzled all three of them. Realtors Susan and Elisabeth had looked at him like he was a zoning-free, lien-free piece of ocean view Abrigo, and Desirée... Desirée had been Zoe's ace in the hole. The woman collected men like connoisseurs collected her stained glass art, and Zoe had counted on Desirée wanting to improve her collection.

That half of the equation had added up as planned.

Yet Yeager, as usual, wasn't so easy to predict. While all three of the women appeared willing enough, what wasn't clear was which woman he preferred. Zoe had no clue which he liked more, the cheerful good humor of Susan and Elisabeth or the blatant sexuality of busty Desirée.

Zoe sent the maddening man a frown. For some illogical, ill-timed, irrational, stupid, and completely silly reason, the very fact that he'd so easily responded to all three of them irritated the dickens out of her.

The least he could do was get out of her living room so she could enjoy her ill humor in peace. She sent him another frown.

"What about Deke?" she asked, sliding a vase of Queen Anne's lace to the spot where the coffee urn had sat. "Don't you think you should find him?"

"Find him? Why?"

Zoe kept her gaze glued to the stalks of delicate white flowers. "I don't know," she said. "Maybe you want to tell him about your evening."

"Oh, yeah." He chuckled, clearly amused. "And then I'll write down all the details in my diary."

Zoe grimaced. Foiled again. The thing was, she just couldn't think with him in the room or think about anything but him anyway. She dried her palms against the sides of her thighs. Him and which woman would fill the starring role in his dreams tonight?

"Are you sure you don't need a breath of fresh air?" she asked desperately, before her tongue betrayed her and just out and out asked him.

"I'm recovering fine right here, thank you very much."

She frowned, turning toward him. "You're not feeling well?"

"I'm feeling fine. I'm referring to all that female charm you exposed me to." He was smiling.

He'd smiled at them too, all three.

Oh, to heck with it. She crossed her arms over her chest.

"Which?" she asked abruptly. "Which one?"

Yeager's head came up and he shifted her way. There was a cookie in each of his hands—one chocolate chip, one oatmeal raisin. He swallowed. "Which?"

She hated herself for needing to ask. "Yes," she said. "Which one?"

His eyebrows rose over the frames of his dark glasses. "Which *cookie*? I like them—"

She cut him off impatiently. "Which *one* of the *cookies*. You know, Susan, Elisabeth or Desirée?"

He pressed his lips together, hard, then *tsked*. " 'Cookies,' Zoe? Isn't that violating one of the tenets of the sisterhood or something?"

She should have known he'd make a joke out of it. Without bothering to reply, she turned her back on him to place the last folding chair in the stack that her part-time housekeeping help would move to the outdoor shed in the morning. Violating the sisterhood—hah! Her feelings toward the three women weren't close to sisterly at the moment, and she didn't wish to examine why.

The only sensible thing to do now was rush through her cleanup. If he wouldn't leave the living room, then she would. By moving quickly and pointedly ignoring Yeager, she made quick work of the rest of her chores. The last thing to go was the plate of leftover cookies she'd palmed off on Yeager earlier.

She grabbed it from the cushion beside him. "All done," she said. "I'm going upstairs now." Upstairs with her curiosity still raging, of course. It might take her hours to fall asleep, the Susan-Elisabeth-Desirée puzzle spinning like a wheel in her mind, but she'd be darned if she asked him again. "Good night," she said firmly.

The sound of the back door slamming announced Lyssa's return.

Yeager cocked his head at the noise and then looked up. "You're not going to walk a guy home?" There was something about the expression on his face, the hint of a dimple in his scarred cheek, that betrayed he was still amused by something.

By her. Zoe frowned. "No, I'm not going to walk you home." It would be cool and moonlit outside, and he should be taking his romantic walks with Susan. Or Elisabeth. Or Desirée. A nasty little twinge of curiosity pinched her again. "Why would I do such a thing?"

That dimple of his dug itself deeper. "Because I can't find my way in the dark?"

Her mouth gaped open. How stupid did she look? Of course he found his way here and back every day in the dark. "N—"

She stopped herself. He wasn't stupid either. He wanted her company for some reason, her private company if she guessed correctly, now that Lyssa had returned to the house.

"Please?" he added.

That hint of a smile somehow traveled the inches between them and started a funny little ache around her middle. She stared down at him, at the glint of gold in his hair and the strong column of his throat and the very male expanse of his shoulders.

She swallowed, tugging at her shirt collar, which was suddenly too tight. It must be the curiosity again, she told herself briskly. If she walked him back, perhaps the night breeze would blow it all away. "All right," she said grudgingly. "Let's go."

Side by side, they walked slowly up the path toward Yeager's cottage. The air was cool, and Zoe buried her hands in the pockets of her jeans and hunched her shoulders to keep warm. After all the interest in her company, though, Yeager seemed to have forgotten she was there.

They were halfway to his cottage when he cleared his throat. "Zoe, about tonight . . ." His voice drifted off.

The fact that Yeager hesitated surprised her. So far he hadn't seemed the hesitant type. But "about tonight" hung in the air without anything to weigh it down, and Zoe frowned. What was he worried about bringing up?

The answer hit her with the cold slap of a wave. It was the women, of course. After all that earlier silence, he wanted to talk about Susan, Elisabeth, or Desirée. It would be Desirée, of course. Sexy Desirée, whose inch-long nails had looked quite at home on Yeager's knee. But what could he want from Zoe—a phone number?

And then another wave of realization struck. Blind as he was, he probably did want a phone number. He certainly couldn't have written one down or read one Susan, Elisabeth, or Desirée passed along to him. A slither of something uncomfortable crawled down her spine. What if he even asked her to dial it for him?

Zoe stumbled. To keep her balance, she flung out an arm, and it glanced off Yeager, who then caught it, his strong hand, his long fingers, closing over it to hold her up.

Heat transferred itself from his palm to her skin, and that inner woman inside her, the one who'd woken like Sleeping Beauty at the first glimpse of him, came completely alert again, without even the slightest need for a stretch or yawn.

He didn't let go of her.

The sweet, bewitching scent of the night-blooming jasmine rose around them. A breeze ruffled the waves of her hair, but she couldn't feel it against the hot flesh of her cheeks. She looked up at him, and the moonlight shone in the dark lenses of his sunglasses.

Silence stretched tautly between them, and she thought maybe she should say something, anything, to break this sudden spell.

"There's a full moon tonight." She whispered the first words that came into her head. Maybe that fat moon explained her too warm skin and the erratic thump of her heart against her ribs.

His hand tightened on her arm. Then he raised his face toward the sky, and in the tick of a heartbeat, he seemed to have forgotten she was there again. But then he suddenly spoke. "Describe it to me," he said, his voice quiet but tense.

Zoe swallowed. "The moon?"

"All of it. The night. The trees. But yeah, describe the moon. And are there clouds? Are the stars out?" His hand tightened again on her arm more urgently. "Tell me about the sky."

There was something she'd never heard before in his voice. Sadness, maybe. Longing.

The blind astronaut wanted to be told about the sky. Her heart slowed down some, and she swallowed again. Forcing her gaze off his face, she stared up and tried desperately to remember which constellation was which. Was the row of three stars Cassiopeia's girdle or Orion's belt? Which had the North Star, the Big or Little Dipper?

"I'm an earth-bound woman," she finally confessed. "I'm more aware of the island beneath my feet than what's above my head."

He shook her arm a little. Not unkindly, but impatiently, as if he really needed her to do this for him. "Tell me, Zoe."

She took a deep breath. "I can see the moon

and a lot of stars. Tons more than people can see on the mainland. I remember that from when I went to college in L.A. Big city lights fade out the sky."

He nodded, his grip on her still strong.

Zoe tried to ignore another surge of heat that came off his hand to slide down her arm. Strangely enough, she was trembling too, though she didn't feel cold any longer.

"The sky. What color is the sky?" he asked.

"Not black. Not yet anyway." Zoe tried hard to think of a way to describe it that went beyond vision. "It's a deep, heavy blue. The moon is full and white, but it looks as thin as those Necco wafers we use to buy at the Island Five and Dime."

Transferring her gaze to Yeager, she smiled a little. "If I was standing on my head, I'd say the moon was floating on the surface of the sky instead of suspended in it."

He didn't reply, and she looked beyond him again. "And the stars." She ran out of inspiration and shrugged. "They're twinkling." When he still didn't answer, she shifted a little, embarrassed. "I, uh, I'm sure you can describe it better than me." She tugged on her captured arm.

He refused to let her pull free. "In space the stars don't twinkle," he said.

She peered at him. The moonlight and her shorter stature let her see that his eyes were closed behind his sunglasses. "Is that right?" she said.

"It's the earth's atmosphere that causes the stars to appear to glitter."

"And from space?"

"They're clearer and brighter, but they're still far beyond our solar system. It's not as if you feel you can zoom over for a visit or anything."

Zoe breathed in a chestful of island air, jasmine and saltwater. "You've been"—she made a gesture with her free hand—"out there, then?"

"A few missions on the space shuttle."

Gee, and she'd spent a few years on the mainland. She sighed. He was Apollo, all right, each foot on a rocket, head in the stars. "So what's the earth look like from there?"

"In the shuttle, you never get far enough in space to see the whole planet at once. Still . . ." There was wonder in his voice. "Still, it's an awesome view. Bright blue oceans and vivid orange deserts against the blackness of space. It's like gliding over a brilliantly colored topographical map. You can see big cities too, and because of their bright lights, some airport runways and bridges."

Zoe dug her island-bred toes into the pathway carved by the hands of her great-grandfather. "But not Abrigo. You'd never be able to spot the island."

He shook his head. "Probably not. But how's this for a trade-off? Every twenty-four hours you get to see sixteen sunsets and sixteen sunrises. And from the moon . . ." His voice lowered to a near whisper. "Well, let's just understate the whole thing and say the earth would be quite a sight."

The moonlight felt cold, and the moon itself

seemed to eye her with an unfriendly glare.
Zoe swallowed. "Yeager..." she started,
without any other idea of what to say.

But then, as if he'd been released from a
hypnotic spell, he shook himself and let go of
her arm. He cleared his throat. "Though that's
not why I brought you on this walk."

She attempted to recover her equilibrium,
now that Yeager's touch was gone. "So you
had a plan, then?"

"Of course I had a plan. I always have a
plan."

His tone and mood were suddenly light,
and Zoe relaxed, chuckling, as they started
walking again. "Okay, okay. I'll bite."

Even his silly "Make that a promise?" didn't
worry her.

Instead, she laughed again. "I feel a request
coming on. What is it? You have a favorite
kind of waffle? Do you want an extra set of
towels?"

"It's about those women."

Zoe's laughter died. Oh. Well. Certainly it
was about those women. All that space stuff
had been just a short sidetrack. "O-Okay."

Phone numbers. She had those. And she
knew the kind of flowers they liked. She knew
the kind of food they liked too. Well, not Desirée, being that it wasn't clear whether she
actually ate meals or just sucked the blood of
the many men she found to date.

"It isn't going to work."

They'd reached the small front porch of his
cottage. "You mean?" She heard the squeaky
question in her voice. But really, it was hard

to think when her stomach was fluttering and they stood so close together in the intimate shadows.

"Zoe." Yeager leaned one shoulder against his front door. He reached out and found her arm again, then pulled her near. "I don't want any of those women."

His thumb stroked under the hem of her short-sleeved blouse to make tiny circles against her skin. Wild shivers rolled down her back.

"Wha-what do you mean?" she said breathlessly.

"What I said." Yeager cupped her other shoulder with his hand and pulled her closer to his hard, wide chest. "I don't want any of those women." He paused, then rubbed her arm again, a tighter circle. "You know who I want."

Oh, God. Oh, God. She wrenched her gaze away from him. From high above, the moon stared down at her again, an unwavering, judgmental eye.

What Yeager wanted was to explore the sky. She was a woman who wanted nothing more than her island. They were miles, planets, *galaxies* apart.

She licked her lips. "None of those women, huh?" she said, hoping to call a halt to whatever was trying to go on here. She even tried out a teasing smile. "My first impression wasn't right about you after all, was it?"

He didn't smile back. Instead, he shook his head as if she was a sad, sad case. "Zoe. Honey."

Oh, boy. He didn't seem willing to be halted.

She could move, of course, but those strong hands were on her. His chest was close and the moon seemed to have quit its role as the Judge Judy of Love. Instead it was acting as a romantic spotlight on something she was half excited about and more than half afraid of.

Yeager lowered his head, and Zoe closed her eyes tight, like a little kid who thinks if she doesn't see the needle coming, she won't feel the shot's sting.

7

Lifting his head, Yeager sighed, Zoe's tension coming right through his hands. It was time to face facts. She wasn't going to help out with the kiss.

It shouldn't surprise him. So far she'd made nothing easy.

But a blind man might require a little help, didn't she realize that? Shortly after his injury, he'd tried to entertain a woman or two and discovered that even a simple kiss demanded cooperation. You'd think after years of doing it in the dark he'd be an expert, but in his new perpetual night his orientation had a way of getting skewed. Once he'd kissed a button instead of a button nose, another time he'd almost choked on a lady friend's feather duster of an earring.

And those women had been relaxed.

He made himself rethink the whole thing. Why was he even touching Zoe? Susan, Elisabeth, and Desirée had left him tonight with lingering good-byes and his promise he'd tattooed their phone numbers on his brain. Not a one of them seemed the type to go as stiff as a broom handle at the threat of his kiss.

Not a one of them smelled like Zoe either.

Yeager sighed. He'd tried to play her way, he really had. But her rules didn't make any sense, not when the other women were as appealing as cold oatmeal and there was this Rice Krispies snap-crackle-pop between him and Zoe. His game would be much more fun for the both of them if she could just pull her head out of the sand and smell the sea air. It was going to come down to this eventually, and with the recent unreliability of his libido, he was going to grab for the gusto whenever he could.

With another breath of that powder-shampoo-Zoe scent, he traced one more figure eight on the smooth, smooth skin of her upper arm. *Come on, baby.*

She was strung so tight, she quivered, and a little anxious sound escaped her mouth.

He gritted his teeth. "Zoe," he whispered, trying to find patience. "Just a kiss." He'd start there, he thought. "I only want a kiss, not your soul."

She tensed even tighter, and he thought she'd break away from him. But then she moved.

Her hand was on him.

Five fingertips, hot as the devil's pitchfork. They tentatively touched his chest and prodded him into the action he'd been wanting to take since he'd heard that worried note in her voice this evening. No, since she'd made him laugh with her description of the island band, or maybe since he'd tasted her home cooking.

No. Since that first breath of her scent had entered his life and swirled around him like a sweet but wicked incantation.

He ducked his head. "Zoe."

"Y-yes?"

God—and it was a prayer—he hoped that she'd look up and make this easy for him.

There. His lips touched down and brushed soft skin—her cheek—and he felt her start. "Easy, easy," he whispered and turned his head to move his cheek against hers.

He knew he didn't shave worth a damn these days either, but already he needed to rub against her somewhere, some way. She made that little anxious sound again, but he smiled now, because she dug those fingers of hers into his chest too in a way that didn't speak of anxiety, but only of anticipation.

He liked anticipating too. Now that he had her skittishness somewhat controlled, he wouldn't hurry her.

His mouth trailed toward her ear. He rubbed his scratchy cheek against that too. Zoe wasn't wearing earrings, and she didn't hide her perfume there either. The scent was everywhere around him, not strangling him, just wrapping him closely, urging him on.

He used his hands now, moving them from her shoulders up her neck to cup her head. Now that she was more compliant, he could risk letting go of her body, and her mouth would be easier to find that way too. He brushed his lips over her temple, across her warm eyebrow and then he used his tongue to trace a tickling line down her short, straight nose.

Zoe didn't laugh.

She didn't do anything but quiver and curl that one hand tighter into his chest. So tight that without his shirt, she'd have made marks.

He'd let her do that later.

He smiled again, then rolled his tongue over the small tip of her nose. Her breath puffed out, moist and warm against his chin. Her mouth was right below his now, no mistake, and ready for the taking.

She made one more pleading sound, and then he obliged her, coming in close for his first real taste.

But she kissed like a kid with braces, her lips all pursed and as stiff as her shoulders had been before. Yeager drew back a little. "Relax, honey."

"I am relaxed." She sounded like her teeth were clenched.

Well, hell, he knew they were clenched.

He rubbed at her scalp with his fingers. "It's just a kiss, Zoe. Give it a chance."

"I am giving it a chance." Now she sounded a bit disgruntled, like he'd found fault with something she'd practiced long and hard.

Jesus. What kind of woman kissed a man like she'd kiss her eighth-grade boyfriend? A terrifying notion entered his brain, and his heart stuttered. He struggled to pull free of the tangle of that bewitching perfume. "Uh, Zoe, uh, exactly how old are you?"

"Twenty-seven."

Whew. His knees went soft in relief. "That's all right, then."

"What's all right, then?"

"This." Determined now, he bent his head. Lips on lips. He found them in the first attempt and he wasn't surprised this time when hers were as tightly puckered as a grandma's. He played with her mouth, outlining it with the tip of his tongue and then taking a tiny bite from her surprisingly full lower lip.

She squeaked.

He sneaked. Just a little touch of his tongue in the new, small opening between her lips.

Her body shuddered, and then she opened for him.

And just before he took her up on her invitation, he realized it wasn't so much that she didn't know how to kiss as that she'd been scared of this one.

Maybe *he* should have been afraid.

She tasted that damn good. The kiss exploded on his tongue with the fire and force of solid rocket boosters. His hands slid through her hair and then shot down her back to haul her close to him.

She was shuddering again, or maybe he was, and he tried to calm whichever of them it was with the soft stroke of his tongue in her mouth. She moaned—it was Zoe for sure—because his body was sending every spare ounce of energy southward. In an instant he went from all systems go to urgently hard. Frantically hard.

Sex.

The need took over his brain and every

other part of him necessary to the task. Still kissing her deeply, tongue stroking in and out, his hands trembled as he pulled Zoe's shirt out of her jeans. Underneath her shirt her skin was warm and the bones of her spine delicate, and he wanted . . .

Sex.

He lifted his head to give them both a chance to get a breath, but she pulled him back down, her fingers biting into his scalp. He groaned into her mouth.

This was good. For once, he and Zoe seemed to be on the same wavelength. If he could just kiss her a little bit more, the last of her nervousness would dissolve, and nothing would distract her from moving into his bed.

Her tongue touched his.

His blood caught fire. It pulsed through his body, hot, but not as hot as Zoe, not as hot as she felt to him when he let his hands wander down to cup her bottom. It wasn't close enough, so he shoved them into the back pockets of her jeans as if he was a junior high boyfriend himself.

He angled his head, and she opened her mouth wider to take him in. Maybe he'd go crazy with her taste. It was like her scent, addictive and sweet and something that he needed to have more of. Like he needed something else.

Sex.

"Zoe." He hauled in a breath and reluctantly took one hand out of her pocket to touch the cold and unyielding front doorknob of his cottage. He wanted her inside.

"Mmm." She leaned into him, and he used the hand left in her pocket to hold her there, his erection pressed against the soft give of her belly. "Kiss me," she whispered.

He'd get her inside in a minute. Their next kiss ignited faster than the one before, and he would have unbuttoned her blouse and unzipped her zipper right there and then, except that without his sight he didn't know how private they were.

"Zoe. We should—"

"This is nice," she murmured. "Just like in the movies. I hear music." She used her tongue again, and he forgot what he was worried about. He forgot what she was talking about. Lost in hot need, he stroked inside her mouth and slid his hand up her arm.

Suddenly, Zoe turned her face so his tongue grazed her cheek. "I really do hear music. What is that?"

"Nothing." Nothing could be as gripping as his need to taste her mouth again. He gently gripped her chin and turned her back to him and what they both wanted.

She went into the kiss willingly enough, but then pulled away again. "Music," she said dreamily.

"Yeah, yeah." He trailed his mouth down her neck and sucked at her scented skin.

She moaned. "Yeager. Don't you hear it?"

He bit her ear persuasively. "Come inside with me, honey. It will be quiet in there."

"Yeager . . ."

The back of his forefinger curled against her

breast. She trembled. "Inside," he said, then found her mouth again.

She let him kiss her, and the blood pounded in him and the need for sex shook him. But despite that he could feel her pulling out of the sexual daze.

"Yeager."

No. He tried pulling her closer.

She pulled back. "Yeager. I hear—"

"It's bells." Isn't that what women heard? Bells? The only sound he was aware of was the rasping intake of his own desperate breaths.

"I hear . . . I hear . . ."

They were *this* close to his bed. He tried desperately to redirect her focus by spearing his hand in her hair and bringing her toward him for another kiss.

But she stiffened instead of softened. "What the—?" she said. Her fingers, cool now, circled his wrist—the wrist with that special watch buckled around it—and she stepped away from him. With a sinking sense of disappointment, he knew he'd lost her.

Zoe's voice entered the night again, completely alert but incredulous. "I hear *Disney*?"

Yeager triple-socked Mickey after that. Well, after a back-to-reality Zoe had taken one long breath and high-tailed it down the garden path and after he had taken his uncomfortably poker-hard and pissed-as-hell self back into his cottage.

Then he flipped on the TV. The noise from it covered the sound of his frustrated curses.

Yeager dropped to his bed, groaning, and

held his head in his hands. Yeah, yeah, yeah. It was a small world after all. He'd turned on the effing Disney channel, of course.

Eyes half open, Zoe dragged her feet like a zombie in the direction of the coffeemaker.

"Good morning."

Startled, Zoe stumbled over her fuzzy yellow slippers. For the first time this morning she opened her eyes all the way. "Lyssa." Her sister sat at the kitchen table, looking as rumpled and tired as Zoe probably would have seen she was if she'd had the guts to pass by a mirror. "You're up early."

Or maybe, like Zoe, she'd never really slept.

"Mm." Lyssa closed the magazine in front of her and shoved it beneath the stack of newspapers they subscribed to for their guests.

Zoe blinked again. "What were you reading?"

Lyssa shrugged. "Nothing, really."

Curious, though, Zoe slid the magazine free. Lyssa was a book reader, not a magazine peruser. The cover was glossy-bright and featured a woman who was mostly breasts with a little red lipstick thrown in. Zoe gaped at her sister. "*Cosmo*?" It was the last thing she'd guess her sister would read.

Lyssa didn't answer.

Zoe checked the cover again. *Cosmo* all right. Lyssa reading *Cosmo*. Maybe Zoe was dreaming. Maybe last night on Yeager's front porch had been a dream!

What a terrific thought. Then instead of worrying over those embarrassing and lustful minutes of kissing, she could dismiss them as the inexplicable meanderings of a slumbering mind.

"What's that on your neck?" Lyssa asked.

Zoe instantly pulled the lapels of her robe up to her ears. "What neck?" *Argh*. She turned her back and scurried to the coffeemaker. *What neck*. What an idiot she was. Of course it wasn't any dream last night. Dreams didn't normally make at-home hickey deliveries. She was going to kill Yeager.

Right after she avoided him for the rest of her life.

"Zoe—"

She didn't want to talk about her neck. "What's with the *Cosmo*?"

An unfamiliar silence filled the room. Zoe frowned and looked over her shoulder. There was rarely any hesitance when she asked Lyssa a direct question. Zoe took her role as her sister's protector seriously, and Lyssa just as naturally confided everything to her. Had her sister caught a glimpse of Zoe and Yeager the night before? Was that the cause of this newfound quiet?

"Zoe." Lyssa swung around in her chair, her long, butter-yellow hair sliding over one shoulder.

Zoe ran a hand over her short waves and remembered Yeager's fingers on her scalp, turning her mouth to his. A shiver tickled the nape of her neck but she ruthlessly ignored it.

"What?" she asked Lyssa, worrying a bit. "Are you feeling okay?"

"I'm fine. I'm just . . ." She made a vague

gesture in the direction of the cover.

Zoe frowned. "The magazine?" she guessed. "Why are you reading something like that?"

"I was . . . looking at the fashions."

Zoe blinked and drew closer to the kitchen table. "What fashions?" She eyed the cover teasers and read a couple aloud. " 'Why He'd Want to Say No.' 'Sexy Secrets He Wants You to Whisper.' "

"Well, um, there's fashion too," Lyssa defended herself.

Zoe riffled through the pages. "Oh, sure, if you want to trek down to Dave Parnelli's Island Grocery in a corset and thigh highs." She grinned. " 'Course, Dave Junior might be willing to forgo cash payment in that case."

"Zoe—"

"Anyway, if you want fashion, there's plenty of pretty things at Rae-Ann's. Didn't she say she was expecting a new shipment at the boutique this week?"

A flush stained Lyssa's cheeks. "Maybe I want something not available on the island."

Uneasiness tickled Zoe's stomach. Something not on the island? "Then there's mail order."

Lyssa didn't look convinced. Nervousness pitched in Zoe's belly again, and the beginnings of a cold sweat broke out at the base of her spine. "What's this about?" she asked her sister. The island was their home. The island was where they stayed and stayed safe. "Is there something you need to tell me?"

"No." Lyssa looked down, the warm color

fading from her face. "Don't worry. There's nothing to tell, more's the pity."

Relief flooded through Zoe, and she dismissed the "more's the pity." Of course everything was fine. The festival plans were proceeding, the firetail would return, their lives would remain secure.

She finished starting the coffee and crossed to the pantry to retrieve their glass jar of homemade granola. "We'll need to eat quickly if we're going to have time for showers before we set up the buffet for the guests."

Lyssa didn't respond, and Zoe looked over at her sister again. She was glumly leafing through the magazine. "Lyssa?"

Her sister continued turning pages. "I do have a question for you, Zoe. What would you do if you wanted something. If you wanted something very, very badly?"

Zoe didn't know if they were talking a dress or a dream. But she thought about Abrigo. About the livelihood of the island and the lives it made possible. Of the safe place they'd found here and how determined she was to keep it from changing. "If I wanted something, I'd make it happen. I'd do everything in my power to make it happen."

For the first time that morning, Lyssa smiled. "You're one smart cookie, big sister."

Zoe toothfully smiled back. "I could have told you that." Inside, though, she felt like a fraud.

She used retrieving cereal bowls as an excuse for turning away from Lyssa's admiring gaze. A smart woman wouldn't have kissed

Yeager Gates. A smart woman wouldn't have
created a situation she'd have to run from for
the rest of his stay.

The problem with working for yourself, Zoe
thought later, was it gave you too many op-
portunities to listen to your own words of wis-
dom.

*If I wanted something, I'd make it happen. I'd
do everything in my power to make it happen.*

She sighed and put the last of the breakfast
china away in the dining room breakfront. The
same woman who'd uttered those words had
spent the entire morning hiding from the one
guest who didn't come down to the dining
room to eat. If she wanted something—like,
say, to clear up this situation with Yeager—
then she had to make it happen.

The fact was, she hated making apologies,
and she owed him a biggie.

This whole embarrassing situation was her
own fault. She'd steamrollered him into meeting Susan, Elisabeth, and Desirée. She'd ac-
quired that ability to single-mindedly push
forward her own agenda more than five years
ago, when it was only Lyssa and her in a
world gone crazy with blood counts and
starched lab coats and terrifying test results.

Lyssa had been seventeen, and Zoe had
been almost twenty-one, enrolled in college,
both of them still grieving for their parents.
But when Lyssa's odd tiredness was diagnosed as leukemia, Zoe realized she had to rise
above her grief. She'd resolved with the help
of her parents' insurance money to find the

best specialists, the most up-to-date treatments, and to fight the most aggressive fight they could.

Nobody liked to tell two young women bad news, but Zoe had fought for every scrap of information, and she'd begun every day by pasting a determined smile on her face. The two sisters had gone out to confront the medical world, her sister with the face of an angel and Zoe with the soul of a shark.

She'd insisted on settling for only one thing—Lyssa's recovery. There was no such word as no.

And if sometimes at night she cried, choking on her own thick sobs, she'd done it under the covers. Lyssa never saw her fear.

Once they'd moved back to the island, after Lyssa's health returned, Zoe had promised herself she'd never have that much at stake again. After her parents passed away, and after Lyssa's brush with death, Zoe knew losing someone else she loved would destroy her.

So even though the threat to her and Lyssa's safety had been beaten back, Zoe held onto that ability to get people to do what she wanted.

It had worked with the Firetail committee when they talked about canceling the festival.

Just as it had worked with Yeager when he wanted to wheedle her into a flirtation.

With the small backfire of those kisses at his front door.

But she realized she was just going to have to face up to the mistake. Admit to him that the matchmaking was a bust and make clear she didn't plan on any more attempts. Make absolutely clear she didn't plan on any more anything with him.

From now on she would only take care of his lodging needs.

The morning sun felt good on her face, and the aroma of the herbs in her garden soothed her as she made her way to Yeager's cottage. She dawdled in the garden for a moment, leaning down to pull up a cheeky dandelion. A bee buzzed by her nose, and a raven cawed hoarsely and flew close enough for its wings to stir the air and flutter her hair.

She sent the thing a dirty look. Really. Was a little personal space too much to ask for?

It cawed again, as if it was taunting her, and then she heard Yeager's voice.

With his plastic friend propped up in the chair opposite his, Yeager was sitting at the table on his porch again, wearing another pair of soft jeans and a shirt open at the neck. Her hand itched, remembering the hot hardness of his chest. She swallowed and tweaked at her own shirt. It was a sleeveless cotton turtleneck, chosen because it covered the mark on her body that told the world she'd spent time with someone other than her sister the night before.

Zoe sucked in a determined breath. *Just get this over with. After you apologize, you can walk away.*

Then Yeager spoke again, and this time she could make out his words. "Dolly, you call the game this time."

Zoe realized he was holding a deck of cards, and as he talked, he pitched them one at a time in the direction of the plastic woman. Dolly made no effort to catch them of course, and in fact one hit her right in the face, knocking askew the pair of kiddie sunglasses she wore— the only thing she wore.

"What's that, Dolly? Five card stud? You want five cards and I'm the stud?" Yeager chuckled humorlessly. "You're a tease, my girl. Did anyone ever tell you that?"

Zoe might have thought he was putting on a show for her benefit, but there was barely controlled emotion in his voice, and he didn't stop with the cards. Instead he kept flicking them in the direction of Dolly over and over, his wrist snapping.

"I know you're tired of the game, hon, but I'm dying here. One little bored minute at a time."

Zoe's heart clenched. *This* she hadn't even considered. He sat in the cottage most of the day, all day long. As far as she knew, he'd only been out in a golf cart with Deke a couple of times. But without the ability to see, he couldn't read or watch TV or play cards.

He kept tossing them at Dolly. "I'm just giving you a chance here, sweetheart. I know you've got a *pair*, but—" His voice broke off and his head went up, his dark glasses aimed skyward.

Zoe heard it a few moments after he did. Squinting against the sun, she spotted a small plane crossing above them. There was an airstrip on Abrigo that was occasionally used. The talk had been for years about developing a full-fledged air service, but to date, no one had seemed interested in taking on the project.

She looked back at Yeager, and her heart lurched again. Even with his sunglasses on, she could read the naked longing on his face.

He sat alone in the dark. Every day missing something he couldn't have.

Zoe bit her lip. No wonder he'd come onto her. He didn't have anything else to do. She was the most convenient distraction at hand.

For some reason, she found the thought comforting instead of insulting. Yeager didn't want her, he wanted something to do with his days.

That she could handle. That didn't threaten the comforting cocoon of her island life. That she could maybe even help with.

But how?

The plane flew out of earshot, but another distant roar took its place, something closer. Zoe looked out toward the Haven harbor. In the glittering water, a speedboat rapidly decelerated to a halt, spewing behind it a white rooster tail of foam. It rocked in its own wake, the red-lettered sign on its side bobbing up and down.

An idea popped into Zoe's mind.

"Hey, Yeager!" she called.

His hand halted in midtoss. "Leave me alone, Zoe," he called back. He didn't sound friendly.

"I'm, uh, here about last night."

"Do you want to start over from where we stopped?"

"No!"

"Gee, now why am I not surprised?" he asked drily. The card flipped from his hand to land in Dolly's lap. "Then leave me alone, Zoe. Just go away."

She frowned. He wasn't going to get rid of her that easily. Not when she understood him now. Not when she could at least make today a little better for him.

She'd learned that too with Lyssa. Sometimes you tried just thinking about today. You watched a funny movie or went out for ice cream or made caramel apples and giggled like a kid.

Sometimes today was all you were certain you had.

Zoe walked closer to his cottage. "Listen. I've had a scathingly brilliant idea."

He didn't seemed moved. "Forgive me, Zoe, but I've already been victim of one of your scathingly brilliant ideas—your matchmaking—and I've had the sleepless night to prove it."

She savored a little spurt of satisfaction. So she hadn't been the only one.

But she reminded herself that dalliance with her had just been his distraction. She had something he'd like even better.

"Why don't we call a friendly truce?"

His lip curled. "Friendly?"

Zoe swallowed. "I think that's fair, don't you?"

"No more matchmaking?"

"I promise. And I apologize."

His lip curled again. "I'm not sure I can trust you, Zoe."

"C'mon. You're going to like what I have."

Now he smiled. "I know that."

"The idea I have," she amended hastily.

When he ignored her, she tried again. "It's better than what Dolly's offering," she said.

"I don't know," he answered, though he sighed and then pushed his chair back to step toward the sliding doors leading into his cottage. "She seems to be offering plenty."

As he brushed by the dummy, he paused to run a careless palm over one *Cosmo*-quality breast.

Zoe pursed her lips and crossed her arms over her own chest.

Yeager gave the plastic woman another lingering touch. "And she hasn't run from me yet."

8

If he hadn't lost two in a row to Dolly—not games, but decks of cards—Yeager assured himself he wouldn't have allowed Zoe to lead him to a golf cart bound for a secret destination.

"Why won't you tell me where we're going?" he demanded.

"Stop being so surly," she answered cheerfully. The cart bounced down what Yeager knew was the steep driveway of the Haven House. "Just relax and enjoy yourself."

He decided to work up a sincere dislike for Zoe Cash. She was treating him like a sulky baby brother when less than twelve hours before they'd been breathing heavy and battling passion. The occasion had apparently, and easily, escaped her memory.

He shifted uncomfortably on the golf cart's cold vinyl seat and tried to remember why he'd been so pleased the day they'd met. All he'd gotten out of the relationship so far was a month's ration of frustration and the hard-on from hell.

A sharp left turn of the cart flung him against her shoulder, and she quickly nudged him upright. "Isn't it a beautiful day?" she gushed.

"Absolutely damn gorgeous," he answered, groping for something to hold onto as she made another fast turn. "I've always liked my world tar-pitch black."

"Oh, stop being so grouchy. Take yourself a deep breath of clean island air."

Grouchy! Yeager drew back in his seat, some emotion burning the back of his neck. "That's easy for you to say. If you only knew—" He bit off the rest of the muttered complaint.

"You're right," Zoe said, apologetic. "Let me give it a try."

She paused a moment, then started gushing again. "I still think it's a beautiful day," she said, the golf cart continuing to hurtle along. "I can smell the salty ocean and hear the birds singing up a storm, eyes closed or not." The cart made another wild maneuver.

Eyes closed? "Shit! Zoe!" Yeager made a mad grab in the direction of the steering wheel. "Open them!"

"Relax," she said again, fending off his hands as she made another hairpin turn. "I can find my way around this place blind-folded."

"Tell me you're kidding," he said.

But then came the screech of brakes on his left and the matching shriek of Yeager's heart. "Shit, Zoe! Open your eyes."

He heard the grin in her voice. "Don't worry so much. That was just Mr. Curtis in his '72 El

Dorado. He drives with cataracts, I drive with my eyes closed. I think that makes us about even."

Yeager's self-pity evaporated as he imagined thousands of pounds of Caddy chrome versus the golf cart's welterweight. It made him sick to think of Zoe broken or even bruised. "Please, Zoe," he said, unwilling to take the chance that she wasn't pulling his leg.

"Oh, all right," she agreed grudgingly. "But you take all the fun out of everything."

He didn't breathe with complete ease until she came to a stop and he heard the grinding protest of the cart's emergency brake. The loud crash of waves and the sharp salt tang in his nostrils gave away their location. She'd brought him to the beach.

Zoe came around to his side and made him take her arm. "Come on, Grumpy. Have I got a surprise for you. You'll never guess why we're here."

He let her pull him out of the cart. The cool slide of her hand against his arm sent a hot stab of reaction in the direction of his groin, and without even thinking, he reached out and touched her cheek.

She was standing so close, he felt her whole body quiver.

The response gave him a strange sense of satisfaction. Maybe she did remember the night before after all. He decided to test the water. "I happen to have one guess."

He heard her take a breath, and then she tugged him in the direction of the surf. "You think you know why we're here? Go for it."

As they trudged forward, Zoe slightly ahead, soft sand kicked up against his ankles, and his healing leg dragged a bit. He bent toward her ear. "You have fifteen women lined up, and I get to find out which one is you by feel alone."

She suddenly stopped, and Yeager smacked against her, his front plastered against her back. He took the opportunity to slide his free arm over her body and pull her closer to him, his forearm nestling between her breasts. Her hair was soft as feathers against his cheek. "I could do it, you know. Find you by feel."

Air shuddered into her lungs, and he smiled to himself. Who was in the driver's seat now?

She slipped out of his hold. "Do you want some fun or not?"

"I think that would be fun," he said mildly.

She just continued walking until the soft sand turned hard-packed beneath their feet. Then she stopped and whistled from between her teeth, boyish and piercing.

"Geez!" Yeager clapped his hands over his ears.

She ignored him and whistled again, then shouted in the direction of the water. "David! Leif!"

Yeager experienced the first tickle of apprehension in his gut. "Zoe, what—"

She yelled over him. "Hey, David! Leif!"

He swallowed, at a loss to guess what she had in mind. "Zoe. Listen. You're not, uh, matchmaking or anything again, are you?"

That amusement reentered her voice. "I promised not to, right?"

His gut made a minor roll. Was that an answer?

Before he could decide, heavy feet pounded toward them on the sand, accompanied by the clink of something weighty and metal. Unfamiliar young male voices greeted them.

"Howzitgoin', Zee? Your big guy here wants a ride?"

Not that he'd admit it in a million years, but it took all of Yeager's military discipline to keep from backing away. "Zoe." He swallowed. "What's this about? Listen, whatever I've done, however I've offended you . . ."

She laughed, actually giggled, and he still couldn't wrap his mind around what was happening even as the men came closer and started to loop their equipment around him.

"You should see your face," she said, between those bubbles of laughter.

Straps went between his legs and across his chest, and a glimmer of what might be happening flared in Yeager's mind.

"You want to go along, Zee?" one of the young voices said. "We can do a tandem hookup."

Zoe finally turned serious. "These feet aren't leaving Abrigo soil, boys."

Yeager frowned, still not certain what was going on. "Zoe . . ."

A hand gave a final tug to a strap. Zoe whistled again, and that unholy glee reentered her voice. "Let her rip!" she yelled. "Listen for Leif's instructions," she whispered in his ear, and then she gave him a swift kiss on the cheek and a smart pat on the ass.

Head reeling, Yeager just stood there, aware the others were moving away from him. What if this was some sort of practical joke Zoe was pulling on him? Truss him up like a turkey and leave him there to find his own way home? Did she think that was what he deserved after talking her into those kisses last night?

The deep growl of an accelerating speedboat broke through his thoughts. He almost immediately felt a pull from behind and above, and then it all came together: the straps, the ocean, the boat, the glee in Zoe's voice. Because she was giving him something all right.

Yeager knew now that air was filling a parachute behind him, a parachute attached by a long tether to a speedboat just offshore. His heartbeat jumped to Mach 1, and then the exhilarated thing climbed into his throat as his body lifted from the ground and Zoe gave him the one thing he missed above all others.

Yeager flew.

As far as speed and maneuverability went, parasailing didn't stand a chance against flight in any kind of plane, but Yeager wasn't complaining. His muscles relaxed into the cradle of the harness, and the metal and canvas squeaked as he lifted his face to catch the wind head on.

Without sight or control, all that remained was sensation. The air buoyed him, lifting his body away from the torn muscles, the irritating stitches, and the headaches he'd suffered since the first days in the hospital.

The air buoyed his spirits too, and just like

that he was a boy again. Eight years old and in some weed-and-gravel air force base playground, where the swings creaked and complained but were the vehicle of his dreams of the sky.

As in those days, Yeager squeezed shut his eyes and imagined himself flying above the earth. The island was below him, and he saw it in his mind. He saw the curling white edges of the waves flinging themselves against the golden shore. He saw there were palm trees and dark green hillsides that rose up to part the pulled-cotton clouds. The sun was hot on his face, and there was the silence—the kind he'd missed—of a man alone with the thing he loved best in the world.

And just like when he was eight years old, his imaginary vision kept moving outward away from the earth. Ocean, sand, trees, hills, all their details dropped away as his imagination soared higher and higher. The island became a dot, and the ocean flattened into a plain of blue. He dreamed himself through the cool clouds and higher and then even higher into the deep dark void of space.

"Yeager!"

He ignored the annoying gnat of reality.

"Yeager!"

Reality buzzed by him again, and he shook himself reluctantly out of the dream, realizing he was dropping and that Zoe and her buddies were shouting instructions at him to direct him back down to the beach.

Without thinking, he responded as directed, automatically reaching up to locate the 'chute's strings, then pulling on one side or the other as they indicated.

Too soon he was back on the hard sand, with all its earthbound noises—waves, clinking harnesses, chatter among Zoe, David, and Leif. It all came to him from a long distance, as if his soul was still in the sky, unhindered and untethered. He wasn't even sure if he thanked the other men before they hurried off to another client.

It was too soon too for Yeager to be left alone facing Zoe.

"Well?" she prompted, still all sass and bubbly good cheer. In his mind's eye he could see her stance, one hand on one feminine hip.

He didn't know what to say.

Almost palpably, the fizz went out of her.

He still didn't know what to say.

"Did I do something wrong?" she asked, her voice hesitant and barely audible over another surge of wave against sand.

He shook his head. After last night, he'd promised himself to stay clear of this woman. She was a ration of frustration and even now that hard-on from hell. But she laughed, and laughed at him, and had driven from the house to the beach with her eyes shut.

Just to show him it was a beautiful day.

He'd promised himself he wasn't going to touch her. She had too much trouble, she *was* too much trouble, and he had enough of his own troubles to want to continue with that annoying dance of attraction-distance-attraction.

And then she showed him what it was like to fly again.

He should thank her, though he wasn't certain of the words. He only knew that his soul could survive a little longer with this damn blindness, now that he'd experienced the sky once more.

"Yeager?" Her voice still sounded unsure.

"Take me home," he said to her gently. She touched his wrist, and he made a lucky grab for her hand and pulled her arm around his waist. He slung his around her shoulder, hugging her close to his body, gritting his teeth as she fitted so easily and completely against him.

He dropped a kiss on the top of her sun-heated hair. Zoe aroma danced around him, and something became quite clear.

Now that he liked her, and now that he owed her, and considering that never-ending hard-on, he was going to have to step into the dance again and hope like hell he didn't end up tromping on Zoe's toes.

Deke hung his head over the peeling balcony railing to gauge the number of feet to the prickly holly below. Thirty painful feet.

Next he ducked inside the third-floor bedroom and made his way back to the stairwell. Peering past the remains of the second-floor landing—it had apparently rotted through some years ago—he wasn't surprised to find the extension ladder that he'd used to reach his present location lying on its side. On the first floor.

He hadn't expected anything different. Not when he'd accidentally kicked the thing down himself when his booted foot had slipped on the dusty hardwood floor.

He was well and truly stranded.

Deke shoved his hands in his jeans pockets and ventured back to the bedroom with the balcony. It was the room he'd slept in those summers when he'd stayed on the island. Damn the nostalgia that had prompted him to get up on the ladder to look it over anyway. If he hadn't succumbed to sentimentality he wouldn't be in this fix.

Grinding his teeth, he stepped back onto the balcony and surveyed the view he remembered from boyhood. Nothing had changed. Perhaps the trees on the hillside and in the canyon leading down to the water were taller, but then so was he.

And just like in the past, he could see his tree house. *Damn.* Deke cursed himself again and blew out a disgusted puff of air. Why couldn't he get the blasted thing out of his mind?

And her. Why couldn't he boot Lyssa out of his brain?

Those initials and that heart around them had blown him away at first sight. But then he'd recovered his breath and hustled both of them out of the tree house and back to civilization. He'd been tensed for some sort of protest on her part, but she'd gone willingly enough.

Willing and with a little smile and a patient attitude that worried him, big time. She'd even said a calm good night with an expression he could read in mile-high letters: *I've made my point and I'm satisfied—for now.*

He gripped the railing and closed his eyes. Since then, he'd been jumping out of his skin at the slightest sound, waiting for the other shoe to drop. Waiting for Lyssa to make another unwelcome appearance.

"Hey, Deke!" a cheery voice called from below.

He slowly shook his head, not even needing a peek to know who it was. That imaginary shoe dropped right on his chest with the weighty thud of an air force combat boot. How did she do that? The instant he allowed her into his mind, she ended up walking into his world.

"Hey, Lyssa," he mumbled.

"Whatcha doing?"

Her face was tilted up to him, sending that long, blond, cover-girl hair of hers swinging against her butt. Deke swallowed. Maybe he could blame his lust on that hair. The straight, parted-in-the-middle look was right out of the sweaty nights of his teens, when he got off by fantasizing with the help of a Cheryl Tiegs poster.

"Whatcha doing?" Lyssa said again.

Deke shifted. Even thinking about sex around Lyssa made him feel guilty, as if he was sullying her sweetness with his dirty thoughts. He swallowed again and thought quickly. "I'm, uh, I'm, uh, working."

A little frown brought her golden eyebrows together. "Working at what?"

"Just, um, some stuff," he answered.

Of course he should stop prevaricating and

just ask for her help getting off the third floor.
But if she figured out he was stuck up here,
who knew what she might do? Looking down
at her, he shifted again uneasily. The clear,
clean-aired sky had nothing on Lyssa. Her
eyes were so blue that their color seared him
even from this distance. Her blond hair, those
laser-blue eyes, that sweet, curvy body hardly
hidden by a soft dress, the whole package terrified him.

Yeah, it was ridiculous, like being terrified
of a kitten, but it was the unwelcome and
surging desire he had for her, even now
changing the fit of his jeans, that wore the
claws.

"See you later," he called down, and turned
his back in preparation for going inside the
house and brainstorming some way out of his
predicament.

"Hey!"

He froze, then reluctantly turned around.

She still wore that little frown. "Are you
sure you're okay?"

*Oh, yeah, I'm fine. Merely prepared to starve to
death before letting you anywhere near me.*

Shit, he was certifiably nuts.

He pinched the bridge of his nose, then
sighed. Really, he had to get a grip. "Actually,
I could use some help. I've accidentally
stranded myself up here."

Her eyes widened and she started forward.

Deke held up a hand. "It's not that simple.
I've knocked over the ladder that I used to
climb up. It's on the floor inside—inside the
front door that automatically locks—and the

keys are in my shirt pocket." He rubbed his bare chest. "The shirt that I left inside too . . . at the foot of the ladder."

He ignored the little smile starting to play over her face. "Would you mind going into town and sending a locksmith out to me?"

She shook her head. "That won't be necessary." One hand dug into the pocket of her dress. "This just happens to be your lucky day."

Frowning, Deke watched her extract a shiny key.

"I've been carrying this around with me for days, and now I know why."

Deke squinted. "Are you trying to tell me that's a key to the door?"

Lyssa smiled. "I'd go to Las Vegas on it."

He frowned. "Where the hell did you get it? My attorney only gave me one key."

Lyssa's smile widened. "It was my lucky day," she said airily. "So I go inside, reset the ladder, and you're free?"

He still couldn't believe she had the right key. "I don't know. The ladder's pretty awkward and heavy. You're probably going to need someone to help, even if you can get in."

Lyssa pursed those give-me-a-kiss lips. "When I'm determined, I'm stronger than I look."

He couldn't argue with that, though he tried. "But—"

She spoke right over him. "Do you want to play Robinson Crusoe or do you want to be rescued?"

Deke stopped trying to protest. "I want

out." *And away from you*, he added mentally.

She took a step in the direction of the front door, then halted. "Wait a minute," she said, her smile turning sly. "I'm letting you off too easily."

Oh, he should have known this was too good to be true. "What are you talking about?" He tried ordering her around. "Go open the door."

Crossing her arms over her chest, she moved back to her original position right below him. "Nuh-uh," she said, shaking her head. "I see this as the perfect opportunity for blackmail."

Deke groaned. "Blackmail? What the hell could I have that you want?"

She laughed. "Among other things, information."

He pretended he didn't hear the "among other things," though his cock heard the words and stiffened even more at the gentle innuendo. Ignoring his body's response, he mimicked her pose. "Maybe I don't mind staying up here."

"Oh, come on," she said. "Answer just a few questions."

"I'm forty-three years old, I work for NASA, and I want to get the hell out of here, so go open the door."

She smiled cheekily. "Tell me something I don't know."

"Like what?"

"Like . . ." Even from this distance he could see the pink tinging her cheeks. "Like is there someone else?"

Deke froze a moment, then immediately grabbed for the out. "Yes. That's why—" He decided against embellishing the lie. "Yes, there is."

She looked down at her flat-soled leather sandals. "Oh." Then she gave him another shot from those laser eyes. "You wouldn't lie to me, would you?"

His eyebrows rose. "Why would you say a thing like that?"

Lyssa cocked her head. "Don't take this the wrong way, but you don't strike me as the type of man to court a woman."

For a moment he did take it the wrong way, and the insult stung. But then he shook himself. "That doesn't mean I don't have one."

"So there's already a woman in your life." Lyssa bit her lip and looked away. "Does she . . . does she have any children?"

Her voice wasn't quite so casual this time, and Deke ran his gaze over her finely etched profile. *She who*? he thought absently, absurdly fascinated by the pugnacious tilt of Lyssa's nose. He caught himself just before echoing the question aloud. Christ, if there was a woman in his life, would he even know if she had children? Would he even ask?

His voice came out gruff. "Listen. I'm forty-three years old. The kind of relationships I have and the kind of women I have them with are something a kid like you can't imagine."

She wouldn't be cowed. "You mean sexual relationships."

He made a sound between a groan and a plea.

Those lips of hers pursed again. "You think
I can't imagine having sex with you?"

Shit. "That does it!" He shoved his hands in
his pockets to stretch a little more room in his
jeans. "Either get me out of here or go back
home and stop torturing me!"

She eyed him with that determination she'd
earlier claimed. "Not until you tell me why
you don't think I'm aware of sex," she said
matter-of-factly. "Is there something about
me—"

"Lyssa." He groaned and rolled his eyes
heavenward. *"No."*

"Good," she said, releasing a big sigh.

Setting his teeth, he shook his head. "Now
get me out of here."

She didn't budge. Oh, God, and she was
smiling again.

One of her sandals drew a pattern in the
dust at her feet. "I'm still thinking about how
you're going to pay me back for the service."

He ground his teeth. "If you stop this non-
sense immediately, I'll rethink strangling you.
Didn't you get that information you asked
for?"

She laughed. "It's not good enough." Her
foot made another circle in the dust. "I want
a kiss."

A kiss! Deke's body went into full red alert
even while his brain was trying desperately to
neutralize the response. He had to swallow
twice before he could make a sound. "Did
anyone ever tell you"—he made his voice cyn-
ical and cool and as bored as all get out—"that
you're too forward?"

She shook her head, and that mass of blond, silky hair swished over her shoulders. "Nope. Because I never have been." Another white, cheeky smile came his way. "Until now."

He closed his eyes. He'd promise anything to get her to stop chattering at him. To get her to stop smiling at him. "Fine, fine," he said, waving a hand in her direction. Once he was no longer trapped, he'd put her off.

Put her off for good.

She was right about the key and her determination. In just a couple of seconds she was inside, and it didn't take much longer for her to horse the ladder around and then hoist it into position. For a delicate little thing, she could get the job done.

She even held the ladder for him as he stepped down, and he had to shoo her away as he neared the bottom. As soon as his boots hit the floor, he reached for his shirt and threw it on, buttoning it quickly and without meeting her eyes.

Finally he had to face her. "Well . . ." He dusted his palms against his jeans.

"Well?" she prompted, widening her eyes.

He took a step back. "Thank you."

She smiled. "You're very welcome."

His shoulders rolled, trying to shrug off the sudden tension. "Maybe I'll see you later at the house. I have some more work to do here."

"Aren't you forgetting something?"

No. He wasn't going to kiss her.

But she stepped close to him and reached for his chest. He went statue-still, and then watched her small fingers nimbly fasten a button he'd missed.

"There," she said, but she didn't move away. Instead, she flattened her palms against his shirtfront.

Deke's heart punched against his chest wall. He just stood there, hands dangling, waiting for that telltale and certain pain to travel down his right arm. It had to be a heart attack. And he'd lay his death at Lyssa's door, damn it.

But the pain didn't come, just more heart punches to the chest, and looking down at her beautiful face and tender mouth, Deke couldn't take it any more.

She was going to get what she asked for.

His breath rasped in and out while his hands finally, finally, came around her young and warm body and slammed her up against him. He pressed his erect cock against her belly, telling her in no uncertain terms what she was getting.

Then he bent his head and saw her eyes dilate, blue to black, as he took her mouth.

Hard and hungry, he didn't give a rat's ass for finesse or persuasion. He pushed against those soft, sweet lips, and they opened for him, opened for him to thrust his tongue into the hot darkness that tasted like . . .

The taste made his head spin so fast he didn't know if there was anything in this world like it.

She moaned, and he almost backed away, but then he ignored the impulse and angled his head for an even deeper kiss. God, he wanted her. And God, he wanted to scare her off.

He sucked on her tongue. He ground himself against her. He ran his hands over the full weight of her breasts and then over her shoulders and down her back to cup her ass and pull her hips into the cradle of his.

He went a little crazy with the touch and feel of her, his mouth traveling away from hers to taste her neck, to bite her earlobes, then back to her mouth.

All the while she made little sounds at the back of her throat. He knew he was frightening her, but he kept on pressing, his lips to hers, his hard, hot body to her softer one. It wasn't until he tasted tears that he stopped, wrenching himself away.

Taking a deep breath, he curled his hands into fists and took another step back. Then he forced himself to look at her, schooling his face into a calm, almost bored mask.

Her eyes were huge and her chest heaved. A lock of hair was stuck to one wet and pink cheek. He reached to free it, but she hastily moved away.

His throat tightened, but he ignored the sensation. This was what he'd wanted. What she'd asked for.

She took another couple of steps back, and her hand trembled as she self-consciously smoothed the front of her dress.

He looked away, her fear sickening him. "That was your kiss," he said roughly.

"No," she said, shaking her head, but still backing away. Her palms wiped at the moisture on her cheeks, and then she dragged the back of her hand across her lips. "That was *your* kiss," she said hoarsely. "You still owe me mine."

Then she turned and ran out the door, leaving the house with a slam and a cloud of dust to join Deke's deep shame and reluctant regret.

9

Lyssa ran as fast as she could down the path leading away from Deke's house, swiping at the last of her tears and trying desperately to rein in her wayward emotions. She had to get control of herself!

Her slick-soled sandals skidded in the dirt as she halted at the turnoff to Haven House. Home wasn't an option. As much as she'd like to hide away in her bedroom right now, Zoe's super sister radar would surely pick up on her distress. Lyssa didn't want to explain or excuse herself.

There were good reasons not to tell Zoe about Deke. Foremost was Zoe's near warrior zeal to protect her. Their parents' death and her subsequent illness had affected Zoe in ways she was certain her sister couldn't even admit. Zoe would break out the spears and breast shields if she thought Lyssa had been in any way hurt.

And nothing would make her believe Lyssa's instant and heart-deep conviction that Deke was the one.

Lyssa took another swipe at her damp cheeks. She was having plenty of doubts on that last point herself.

Turning right, she scrambled down a little-used path that wandered over the hills, ignoring a renewed desire to cry and an unfamiliar anger burning inside her. With a deep breath, she purposely slowed her steps and tried releasing her turmoil, letting her mind go to the cloud place she'd discovered years before.

The cloud place was the wellspring of her customary serenity, though she couldn't claim to have discovered it on her own. An eight-year-old named Danica, in the last stages of the disease that killed her, told Lyssa about it during her very first kids-with-cancer support group meeting.

Bewildered and still numbed by her own diagnosis, Lyssa had stared at the bristly headed little girl as she described how helpful it was to let her spirit go to the cloud place while her body stayed behind to deal with the realities of treatment.

During the course of her own cancer, Lyssa hadn't always been able to find the cloud place. But with time and practice she'd reached that spot more and more often.

Though she didn't need the cloud place any more to escape fear and pain, Lyssa still found it a valuable refuge from everyday annoyances and failures. While Zoe tangled herself in knots worrying about what-ifs and might-bes, Lyssa accepted life's events as they came to her.

Except this! Except Deke rejecting her!

Lyssa grunted out loud in aggrieved frustration, then hastily looked around, embarrassed by her outburst. But she was alone, thank goodness, having marched herself to a hill so remote that it would require even her, an island-bred woman, a bit of time to get her bearings.

Turning in a circle, she saw only hill and scrub and bright blue sky.

Lyssa made a face. Fine, then. She needed time alone, didn't she? Time to get this stupid anger under control. Wrapped up in emotion, she set off at random in a downhill direction.

Why was Deke making everything so difficult? Was she truly so unappealing?

The stinging started behind her eyes again, and as she blinked it away, she missed a deep rut of dried mud and went down gracelessly and heavily on one knee.

"Ow!" A sharp rock had dug a deep gash, and bright red blood welled up, then oozed down her leg.

Lyssa stared at the wound, aghast, then her heart thrummed to hummingbird speed, and she hurriedly reached into her pocket. No tissue, so she quickly clapped her palm over the cut.

Ten minutes, she reminded herself. Direct pressure for ten minutes and then she'd get home fast and clean it. An infection could kill her.

Kill her.

The words sank in, and Lyssa fell back onto her rear end in the dirt. She forced a long, deep breath past the lump in her throat.

There was nothing to worry about any more. That was an old panic. She was cured. Chemotherapy was no longer destroying her healthy, infection-fighting cells as well as her cancer.

She knew that of course. This situation with Deke was messing with her head. But a survivor like herself should be able to control things!

Gritting her teeth, she picked up the offending rock and threw it as hard and far as she could. "Damn him," she said out loud, then looked around guiltily.

But she was still alone, of course, and the words felt good. Astonishingly good. "Damn him!" she said again louder.

She grabbed a rock in each hand and, taking a deep, angry breath, flung them both for all she was worth. "Damn him all to hell!"

An unexpected male voice sounded from behind her. "Should my ears be getting red?"

Lyssa gritted her teeth. No. She refused to turn around. "Go away," she told Deke.

His footsteps dislodged a powdery shower of dried mud as he disobeyed and came closer.

Lyssa frowned. The last thing she wanted was for him to see her sitting in the dirt and crying over her bloody cut like a little girl. She was a dignified, calm woman who had survived a lot worse than this. "Go *away*."

He hunkered down beside her. "What happened?"

She opened her mouth for a sharp retort, then closed it. The cloud place. Find the cloud place. She was known for her serenity, wasn't she? All she had to do was recover it, and her dignity couldn't be far behind. "I fell," she said, keeping her palm firmly over her knee and her gaze off him.

He moved as if to peel her hand away.

"No!" Lyssa hunched her shoulders and drew her knees closer to her chest. *The cloud place. Serenity.* She quieted her voice and allowed herself to look at him. "No, thank you. I'm fine."

There was a smudge of dirt next to Deke's mouth, and Lyssa shivered, remembering their kiss. His lips had burned her, like hot water burned cold hands. She'd welcomed it, wallowed in it, and all the while this great iciness inside her had broken up, then melted to run in rivers of heat down her arms and legs. She'd wondered if he could sense she was ready to flow right over him.

But then *she'd* sensed something. There was tension and a bitter intent in Deke and in the kiss, and then . . . and then she knew. He thought she'd cried because he'd frightened her, but he hadn't. She'd cried because he'd *wanted* to. He'd wanted to scare her away.

"Let me look at it."

She found herself glaring at him. "No."

His lips twitched. "Are you pouting?"

Lyssa blinked. "I haven't pouted in years." A raven crossed the sky overhead, and she followed it with her gaze. "Didn't I already ask you to go away?"

"Crabby, too," he said pleasantly. "I'm thinking you must have really hurt yourself."

Lyssa let out a strangled sound. "How did you find me, anyway?"

"I'm not exactly sure." Deke reached into his back pocket and pulled out a white handkerchief folded in a square. "I just had this sudden urge to explore."

Lyssa stared at the cotton square in his hand. "My dad used to carry a handkerchief. I haven't seen a man with one in years."

Something that wasn't quite a smile turned up the corners of Deke's lips. He shrugged. "Must be a generational thing."

A red haze clouded Lyssa's vision, and a hot irritation built that she didn't even try to rein in. *Screw serenity,* she thought, aware it was personal blasphemy. "You're not my father," she said tightly.

Ignoring her anger, he pinched the ends of the handkerchief and twirled it into a makeshift bandage. With amazing deftness, he lifted her hand from her leg and tied the handkerchief around her cut with the briefest and most impersonal of touches.

Lyssa's skin goose bumped like a plucked chicken anyway. And oh, it made her so mad.

A muscle in Deke's jaw jumped. "I'll take you home," he said. "The golf cart's not too far." He gestured behind him.

To her mortification, she felt the betraying tears rising again. She had most certainly been wrong about him. He was not the one. No way could she fall for a man who turned her into an uncontrollable, wobbly mass of emotions and then turned away from her.

She stood up and glared at him through the wetness. "I am not a cryer," she said. "And I'm not someone who falls down or ever loses her dignity. Dammit, I'm not a person who even gets angry!"

His eyebrows rose and his lips twitched again. "And I'm Pat Boone."

Lyssa let a long pause go by, then blinked, releasing one rogue tear down her cheek. "Pat who?" she said, as if bewildered.

He stilled, his face stiffening to preacher-serious again, and that little flare of humor died in his eyes. "Let's go."

It was Lyssa's turn to smile. And she did it, smugly, and then pointed her finger at Deke, pistol-style. "Gotcha, *old man*." She flounced ahead of him—Lyssa, flouncing!—and shot him another smile over her shoulder. "But admit it, I'm pretty sure Pat Boone's before your time too."

It took a minute for him to catch up with her, but that smile was teasing his mouth again, and those gray eyes of his had warmed to almost blue. "Not so, little girl," he said, and this time the name didn't seem so insulting. "He put out a heavy metal album right up my alley." Then he winked.

Warmed by the little taste of humor, Lyssa tried another, friendlier smile as she clambered into the golf cart he'd parked just over the rise. But he had quickly reverted to his cautious self again, and she knew he pretended he didn't see it.

They drove back to Haven House in silence, Lyssa still annoyed and embarrassed by her uncharacteristic outbursts. When the cart braked to a stop at her front door, Lyssa looked at Deke and swallowed. She squeezed her fingers together in a tight ball.

"About before." God! She didn't want him to think she meant about the kiss. "About before, on the hill, when I hurt my leg . . ."

Deke just sat there, staring at his hands on the steering wheel.

Lyssa swallowed again. "I'm sorry. I guess I acted like a—like a—witch."

"Funny." He looked at her now, shooting her an unreadable glance from those cool, cool eyes. "I thought you acted like a woman."

Lyssa's jaw dropped. A woman! Flabbergasted, she froze, as if bolted to her seat. A woman.

She suddenly realized that she hadn't been one before. Never in her whole life. A woman.

Not a cancer victim or a cancer survivor but a breathing, living, sometimes fickle, sometimes unserene woman.

Surviving her long stretch of illness had given her ample time to examine herself and examine life. She thought she knew and understood them both well. Then along came Deke, and she suddenly wasn't so sure about anything. Who was she? What was the point of all the emotions he stirred inside her?

Her heart pounded, awake and alive, in her chest. There was a point to all these feelings. There was a reason she'd fallen for Deke. Yes, she'd survived, but love, love was what made her finally alive.

Another round of tears pricked her eyes, but she didn't bother hiding from them this time as she automatically climbed out of the cart and up the porch steps. At the front door, she whirled to say something to Deke, but he was already turning the key over, and the cart rolled away.

Lyssa watched until he rounded the corner. Her man had gone away again, but he'd taken her very womanly and very won heart along with him.

The day following their parasailing adventure, Yeager showed up in Zoe's kitchen just as she put away the last of the dishes from the breakfast buffet.

"What are you doing?" he asked, coming through the back door.

The late-morning sun streamed in behind him. Zoe grabbed with both hands for her heart, tugging it back as it tried to leap toward the golden figure that he made, striding into her kitchen and bringing with him all that attractive and otherworldly glitter.

"Zoe?" He leaned against the doorjamb, crossing his arms over his chest.

"Hmm?" She turned away from him and stowed a chafing dish in the lower cupboard.

"Entertain me," he said.

She couldn't help smiling at that. The command was cocky and charming and so very like him.

"Please," he added belatedly, grinning.

So very like him. "Entertain me," he'd said. Yet it confirmed for her why she was safe around him. Everything he'd done to this point had been about his entertainment. All that flirtation. The kisses, even. Once she'd proven she could amuse him in another way—like the parasailing—he was willing to forgo what was probably a mere mechanical response to any available woman. She'd suspected that from the very first, hadn't she?

Still, even a friend wasn't easy. "I've got things to do this morning," she said.

The smile didn't leave his face. "C'mon, Zoe."

She bit her lip. "Do you want to parasail again?"

He shook his head. "I enjoyed it, Zoe, but I don't think . . . I don't think I can do it every day."

It didn't surprise her. He'd been almost dazed at the end of his sail, and she'd hadn't known whether her idea had been a bust or a boon. But then after a few moments he'd seemed happier, or at least less edgy. And calmer, as if he'd come to a decision that settled him down some.

And she'd been glad for him.

"I want to be with you today," he said.

Zoe shot him a startled look.

"Just to give me something to do," he amended, his casual smile putting her back at ease. "What are you up to today? Maybe I can help you."

"Yeager . . ."

"Please, Zoe."

She checked her watch. "I have an errand to run and then . . ." For all her brilliant analysis—he was safe as long as she was entertaining him—was it really a good idea to hang around him? "And then I'm free for a while," she ended reluctantly.

"Zoe, I'm begging you here." He grinned again. "Any more time in Dolly's company, and I won't be responsible for what happens."

She laughed. How could a man with a plastic doll scare her? "Oh, all right." Bending down, she rummaged in the cupboard again, searching for a small basket in which to pack a picnic lunch. She had him figured out now, right? Being a playmate wasn't the same as being a Playmate. "I'll take you on a picnic."

"Have I told you I love you?"

Zoe shook her head and chuckled. "No, and I don't expect you will."

He laughed too and even made himself partially useful by staying out of her way as she packed their lunch. He sat at the kitchen table and regaled her with silly stories about the kind of questions he often fielded from kids. She relaxed, and the last of her misgivings about spending time with Yeager went the way of the old tuna salad she found hiding away in the back of the refrigerator.

He voted for adventure by scooter. She'd suggested the golf cart, but he said he wanted a better shot at being able to control the vehicle himself in case she got it in her mind to drive blind again.

Laughing at the blind-leading-the-blind image, she strapped their lunch on the back and obligingly moved forward on the banana seat so he could sit.

Only when he fitted his body behind hers did Zoe feel the first real spurt of misgiving.

She wriggled her backside to give herself some more room, but that only caused him to wrap one arm tightly around her midsection.

"Hold still," he said in her ear, his voice almost a growl.

"You're too close," she complained, a chill rolling down her spine and lingering where his torso met the small of her back.

He cleared his throat. "Don't you have an errand to run?"

She sighed. Okay, so the chills were one-sided and should just be ignored. Nerves made her start off with a little lurch, and he grabbed her around the middle with his other arm, this one clamping over her right under her breasts.

It was just the cool breeze making them peak, of course.

With gritted teeth she drove to her first stop, leaving Yeager on the scooter at the curb while she ran into the Shear Terror Styling Salon. She took the box Marlene had for her and told her friend she'd chat another time. Back at the scooter, she used a bungee cord to fasten the box on top of their lunch basket and then propelled the scooter to the biggest and priciest of Abrigo's hilltop homes.

Ignoring the buzzer at the bottom of the driveway, she zipped through the open wrought-iron gates and braked to a stop right beside the front door and under the surprised noses of two Italianate marble lions. They each wore a feral expression and held up one paw, as if poised to squash flat any mice—or visitors, for that matter—with uppity ideas.

The front door immediately opened. Behind the uniformed housekeeper, Donna, was the pouting but beautiful face of Randa Hill.

"I was expecting you hours ago, Zoe," she said, the disapproval in her voice turning down the corners of her lush-lipped mouth.

Zoe removed her helmet and struggled off the bike. "Sorry, Randa. Hi, there, Donna." She pulled the box Marlene had given her free of its cord. "I have the crown right here. I just had a slow start this morning." There was no sense pointing out that Randa could have retrieved the darn thing herself and for that matter cleaned it herself, instead of relying on Marlene and Zoe to take care of it for her.

But Randa had already lost interest in Zoe and her excuses. "Well. Who is this?"

Zoe swung around, not surprised to see that Yeager had removed his helmet too. He was smiling politely in the direction of Randa's voice.

"This is Yeager Gates," Zoe said. "One of my guests. Yeager, this is Randa Hill. Mrs. Randa Hill. And Donna Kelly."

He nodded. "Ms. Kelly, Mrs. Hill."

Randa shot Zoe a look. "Randa. The only person who calls me Mrs. Hill is Mr. Hill."

Zoe shrugged. That was true. One of them had to remember they were married. She mounted the steps and handed over the box to Donna. "How is Jerry? Still on a business trip?"

Randa cast a speculative look in Yeager's direction. "For another few days. I am so lonely."

Zoe smiled to herself when Yeager, who couldn't see the little glances Randa was throwing his way, appeared unmoved by her innuendo.

Frowning, Randa turned on Zoe. "And he said he wants to have a long talk with you when he returns."

Uh-oh. Time to move. "Gotta go, Randa!" Zoe trotted down the steps and swung her leg over the scooter seat, kicking Yeager's stomach in her hurry.

"Umph."

"Get your helmet on," she said by way of apology.

She zoomed down the driveway while he was still wrestling with his helmet's chin strap, and he made a mad grab for her waist as she leaned into a quick turn onto the road.

"Jesus, woman!" He clamped his hands firmly about her middle. "What are you doing, trying to kill me? I've already been in one motorcycle accident, thank you very much!"

Zoe guiltily reduced her speed. "Sorry," she said, over the *putt-putt-putt* of the scooter. "I didn't want to listen to Randa any more, okay?"

"You afraid of what Jerry has to say? And what's this about a crown?"

Yes, she was afraid of what Jerry had to say. Jerry owned the Island Realty and the Island Bank and about half the rental property on Abrigo. He also contributed more than half the cash necessary for the Firetail Festival. Lucky for Zoe, he'd been traveling on an extended business trip for the last couple of months. If he knew just how dire the stupid warnings of the marine biologists were, Zoe wasn't sure those Festival flags would have gone up after all. Jerry wasn't much of a speculator. He expected a return on his buck and if the firetail weren't going to show Jerry would question the need for a festival.

"Zoe?"

She decided on answering the easy question. "Randa is Miss Abrigo Island. She wears the crown during the Firetail Festival, and we just had it cleaned for her."

There was a brief silence. "Miss Abrigo? Correct me if I'm wrong, but didn't you tell me that Randa was *Mrs.* Hill?"

Zoe shrugged and turned the scooter onto the dirt path that would lead to one of her favorite spots on the island. Her voice shook as they rode over the uneven ground. "Randa's been Miss Abrigo since 1989, when Jerry spotted her, then married her. Since Jerry puts up most of the money, Jerry gets to pick Miss Abrigo. He's been choosing his wife, or she's been making him choose her, for more than ten years."

Thankfully, Yeager was silent for the next several minutes. When she finally stopped at the shady spot beneath the oaks and beside Gumbee Creek on Harry's Hill, she figured he'd lost interest in the subject.

That suited Zoe just fine. She spread out the blanket she'd also brought and put the basket on one corner. With Yeager's hand tucked under her arm, she led him from the scooter to the picnic spot she'd prepared.

"There." She pushed him onto the blanket and followed him down. "Welcome to Zoe's secret place."

He stretched his legs out in front of him. "What makes me think that I'm only welcome because I can't find my way back alone?"

She smiled. "I have to keep some parts of myself private."

"And why do I keep getting the feeling this isn't your only secret?"

Zoe's throat went dry. "Give me a break. What would you know about secrets, a man whose life is out there for all to examine?"

The sun shot gold strands through his hair. "What do you mean by that?"

She was glad to deflect his attention. Talking about *him* was perfectly safe. "Lyssa told me all about it. I saw a magazine article myself."

"Don't believe everything you read."

"So you didn't date an actress with—" She made an imaginary buxom bustline with her hands, then realized he couldn't see the gesture. "Well, you know."

He leaned back on his elbows and grinned. "How well do I know? Is that your question?"

"I don't have any questions at all," she said primly. "Your past, or for that matter, your future," she added hastily, "are none of my business."

Yeager rolled closer to her. "How about my present? You interested in that at all?"

Zoe moved away. He was starting that silly flirtation with her again. "I bet you're hungry."

"Yeah."

She ignored the amusement in his voice. "Nothing fancy. Chicken salad sandwiches, grapes, and brownies."

"I have told you I love you."

When he went over the top, she could easily dismiss him. She giggled. "You're a pushover for home cooking, do you know that?" She rummaged through the picnic basket, then placed an unwrapped sandwich and a small bunch of grapes on the washboard flatness of his belly.

"Because I never had much of it. My mom died just after I was born, and the brigadier general—that's my father—makes filet mignon taste like fish sticks. It's an air force requirement."

"What's he think about your . . . situation. The blindness?" she asked curiously.

Yeager adjusted his dark glasses. "We both know it's only a temporary setback."

He suddenly exuded a very patent uneasiness, and Zoe struggled to get back on their easier, comfortable footing. "So. Your dad was in the air force?"

She saw his shoulders relax. "Still is," he said. "He's with a UN peacekeeping force in Europe right now. When I was a kid, we lived on eight different bases in twelve years."

Zoe couldn't fathom his matter-of-factness about moving. She'd hated it.

He swallowed the last bite of sandwich. "Never lived on an island before, though."

Zoe looked about her at the creek bubbling over the rocks, at the view of rolling hills and then the flat, blue ocean that surrounded her like a security blanket. "Then you really missed out."

He shrugged, popping a fat grape into his mouth. "There are Jerrys and Randas everywhere."

"You may be right about that." Zoe stretched out on the blanket and stacked her hands behind her head as a pillow. "But other places don't have my friend Marlene or my sister Lyssa or Gunther our quasi-postman, or the hundred other people and things that make Abrigo just about the best place on earth."

He laughed at her enthusiasm. " 'Just' about?"

She smiled at the clouds drifting over her head. "Okay. The best place. I think there's a reason the firetail fish have chosen our island all these years. We've got something going here, our community is like a family. And we have the island that always stays the same and always keeps us safe."

Yeager lay down beside her and stretched his arms over his head. His ribs lifted and his shirt rode up, showing her a golden-tan slice of his stomach. Above the snap of his jeans was the spiral of his belly button and a sprinkling of blond hair.

"Zoe?"

"Hmm?" When Yeager breathed, his shirt edged higher.

"I asked you about your parents. Did you fall asleep on me or something?"

Zoe blinked, then hastily redirected her gaze toward the blue sky. "Oh. Sorry. They, uh, died when I was in college. On a trip to visit me, actually. I was going to school in Los Angeles, a private womens' college, and they were on a bus—" She swallowed. "It was Lyssa who had to call and tell me. Their ID had the island address, of course, though they'd been taken to a hospital only fifteen minutes away from my dorm." Leaves rustled cheerlessly in the oak above them.

Yeager's hand touched her face. He turned it toward his. "I'm sorry," he said. His thumb brushed over her skin, as if checking for tears. "You okay?"

"Mm." She wanted to turn her cheek into his hand. There hadn't been anyone to comfort her on that afternoon when she learned her parents had died. It had been unseasonably cold that day and it seemed like months— years, maybe—before she felt warm again.

He continued stroking her cheek. "So," he said, his voice deliberately light, "tell me about what makes this Zoe's favorite spot." He didn't take his hand away all the while she described the ring of hills enclosing them and Gumbee Creek that ran year round except during the driest of Septembers.

His fingers found, then traced one eyebrow. She thought about moving away, but his touch was soft and friendly. "Is this your private make-out location? Have I wandered into the box seats for the local submarine races?" he asked.

She figured he could feel her little frown. "I'm only going to say one thing, pal. There were twenty-six students in my high school graduating class. Eighteen were girls."

His fingers moved to her hair. It stroked through the feathery stuff at her temple. "Now them's odds I like."

Zoe kept her sigh to herself and stayed as still as she could, afraid he wouldn't stop, afraid he would. "I don't doubt it."

He shifted closer. "So you're saying I'd be the first to get a kiss from you here?"

"Oh, Yeager." He shouldn't. She shouldn't want him to. But that hand just kept patiently stroking her hair, letting all her doubts and desires roll around and around in her head. His hand was warm and big—so seductively masculine—and a traitorous, urgent breathlessness overtook her.

She swallowed, trying to discipline this unfamiliar surge of neediness. Wasn't she supposed to have him under control? "Entertain me," he'd said. And she'd thought a ride around the island and a picnic lunch would do that very thing.

His shoulder rubbed against hers. "Show me we're friends, Zoe. Kiss me."

10

Zoe's heart pounded. It wasn't supposed to be like this. She wasn't supposed to have to make this kind of choice. Living on her island was supposed to protect her from the sort of mistake she was making right at this moment, leaning toward a beautiful man— a famous man!—a temporary man, who in the end would leave her.

But his breath smelled like grapes, and his lips were so close. They moved as he whispered her name again. "Zoe."

Maybe she knew why the sailors had crashed against the rocks on the west side of the island a hundred and fifty years ago. There were sexy, sneaky, sirens around, and some of them were male.

Yeager's hand slid around to the back of her head and brought her mouth toward his. "Kiss," he whispered.

And so she did.

He tasted like grapes too, or maybe wine, because the sweetness of it was intoxicating and the gentle pressure of his lips so, so arousing.

The heat kindled in her belly, and when he angled his mouth against hers, Zoe couldn't help but roll her body closer to his. His chest was warm and hard, and his hand slid down from the back of her head to her waist. She remembered him there from the scooter ride, the feel of him against the small of her back, and she moaned into his mouth.

He pulled her hips against his. She felt maleness there too, his erection pressing against the placket of her jeans. She went hot all over.

She'd done this to him. She'd made him hard and she'd made him want. Her skin prickled, and needy heat speared through her.

Rubbing over her T-shirt, his hands slid up her back. She knew the instant he realized she wasn't wearing a bra. His fingers froze, and he lifted his head as if he needed a breath.

"Zoe?"

She ducked her head against his shoulder, embarrassed. He bumped his forehead against her cheek and then located her mouth again. This kiss went on and on, firing up that heat in her belly, sending tingling waves of sensation down her arms and legs. His fingers edged over to her sides, then smoothed up to palm her breasts.

Oh. Zoe pulled her head away from Yeager's kiss. Apparently size didn't matter when it came to enjoying the sensation of a man's hands on her breasts. He didn't seem to care about her lack of cleavage either. Even with the soft cotton of her shirt between them, he appeared fascinated by the shape of her breasts, smoothing his palms over and over the small curves and then zeroing in on her nipples. They immediately hardened into points.

Flat on her back, Zoe froze, stunned by another surge of excitement. Something was happening to her. Her limbs felt liquefied by the heat Yeager ignited inside her. Her breath stuttered in her lungs as he slid lower, and she bit on her hand to stifle her scream when his mouth located her stiff nipple.

Blind or not, he knew exactly what to do. He licked, wetting the fabric over the hard point, then drew it into the cavern of his mouth. Just when she thought she'd melt all over him from the heat of it, he sucked at her strongly and grunted with satisfaction, like the taste was just as satisfying as any dish she'd ever fed him.

She couldn't stop herself from running her fingers through his hair as he unerringly located the other nipple and wet and sucked on it too. There was something building in her body, a sort of tension in her legs and in her belly that made her shift restlessly. Heat was everywhere, her face, the palms of her hands, the backs of her knees. She tried pulling back, tried to stop herself from moving her hips in such an embarrassing and obvious manner.

Maybe Yeager thought the same, because he laid one hot, big hand over her midriff and held her down, causing that tension to twist higher.

He took her mouth again. Somebody—of course it was her—sobbed a little as she pushed up the fabric of his shirt. Finally she had that golden chest partially bared, and she rubbed her wet T-shirt and hard nipples against him. She sobbed again.

"Sh, sh." He tried soothing her, but something was happening inside her. Outside her too. Everywhere there was heat and arousal and Yeager's touch.

"It's okay," he whispered against her mouth. "I've got it."

Got it? *Got what*? But then she couldn't think, because his tongue plunged in her mouth and he ripped at the snap of her jeans. His hand, big and wide and almost as hot as her skin, insinuated itself between the denim and the satin fabric of her panties.

The flesh of Zoe's belly quivered in reaction, and then the trembling was everywhere.

"Yeager?"

His mouth had found her neck, and he licked a line toward her throat to match the path his hand made toward the place that was so hot and needy.

Still with her panties between them, he touched her there, and she jumped.

"Sh, sh," he soothed again. "I know, honey. I know."

She felt him against her through both their jeans, his hard penis against her thigh. It made it okay, somehow, to let him stroke her. And then he kissed her again, and his knuckles brushed someplace that, beneath her underwear, was hot and mortifyingly wet.

But he seemed to like it. "Oh, honey," he said, almost reverently, she thought, her mind dizzy. And when he licked her bottom lip and stroked her with his finger, all at once all of her burst. Burst free of that spot on Harry's Hill, burst free of the island, of the whole darn world, maybe. Then she showered down in little tiny pieces, falling over her favorite spot and the man whom she had thought would be so easy to handle.

The minute it was over, he rolled away from her. "Zoe," he said, then stopped. "I didn't . . . I don't . . ." he finally said, his voice hoarse.

Her cheeks burned with humiliation and embarrassment. Zoe turned her face away as she zipped up her jeans and tucked in her shirt. Of course. Of course he didn't mean to take it this far. Of course he didn't really want her. He was Apollo, and she was . . . someone he should never have met.

He'd been looking for a few kisses, an afternoon's entertainment, just some fooling around, probably, and he'd ended up having to hold down some desperate woman who'd popped off like a firecracker at nearly his first touch! Another wash of shame rushed over her face.

Maybe she would have felt better if he'd tried to satisfy himself too, but it was obvious from how quickly he moved away that he knew she wasn't enough for him.

She scrambled to her feet and was never so glad that he couldn't see her face. "We better get back."

"Yeah." He stood there while she gathered

the remains of their picnic and folded the blanket and stowed them on the scooter. Luckily she'd packed a sweatshirt too, and she pulled it over her T-shirt and those mortifying circles of wetness.

She handed him his helmet. He didn't sit so closely to her on their return ride. He didn't sit close at all, and Zoe felt chilled by the time they returned to the Haven House.

"Zoe—"

"Don't say anything, okay?" she said tightly. "Just do me this one favor and leave it alone." The last thing she wanted was a rehash of this episode of unseemly lust. Lust that had apparently left him almost completely unmoved.

He shook his head, and as he turned up the path to his cottage, he stumbled. For the first time, Yeager really seemed to be blind.

Ready to prepare their afternoon buffet, Zoe entered the kitchen later that afternoon to find Lyssa slicing water chestnuts.

She frowned. "What's up? I thought we agreed on guacamole and chips and a platter of crackers and cheeses."

Lyssa kept her gaze on the knife. "Mm-hm. I made the guacamole already. But this is for dinner. We're having guests."

Zoe blinked. "What?" She questioned the most astonishing piece of information first. "Are you telling me you're cooking?" Zoe knew that running the bed-and-breakfast was more the work of her heart than Lyssa's. Though Haven House was a joint venture,

Zoe—maybe because she was the oldest and because of Lyssa's illness—took the lead when it came to any of the household matters.

Lyssa shot her a look from under her lashes. "I have my specialty," she defended herself.

"Your specialty is usually eating," she retorted, but smiled. "I'm kidding. Who's coming over?"

"Yeager and Deke."

Zoe's stomach swooped like a seagull in the direction of her toes. "What?" She took a breath to quell her brief panic. "They won't come." Yeager wouldn't anyway. She still didn't have much of a read on Deke.

"They'll come," Lyssa said serenely. "I left them each a message saying we have a problem with their bill."

Zoe's eyebrows rose. There wasn't anything wrong with their bill. "What?"

Lyssa ignored her confusion. "When they get here, slap a cold beer in their hands. They'll stay."

Zoe crossed her arms over her chest and stared down her angelic-looking younger sister. "What's this about, Lyssa?"

"Maybe I think we hole ourselves away too much," she answered, avoiding Zoe's gaze.

Zoe shifted uneasily. She liked holing herself away. As a matter of fact, she'd been calculating madly how she could do that very same thing for the rest of Yeager's stay. Yes, she'd tried that tactic before, but this time she meant to make it stick. After what happened between them—what happened to *her* on the hilltop—how could she be anywhere near him anyhow?

She'd either expire of embarrassment or experience another attack of unmaidenly lust for the man. Neither was pleasant to contemplate.

Zoe swallowed. "Well, then, we can invite some of our friends over. Our island friends."

"Yeager and Deke. That's who I'm cooking for. I want to get to know him—I mean *them*—a little better."

Zoe shook her head in surprise. "But—"

"Is there any good reason you don't want them here?"

Zoe opened her mouth. There were cartloads of good reasons. She shut her mouth. But none she wanted to share, even with Lyssa.

Maybe especially with Lyssa. There was no need to worry her sister over something so . . . so . . . inconsequential. Something that would never happen again.

Still. "It's going to be a disaster," Zoe said. Even if Yeager did stay, he certainly wouldn't want to be around her.

"No, it won't," Lyssa said sharply.

Zoe blinked. Serene, calm Lyssa sharp? "Is there something wrong?"

Her sister compressed her lips and shook her head. "Can't we just have a pleasant dinner together?"

"Well, uh, sure." A surge of sister loyalty made her automatically agree. There was some unfamiliar tension running beneath Lyssa's outer calm, and Zoe would do anything to help alleviate it.

Even if it meant faking pleasantness at dinner with Yeager.

The rat. Because when she thought about it, he was the one who should feel uncomfortable. He was the one with all the experience. He should have known what was happening.

She tended the little fiery burst of anger, because it sure beat the heck out of embarrassment. Oh, she'd be pleasant, all right, if they all sat down to Lyssa's dinner.

She'd be so pleasant he wouldn't know what hit him.

Deke thought it was the strangest goddamn dinner party he'd ever been tricked into attending.

And it didn't even matter that it was the only goddamn dinner party he'd ever been tricked into attending.

He had no idea why the women wanted him and Yeager here, but there were rivers of emotional undercurrents running beneath the four of them—he and Lyssa on one side of the table and Yeager and Zoe on the other—that even he couldn't pretend to ignore.

Lyssa wasn't talking to him or her sister. Yeager wasn't talking to Zoe. Zoe wasn't talking to Lyssa or Yeager or him. It was making for zero conversation and a lot of unnecessary utensil-clattering.

And something in the deep crystal blue of Lyssa's eyes gave Deke this weird impulse—responsibility, even—to ease the tension at the table.

Shit. He must be getting soft.

Old age did that to a man.

"Well," he said, struggling to find some small talk that he'd never bothered with before. "Is this great weather or what?"

Zoe *hmm*d. Yeager *umm*d. Lyssa was conspicuously without any mutters at all.

He shot a surreptitious glance at her. If anyone that lovely could be called miserable-looking, then she was. The regret and shame he'd felt earlier in the day burned in his gut like an ulcer.

He'd made a big mistake, he knew, and he planned on doing something about it, something to stop cold everything going on between them. First, though, they had to get through this travesty of a meal.

He let out a quiet sigh and tried again, directing his remarks across the table. "Great dinner, right, Yeager?"

"Yeah," the other man grunted, though his food hadn't been touched. He lifted his sweating beer bottle and took a long chug, and when he set it back down, it clacked against one of the other two bottles he'd already finished off.

It was Zoe that saved the empties from going down like bowling pins. She grabbed one in each hand and stood up. "I'll just—"

"Where are you going?" Yeager jerked his head in her direction.

Zoe ignored him. "Anyone need anything from the kitchen?" She addressed the polite remark to the old-fashioned light fixture hanging over the dining room table.

Yeager grunted again. "Bring me another beer. Please," he added, a tad too late.

Zoe rolled her eyes but headed through the swinging door to the kitchen. Silence fell like a wet blanket over the three remaining.

Once she returned, Deke tried again. "I'm making progress on the house."

It appeared to be a boring subject. Lyssa and Zoe stared at their plates instead of looking at him, and Yeager started on his fourth beer.

Deke watched him carefully. There was an edginess to his friend that he'd thought this time on the island had dulled. Zoe had something to do with the renewed tension, that was obvious, but Deke didn't think it was only woman trouble that was getting Yeager so down. They'd been friends for a long time, and women had never been a problem for Yeager. He charmed them, he entertained them, he left them, all in those three easy steps.

It wasn't that Yeager didn't have complexity. A man had to be driven to perfectionism and achievement to be one of NASA's best. Deke had also met Yeager's father, the brigadier general, and it didn't take more than two brain cells to comprehend the extreme level of expectation Yeager had grown up with from his father and from himself. That kind of pressure needed a steam release, and women had always been Yeager's.

But now, with no ladders to climb, no risks to take, and so much lost for good, Deke didn't know if there was any kind of release possible, or even conceivable, that could ease Yeager's tension.

The fourth beer went down in seconds. Apparently his buddy was going to see if alcohol would do the trick.

Yeager slapped the empty bottle against the table. "Did any mail come for me today?"

No one answered him.

Deke looked from Lyssa, to Zoe, to Yeager, and then made the rounds again.

Yeager pushed his sunglasses farther up, crossed his arms over his chest, and angled his body in Zoe's direction. "Did any mail come for me today?" he asked again

"Why? Are you expecting another plastic girlfriend?" she answered sweetly.

Deke held onto his grin. He liked Zoe, and he knew Yeager did too, though she didn't have the lushness of her younger sister or the self-involved beauty of the women Yeager usually dated. There was a liveliness about her that was unmistakably appealing.

Yeager bared his teeth. "No."

"Are you sure? Aren't two in the hand better than one in the bush?" Zoe continued.

"No."

Zoe acted as if she hadn't heard him. "You know, I just might have to contact your supplier myself."

"Why would you want to do that?" Yeager's voice had a nasty edge that surprised Deke. "Flesh and blood men seem to satisfy you."

Zoe blushed. "Not for me, for you. I'm convinced your current companion just isn't enough for you."

Yeager's eyebrows rose. "Would that be you you're referring to?"

Zoe went even redder. The two of them seemed to have forgotten they weren't alone. "Of course not. I mean Whatever-you-call-her. Dolly."

"At least she doesn't play games and run hot-cold-hot."

"Games!" Zoe exclaimed angrily. "She probably doesn't realize she's just a distraction to you yet. Some little bimbo to pass the time with."

"I don't think you're a bimbo," Yeager said quietly.

"You don't think much of me at all."

Yeager made an angry gesture that knocked over the empty beer bottle. "Damn it, Zoe, what's that supposed to mean? So we're having a little fun. So what?"

"The 'so what' is that you let the fun get out of hand."

Deke exchanged a look with Lyssa, who was all wide blue eyes. She shrugged.

There was a long silence, and then Yeager's expression turned even grimmer. "You're mad because I stopped. That's it, isn't it?"

"If I was really . . . If you'd wanted . . . You just didn't care about continuing!"

Deke shot another look at Lyssa and found her nearly as fascinated with this byplay as he was. He didn't know what exactly was happening between Yeager and Zoe, but it was enough to seriously rile his friend. Even as he watched, one of Yeager's hands curled into a fist.

"Damn it, Zoe, I stopped because of the

other times *you've* stopped. It doesn't take a rocket scientist—"

"Which he is, by the way," Deke couldn't resist adding sotto voce.

"—to figure out you weren't ready for a quickie on the blanket of the shores of Gitchee Gummee."

"Gumbee Creek," Zoe corrected.

"Whatever." Yeager's face was fierce. "I stopped for you."

There was a long pause.

"Oh," she said then.

" 'Oh,' " Yeager parroted in disgust.

"All right, then." Zoe wiggled primly in her seat. "All's well that ends well."

"Jesus Christ," Yeager muttered. "That's easy for you to say." Then he pitched his voice louder. "Now, would somebody just tell me if I got any mail? When we got back this afternoon, I put in a call to Houston and was told to expect a report any day."

Deke frowned. "A report?" Yeager was on an extended disability leave. Houston shouldn't be bothering him with paperwork right now.

"My medical report," Yeager said tersely.

"Medical report?" Deke echoed. What the hell was he going to do with that?

Yeager waved his hand. "You might as well know. Before we came to the island, I appealed the decision that took me off the Millennium list."

Deke stared at Yeager. From the corner of his eye, he saw Zoe straighten in her chair and look at Yeager too. Deke shook his head. "You know what the doctors said. Yes, you're going to get your eyesight back. No, you won't be going into space again."

Yeager's expression didn't change. "I asked for a review of that decision."

Deke couldn't believe it. He thought Yeager understood the situation, even though he was having a hard time living with it. "Why the hell would you do this to yourself? You know as well as I do they won't compromise on this."

"I'm going up again."

Shit, this was worse than he thought. Deke kept his voice carefully neutral. "What did Houston say?"

"They said they'd review my case. When I called today, they'd already sent out the report, but they wouldn't discuss it over the phone."

"For God's sake," Deke said. "Did you explain to them you won't be able to read it when it gets here?"

Yeager ignored the question. "Lyssa?"

"Yes?" she answered quietly. Her eyes were as big as the china plates on the table.

"Did I get any mail?"

She shook her head, then quickly added. "No. No mail for you today. But Yeager, sometimes"—she hesitated a moment and then the rest of the words rushed out—"sometimes destiny has a plan that you just have to wait for."

The words seemed to set off an explosion. His face a tight mask, he abruptly stood, and his chair tipped over, crashing to the floor. Zoe

jumped up, righted the chair, and dragged it
back. "Okay," she said, lightly touching his
arm. "It's out of the way."

Without another word, Yeager stalked out
of the dining room, going through the kitchen.
Zoe jerked at the slam of the back door, sig-
naling he'd left the house.

For the first time since Deke had sat down,
Zoe looked at him. "What's going on?"

Deke shook his head. "I wish I couldn't
guess."

"He told me his injuries were just a temporary setback," Zoe said, her face troubled.
"He never told me he wouldn't fly again."

"He won't fly again for NASA or the navy,"
Deke amended. "He knows, dammit, he
knows that they won't let him back up with
this injury in his past."

Zoe's eyebrows rose and she shook her
head. "I don't think he does."

Deke groaned. "He walked out of rehab,
you know. He was doing fine getting around
with his impaired eyesight, but they wanted
him to go through some counseling."

"To help him accept the changes in his life,
I suppose," Lyssa said, nodding.

Deke nodded back. "When he left early, I
thought it was a good sign. I thought it meant
he had the situation under control."

"Men," Lyssa scoffed, but there was a faint
smile on her face.

Deke ignored her. "And the press was
rabid. They were crawling all over the place,
and Yeager didn't want their attention or the

public's pity. I thought that was a good sign too."

Lyssa made a face. "Pity stinks."

Puzzled, Deke shot a glance her way, but then his eyes were drawn back to Zoe, who had gone paler the longer the conversation went on. "Are you okay?"

"Yes. I just didn't understand what he was really facing. His life will never be the same." She stood up and pushed her chair in. "I think I need to take a walk." Her gaze found her sister. "Leave the dishes for me."

"Don't worry about it," Lyssa answered. "Deke will help me with them."

He raised his eyebrows, surprised. The way Lyssa had been avoiding even looking at him, he thought he'd have to tie her down to get a chance to speak with her privately. "No problem."

Zoe shook herself a little, then narrowed her eyes. "There better not be."

Deke's lips twitched, but he controlled himself as Zoe left the room. A warning from Lyssa's big sister was about as dire as a mosquito threatening a vampire.

Finally, the only two at the table were him and Lyssa. She nudged her plate toward the center of the table and tilted her head. The soft light from the old-fashioned chandelier brushed against her cheekbones, leaving shadows in the hollows.

His heart punched against his chest wall again, and that ulcer-burn started firing up in his gut. She was so beautiful he hurt.

She put her elbows on the table and laced

her fingers. Her chin rested against them as she looked at him. "Why do I get the feeling," she said, "that you're about to tell me Yeager isn't the only one kidding himself?"

11

Deke stalled for more time by clearing the dishes. Lyssa followed suit, her long hair swishing against her shoulders and her soft pink dress floating around her calves.

He tried to keep his mind off her and on what he had to say. The kiss at the house hadn't worked, that was obvious. Even after her tears and anger this afternoon, she still looked at him in a way that he was afraid he was returning.

What middle-aged man wouldn't be flattered, fascinated, and turned on by the attention of a blond, blue-eyed twenty-three-year-old?

But he also had to look at himself in the mirror every morning, and for once, for all, he had to squelch her interest. It was the right thing to do. She was young and sweet and pure, and he was a mean old dog that had been kicked around a few times—and who was just about to kick back.

He leaned against the kitchen counter and scrubbed his hand over his face as Lyssa moved about, rinsing plates and inserting them in the dishwasher.

"Listen," he finally said.

She continued rinsing dishes.

"Listen," he said louder.

She looked at him over her shoulder as she bent over the dishwasher. Her artless pose made him think guiltily about wild and nasty sex, and then he focused on her mouth. It was pink and moist, and he barely suppressed the shudder that rolled down his back. Strawberries and peaches. Her kiss had tasted like summer fruit.

"I *am* listening," she said.

He scrubbed his face again. She looked too calm, too relaxed. Sure, he didn't anticipate a big scene, but this wasn't going to be easy for her to hear, and she had to realize what was coming. He knew she did.

"I don't like to do this," he started again.

"But you're compelled to be honest with me," she finished.

"Well, yeah." The way she'd jumped in put him off track for a moment, and he tried to remember the points he wanted to make. "First, I need to apologize."

"I accept," she said.

"You don't even know what for!"

She ran a handful of silverware under the tap and then dropped them in the dishwasher's basket with a cheerful clatter. "You're sorry you kissed me like that."

"Well, yeah." He shoved his hands in his front pockets. "I didn't mean to scare you."

At this, she turned completely around, one

blond eyebrow winging high on her forehead.

He felt like a bug about to be pinned. "Okay," he muttered. "I wanted to show you . . . how it could be between us."

Her other eyebrow rose to match the first one. "And that was supposed to scare me?"

Something about the way she said it caused the memory of the kiss to explode in his head. His blood slowed to a crawl and his pulse beat heavily. She hadn't been afraid. Her mouth had tasted like summer and her skin had smelled like honey and her arms had twined around him, young and supple. He'd wanted to bury himself in her ripeness.

He cleared his throat and looked away. "Okay. So maybe it was a bad idea. But so is . . . this." He waved a path back and forth between them.

She turned back to the sink. "Because I'm younger than you."

It was easier when she wasn't looking at him. "Lyssa." He had to clear his throat. "I've been your age before. I've believed what you want to believe, okay?"

"But that was a long time ago."

It ticked him off that she was reading his mind and speaking his thoughts. "Right," he said tightly. "I was even married once." Probably one of the shortest marriages on the books.

She took a big sponge and dipped it in a pot of soapy water. "You're divorced?"

"Yeah." No sense telling her the marriage ended after three days and so was technically annulled.

She scrubbed at the countertop. "And that turned you against marriage."

Apparently the idea didn't surprise her. "Right."

"Did it turn you against women too?" she asked matter-of-factly.

"No! Yes. No." He ground his teeth in frustration. How could he explain how the experience changed him? "I just became different, okay?"

The sponge moved in continuous circles over the tile, but Lyssa didn't say anything. He knew he was likely hurting her, and he hated himself for it, but somebody had to save her.

From him.

Because if she kept coming to him day after day, if she kept looking at him, if she kept breathing near him, her breasts straining at the fabric of her dress, he wouldn't be responsible for what happened.

"Lyssa," he said gently. "Do you understand what I'm saying? I—"

She turned around and fixed that bug-pinning stare back on him. "You distrust women now and emotions. Maybe you think you can never love like you did that time. You probably never want to."

Deke gaped at her. She'd stolen the words right out of his mouth. Maybe she'd prettied it up a bit, but that's what he needed her to understand.

Except she'd said it all so coolly, so unemotionally, he wasn't convinced she did understand.

"Lyssa—"

"You don't ever want to be that close to a woman again."

He gritted his teeth. She was discussing him as if she was discussing a character in a movie. As if it wasn't real to her. But she had to understand what he was talking about. He couldn't fight both himself and her.

"You see—"

She tried to interrupt again. "Deke—"

"Let me finish. Let me say it, okay?"

"But—"

"*I've got to say it.*" He stared back at her, determined to get everything out. "Promise me you won't talk."

Lyssa pressed her lips together. "Fine." She threw up a hand. "Go ahead."

He blew out a sigh. "I have years on you. Experience. Whatever you're dreaming up in your head is just that, a dream, okay? A fantasy."

To avoid seeing what his words were doing to her, he cut his gaze away and remembered he was an old grizzled dog and she was an innocent young creature. They had no business even playing on the same street. "You've been sheltered, and yes, you're naive. What do you even know about life?"

Without looking at her face, he backed away toward the door leading out of the kitchen and away from the temptation of her youth and innocence. His chest hurt again, that tight, quasi-cardiac-arrest pain constricting his breathing.

"We're too far apart, you see?" He put his hand on the cold doorknob and turned it be-

fore he could change his mind. She had to realize the distance between them. "Give
yourself some time to grow up, little girl."

Deke shut the door quickly behind him and
walked out into the quiet, cool night. He
wasn't sure if he expected to hear Lyssa's tears
or protests, but as he strode up the path to his
cottage, he heard nothing at all but the sound
of his own rasping and desperate breaths.

The squealing of the brakes on Gunther's Jeep
brought Zoe out of the kitchen and to her front
door. It was one of the gray-haired man's
postal-play days, and even as she opened the
front door, he was turning from his vehicle,
parked with exaggerated importance at a di-
agonal on the narrow street in front of the
house, to mount the steps. As if it was a
platter, he held a large flat box before him,
with a stack of envelopes scattered like hors
d'oeuvres across its top.

"Hey, Zoe!" Gunther smiled as he reached
the last step. "Bills, a letter for one of your
guests, and a package for you from Island
Dreams that Rae-Ann asked me to bring along.
Something special?"

Zoe smiled back. Gunther wasn't a big be-
liever in the privacy of the mails. It wouldn't
occur to him to even pretend he didn't know
what came for you or that he hadn't read the
backs of your postcards. Of course the Island
Dreams package wasn't mail exactly. Rae-
Ann's shop was right next door to the post
office, and she'd merely saved Zoe a trip by
asking Gunther to deliver the package.

"It must be my dress for the Firetail Dance," she told Gunther. The kickoff event of the festival was an evening dance in the school auditorium. The dress she'd found at the local boutique had been too long, and Rae-Ann had done the hemming for her.

Gunther nodded approvingly as he passed over the package and envelopes. "An island girl after my own heart," he said. "When it comes to shopping, every other female around here insists on going to a mainland mall."

Zoe shifted uneasily. "Well, uh . . ."

Gunther kept right on talking. "Your sister took the ferry over just yesterday, didn't she?"

Zoe shrugged. "She had a few things to do and some purchases to make."

Gunther nodded his head. "But there you go. You, Zoe, you find everything you need right here. When was the last time you went off island?"

Zoe hesitated, and then was saved from replying when a car drew up behind the Jeep and honked its displeasure at being blocked from passing.

Gunther jerked around. "Oops! Gotta go, Zoe. People are counting on me, you know."

She grinned as he hurried down the porch steps, his gray ponytail fluttering against the smartly pressed light blue shirt of his old uniform. He paused before clambering into the driver's side. "See you at the Festival meeting?"

Zoe nodded and waved.

"Jerry's back!" Gunther shouted as he trundled off.

Zoe groaned. Jerry. Forcibly putting the idea
of another naysayer out of her mind, she
looked down at the envelopes spread atop the
package.

One immediately caught her eye. Addressed
to Yeager, in the top left-hand corner it read
NASA.

She barely made it inside the house before
she had to sit down on the little seat that was
part of the mirrored hall tree. She set the dress
box and the other mail on the hardwood floor
at her feet and held the manila envelope addressed to Yeager, weighing it in the palm of
her hand.

She shivered.

For two days she'd tried not to think about
what he had revealed at dinner that night. Not
an easy task, even though she hadn't spoken
with him privately since then. Yeager still
came in for breakfast, but they had some new
guests visiting, and he would ask Lyssa to
grab him a piece of fruit and a muffin and then
he was gone, probably to avoid them.

Or Zoe.

She ran her finger over the sharp edges of
the envelope. It was one thing to find out that
the reason he'd stopped that day by the creek
wasn't because he didn't want her—that had
been a strange kind of relief. It was quite another to also find out that he'd been lying
about returning to space.

But you couldn't really call it lying. She
knew he'd been fooling himself as much as
anybody else.

She peered at the envelope, weighed it in

her palm again, then held it up to the light and squinted. With a guilty pang, she jerked it back down. She was getting as bad as Gunther!

The smart thing to do was to give the envelope to Deke when he got back to the house that evening. Yeager couldn't read it himself anyway, and that plan would save her from any further involvement.

But she knew he was waiting.

Zoe swallowed against the ache in her heart. This was the kind of feeling she should be afraid of. This was why she should leave it to Deke.

She had spent the last three years protecting herself from scary situations like this one, situations that involved that fragile organ pumping inside her chest that she knew could so easily be broken.

The envelope either gave back to Yeager the freedom he craved or was the death sentence to his dreams. Neither should concern her. Yeager shouldn't concern her. He was the golden Apollo accustomed to an orbit way out of her reach.

But still, he was waiting.

An ache pierced her heart again deeply, and despite all her intentions, Zoe found herself getting to her feet. When they'd been beside the creek, when he'd stopped short of going further, he'd been thinking of her. It seemed only fair to return the favor.

From the path below his cottage, she spied him. He was sitting in the shade against the back wall of his cottage, across the table from

Dolly. The dummy still wore the yellow-framed kids' sunglasses, and now she also had on a shell necklace slung wildly around her neck and looped under one voluptuous breast.

"Hey!" she called up to him.

His head turned toward her, and in the shade the dark lenses of his glasses looked like bottomless, unfathomable wells. "Zoe?"

She swallowed. "Mail," she said, waving the envelope, even though she knew he couldn't see it.

His chair clunked against the wall as he hastily stood. Just then, their newest group of guests—three women and two men—joined her on the path, exclaiming over the herb garden and asking her to identify some of the plants. One couple dropped into the nearby loveseat and stretched their legs in front of them comfortably.

By the time she'd exchanged smiles and the information they'd requested, she found Yeager at her elbow. She pulled his arm through hers. "Shall we go to your cottage?"

"How about if you take me a little further away?" he murmured.

Aware of the speculative looks from the other guests, Zoe didn't bother answering but instead tugged him further up the flagstone pathway. Once it turned to dirt, she kept leading him along, past the row of date and fan palms that delineated the cultivated grounds of Haven House from the wild hillside. Nobody would disturb them up here.

Not far from a rusty water spigot complete with green garden hose coiled nearby was the

cleared patch of earth that Zoe and Mr.
Duran—the male half of her part-time help—
were slowly preparing for a vegetable garden.
Though they'd already missed the optimum
time for planting, they were determined to get
a vegetable garden in this summer.

As Zoe invited Yeager to sit on an upturned
black plastic bucket and took a seat on one
beside him, she noticed that the twenty-by-
fifteen rectangle had been soaked with water,
just as she'd directed Mr. Duran. She'd
planned on turning the dirt over with a shovel
this morning, and the hard-packed earth had
needed softening up. It looked properly satu-
rated now, even a bit gooey.

"Well?" Yeager asked impatiently. "You
said mail came for me?" A cool breeze ruffled
his hair.

She swallowed. "Yes."

His face gave nothing away. "What's it
say?"

"I—I didn't open it."

"Do it, then." He rested his elbows on his
knees and linked his hands between them, his
head down. A deceptively relaxed pose.

Zoe swallowed and tentatively picked at the
seal with her fingernail. "I could get Deke . . ."
She let the offer trail off.

"Do it, Zoe," he said, and tension started
buzzing around him like a swarm of hornets.

The stiff envelope didn't open easily, and
she finally lifted it to her mouth and ripped at
the corner with her teeth. Once she could get
her finger in the edge, she ripped forcefully
across the top.

Yeager flinched.

Zoe swallowed again and drew out the double sheets of paper. "Are you sure you don't want Deke?" Her heart was pounding with worry.

"Zoe."

She heard the command in his voice. Taking a deep breath, she unfolded the pages. "It's from a Dr.—"

"I know who it's from," he said tightly. "Just tell me what he says."

She held the letter in one hand and wiped the other sweaty palm against her cutoff shorts. " 'Dear Commander Gates,' "

"Cut to the chase!" His voice was harsh.

Zoe quickly scanned the lines, her hands trembling and her stomach queasy. Then she dropped the letter into her lap and wrapped both her palms around one of his corded forearms.

"Yeager."

He froze. "So it's over," he finally said. He shook off her hands, blew out a long breath, and then ran his fingers through his hair.

"Yes," she whispered.

He pressed his lips together and was silent for a long moment. "I knew it, of course. Or at least I should have known it. Deke was right."

Zoe didn't like the tight control in his voice. "I'm sorry."

"Don't be." He waved a hand in a dismissive gesture. "This was over a long time ago. Weeks ago." His humorless laugh grated against her nerves. "I was just playing a stupid game with myself."

Despite his careless words, a muscle was ticking in his jaw.

She put out a hand and tried stroking his shoulder. "It's all right. You had to ask. What if they had changed their minds?"

He shrugged away from her touch. "What if?" he said harshly. "Now there's a question for you." She saw him struggle to take in a long breath, and then his voice quieted ominously. "I've got a stack of those what ifs."

"You do?" She didn't know what else to say.

"Yeah." He laughed again, the sound so raw it was painful to hear. "Here's one I can't get out of my head. What if I had never decided to go out that night?"

Zoe bit her lip. "Yeager—"

"What if I'd done something smart and stayed home with a six pack and a night's subscription to the pay-per-view porn channels?" He laughed again.

Chills prickled at the base of Zoe's skull and trickled down her spine.

"What if I'd taken my car? Or what if that little old lady had caught a cold, and instead of the urge for a bingo card had stayed home with her hankies and Vaporub?"

He turned to Zoe, the smile on his face so stark that another round of chills escaped down her back. "She came to visit me in the hospital, you know. This little old lady came to apologize for running into me. I couldn't see her, of course, but she smelled like Vaporub and she told me she'd caught a cold."

"Wh-what did you say to her?"

The corner of his mouth kicked up, and he ran a hand over his shiny scar. "I told her my grandma always swore by hot tea and honey. A cup of that stuff and you were cured."

Zoe smiled a little. "True?"

"Hell, no. I didn't even know my grandma. Either one." He shrugged. "But we didn't have much else to say to each other."

Zoe rubbed a hand over her chest, picturing the whole scene. Yeager laid up in the hospital, blind, talking to the elderly woman who'd caused the accident. Giving her cold cures instead of hell for what she'd done to change his life. Irrevocably.

Silence fell between them, but it was noisy with Yeager's unspoken thoughts.

"You must feel powerless," she said, to break the tense quiet.

"Don't tell me how I feel."

She ignored his brusqueness. "I know it's not easy." Every day of watching Lyssa fight her illness had torn at Zoe's insides.

"Yeah, like you'd know." He ran his knuckles over his scar, down, up, down.

"But I do. I know how it feels to lose something." Her sense of security hadn't reappeared until they'd returned to the island.

"You have no goddamn idea how it feels."

Zoe's heart fluttered in her chest, and she swallowed. He didn't appear golden and godly now, but just a man. A hurt, moody man. The idea that he wasn't so out of her reach terrified her. But she shoved the fear away, because he was also helpless and lost and full of emotions she knew he needed to lay aside if he was going to survive. Zoe shifted restlessly and stretched her legs, the garden's mud squishing beneath her shoe.

Racking her brain for a way to help him, she bent down and grabbed a handful of the wet dirt. It was fashioned easily into a sticky ball, and she drew back her arm to give it an aimless toss.

And then halted. And then she looked over at Yeager.

"Here," she said, grabbing one of his hands and putting the mudball in the cup of his palm.

His fingers curved over it reflexively. "What—?"

"It's a mudball." She looked around her and spied a volunteer date palm sticking up a few feet out of the ground not far away. "Throw it at that palm tree over there. You'll feel better."

His eyebrows rose over the frames of his sunglasses. "Zoe, I can't even see any effing palm tree."

"Oops," she said. "You're right." Yet she didn't let the slip deter her but bent over again and fashioned her own clod of wet dirt. "Just throw it anywhere, then."

"Zoe."

She flashed him a smile. "Give it a chance, 'kay?" She drew back her arm and flung her mud in the direction of the tree. It exploded a few feet short of the target, but she whooped anyway. "Perfect hit," she told her blind partner.

He was shaking his head. "What was that for?"

She scooped up more wet dirt. "For those stupid marine biologists who claim the firetail won't return." She flung another one that landed closer to the tree with an audible *plop*. "And that, that was for the El Naughty Niño that messed with our ocean currents."

"You're nuts."

She reached over and squeezed his fingers around his mudball. "Don't knock it until you try it."

She held her breath, and then, with another shake of his head, he limply tossed the mud.

Zoe *tsked*. "Oh, man, now I know why they kicked you out, Mr. Spaceman. You throw like a wuss."

There was an instant of charged silence. And then Yeager bent down, an unreadable expression on his face. "Them's fighting words."

Yes! Zoe thought proudly, and she watched him make a mega-orb, one that required packing with both hands. Then he hefted it in his right palm and jettisoned it with a grunt, causing the ball to sail over the little palm target and hit a unsuspecting manzanita bush several yards past.

She let out a triumphant yelp. "What was that for?"

He was already packing more mud. "For the NASA doctors, of course."

She clapped her hands. "Go for it, dude!"

His next mudball slammed the ground just short of the manzanita. "That's for the slick roads and the rain in Houston."

Zoe got into the spirit of the thing. She made another herself and took a third toss at the lucky palm. "For Jerry and Randa and anyone who mentions one word—one word!—of criticism against the Island Band."

Yeager groaned. "You're not seriously still thinking of letting them play? Whoever is their leader should do the festival a favor and bow out gracefully."

Eyes wide in insult, Zoe looked over at him. His hair was sticking up, and there was a streak of mud on his cheek. "*I'm* the bandleader," she said. "Didn't you know that?"

"No." Yeager's lips twitched. "Cross my heart, Zoe. I had no idea."

She suddenly didn't like his twitching lips or his clean shirt or that lonely streak of mud on his face. Her hand scooped quickly in the mud and, without bothering to make a mudball, she wiped her sticky fingers over his cheek and down his shirt.

"Oops," she said contritely. "I missed my target."

Yeager froze. A fat dollop of mud ran off the edge of his jaw. "That was no accident," he finally said.

At his overly calm tone, she edged her seatbucket away. "Sure it was," she said.

"No." Leaning sideways, he gripped her shoulder with one hand and dumped the mud in his other on top of her head. "*This* is an accident."

Zoe gasped and sprang to her feet. "You shouldn't have done that," she said.

"Yeah?" He reached down and scooped up two handfuls of mud. "Why not?"

Because she had the advantage of sight. Keeping one eye on him, she quietly moved farther into the muddy garden area and armed herself too. Then, tiptoeing, she circled back around him.

"Zoe?" he asked suspiciously. "Where are you, darlin'?"

"Right here," she whispered in his ear, then quickly pulled out the collar of his shirt and dropped the wet dirt down his back.

He shouted and twisted toward her, but she danced out of his reach.

"Gotcha, gotcha, gotcha!" she yelled triumphantly.

He was packing the biggest mudball yet. A little thrill of excitement zinged through her body, and she couldn't resist torturing him.

"I'm over here!" she called, then dashed a few steps away. "And here!"

He spun toward her first call and then her second. "Don't play with me, Zoe," he warned.

She bit a clean patch on the back of her hand to stifle her giggle. Oh, goodness, she knew where she wanted the mud to go next. Cautiously, she shifted over another couple of feet and stood in the middle of the garden to gather up the gooiest, messiest, wettest denouement of dirt balls.

Yeager was standing at one edge of the cleared area on a patch of trampled weeds, apparently waiting her out patiently. Zoe walked softly toward him again, knees bent.

Something rustled in a nearby bush, and he instantly swung around. "Zoe?"

Her hands were too full to stifle her next rash of giggling. She swallowed the sounds as best she could, but he apparently heard something and turned back in her direction. That suited her plans just fine. A couple feet from him she halted, planting her feet in the thick mud and trying to take quiet, shallow pants of breath. Then she slowly, slowly, reached her hand toward the waistband of his jeans.

She was going to have to be quick.

One deep breath, then she grasped the denim. She pulled it forward, shoved her wad of mud against his belly and his—

He circled her wrist in a dirty but iron grip.

She yelped.

"Hey. Were you looking for something?" he said.

She tried scrambling back, but her feet couldn't gain traction in the mud. Her frantic movements pulled him forward, though, and suddenly they were both scrabbling for footholds in the squishy mud, his hand still on her wrist, her hand still on his—

Zoe toppled over in the mud.

Yeager toppled after her.

Stunned, she lay flat on her back, Yeager beside her, his hand still on her wrist, her arm still awkwardly shoved down his pants, her fingers around his—

She looked over at him. There was mud smeared on the lenses of his glasses, and the rest of him looked like the Creature from the Slimy Lagoon. The silence between them turned tense and threatening.

Zoe swallowed. "Is that a banana you've got in there or are you just happy to see me?"

He shouted with laughter. She couldn't suppress a mad fit of giggling. They rolled around in the wet garden, laughing like a pair of hysterical kids, and the sun was as hot as the mud was cold. At some point they stopped squirming, and she realized she had her hand back, and she used her whole arm to hug Yeager close to her, her cheek against the steady thudding of his heart.

His arm came around her for an answering squeeze. Zoe looked up. He was still smiling, but in the mud on his face, a clean streak ran down one cheek. Maybe he'd laughed so hard he'd cried.

Maybe he'd just cried.

She rubbed her muddy face against his filthy shirtfront and decided against asking which it was.

12

Deke pushed open the door of Yeager's cottage without bothering to knock. "I just found out you got your letter from NASA."

Yeager didn't stop what he was doing, which was nothing, unless you counted lying on the bed and letting CNN drone on as background noise. He grunted to show Deke he'd heard him.

"I understand the news wasn't good." The front door shut, and Deke moved further into the room. "Why didn't you say anything?"

Yeager shrugged. "You knew the answer the minute I told you about my appeal." What was the point of talking about it anyway? The verdict, coming down for the second time, was just beginning to burrow its way under his skin. He was never going to be an astronaut again. He'd spent two days hibernating in his room and trying to get used to the idea.

"Zoe asked me to check on you."

Zoe. Oh, yeah, there was something else that was getting under his skin too. Someone else.

Zoe. He been avoiding her, spending most of
his time on the patio of his cottage, listening
to the rhythms of the island. In the daytime,
he did okay, soothed even by the cool breeze,
the sounds of the birds, and the *whush-hiss* of
waves crashing on the distant rocks, but at
night . . . At night he sought out cool places on
his sheets and tried not to sleep, because then
he dreamed of flying, or worse, he dreamed of
Zoe in the bed beside him, her cheek on his
chest and her arms hugging him to her. Just
like at the end of their mudfight.

Something had happened to him at that moment, with her in the circle of his arms, and
he didn't like it. He'd felt close to her, intimate
even, and it had occurred to him that he'd
never felt this friendly with a woman. How
could that be, when they'd both been completely clothed and covered in dirt! The whole
idea made him itch all over just thinking about
it, as if two-day-old mud was drying on his
skin.

"She wants to know how you're doing,"
Deke said.

Suddenly, a bubble of angry resentment
burst in his gut. She wanted to know how he
was doing. Right. What she wanted was to get
in his head. Two mornings ago she'd tried to,
and she needed to learn she wasn't welcome
there.

Women were a distraction for him, for
God's sake, and that's all. He liked it that way.

Where she'd gotten the idea he'd play
touchy-tell-me with her he didn't know, but it
was time to put a stop to the game if he was

going to have a moment's peace during the rest of his stay on the island.

Deke opened the small refrigerator in the kitchen area, and Yeager heard the squirt of air as the other man twisted the cap off a beer.

"Hand me one of those, will you?" he asked.

The comforting sweat of a cold bottle slapped his palm, and Yeager sat up and took a long swig. Yeah, when it came to Zoe, the problem was there'd been too much talk about feelings and not enough *feeling*. He smiled to himself and remembered that day by the creek and the unforgettable taste of her mouth and the heat between her legs when he touched her there. Just one little push of a button, and she'd reacted with a hot, unexpected passion.

The memory was damn sweet. What the hell had he been thinking that day, going for nice guy points? Some misguided notion of waiting for flowers and feather mattresses had stopped him, but if he'd pressed ahead and they'd done it, he wouldn't be in this uncomfortable predicament. Any time after, if Zoe showed signs of trying to x-ray his brain, he could have simply shown her what part of him really required her attention.

Deke rattled around in the bags of junk food Yeager had been forced to live on while skulking inside, evading Zoe. "She also wants to know if there's anything you need," his buddy said.

Yeager took another long, cold drink of his beer. Oh, yeah, there was something he needed. To put things back on a comfortable, familiar footing. And to accomplish that, he needed to do something familiar. Something he'd been wanting to do since the moment they met.

He smiled to himself smugly. Having sex with Zoe wasn't purely selfish on his part. If he remembered her nasty repartee at dinner a few nights before, she'd been miffed when he'd stopped short of taking her all the way. Insulted, even.

So, come to think of it, he was straightening out something between them that had been waiting to be put to rights.

He chugged down the rest of his beer. "Let's go down to the house."

Deke choked on his own drink, then coughed. "Nah. It's past dinner. They're not expecting anyone now."

Yeager got to his feet. "All the better." His shirt fluttered open, and he fastened one button, his only concession to a formal visit. If he had his way, he wouldn't be needing his clothes for long anyhow.

Deke wasn't budging. "You go ahead. You know your way down there."

Yeager shook his head. He didn't want to waste time fumbling around tonight. "I might have trouble finding them if they're not in the kitchen." To underscore the thought, his shoulder banged into his buddy's on his way to the door.

Deke heaved a resigned sigh. "What if they don't want company? How will we get them to even let us in?"

Yeager grinned, anticipating all that lay

ahead. "Haven't you learned anything? We'll tell them we have a problem with the bill."

Having Deke be his eyes left a whole lot to be desired, Yeager thought. They were making it down to the main house just fine, but Deke started balking again just as they closed in on Haven House's back door.

The other man finally came to a complete stop. "You're on your own," he said.

Yeager frowned. "Huh?"

"You're on your own."

This wasn't like Deke. "What's your problem?"

"I have a bad feeling about this."

Yeager still didn't get it. "What?"

"In my gut," Deke said. "Something's telling me I don't want to knock on that door."

"For Christ's sake, when did you go mystic on me?"

Deke muttered something unintelligible.

"Say it again?" Yeager said.

"Bad influences," he repeated, more clearly this time.

Baffled, Yeager shook his head. "Just get me within five feet of Zoe, and you're off the hook. Thirty more seconds, tops."

His estimation proved to be overoptimistic, however, because once they reached the back door, no one answered Deke's polite knock.

"Try again," Yeager urged, though it was obvious why they weren't getting a response. Even through the closed door, the sounds of party came through clearly: a warbled chorus of "Girls Just Wanna Have Fun" followed by

a fit of feminine laughter. More off-tune war-
bling.

Zoe wasn't any better at singing than she
was at bandleading.

Their second knock didn't produce better results.

"C'mon—"

Yeager didn't let Deke finish, but instead
turned the kitchen doorknob. It opened, and
he started through the door, his arm still
linked with his friend's. "I think they're in the
next room. You distract Lyssa while I talk to
Zoe."

He ignored Deke's groan, and the two of
them made it through the kitchen. Deke
pushed open the swinging door to the dining
room, where all the sound was coming from.

"Hello!" Yeager started cheerfully, but nobody helloed back.

Deke took a step backward. "We're interrupting."

Neither of the women denied it, which surprised Yeager. The sisters were usually very
hospitable.

Yeager didn't move. "What's going on?" he
said for Deke's ears only.

His friend didn't reply, and Yeager's imagination took a wild turn. What was going on?
Giggles, girls having fun. Were Lyssa and Zoe
. . . entertaining?

"It's a little private party," Lyssa said
clearly. "You're welcome to some cake,
though."

Deke stepped back, dragging Yeager with
him. Their shoulders hit the swinging door.

"We'll come back some other time."

A little private party? Yeager didn't like Zoe's silence. She was in the room, all right, because her scent tickled his nose and nudged something lower. "Zoe?"

"I'm here," she said quietly, a note in her voice, almost protective, that he didn't understand.

Someone had turned down the music, but the girls were still wannaing, a tinny counterpoint to the awkward silence that filled the rest of the room.

"It's been five years," Lyssa said suddenly.

Yeager felt Deke's flinch, but he didn't understand it. "Five years since what?" What the hell was going on?

Lyssa spoke right up. "When I was a teenager, I was diagnosed with cancer—leukemia. I've been free of it for five years. Tonight is our annual celebration. We have our favorite kind of cake and act crazy and . . ."

"And what?" Deke asked hoarsely.

"And . . ." There was a smile in Lyssa's voice, and Yeager didn't get that either. "And pretend we're young again."

Yeager ran a hand through his hair. Sweet Lyssa—cancer? When her sister was diagnosed, Zoe would have been twenty-one. Their parents were just dead, and Zoe would have still been in college, and then her younger sister was diagnosed with cancer.

"Let me get you each a piece of cake." That was Zoe. Her scent brushed by him as she bustled around the room.

"No," he said. At that same time, when he'd

been busting his ass trying to prove himself at
NASA, congratulating himself on being the
hottest, youngest pilot ever in the astronaut
program, Lyssa had been undergoing treatment for cancer.

Zoe had been alone by her side.

He backed into the door and felt it swing
out with his weight. "We've got to go, don't
we Deke? We shouldn't have barged in."

"*We* didn't want to," Deke muttered.

They made it outside without bothering
with cake or good-byes. The night air was
cooler than usual, and for once Yeager didn't
picture the moon in his mind or yearn for the
dark, almost spacelike sky.

"Jesus Christ," he said.

"God," Deke echoed.

"They were eating cake and singing,"
Yeager said, as if Deke hadn't been there himself.

"That's not all."

"What?" For lack of a better reaction, he
tried to go for a little bit of humor. "They
didn't have men in there, did they? I wondered if pretending they were young again
meant they were playing with boy toys."

Deke blew out a heavy sigh, as if he hadn't
heard Yeager.

A chill rolled down Yeager's back. "What?"

"The room was dark," Deke said, "but lit
by candles. Candles all over the room, and a
chocolate cake the size of a hubcap."

Yeager didn't like the grim tone to his
friend's voice. "Maybe we should have taken

some slices of the stuff after all," he said, trying to distract him.

Deke ignored his second stupid attempt at humor. "A boombox sat on the table. And some pretty china plates and a silver coffee pot. It reflected the light of a thousand flames."

"Whoa, Shakespeare," Yeager said, still trying to derail the conversation.

"There was a silver frame too. With a photograph inside."

Candlelight, cake, cancer. Yeager thought he'd heard enough. He didn't need to know about any picture. "I'm going back to my room." He started up the path.

Deke caught him by the arm. "You need to hear the rest."

"No, I don't."

Deke laughed shortly. "Yes, you do."

He shook off his friend's hand. "Shit, man, why tell me more?" Anger came onto Yeager suddenly, and he couldn't quite put his finger on why. The cancer, maybe. Or the memory of himself telling Zoe she couldn't know what it was like to be powerless.

"Don't you think we invaded their privacy enough?" Yeager said, acting as if it was all about them, about Lyssa and Zoe, though it shamed him to realize he was really trying to protect himself. He could already imagine the scene without putting a photograph in the effing frame. For damn sure, he wouldn't like what it was a picture of.

Deke put his hand on Yeager's shoulder.

"It's just something you need to know, I think."

Yeager gritted his teeth and squeezed shut his eyes. "Fine," he said. "Go ahead."

"The photo, it was a close-up of Lyssa and Zoe. They were smiling, but they looked like hell. All skin and bones and big eyes and no hair."

Yeager made a gesture. "Chemotherapy. You lose your hair."

"Both of them. No hair."

"Both of them? I don't get it. Wha—"

"I'm guessing Zoe shaved hers off. She was as bald as Michael Jordan, buddy. I'm guessing as a show of solidarity for her death-defying sister."

Another cold chill raised the hairs at the back of Yeager's neck. When Zoe thought her little sister was dying, she'd shaved her head. Just a little show of solidarity, as Deke put it, for her only family left in the world.

"Zoe," he said.

"And Lyssa," Deke added. "She almost died."

And Zoe'd had to keep her sister alive. Yeager shook his head. "Jesus Christ," he said again.

"God."

It almost felt like they were praying.

Zoe realized Yeager was avoiding her. She tried to feel relieved. Yeager had felt too warm and solid and permanent when she'd held him in her arms in the muddy garden. She'd wanted

to hold him and heal him and have him forever. Wasn't that silly?

Just plain silly.

With her energy focused on the Firetail Festival instead of her guest, Zoe had been a whirl
of activity lately. More flyers, more band practice, a meeting with the island chief of police
to pin down the parade route and which
streets would have to be cordoned off.

Then there was her promise to make one
hundred tinfoil stars to decorate the school auditorium for the festival dance. The Abrigo
Anglers' Club had volunteered to gather all
one thousand stars being made and hang them
with fishing line from the acoustically tiled
ceiling.

Sitting at the kitchen table and massaging
her scissor-cramped fingers, Zoe wished
they'd stuck with last year's theme, A Garden
of Island Delights. Somebody's garage held
boxes of papier-mâché fruit, made by the high
schoolers, and tissue-paper flowers, courtesy
of the elementary grades.

The Sky's the Limit!, this year's theme, complete with exclamation point, just seemed a tri-
fle too optimistic. But Zoe reined in her doubts
and grabbed up another sheet of tagboard full
of pencil-traced stars. She was optimistic. She
was.

As punishment for her brief bout of negativ-
ity, she fitted the scissors to her hand and
started cutting again.

Her aching fingers appreciated the interrup-
tion of the knock at the front door, however.

So did Zoe—until she saw who stood on the other side.

"Jerry."

He bustled through the door, belly first, his expensive knit shirt rolled over his expensive plumpness and tucked into his expensive white slacks. With a sinking heart, Zoe followed him into the living room.

Gunther had told her Jerry was back days ago, and she'd counted each one as a blessing when he didn't show up with some complaint or correction about the festival. Jerry mostly paid for the thing, and he expected value for his buck.

He settled on one of the couches with a little sigh. "We need to talk, Zoe."

"Sure, Jerry." She perched on a straight-backed chair and wondered how to get rid of him. "I hope you had a successful trip."

He waved a ringed hand—expensive jewelry, plump fingers—as if her polite hope was a given. "I see you've continued with the plans for the festival."

Zoe swallowed. "Well, of course, Jerry. We decided—"

"*You* decided is the way that I hear it."

She swallowed again. "It was a majority vote of the committee, Jerry. You know we need the festival to keep our tourism numbers up."

"The fish, Zoe. We need those G.D. fish."

"They're coming back." The nape of her neck burned, a sure sign of stress.

"Those scientists aren't swayed by words, Zoe. They haven't changed their opinion."

"I don't know what you'd have me do, Jerry." Zoe rubbed her suddenly sweaty palms over the front of her cutoffs. "The flags are up, the flyers are out, the Scouts are making their parade floats."

Jerry scowled. "That's a lot of my money on the line."

"Jerry." Zoe couldn't think of anything else to say, so she ended up repeating herself. "The flags are up. The flyers are out. The Scouts are making their parade floats."

He stood up and put his hands in his slacks, jingling his change ominously. "And I think—"

Another voice entered the conversation. "You're just pestering Zoe for no reason."

She swung around. Yeager. Leaning against the arched entry to the living room, one foot crossed over the other, wearing a silk sports shirt and wrinkled linen slacks. With his sunglasses and the dark stubble covering the stark planes of his face, he looked like a dissolute Hollywood celebrity. He wore a faint smile on his face, and you wouldn't guess he was blind.

"Excuse me?" Jerry said.

Yeager smiled wider, but there was something in the way he held himself, however casually, that spoke of command. For the first time Zoe remembered he was an officer in the navy. "I said, there isn't any reason to bother Zoe about this now. Not when the festival plans are going full speed ahead. A businessman of your caliber must see that now's the time to just make the best of whatever happens."

"Well, I—Well, I—"

"I'm sure you realize that it doesn't make a whole lot of sense to badger Zoe about this." Yeager then turned his head toward her. "Zoe," he said. "I need to speak with you privately."

She smiled. "Something about your bill?" she said sweetly.

"Exactly." Even blind and even with his sunglasses on, he managed to send Jerry a pointed look.

The other man took the hint. "I'll let you get back to your business, then." He strode toward the door, then turned to look at Yeager. "Aren't you—?"

Yeager nodded. "Exactly. The second-in-command of the IRS."

Jerry couldn't get out the door fast enough.

Zoe clapped her hands over her mouth to stifle her laughter. Once she had control of herself, she shook her head. "He's going to realize his mistake in about twenty-two seconds. Jerry isn't stupid, you know. He won't really believe you work for the IRS and he'll realize who you are."

Yeager was already turning away. "Who knows? I'm looking for a job."

Zoe ran to catch up with him. "What did you need?"

He let her push open the swinging door to the kitchen for him. "Nothing. I heard voices. I was curious."

"Well, you saved me." At the thought, warmth blossomed in her chest. Nobody had come to her rescue in a long time.

"You would have handled him," he said brusquely. "I shaved maybe three minutes off your hassle quota for today."

She followed him out the kitchen door. "Are you okay?"

"Dandy." He strode up the path toward Basil Cottage.

Zoe lengthened her step to keep up with him. "I haven't seen you in a while. Is there something the matter?"

"Not a thing."

But something was definitely wrong with him, very wrong. Now that Jerry was gone, Yeager's shoulders betrayed his tension, and a muscle ticked in his jaw. He started to walk even faster, and Zoe noticed he was limping heavily on his right leg.

Frowning, she jogged to stay beside him. "Is Deke around?"

"He's at his uncle's old place, I think."

Meaning Yeager was alone. Zoe bit her lip. She could fathom part of his abrupt mood change—he'd been putting on a relaxed pose as a way of disarming Jerry—but what was beneath it seemed darker than anything she'd ever sensed in him.

She bit her lip again. The man had just done her a favor. Was it right to leave him alone in this mood? She continued dogging his footsteps, unsure what to do.

At the doorstep of his cottage, he halted. "Zoe," he said clearly. "Go away."

She shoved her hands in her pockets. "But—"

"Go away." He reached out, found her

shoulder, and gave it a little push. Then he turned and opened the door.

Zoe could see the cottage was a mess. The bedcovers sprawled on the floor like a drunken party guest. Chip bags, beer, and soda cans littered the small countertop in the kitchen area. The bed pillows and a tray of store-bought cookies lay on the floor between the bed and the patio doors. Only the patio itself was neat. Dolly still sat in her chair, her inflated feet, stuffed into purple rubber thongs, propped up on the table.

"Mrs. Duran told me you wouldn't let her in," Zoe said. "Would you like me to tidy up for you?"

He rubbed his hand down his scar, even the stubble on his cheek unable to disguise it. "I'd like you to close the door and go away."

She closed the door anyway.

He must have thought she'd followed his orders and left, because he crossed to the mussed bed, sat down on it, then flopped backward. The mattress bounced in response to his weight.

She hesitated. That dark mood—or whatever you'd call it—still came off him.

"Zoe, why are you still here?"

Apparently his other senses continued to maintain that fine tune.

She rubbed her palms down her shorts. What to do? She'd seen him charming and teasing and seductive. Friendly and frustrated. But now all those were gone. Instead he seemed raw and tense and hurting. Should she just leave him to it, or try to help him in some way?

"Are you in pain?" she asked.

He let out a short, unfunny laugh. "Yeah, I'm in agony."

She didn't know what to make of his caustic tone. "Is there something I can do?" She drew nearer the bed. "Where does it hurt?"

He didn't seem inclined to answer. Taking a breath, she eased down on the mattress beside him. "I saw you limping earlier." Her fingers tentatively touched the middle of one hard thigh.

His fingers clamped over her wrist.

She froze. "Is that where it hurts?"

"Don't, Zoe. Don't do it." His fingers tightened on her wrist.

"Don't do what?"

"Don't make a fool out of me."

"What?" She tried tugging her arm from him, but he wouldn't let go. "I don't know what you're talking about."

"It started that day in the garden. Should I refresh your memory? You told me you knew how it felt to lose something." He sat up. "Yet you didn't counter my pleasant little comeback. What was it I said? 'You have no goddamn idea'?"

"I *haven't* been an astronaut—"

"Please, Zoe." He sounded disgusted. "You let me whine and moan and expose every piddly-ass complaint I could dredge up."

She swallowed. "I—"

"And when I'm sitting there whimpering about my life, all that time you're keeping quiet about a few important details of your own. Like your sister had cancer. Like you were the only family she had to get her through it. Like you fucking shaved your head so she wouldn't feel so alone."

"I don't know what—"

"That has to do with anything?" His voice rose angrily, and he dropped her arm. "How about making me feel like a jerk? How about showing me up as whining and selfish? How about making it clear I'm a wannabe hero? One who doesn't have enough courage to go to sleep at night because he hates waking up and remembering the truth."

"Yeager! For goodness sake. You haven't been sleeping?"

"Just get out of here, Zoe." He stood up and turning his back on her, stalked toward the patio doors. "For 'goodness' sake, get away from me."

At the pain in his voice, a sharp ache pierced her chest. The emotional roller coaster he was riding was too familiar. She swallowed, knowing she should at least tell him that much.

But in the years since Lyssa's diagnosis, Zoe had sought out ways to protect herself as well as ways to cope. She'd developed a habit of not talking freely about Lyssa's cancer to other people, in order to insulate herself from fears she couldn't quite let go of and from the terrible memories of that time.

Against the sunlight streaming through the patio doors, Yeager was a dark, lonely shadow. That ache pierced her chest again. No matter what, she couldn't leave him like this.

Not even if it meant reaching inside herself and exposing a few pieces of her heart.

She swallowed again. "Okay, so I did leave out a few things about myself. I should have told you that when I was almost twenty-one years old, and my parents had recently died, my sister came to my apartment in L.A. for the summer. She seemed tired a lot, but because we were both grieving, I didn't think much about it. Then, though"—Zoe gulped a breath—"then came these strange bruises. We went to the doctor, and it didn't take very long for him to tell me I might lose my sister too."

He said nothing, so she started talking again.

"You think I wasn't mad at the world? But what could I do? We got the best treatment. I smiled as many times as I could fake it. And when Lyssa came home from the hospital, I made myself a bed on the floor in the hallway outside her room." Zoe had never told her sister or anyone else about this. "I didn't want to scare her, but I was also terrified something would happen to her in the night. I didn't sleep much then either."

Her impromptu confession didn't immediately seem to ease Yeager's tension. He still didn't talk to her or even turn her way. After a few more moments of silence, Zoe approached him, moving carefully. "Yeager." She touched his back. "Talk to me—"

He whirled and both hands shot out and gripped her shoulders. "God damn it, Zoe! Won't you just leave me alone? Don't you get it? I don't want you here. I don't want you touching me. I don't want you inside my head. I don't want to think about you as twenty-one and hairless as a billiard ball and sleeping outside your sister's room in case death decided to make a visit."

She froze. "I—I thought you were angry that I hadn't told you before."

He shook his head. "Oh, yeah, I was angry. And I'm angry now. But don't you understand?"

"I don't think I do," she said, then took a breath. "Go ahead and explain it to me."

His hands tightened on her shoulders. "You don't want to know."

"Tell me, Yeager."

His arms started to shake, and his whole body trembled with tension. "Fine. Okay." He heaved in a quick breath and spit out the words, each more furious than the one before. "I'm angry at myself. I hate how weak and stupid I am, that even knowing about what happened to Lyssa—and to you—it doesn't change a thing about how I feel about *me*. Do you get it now?"

His anger had reached a crescendo. Zoe tried to pull away, but he wouldn't let go. Instead he drew her close to his taut, furious body. "Yeah, there are other tragedies in this world, but I still want to know." His voice lowered in quiet rage. "*I want to know, Zoe, I want to know why the fuck this happened to me.*"

She was utterly silenced. Then, stunned by his fierce despair, Zoe let out a soft whimper.

"Oh, God." His bitterness instantly evaporated, and his hands softened. "Oh, God." He patted her shoulders gently, then ran his palms down her arms. "Tell me I haven't hurt you," he said, his voice hoarse.

But Zoe couldn't get words past the lump in her throat.

"Talk to me. Please, Zoe, tell me I haven't done something to hurt you." He gathered her up against his body, his hands roving down her back as if to make sure he hadn't broken her.

She turned her cheek against his chest. A button pressed into her skin. "I'm okay," she whispered.

But she wasn't.

"I scared you. God, honey, I didn't mean to scare you."

She wrapped her arms around his waist. "You didn't."

"You're shaking. I can feel you shaking." He pulled her even closer and groaned. "Zoe."

Tears stung the corners of her eyes, but she ignored them and looked up at Yeager. "It's okay," she said. "Everything's going to be okay."

He groaned again and buried his face against the side of her neck.

She turned her face to brush her lips against his cheek, and then he turned too, so that their lips met and they kissed gently, their mouths open and wet.

But then he abruptly broke the kiss and held her away from him. "Stay away from me, Zoe. I'm not worth another moment of your time."

"Yeager, no," she whispered.

But he suddenly let go of her, and she stumbled back a step. "Please," he said. "Just get away from me."

The sting of tears started in the corners of her eyes, but Zoe ignored them. She focused on Yeager instead, on finding some way to take away the terrible burden he'd put on himself.

"I think you've been reading way too much of your own press," she said quietly. "No one expects you to be a hero every minute of your life. Anyone would feel as you do. Yeager, you're just a man."

He let out a crack of laughter sharp enough to cut glass, yet he reached out and ran his knuckles down her face in a strangely tender gesture. "Even that's in question, honey, believe me. So just leave me alone."

But she wouldn't. Not this moment when he needed her and when she knew so well, so rightly, what she could do for him. A now familiar yearning kindled from spark to fire inside her. She stepped forward, her arms going around his waist. "Yeager."

He groaned. "Zoe, go—"

"I won't." She pressed her body against his, and the warmth of him caused that woman inside her to become instantly and demandingly awake. "Let me stay."

Not that she fooled herself he'd be hers forever. Or that in any other circumstances she would have had a chance with him. *But I can be what he needs right now, and he can be what I need.*

"Kiss me," she whispered, and brought his mouth down to hers.

13

Yeager tried pulling away from Zoe. "No," he said.

But she tightened her arms around his back, lifted her face, and found his mouth. She needed this. He needed this.

The kiss began as a gentle comfort, but then it quickly changed, and he seemed hungry, his mouth demanding. Zoe found herself demanding too as she crowded him, bumping against the hard heat of his body.

His palms cupped her bottom and tilted her against his hips. He groaned.

Zoe's head spun, and she eagerly pressed herself forward. His erection was imposing and impossibly hard against her belly, and her heart pounded. He wanted her.

And she wanted him.

He groaned again and inched back from her body, but then buried his face again in the curve of her neck and shoulder. The air felt cool against her wet mouth, and Zoe lifted her hands to sift through his gold-shot hair and hold him against her.

She was going to make love to him.

The idea more excited than surprised her. She knew Yeager needed her. He needed her right now. He needed her to accept his understandable anger and he needed her to give him some respite from it.

She started shaking a little just at the thought of what she was contemplating.

But she wanted to do it. Zoe wanted to take Yeager into her arms and into her body, and she'd lie beside him in that mussed-up bed and keep away any demons that tried to reach him.

He pressed his lips against her neck, a soothing kiss, but it made her moan, and goose bumps skittered down her skin.

Okay. So she couldn't kid herself and say it would be all for him. The truth was, he was right about how stingy she'd become with herself. She needed him too, to prod her to expose her heart to a little sunshine, however briefly.

Savoring the decision, she closed her eyes and let herself fantasize for a moment how it was going to be. Since she'd never actually done it before, a gossamer-curtain haziness floated over her imagination. In her mind there were dim lights and mosquito-net canopies and a melting, melding of bodies that was as lyrical as a Rodgers and Hammerstein score.

Hearing the music in her head, she whispered to Yeager. "Make love to me."

He stiffened, and then his arms tightened, his mouth still against her neck. "Zoe—"

"Please." Her insides felt warm and soft, like toasted marshmallows, and she added sweetness to her fantasy, soft touches and gentle, languid kisses. Their lovemaking would be a slow, patient give and take, and at the end she'd be satisfied. Okay, smugly satisfied, that her first experience with lovemaking had been with a man she cared for and who had luckily found the way into her tiny corner of the galaxy for a little while before moving on to explore the wider universe.

"Zoe. Do you really want—?"

Want. Yes, she did. But this time she'd slowly slide into the romantic moment. She put from her mind the combustible quality of their other encounters. Mere preludes. Now that she was planning on going the whole nine yards, that overheated urgency she usually experienced with him would disappear. She wouldn't ruin their lovemaking by letting desire run away with her.

She remembered that time by the creek. It had taken too little of his touch before she . . . detonated. She wasn't going to let her inexperience ruin this for him.

Zoe dug her fingers in his hair and gently pulled back his head. "Make love to me," she said again, smiling.

His hands moved from her back to frame her face. "Don't fool with me, Zoe."

There was an intensity in his expression that didn't quite fit in with her sugar-frosted fantasy, and her smile died. But there was no backing out now. She didn't want to. "Please, Yeager," she said again.

He hesitated another moment, and then Rodgers—or was it Hammerstein?—struck up the band in her mind as he kissed her once more. He started out gentle, and then his tongue fluttered over the seam of her lips. She knew what he wanted, and she opened for him.

Her eyes drifted shut as he explored her mouth, and his hands traveled down her back to her rear end again.

Yeager hauled her body close to his. "Spread your legs a little, honey," he said against her lips.

Zoe half opened her eyes. Spread your legs. She shivered. It wasn't exactly a phrase that matched her ruffles and lace daydream. As a matter of fact, it sounded raunchy. She swallowed and felt an urgent heat crawl over her skin. Delightfully raunchy.

The tempo of her mental musical score sped up a notch.

"Spread your legs," he murmured again, and she obeyed. When he settled against her body this time, he tilted his hips into the vee of her thighs, pressing his hard erection against the lower part of her belly.

Zoe gasped, the sensation of him aroused—the idea that she had aroused him—startling her all over again. With his hands cupping her hips, he held her against him and bit her bottom lip.

The mental violins squealed in surprise. Zoe gasped again, and hot goose bumps burst over her skin. She sagged against Yeager, and he angled his head to kiss her again. Slowly kiss her. Deeply kiss her.

It took the kind of time that she'd imagined.

He brushed his tongue against the place he'd bitten. He moved inside and stroked her tongue gently, then teased her by moving in and out of her mouth. The strings started up again, languid and seductive, and for some reason, when he retreated, her own tongue followed.

He sucked.

He sucked on her tongue.

Zoe moaned helplessly, and her nipples instantly tightened into embarrassingly hard points. Maybe he wouldn't notice. But he must have, because he dug his fingers into her hips and slowly, with excruciating care, brushed his chest against the sensitive tips of her breasts.

Where were Rodgers and Hammerstein? But the music inside her was gone, to be replaced by the demanding pound of a hammering drum that was her heartbeat.

She opened her eyes. Yeager's mouth was wet and his nostrils flared. One of his hands slid up her back then down, then it came around between them. She watched it inch over her ribcage.

"Promise me you'll never wear a bra," he said hoarsely. "I love to be able to touch you like this." Her nipples stood out against her T-shirt, and he found one, flicking it with his thumb.

Zoe whimpered as something deep inside her clenched like a fist. She hastily shut her eyes, trying to reconjure that fuzzy and candyfloss fantasy. Wasn't it supposed to be like that?

But instead, there was a hot, insistent pounding in her blood, and she didn't think it was exactly feminine to feel this way.

His thumb pressed her nipple again.

Zoe's knees and ankles buckled. "No. Please."

Yeager licked her neck on his way to her ear. "What's wrong?"

Her face burned, and she held onto his shoulders. "I think—I think I'm feeling a little too . . . hot."

He chuckled. "There's no such thing." He bit down on her earlobe.

The spunsugar daydream exploded in a burst of brilliant sugary crystals. Zoe desperately dug her fingers into Yeager's hard muscles. "We better slow down."

He drew away, his hands cupping her upper arms. "Did you change your mind?" he said quietly.

"No! Yes. No." She took in a calming breath. "I just want to go a bit slower, okay?" Somehow she had to get control of herself before she terrified the man with her lust by throwing him down on the bed and rubbing herself all over him.

"You're sure? Zoe?"

She swallowed. "I'm sure."

"Thank God." He took one hand off her and started unbuttoning his shirt. He grinned. "Speaking of hot . . ."

Zoe's eyes widened. Her mouth opened, but she couldn't suck in air and stare at all the bare skin of his chest at the same time. Inches from her nose. Inches!

"Oh, no." She pulled away from him and went over to the bed and sat down. Her hands covered her eyes. "I'm sorry, but we can't do this."

"Zoe?"

"I'm just too . . . Oh, goodness, there just isn't another word that fits. I hate to say it, I hate to shock you like this, but . . . I'm too horny." She bent her head lower, humbly humiliated.

"Hor—" he started, and then broke off, stumbling over a pillow on his way to the bed. "This is a big joke, right?" he said carefully, his voice raspy. "Who put you up to this? Deke? The guys in Houston?"

She looked up at him, frowning. "Nobody put me up to anything."

His head swung around wildly. "It's *Candid Camera*, then. Where are they? If they're in here, I'm gonna strangle them."

"What's wrong with you? There's no *Candid Camera* in here. Just me and you and nobody else."

The mattress dipped as he sat down beside her. "Then who the hell are you?" he asked. "Because I don't get it. I just don't get it. One minute you're moaning and melting in my arms, and then the next minute you're pushing me away because you're too—too—"

"Horny," she supplied helpfully.

He threw up his hands. "I think I'm losing my mind as well as everything else I ever cared about."

Zoe swallowed. "Maybe I do owe you an explanation."

"Oh, there's a good idea," he said sarcastically. "Now, if you can only guarantee I'll understand any explanation you could possibly provide!"

"I'm a virgin," she said quickly.

His mouth shut with an audible snap.

"I'm sorry," she said, "but it's true. And I'm also sorry that it's made me kind of hor—*intense*, when it comes to you."

He didn't respond right away. Instead he just sat there, still as a statue. "Virgin?" he finally echoed hoarsely.

She nodded, then caught herself, remembering he couldn't see. "I guess, I guess I'm sort of in a time warp or something. I was just shy of my twenty-first birthday when Lyssa got sick. I'd come from a little teeny place—remember, there were eighteen girls and eight boys in my high school graduating class? And my college classmates were all women. So when my parents died and Lyssa was diagnosed—" She sighed. "Well, other things took precedence in my life. First it was Lyssa's health, and then it was getting us here and creating this place where we could be secure. So you see—"

"You're a virgin," he said again.

"And I apologize for it. Not that I think a woman should sleep around or anything, but goodness, I'm twenty-seven years old! So when you kiss me, and when you touch me, I go just a little bit . . . crazy."

"You get horny," he said.

"That's right. And I don't mean for it to spoil things between us, I really don't, but af-

ter just a few kisses and when you touch my—
me, I know I'm this close to exploding and
ruining everything."

"Ruining everything," he said faintly.

"I'm sorry," she said sincerely.

He fell back on the bed like she'd shot him.

Concerned, she bent over his body, trying
not to be distracted by the wedge of masculine
chest she could see in the vee of his half-
opened shirt. "Are you okay?"

"No."

Alarm widened her eyes. "What is it? Does
it hurt somewhere? Can I do something?"

"Yes," he said. "If you don't unleash your
horniness on me, I think I'll die."

Embarrassment burned her cheeks, and she
slapped at his arm. "That isn't funny."

He caught her hand. "I'm not kidding, Zoe.
It sounds to me like you got your ideas about
sex from an outdated high school hygiene
book."

That was perilously close to the truth. "I
watch movies! I read books!"

"Not anything made after 1950, I'm guessing."

Perilously closer to the truth. She bit her lip.

Yeager dragged her over on top of him.
"Listen. There are no unacceptable outer limits
to a woman's desire."

She felt him throbbing between her legs, or
maybe it was her again. "But what if we're
kissing and touching and I, um, I, you know,
before you, um, I—"

"Explode and ruin everything?"

She was glad he couldn't see her red, red blush. "Yes."

"Then we just start the kissing and touching all over again."

Yeager figured that a horny virgin might just make up for all the bad luck that had come his way lately.

He experienced a slight twinge of guilt at the unapologetic machoness of the thought, but then dismissed it. Guilt didn't have a place in his bed right now. There was only room for him and Zoe.

And he was strangely—and again, unapologetically—glad that she was a virgin.

He didn't have a good explanation for the feeling, so he dismissed it too and concentrated on Zoe. He'd lifted Her Horniness on top of him on the bed, and now he snuggled her closer then slid his hands to her thighs and pushed them wide, so they bracketed his hips.

She moaned a little, then wriggled her little behind to wedge him *there*.

Yeager moaned a little too.

"I like this," Zoe said, wriggling again.

Yeager gritted his teeth. "I think we need to get a few things clear." He put his hands on her hips then shoved them in the back pockets of her shorts to still her movement.

She started playing with his hair, sifting her fingers through it. "Okay." She kissed his chin.

"Just so we're on the same page."

"Hmm."

"You want to have sex with me."

She tried that little hip grind again, and he had to squeeze her rounded butt to make her stop. "Yes."

"Okay. Fine." He bit back a groan as the heat between her thighs became the call of the wild to his penis. "But first"—he had to get this part out—"I just want to be sure you understand that . . . that . . ." How did you tell a virgin who you want to be inside more than anything you remembered in your life that it was a short-term kind of thing? "That . . . that . . ."

Zoe kissed his chin again. "That you'll marry me in the morning?"

He froze.

Her fingers poked him in the ribs. "Kidding. Sheesh. You should see your face."

Relief met another upsurge of lust. "You're sure, Zoe?"

Suddenly, instead of answering, she sat up, her body pressing against his erection. Sheer, don't-ever-stop torture. Her fingers made fast work of the rest of the buttons of his shirt, and she spread the sides, her fingertips brushing against his hot skin.

"Oh," she breathed.

In response he found the hem of her T-shirt and ran his fingers under it, inching over her warm, smooth skin to the small curves of her breasts. He cupped them in his palms and smiled. "Oh," he echoed.

She wriggled again. He was going to have to get her to stop that pretty soon.

"Did I say how much I appreciate the fact you don't wear a bra?"

"You seem to have mentioned it," she said primly, then gasped as he squeezed her softness.

Taking his time, he reveled in the contrast of soft breast and hardened nipple. He'd never noticed it before, when he could see, how good it was to run his thumb in circles around a woman's puckered aureole. Zoe gasped, and her hips bucked against him when he lightly pinched her nipples.

He smiled. "Are we in any immediate danger of you exploding?"

She moaned as he rubbed his thumbs over the sensitive flesh.

Yeager was feeling a little explosive himself. Dropping his hands to her waist, he lifted her off his lap and laid her on the bed, then shoved her T-shirt toward her neck.

The skin over her ribs smelled like her and tasted as sweet as her mouth. He ran his tongue across her stomach, then traveled up to her breasts. When he found his way between them, he kissed her there, sucked lightly at the skin, and listened to her whimper.

"Yeager . . ."

He reached up and smoothed back her hair. "Hold on, honey. It'll be better if we just stretch it out a while." His thumb brushed over her nipple again, and her whole body jerked.

"Don't wanna . . . stretch it out."

He smiled. "Do it for me, sweetie." Bending over, he licked his way down her skin until he found her nipple and took it in his mouth.

When he sucked, desire traveled like a comet to his groin, heating him white hot.

"Yeager!"

He pulled away and blew a stream of air in the direction of her breast. "Okay, okay, let me cool you down." Another blow.

She bowed in his arms, he could feel it, her breasts lifting toward him, her hips grinding into the mattress. "That's not helping."

He shrugged. "Well, then." And then he bent to taste her other nipple, sucking strongly while dallying with the first one, his fingers gently pinching, then thumbing the hard point.

"Yeager." Her hips pushed into the bed again.

He forced himself back. "Hmm?"

"Take off your clothes," she said.

He couldn't stop his grin. "I thought I told you we were stretching this out. One look at my great physique and—"

"Take off your clothes."

"Well, aren't you the bossy virgin." But it was no hardship to obey the urgent demand in her voice. He tossed his shirt away and shucked the rest of what he was wearing in two seconds flat.

When he was done, he stood beside the bed, facing Zoe. "Oh, my," she said.

A little chill of worry crept over him. Maybe he shouldn't have complied so quickly. He couldn't see her face, and it probably wasn't such a great idea to let a twenty-seven-year-old virgin take a daylight, up-close-and-personal view of the organ that was standing at the ready to invade her body. "Zoe—"

Something brushed his penis. Her fingers. They touched him again, and he clamped down on his groan and his immediate need to spread her legs and bury the thing inside her.

He swallowed. What was she thinking? "Zoe, honey. You need to remember my disability here."

"What disability?" she replied absently.

He felt another brush of that curious touch. "You gotta remember I can't see, honey. I don't know. Am I scaring you to death, or are you ready to be my love slave?"

A little giggle escaped. A good sign. "I've just never—"

"Seen one, I know."

"Such a big one," she corrected, another giggle in her voice. "That's what I meant to say."

Zoe. Even now she could make him laugh. "God forbid I ever try to finish your sentences again."

"That's right. You just might underestimate yourself."

He laughed again, and then knelt on the bed. "Your turn, please."

"My turn?"

"Take your clothes off."

"But—but—"

"Zoe, honey, there's nothing to be modest about. Remember?" he coaxed. "I can't see a thing."

He could almost hear her blink. "Well, of course, that's right."

The *vriiip* of the zipper on her shorts nearly undid him. But he hung on, and when he

sensed she was finished undressing, he held
out his arms. "Come here, sweetheart."

She was small and sleek, and when her nipples pressed against his chest, he thought com-
ets and heat and white-hot explosions again.
He pushed her back against the mattress and
then pushed her thighs apart and settled between them.

He gave her a mock frown. "You didn't take
off your panties," he said.

He heard her swallow. "Stretching it out, remember? I—I—"

"Did exactly the right thing," he answered,
pushing against the damp silkiness.

Tilting her hips toward him, she moaned.

Need clenched deep in Yeager's belly. Bending his head, he took her mouth, pushing it
wide with his own. She opened for him immediately, and he thrust his tongue inside and
pushed against her panties too, letting the fabric barrier prevent him from going in too far
and too fast.

They moaned together.

Heat gathered at the base of his spine. He
ran his palm over her breast, down her ribs,
then lifted himself a little so he could insinuate
his hand under her panties. Still kissing her
deeply, he shifted his weight to the side and
eased his hand through the wispy hair between her thighs until her found her hot, soft
wetness.

He lifted his head and, clenching his teeth,
slowly pushed one finger inside her.

Her hips tilted, and her inner muscles
grabbed his finger. "Yeager."

Shit. She was so tight, just the thought of going inside her body was enough to burn him up. He panted a little, slowly withdrew the finger, and then sent in two.

"Yeager!" She writhed around him, against him, her hands biting into his shoulders and her body pulsing against his fingers.

He groaned, just barely holding himself back. He rode through the climax with her, and when it was over, he bent to her mouth and kissed her sweetly, his tongue stroking soothingly over hers.

When she'd quieted, he raised his head. He smiled. "Okay, honey?"

"Yeager." There was a shade of tears in her voice. "I thought, I thought. You know I wanted this. With you. You just said we were stretching it out."

He smile ruefully. "And then when it was almost too late, I realized there was a little something we'd left out of this good plan. Protection."

"Protection?"

His little virgin. It scared the hell out of him that she hadn't given a thought to it herself. "Condoms? Protection against pregnancy and disease?"

"Oh. Well, why didn't you just say something, then?"

"I wasn't in much of a mood to send you to the corner drugstore."

"No need to go that far." She rolled away from him and she got out of the bed. He heard her head in the direction of the bathroom, and then came the unmistakable sounds of a cupboard opening and closing.

The mattress dipped when she came back to him. "I keep the bathroom cupboard well stocked with toiletries. Razors, toothbrush, toothpaste, that kind of thing."

Yeager lifted himself onto one elbow but didn't know if he dared hope. "And condoms?"

"It was Lyssa's idea," she said.

"Remind me to kiss your sister." Yeager held out his hand, and she dropped something into his palm, a foil-wrapped square. He looked in Zoe's direction, trying to sense her mood. Now that she'd had an orgasm, maybe she wouldn't—

"Let me put it on you," she said.

Yeager sent up a brief prayer of thanks. But he didn't comply immediately with Zoe's request. Instead he pushed her back on the bed and started kissing and touching her again, running the cool condom package over her belly, breasts, and inner thighs.

When she was trembling and moaning his name, he gave her instructions but let her put the rubber on him herself.

He had to grit his teeth before she was done, but then she was finished, and he laid her on her back and slipped off her panties before spreading her thighs and positioning himself at the hot heart of her body.

She was so damn tight.

He held his breath as he tried easing into her, but she was writhing and begging and pushing her hips up to meet him, and so finally he just drove into her.

He froze when she sobbed, his arms aching as he held himself above her, his penis so tightly encased by her body he thought he might come without moving at all. She sobbed again.

He inhaled a shuddering breath. "Zoe? Honey?"

Her hands slapped down on his ass and pushed. "*Please*," she said.

Given permission to love her, Yeager squeezed shut his eyes and buried and reburied himself inside Zoe's body. He felt heat and joy, and when he knew she climaxed again, he finally let himself go in a violent burst of pleasure that rivaled any rocket known to man.

14

 As sure as God made little green apples, he'd created another perfect miracle—a man's naked body.

Zoe sat on the edge of the mattress, running her gaze over Yeager. The covers had never made it back on the bed, and he lay stomach down and spread-eagled on the sheet, his face buried in a pillow.

Sometime before he'd fallen asleep, he'd taken off his dark glasses. For the first time she could truly enjoy the complete beauty of his face—the high cheekbones, the blade of his nose, the clean angles of his jaw and chin. She ran her tongue over her bottom lip, remembering the taste of his kisses and appreciating again the sensual cut of his mouth.

Goose bumps popped all over her, and her blood started a ginger-ale fizz as she let her gaze wander past his face. His shoulders and upper arms were heavy with muscle. She'd never before considered the pure beauty of a man's body. The long, deeply etched valley of Yeager's spine bisected the width of his back and led to the hard, curved roundness of his buttocks. Biting her lip, Zoe glanced away, but then couldn't stop herself from looking back.

Her air huffed out of her lungs. She remembered holding those curves in her palms as he pushed inside her and the exquisite feeling of being filled by him and filling her hands with him as he became her first lover.

Chills ran down her arms, and Zoe twisted her hands together to prevent herself from reaching out and caressing him. Her skin was heating up again, and that wild effervescent desire was surging through her body. But she didn't want to wake him.

He slept like a man finally at rest, and he hadn't budged when she'd uncurled from the thirteen inches of mattress space he'd left for her. Determined to control herself, she lifted her T-shirt from the floor and pulled it over her nakedness.

It was time for her to go.

She slipped into the rest of her clothes and then grabbed fistfuls of the bedclothes to tuck them around her sleeping Apollo. He'd blazed in her arms, golden and hot, and she'd never forget how beautiful he'd made her feel with the tenderness of his touch and the sweetness of his mouth.

But it was time for her to go.

She lingered at the doorway, taking another look back at the bed and the man who had irrevocably changed her life. He'd introduced her to physical passion between a man and a woman. It had been so much more than she'd expected, less awkward and more awesome.

Maybe it was because he was blind, freeing her from worrying about her own physical imperfections.

Maybe it was because he was Yeager.

She turned away from the thought and forced herself to leave the cottage. She'd gone to his bed with eyes wide open, knowing that her heart was protected by the very fact that he was temporarily in her life. She wasn't going to let her emotions get involved.

As a matter of fact, she'd make sure of that by not going to bed with him again.

Back at the house, she took a quick shower, using cold water so she wouldn't be tempted to linger. Dressed again, she forced herself back to the kitchen and the half-completed tinfoil stars. Pursing her lips in determination, she refitted the scissors to her hand and began cutting more tagboard.

She hummed an Island Band piece loudly to occupy her mind.

To forget that these very same hands had so recently stroked the hot skin and hard muscles of Yeager.

To avoid remembering that after they'd made love, he'd found her hand and kissed each fingertip and then her palm and then folded her fingers over the kiss so that she could feel it even now, sizzling like a brand in the sensitive curve.

The scissors clattered to table. "Darn," Zoe muttered, and then decided before she hurt herself to move onto wrapping foil around the stars she'd already cut.

She could see herself in the silver tin. The

reflection was blurry, but her lips stood out, redder and fuller than normal.

Redder and fuller from Yeager's kiss.

Disgusted with herself, she abandoned the stars and, grabbing a dustcloth and furniture polish, headed for the living room. She picked up a crocheted throw made by her mother from the back of a chair and wrapped it around her shoulders, relishing its comforting security.

Hugging herself, she stood in the center of the living room at the heart of the house that represented everything familiar and safe to her. *This* was where she belonged, here in her very own haven.

Comforted, she took a breath and then began her dusting ritual, spraying the lemony wax over occasional tables, the sideboard, and then finally the wide pine coffee table. There wasn't any dust to speak of—Zoe had already performed this task first thing in the morning—but the slow polishing was soothing, almost hypnotizing.

With the last stroke on the coffee table, she stood back to admire the high gloss.

And there was her reflection again.

Yeager hadn't made any promises to her. In fact, he'd made a point of pointing out there were no promises.

But she looked like a woman with promises on her mind.

And love in her eyes.

She pulled the crocheted throw tighter around her shoulders and tried denying it. She couldn't have fallen in love with him!

But she had.

With every complex, cranky, charming, and seductive inch of his body and mind.

Oh, no.

She was only going to end up hurt.

Sighing, Zoe dropped to the couch. It was the truth. When Yeager left the island, he was going to break her heart.

But he wasn't gone yet. Not yet.

The hairs stood up on the back of her neck, and she didn't know whether to interpret this as excitement or as a warning. Gripping her hands together, she tried getting tough with herself.

Could she do it? Did she have what it took?

Could she be with Yeager now and until he left the island and still survive?

It seemed a silly question, since he was going to leave no matter what she decided. And she was going to love him, no matter what she decided. And her heart was going to break, no matter what she decided.

Zoe shrugged off the throw and tossed down the dustcloth. There wasn't any point in making a decision at all.

The kitchen door slammed behind her, and then she ran up the path to Yeager's cottage. To Yeager's bed.

To Yeager.

When he woke up, she wanted to be beside him.

Deke was having as much trouble keeping his mind on the house repairs as he was keeping his mind off what he'd learned about Lyssa.

It was late afternoon when he finally allowed himself to give up. His carpenter's belt dropped to the floor with a *clunk*, and then he walked onto the porch, unsure what to do next.

If he went back to Haven House, he might run into her and for once he didn't have any bright ideas about how to handle that.

Shoving his hands in the pockets of his grimy jeans, he left the dilapidated house behind him and wandered down the hill, past the old tree house, toward the ocean. There were faint signs of a trail, and he idly followed it as it traversed the steepness.

As he moved lower on the hillside, the salty smell of the ocean deepened in the air, and birds twittered in the rustling leaves of the chaparral. He surprised an alligator lizard sunning itself in the weeds, but it didn't appear appeased by his quick apology.

Just as he rounded a turn in the path, the deep *caw* of a nearby raven startled him. He stumbled, glanced down at his feet, then back up, and looked straight into Lyssa's eyes.

His heart made that now familiar, pseudo-attack slam against his chest. How could she be so impossibly beautiful?

She was kneeling in a small clearing beside the path, wearing an embroidered white Mexican blouse and jeans. Her hair, as straight and yellow as cornsilk, hung down her back, and her eyes, like faceted drops of the sky, regarded him solemnly. She looked so young and tender and yet it was he who suddenly

felt as awkward and clumsy-handed as a teenager.

She held a crust of bread. "He almost ate
out of my hand." Lyssa nodded toward a
dusty-leaved manzanita bush. A raven
perched on one of its branches, regarding the
pair of them with its gleaming eyes.

"It was so close," she said.

Deke shuffled his feet, just like he used to
do in high school when he found himself near
the prettiest girl in class. His Adam's apple
swelled with nervousness. "I'm sorry," he
said.

She shrugged and rose to her feet, tossing
the bite of bread away. "I'll have another
chance."

The words bit into Deke, reawakening every
thought that had tortured him the past few
days. This young woman had battled cancer.
She'd almost had no chances. "Why didn't
you tell me?" he said hoarsely.

"About the leukemia?"

When he nodded, she turned to face the
ocean, her hair rippling with the movement
and then falling back into perfect smoothness.
"I didn't want to be a pity fuck."

Deke jerked back, the outrageous words hitting him like a slap. "Is that what you wanted,
little girl?"

She turned to look at him over her shoulder,
sloe-eyed and close to angry. "You know I'm
not a little girl, *now*, don't you?"

His pulse beat heavily. He wanted to continue thinking of her as a little girl. He wanted
to remember that if his friends saw him with

a woman as young as Lyssa, half of them would slap him a high five, and the other half would frisk him for gold chains and the keys to a brand-new Ferrari. A midlife crisis didn't get any more beautiful and typical than this woman.

Except she wasn't typical at all.

Without wanting to, he took a step closer. "Is that what you want from me?" he asked again. "A f—" He found he couldn't say it, not to her. "Without the pity?"

She didn't turn around. "I want to make love with you."

Deke's heart slammed against his chest once again, his mind going into sudden overdrive. He imagined lifting that weight of Goldilocks hair off her neck. He imagined smelling her skin and kissing her mouth and breasts. He imagined how soft and gentle he could be.

He closed his eyes. That's what a man of forty-three could give to someone like Lyssa. His experience and age could make the event if not perfect at least tender and caring.

What he couldn't imagine was why she wanted him.

But perhaps experience was something she wanted too. To experience an essential part of life that he deduced she hadn't had yet. And experience in the man who provided it for her.

She was smart. Some young hothead near her own age wouldn't take the time to make it good for her.

He could.

He would.

The rationalization came that easy to him.

Leaving behind his doubts, he took another step closer, and wrapped his arms around her to draw her back against his chest. She trembled in his arms, and he barely managed to control his own answering shudder. "Is this what you want, baby?"

She nodded quickly, and he half smiled, noting her lack of protest at the endearment. She wouldn't be a little girl, but she was happy to be his baby.

He tried thinking about other things too. The delicious mix of sun and salty air. The wisp of white cloud trailing across the sky.

But the sensation of Lyssa in his arms overshadowed it all. Blood pumped to his groin, and he grew hard and hot, and it was only all that inner boasting about experience that kept him from pushing against her round bottom then and there.

After a few moments he had to turn her in his arms. He had to look into that beautiful face. He had to kiss her, greedy but soft. *Soft, soft and slow*, he reminded himself.

His heart banged wildly in his chest, and he licked his lips to retaste her kiss on him.

God, he wanted her. God, he wanted to do this right.

He tilted up her chin with his finger. "I'm going to make you mine," he said.

She smiled, and there was only happiness in her eyes. "I know."

He didn't remember how they got back to his cottage. He only knew that with each step his body wound tighter and her breathing became quicker.

By the time he had her inside, her pupils were dilated, and he could see her nipples standing out beneath her white blouse and bra.

He held her loosely in his arms. "About protection—" he started.

"I'm sterile," Lyssa said quickly.

His heart stopped cold, then took an elevator fall toward his belt buckle.

She swallowed. "The treatment—"

Deke gathered her up against him. "Okay," he said, rubbing his hands down her back. "But I'll still use a condom."

She ducked her head against him. "If it's all right, if you're all right, please, don't."

Air stuttered in Deke's chest.

"I want to feel you as close as possible to me," she said quietly.

So that's how it went. He reined in every slam-bam impulse and concentrated on getting as close as possible to Lyssa.

Her blouse and jeans he drew off.

He licked around the edges of her bra and panties, then licked her nipples through the stretchy lace, then licked her matching panties, right over the center of her damp heat.

Every time he glanced up at her, she was smiling, dreamy, and aroused, and he had to clamp down on his own desires in order to continue slowly pleasuring her.

Once he pulled off her underwear, he had her writhing on the bed, and he ditched his clothes quickly so he could join her on the mattress skin to skin.

He swept his hands over her breasts and

belly toward the soft blond curls between her legs. She pulled his head down with her hands and kissed him deeply, her tongue moving in his mouth and making him so achingly hard that he couldn't hold back from finding his way between her thighs and positioning himself to join with her.

"I don't want to hurt you, baby," he said, and the air rasped heavily in and out of his lungs.

She opened her thighs wider. "You won't."

He hesitated. Despoiling a virgin was something he could barely remember. He'd hate himself for putting more pain in her life.

"Love me, Deke," she urged.

And it was a command and an invocation and a plea and something he couldn't resist any more than he could resist Lyssa herself.

He surged forward into her body and was surprised and relieved to find that though she was incredibly tight, there was no resistance. Then both emotions burned away in the slick heat of Lyssa, in the odd yet exhilarating sensation of looking into her crystal-blue eyes and seeing a heady mix of trust and surrender.

Afterward, she lay against his chest and ran her fingernails lightly against his skin. His oh-so-aged-and-experienced cock stirred immediately with an astonishingly youthful recovery. Deke gritted his teeth.

No matter how good it had been—oh, so damn good for him—this was a one-time deal. That's what he'd promised himself.

He'd gone against his better judgment for this one time because he'd thought she was a virgin who'd wanted to experience a taste of life she'd hadn't had a chance for yet.

Her thumb caught on his nipple, and his cock jumped against his thigh. He gritted his teeth again and caught her hand, squeezing it a little.

"I thought you said you were a virgin," he muttered, trying to think of a five-gallon tub of ice cream chilling on top of his groin.

She pulled her hand from his and went back to making circles on his chest. "I never said any such thing," she said, unperturbed.

"You implied it."

Her hair tickled his arm as she shook her head. "It bothers you that you're not the first?"

"Hell, no. It's just that . . . that . . ." Her virginity had made what she wanted from him if not sensible, at least explainable. But now, instead of a once-in-a-lifetime good deed, he found out that he'd had sex with a twenty-three-year-old beauty and that the lower half of him wanted to do it all over again!

He rolled away from her, ready to leave the bed completely if his good sense showed signs of giving way to his aroused body.

She edged closer. "You're number two, if that makes you feel any better."

He stifled a groan. What would make him feel better was a cold shower, but he couldn't quite command his arms to stop surrounding her.

"I was at a cancer camp for young adults. The first summer following my diagnosis."

Deke froze. That image of a bald and fragile Lyssa jumped into his mind. He tightened his hold on her.

"There was a boy, Jamie. I liked him. I liked him a lot. And . . ."

Deke inhaled a long, careful breath. "And?" he prompted softly.

"And we both didn't want to die without . . . without knowing."

Deke squeezed shut his eyes. He didn't want to think about Lyssa—gorgeous, smile-like-sunshine Lyssa—thinking about dying.

"So we snuck away and did it."

Her hair felt silky against his palm as he stroked her head. "And Jamie? Did you ever see him again?"

He could feel her little smile against his chest. "We exchanged E-mails for a while," she said. "Then he died. The next spring."

Deke swallowed. The boy she'd first made love to had died the spring after they'd come together. She said it so matter-of-factly, as if death of the young was a regular part of her world.

And he supposed it was.

Deke bent his head and found her mouth. He kissed her and then kissed her again.

His blood suddenly heated, pushing him to open her mouth wider, to kiss her roughly, primitively. He wanted to kiss her hard and furious and take her that way too.

She moaned, a woman's sound of desire, and Deke rolled and then rose over her. He drove into the hot, womanly center of her body again and again, and she cried out, brazen with need. And he filled her, hot and pulsing and brazen too, brazen with the need to make them both feel alive.

15

The second morning after Yeager made love to Zoe was just like the first. She'd already left his bed, but her scent lingered on the sheets. And for only the second time since the accident, his dread at awakening was gone.

He still woke up blind, but now there was reason to anticipate each day, and not only Zoe joining him later, although that was a certainty that could be savored. But he also looked forward to the taste of the food she prepared, the sound of her laughter floating through the warm, salty air, and the seductive rhythms of island life. He'd thought she might be his cure and damned if he wasn't nearly right.

The island was getting to him. He'd expected to be bored at the least, claustrophobic at the worst, but neither had happened. His blindness hemmed him in, but the island didn't. In fact, the pulse of the waves along the beach, the freshness of the breeze, and the sounds of island life had kept him feeling alive in the cloying darkness.

He rolled to Zoe's side of the bed and buried his face in the fragrance of her hair. He couldn't get enough of touching the stuff. Her short curls seemed to wrap around his fingers, holding him to her warmth, and he loved rubbing his whiskery cheeks against it, feeling that part of her cling to him when the woman herself wouldn't.

Because she was leaving him plenty of space. You'd think he'd be happy about that, but the night before, she'd needed coaxing to return to his bed. He grinned, thinking how sweet it was to persuade Zoe, and what little resistance he'd found in her small, light body.

No doubt about it, he was going to miss her and the island when he left.

The thought took the sunshine out of his mood. Frowning, he told himself he was uneasy because he still didn't know what he was going to do if—*when*—he regained his sight and returned to Houston. He'd retire from the navy for sure, and then he'd probably end up in some kind of big-desk-and-big-bore consulting position in the space industry.

He pulled Zoe's pillow over his head. The idea of searching for tie clips every morning for the next thirty years was about as appealing as screwing one of the space bunnies that hung out at The Nest, the astronauts' favorite Houston bar.

To push away the encroaching dark mood, he hustled into the shower and then his clothes. Zoe would cheer him up.

Yeager made his way to the house, automatically maneuvering the sixty-four steps, but then didn't go any further than the kitchen. He wanted to be with Zoe, not the other guests. He found the room empty, but the murmur of voices in the dining room told him she was close by.

Sitting at the kitchen table to wait for her, he half listened to the *Today* show coming from a TV in the corner. Katie Couric bubbled like an old-fashioned coffeemaker as she introduced her next guest, the designated pilot of Millennium I.

They'd replaced him.

Yeager stilled, cocking his head to listen more intently. The last thing he knew, NASA had announced that he, Yeager, wouldn't be piloting. But apparently they'd now notified the press that Marquez Herst would take his place. No surprise in the choice. The other man had always been Yeager's backup. But to hear the announcement on television and then to hear the distinctive lilt of Mark's voice— Spanish was his first language, and now he had five others—was a shock.

Yeager gritted his teeth and hung onto the table edge with both hands as Katie ended the interview with a brief good wish for the speedy recovery of Commander Yeager Gates.

Mark, bless his ever-lovin' but second-best heart, graciously echoed it, though Yeager knew that inside Mark was executing barrel rolls at the chance to pilot the first Millennium launch. Hell, if the shoe was on the other foot, he would have been wiggling his butt in a touchdown boogie himself. He couldn't hold it against the other man, but when they both got back to Houston and Yeager could see again, for damn sure he'd have to beat the crap out of Mr. Fernando Lamas Voice "You-look-mahvelous" Marquez . . . in racquetball.

Again.

"Yeager."

He started, suddenly realizing Zoe was in the room. Smiling, he turned away from the TV. "What's up, honey?"

"Are you okay?"

Ah. She must have been in the kitchen for at least some of Katie and Mark's interview. He pasted on that grin again and patted his knees in invitation. "Dandy and randy."

"Don't say it like that."

Something in her voice bothered him. Something that was about her, not him. Frowning, he pushed aside his own concerns. "What's wrong with you, Zoe?"

"Nothing," she said quietly. Too quietly.

Looking in her direction, he saw a shadow— he'd noticed these in the past few days, some small distinctions to the darkness—and he snaked out an arm and found her.

He reeled her in by the cloth of her apron skirt, and pulled her into place between his knees. "Works both ways, honey. I talk to you, you talk to me."

"It's nothing," she tried again.

He pushed her down onto his lap and pulled her head—that clingy, sweet-smelling cap of waves against his palm—to his chest. At night, after she left him breathless from their mutual explosive lust, she would put her cheek just there, her soft breath blowing softly, teasingly, against his nipple. His groin tightened at the thought.

She didn't seem to notice the state of his body, holding herself so stiffly. But after a few strokes of his hand against her hair, she sighed and relaxed against him. He closed his eyes, savoring the warmth and the new sensation of offering her some comfort.

What a lucky bastard he was. If he hadn't come to Abrigo, he wouldn't have met this woman who'd helped him bear the darkness. Maybe, once he returned to civilization, he'd put his island princess on a lifetime flowers-a-month plan. It tickled him to think that Zoe wouldn't be able to forget him either, that even if someone else landed in her bed, every month there would be a new delivery to remind her of the man who'd been there first.

He rubbed his chin against the top of her head, perhaps a bit roughly, punishing her a little for that next lover.

"Ouch," she said, sitting up.

"Sorry." His arms tightened around her.

She heaved another huge sigh.

He frowned. "I know something's wrong." But not as wrong as the crazy image he had of Zoe sharing a bed with someone else. "What is it?"

She leaned back against his chest. "Jerry's going to kill me."

"That prick?" Yeager drew a finger down Zoe's arm and savored her answering shiver. "Do I need to pay a call on him? I'll bring

Deke with me—all legit IRS agents travel with bodyguards, I'll bet—and I swear, by the time we're through with him the only thing you'll need to worry about is how pretty you'll look as this year's Abrigo Queen."

Zoe giggled but shook her head. "I want something more than that rhinestone crown. This festival *must* go off without a hitch."

Yeager found her hand and squeezed her fingers. "I've been around here long enough to know you've done more work than any ten people, Zoe. It's going to be fine. Stop worrying."

"The firetail won't come unless everything is perfect."

Yeager's eyebrows rose. Thinking that the fish gave even a bubble of thought to the festival was a bit of a stretch. But he shrugged. "It'll be fine."

She shook her head again. "Perfect, I'm telling you."

"Okay. Perfect," he reassured her.

"Not unless we find a new parade grand marshal," she said, her voice glum.

"A who? For what?"

"And you claim you've been around. The festival is really three separate events. The dance at the school the night before the firetail are due. The parade the following morning. And then the big bonfire on the beach that's lit the moment the fish arrive. Of course the shops and restaurants have promos running too, but our committee is only responsible for those three."

"And you're short one—"

"Parade grand marshal. You know, the dignitary who leads it off. He was a second cousin of Marlene's, and he agreed months ago, but I just found out he apparently decided that running off with his administrative assistant took precedence over presiding over our parade."

Yeager laughed. "The scum. Who was he anyway?"

"The head of the big planetarium in L.A."

Yeager laughed again. "Not much of a dignitary."

Zoe sighed. "Well, you're right about that, but he was the best we had. We even built a whole theme around him. The Sky's the Limit!" She sighed again. "Jerry loved the whole sky thing. He thought it would take people's attention away from what was—or wasn't—happening in the water."

Yeager wrapped his arms around her and lightly squeezed. "It's not the end of the world."

"If this doesn't go right, it might be the end of mine."

Guilt stabbed Yeager. He remembered what Desirée had told him weeks ago. If the fish didn't show up, it could very well be disastrous for Abrigo's tourism and economy. How a parade grand marshal was the linchpin in the festival's success Yeager couldn't figure, but it seemed to be so to Zoe.

A foreboding chill wormed its way down his spine, but he ignored it, instead pulling Zoe closer and breathing in the warm scent of her fragrance. "The Sky's the Limit!?"

"Yeah." She sighed again.

The words just tumbled out of his mouth. "How about a broken-down astronaut as grand marshal? Do you think that I would do?"

She was silent, stunned probably.

He was bewildered too. Never before had he wanted to play Dudley Do-Right, but something about Zoe, this island, and the whole notion of a place that lived off a spectacular fish that visited once a year had him rushing to don his Mountie coat and goofy hat.

To be honest, the island had enchanted him, and he couldn't stand the thought of anything disturbing the spell.

"You'd do that?" Zoe's voice was small. "But you don't want publicity. Your condition . . ."

She was right. He didn't want the world to find out about his blindness, his weakness. But then he thought of all the things that Zoe had done that she hadn't wanted to do. Of how she'd let herself be seen bald and vulnerable so she could support her sister. And he knew he'd go through with it.

"I'll do it for you, honey," he said honestly.

She made a funny little noise in the back of her throat and threw her arms around him. Hot tears landed on his neck, and a big ol' wet kiss was pressed against his mouth. He didn't hesitate to press back.

And damn if for the first time in his whole achievement-filled life he didn't feel like the hero the rest of the world had always called him.

*   *   *

Zoe bounced around the kitchen on her toes, exuberant. After nearly a year of worry, the festival was finally on a smooth and certain track.

Marlene looked up from the placard she was lettering on the table, the placard announcing Yeager Gates as the Firetail Festival Parade Grand Marshal.

"Why are you so happy?" she asked, throwing a worried look in the direction of Yeager, who stood nearby, leaning against the butcher block island.

Zoe restrained herself to a skip and topped off both her friend's and Yeager's glasses of iced sun tea. "I'm happy because we have a parade grand marshal. I'm happy because we're minus five days and counting until the firetail return. I'm happy because—" She stopped herself from mentioning Yeager by name, but didn't try to hide her smile from Marlene. "I'm just happy."

Her friend shook her head. "If we bottled and tried to sell the kind of mood you're spreading, I swear we'd never get approval from the FDA."

Zoe threw one hand in the air. "I'm unbottleable!"

A hard masculine arm reached out, grabbed her, swung her close. Yeager's voice whispered against her ear. "You're adorable."

Her stomach flip-flopped. Just his touch, his breath rushing past her cheek, could turn her inside out. But even with woozy knees, she managed to dance away from his touch. Marlene was watching closely, and Zoe wanted to keep what was between her and Yeager private.

She hadn't even told Lyssa.

Her sister had seemed preoccupied herself, and Zoe wasn't ready to talk. For years she'd remained strong for Lyssa by holding her own worries and fears inside, and the habit wasn't easy to break. Or necessary.

Not yet. Not when the short rocket ride she was on with Yeager was still climbing high. She was being sensible, though. Even since sharing Yeager's bed, not for one second had she kidded herself that what an ordinary woman like herself had to offer him could replace what he had lost.

Well, maybe for one second she'd kidded herself.

For a few. Just for a few seconds she allowed herself to dream. Sometimes, from within the security of his embrace, she imagined Apollo in her arms forever, keeping her warm and alive with his heat and light.

She'd started to daydream a little. Maybe— and she felt half guilty and half giddy putting it into words—if his vision didn't return, she could have him. If he couldn't see again, perhaps he wouldn't leave her.

Marlene cleared her throat. "Jerry seemed as nearly happy as you at the festival meeting today. Doesn't that worry you a little?"

Zoe ignored the warning in Marlene's voice. "Why shouldn't he be happy? We needed a grand marshal, et voilà, I provided one."

"In French, even," Marlene said under her breath. "I'm getting worried about you, kid."

Zoe frowned. "I'm fine, Marlene. Everything's fine."

Her friend pursed her lips. "I'm just saying Jerry went out of here this afternoon looking a little too happy. Rubbing those too soft hands of his together. I have the feeling he has something up his sleeve."

Zoe refused to let her mood be dampened. "Maybe it's a firetail or two," she said, grinning. "I wouldn't put it past Jerry to try and stock the entire Pacific Ocean if he thought it would guarantee a return on his investment."

Yeager entered the discussion, his face unreadable behind his habitual dark glasses. "Zoe, just so you don't forget. A grand marshal, a parade, and all this positive thinking doesn't guarantee anything. The fish may very well not return."

"They're coming back," Zoe insisted stubbornly. "Haven House has bookings through October," she said, as if that meant something. But if the fish failed to show, visitors would certainly follow their lead. And Haven House couldn't weather a wave of cancellations.

She shook herself. "Come on, you two. Enough of all this doom and gloom."

"Zoe!" Marlene and Yeager said together.

"What? You act like I have my head in the sand."

"Don't you?" Marlene said quietly. "I'm at least certain your feet are buried there."

Zoe wouldn't meet her eyes. "I don't know what you're talking about." Yeager had his head cocked, as if sensing trouble in the air.

Marlene shrugged, then pitched her voice in

Yeager's direction. "Okay, I'm about ready to letter in your name, Mr. Hotshot Astronaut."

Yeager grinned. "You can leave off the Mister."

Both Zoe and Marlene groaned, then Zoe sent a smile toward the other woman. "See what I've had to put up with?"

Marlene raised her eyebrows. "You don't appear to be hurting, hon."

Zoe found her heels bouncing off the hardwood floor again, her mood soaring with euphoria. Not hurting at all, thank you very much. During the day she took care of her house and her guests. At night she stole into Yeager's bed, and they took care of each other.

Holding back another smile, on the return trip to the refrigerator with the iced tea pitcher she managed to brush her shoulder and hip against Yeager's. A current of sensation, sweet and hot, stretched between them. Oh, it was so good.

She could barely hear Yeager spell his name for Marlene through a haze of almost painful happiness.

Marlene dropped her brush into a jelly jar of water and stepped back from the table. "All done," she said, moving her head this way and that to inspect her work.

Zoe examined it too. "NASA Astronaut" in blue. "Commander Yeager Gates" in scarlet. Her heart jumped a bit when she remembered walking in on Yeager a couple of days before, during the TV interview of the new Millennium pilot. She wished she couldn't recall the expression on his face, but it was too easy to conjure up.

He'd looked bereft.

Zoe forced her mind away from the uneasy memory to focus on Marlene. Her friend was making small talk with Yeager, letting him know how popular the parade was and how many would turn out to cheer him on.

Zoe frowned at her friend. "Don't start him worrying, Marlene." She looked back at Yeager. "I'll get you positioned on the float before the parade begins. Do the Queen Elizabeth wave, and no one will even know you're blind."

"Zoe—" Marlene started.

"I'm hoping by then I won't be," Yeager said. "Completely anyway."

Zoe jerked in surprise. "What? You won't be completely what?"

He leaned back against the countertop and gave a little shrug. "I'm seeing shadows. Movement. A little more, a little clearer, every day."

Marlene beamed. "Good for you."

The muscles of Zoe's cheeks felt stiff. She hoped that meant she was smiling. If he was seeing a little more, a little clearer every day, maybe he could see if she was smiling or not.

Maybe he could see her.

Marlene swung toward her. "Isn't that wonderful, Zoe? Tell Yeager you think it's wonderful."

"Wonderful," Zoe echoed, only partly aware that Marlene was trying to help her out.

She must have been standing like a zombie for several seconds. "Wonderful."

But Zoe's sweet euphoria had dissolved. Yeager was regaining his sight. And once it came back, he'd see her, really *see* her, in all her ordinariness, in her too short hair and her boyish body. He'd see Abrigo too, and what was safety to her would surely appear too small for him.

She'd be too small for him.

Her stomach flopped over. It was the kind of feeling she remembered from her one and only roller coaster ride as a little girl. After the car crested the hill, it was that terrifying inner *oosh* that came just as the car succumbed to the laws of gravity.

Zoe turned away from Yeager, unable to look at him, unwilling for him to see her. Maybe her rocket ride wasn't yet quite over, but it had just surrendered to the inevitable and was heading nose down for a great, long fall.

Zoe started walking in the direction of downtown Haven just as the streetlights switched on. A round of distant laughter assured her that at least some of the Haven House guests were enjoying themselves, but she couldn't drum up even half a satisfied smile.

Not when she could hardly inhale half a breath.

Despite the discomfort of her ever tightening chest, she continued putting one step in front of the other, descending through the narrow streets of town toward the Haven Bay ma-

rina. Ahead, she caught a glimpse of Randa
emerging from Mr. Wright's jewelry repair
shop, and she dove down a side street to avoid
the other woman.

The test she was about to put herself
through required no distractions and just as
few witnesses.

The detour only delayed her journey by a
couple of minutes. Too soon, Zoe stood in the
shadows surrounding the Abrigo Ferry's ticket
office. The small clapboard shack was lit
brightly by another streetlight and from inside
by a fluorescent fixture. Billie Wade manned
the booth, her soft gray curls bobbing slightly
as she counted out change to the sole ticket
buyer. According to the schedule posted in
bright green lettering, the next ferry left in fifteen minutes.

The ticket buyer turned around, and Zoe
shrank further into the shadows. As his footsteps receded, she closed her eyes and imagined herself walking up to Billie. She even
slipped her fingers inside the front pocket of
her jeans, touching the wad of cash she'd
placed there to eliminate the need to fumble
through purse and wallet.

She licked her suddenly dry lips and
mouthed the words she'd speak to Billie. A
ticket, please. No! A round trip ticket. That
shouldn't be so hard, should it?

Steeling herself, Zoe slid one foot in the direction of the booth, though her desperate
breaths sounded like sandpaper in her ears.
Three years had passed since she and Lyssa
had landed on Abrigo, finally leaving behind

the long months of heartache and fear on the mainland.

She gulped and opened her eyes, only to see the ocean stretching darkly and hungrily before her. A sick chill washed over her skin. Already she could imagine the unsteady roll of the ferry's deck beneath her feet and the oppressive drone of the boat's engines as they carried her away from safety. Her muscles froze, and her heart stuttered, then sank like an anchor toward her belly.

She couldn't do it.

Her foot slid back into the comforting darkness, and she shoved the money deeper into her pocket. Then she turned away from the ferry and toward the comforting lights of Haven.

Three years had passed since she and Lyssa had returned to the island, and not now, not ever, could she make herself leave.

That night, for the first time, Zoe didn't go to Yeager's bed.

After what happened—or didn't happen—at the ticket office, she knew it was past time for getting used to living without him.

But she wasn't surprised when the house phone, the one that connected all the cottages to the main house, sounded at about ten o'clock. Zoe considered letting it ring, but Lyssa had gone out right after dinner and that left her alone with the insistent phone.

What if it wasn't Yeager at all, but one of her other guests?

Sighing, she picked up the receiver.

"Where are you?" he said. "Don't bother answering. I know you're not here, and that's where you should be. What's keeping you?"

Zoe swallowed. "I thought maybe you'd prefer to be alone tonight."

There was a moment of silence on the line. "What are you, nuts?"

I'm trying to help myself. I'm trying to remember what it feels like to be myself, plain old Zoe Cash, again. "Thanks," she said drily.

A suspicious note came into his voice. "Zoe, are you relying on some book you've read again? Another outdated tome on male and female relationships?"

"No. Maybe . . . maybe I just want to be alone tonight."

There was another silence. She could imagine him lying on his bed, a pillow doubled behind his head. When she'd come to him in his cottage the previous nights, the room had been dark and his hair had been wet from the shower and his skin tasted like the sweet island spring water. She shivered.

"Is this what you want, Zoe?" he asked quietly.

She squeezed the phone. "Yes."

Another long pause. "Give me something to dream about, then. Just a little hint of what you're doing and what you're wearing."

She shivered again. No matter what, he was still so achingly irrestible. "I'm in my bedroom on the second floor."

"Is it to the right or left of the stairs?" he asked softly. "Tell me so I can paint a picture of you in my mind."

"To the left. It's the first room on the left."

"Are you in your nightclothes?"

"Yes," she said huskily.

"Turn out the lights, Zoe," he ordered. "Then get into bed for me."

She shivered once more, unable to disobey him. Once she flipped off the light, the sheets were cold along her bare legs, and she had to steel herself against surrendering and going to him and the warmth and delight of his bed.

"Covers up to your chin, honey?"

The heavy, whispering note in his voice stroked her skin like a hand. Zoe closed her eyes. "Yes," she said.

"Mmm." His breath sounded loud in her ear. "I've changed my mind. Take off your clothes."

"Yeager!"

His voice softened, turned coaxing. "For me, honey. Just do it for me."

Zoe went hot all over.

Too hot for the oversized T-shirt she was wearing. Feeling half excited and half embarrassed, she put the phone down for a moment to pull the garment over her head. The covers went back up to her chin, but now the sheets abraded her nipples. They tightened, and she blushed again.

"Zoe?" She heard Yeager's voice coming through the phone receiver.

She slowly picked it up and held it to her ear. "I'm here."

"You took your panties off, didn't you?"

His breathing sounded loud and deliberate.

Her legs shifted restlessly. "Yes," she lied.

He was too smart for that. "Zoe."

"I don't know why I'm even doing what you say—"

"Because I'd be doing it for you, if you'd just come to my bed."

She licked her lips. "Yeager—"

"The panties, Zoe," he ordered.

Her flesh was burning as she pushed them down with one hand and then wriggled her legs free. "There," she said. "Are you satisfied?"

There was a long silence, and then he laughed. "Not even close," he said, his voice sounding raw. "Hang up, Zoe."

Click.

In the dark, Zoe stared at the receiver in her hand. He'd hung up on her! He'd stripped her naked and then hung up on her!

She lay still, buck naked in her own bed and unsure if she was miffed or relieved. Then came the distinct sound of the back door opening.

Lyssa, Zoe thought. Worried her sister might want to come in for a late-night chat, Zoe jackknifed up in bed and frantically ran her feet over the sheets, searching for her panties, even as she reached over the side of the mattress for her T-shirt. But just like a dream, what she reached for kept eluding her.

There were slow footsteps on the stairs.

Zoe's heart sped up, and suddenly the door was flung open.

The dark shadow silhouetted in the doorway was much too big to be her sister.

The shadow's voice was deeper and sexier too. "Don't tell me you have your clothes back on."

Zoe pressed back against the pillows, strangely nervous at the dark intent in his voice. She grabbed for the covers again and pulled them tightly to her neck. "Why are you here?"

He must have been waiting for her voice to find his way to the bed, because he came closer now. "You can call me Mohammed."

Zoe swallowed, trying to lighten the atmosphere in the room. "I guess that makes me the mountain."

He didn't appear amused. His dark shadow just came closer, and his breathing was harsh and loud in the room.

She could have told him to go away, but she didn't.

With his big hand outstretched, he found the edge of the mattress, found the covers, then pulled them out of her grasp and flung them back. His fingers brushed over her bare skin. He grunted in satisfaction. "Good."

"What are you doing?" She detested the little squeak in her voice, but he was crawling onto the bed, and then his hands found her ankles.

Instead of answering, he grasped them strongly to slide her down flat on her back against the mattress. He had on a pair of jeans, but he was bare-chested, and she felt the hot skin of his wide shoulders against the inside of her knees as he pushed apart her thighs.

He lowered his head.

Zoe squeaked again. "What are you doing?"

He lifted his face. He wasn't wearing his sunglasses, but his eyes were just dark mysteries. He smiled, and his teeth gleamed whitely in the dim room. "I'm proving that you don't want to be alone."

And then he ran his hands down the inside of her legs, stretching her even wider. His head ducked, and she felt a whisper of hot breath against her—there.

Her heart shuddered. "Yeager."

Now she felt a wet stroke, and her whole body trembled. "Yeager!"

He licked her again and then again, soft explorations that lingered here and tarried there. Her heels pushed into the mattress, and she scratched at the sheet to hold onto something, something, as the rest of the world tipped and rolled and tumbled in every direction.

She couldn't believe she was letting him do this.

But he'd found a spot—oh, God!—that he'd stroked during their previous lovemaking, but now he stroked it with his tongue! Her thighs opened wider, her heart banged against her ribs, and when he reached up to gently pinch one nipple, she thought she might rise off the bed and fly out of the room.

"Zoe."

She panted. He'd taken her to a point with his hands and mouth where that was all she could do—try to bring a little air into her lungs. Her nerve endings were buzzing, and her blood was burning.

"Zoe."

She panted some more. "What?" She wanted to beg him to finish it, finish her, and she plucked at the sheet again to keep herself from pushing him back where she wanted him.

"Tell me, Zoe." He breathed on her hot wetness again.

What did he want? She was so close, so, so close, she'd tell him anything he wanted to hear if he would just touch her once more. She whimpered. "What?"

"Tell me you didn't want to be alone. Tell me you want me. Tell me you need *me*."

Zoe almost sobbed. He was asking her to lay out her heart. He wanted her to serve it up to him on a silver platter, one that she polished herself to a gleaming sheen.

He ran a finger down her slickness, and she moaned.

"Tell me, Zoe," he said again.

Why was he asking for this? Why did he have to hear it?

His finger traced her once more and then slid up inside her body. Zoe moaned, and then she broke. "I want you. I need you," she said, her voice a hoarse whisper. "I don't want to be alone."

He immediately bent his head to her, as if the words inflamed him. She felt his tongue again. He found that special place on her body, and the kiss he gave her there was demanding and knowing. And then her whole body shook, and she cried out with the beautiful intimacy of the act—and of the words she'd shared.

With her body still trembling, he moved over her and drove inside, and she cried out once more, the hardness of him pleasuring her again. He started up a rhythm, fast and unrelenting.

His back was slick, and she held him against her, lifting her hips to take him deeper. Then he stiffened, groaned, and pumped into her even faster. Collapsing against her, he pressed a kiss against her shoulder.

"I need you too, honey," he said.

Zoe closed her eyes and stroked his hair. "For a little while," she whispered. For a little while he needed her. For a little while longer they'd be together on the island, and that little while would have to be enough.

16

Yeager stood at the bottom of the Haven House stairs, his hands shoved in the pockets of his slacks, waiting for Zoe. Deke, Lyssa, Zoe, and Yeager were all supposed to attend the kickoff event of the Firetail Festival that night, the dance in the school auditorium. Deke and Lyssa were waiting in the golf cart outside, and Yeager had drawn the short straw, getting Zoe down the stairs and calm enough to enjoy the evening.

He would have preferred to ditch this event altogether, but both Lyssa and Deke had bent his ear about attending. Something was going on between those two, and half of him had been curious enough about it to agree. The other half merely wanted to be where Zoe was.

"Hey, we're leaving!" he yelled up the stairs. Again.

Only a muffled cry, high pitched, came back at him.

He shook his head. In the days leading up to the dance she'd wound herself tighter and tighter. She'd started carrying a clipboard around too, and it had become a kind of armor, which left him increasingly frustrated. Want to steal a kiss? A man had to first break through her plastic board and inch-thick stack of lists.

She hadn't tried that sleeping alone thing again, though. He had his own breaking point, and by God, that was it. He didn't have much longer on the island, and he wasn't going to deny himself a moment of pleasure in Zoe's arms. The night before, she'd been asleep on his pillows by the time he'd stepped out of the shower, but that had been pleasureful too. Lying beside her, he'd listened to her breathe, and when she'd turned to burrow into his arms, he'd held her close, guarding her.

Guarding her from what? From disappointment. If those damn fish didn't show up, he didn't know what he'd do. He didn't know what *she'd* do.

"Here I am," she said breathlessly, her footsteps fast on the stairs.

Her scent wafted toward him, and he drank it in, squinting through his dark glasses, wishing he could see her better. Like a developing Polaroid, his vision had changed in recent days from darkness to outlines to the hazy beginnings of details. Shapes were distinguishable enough for him not to walk into trees any more, but he couldn't make out the distinctions of the leaves.

So while he could see the outline of Zoe, it wasn't any more than his hands had already memorized. Details like her eyes and the other features of her face were still lost to him.

Deke's work on his uncle's house was winding down, and just this morning they'd been discussing departure dates. Yeager wondered if he'd ever see Zoe, really see her, before he left the island.

"What's wrong?" Zoe asked, her voice puzzled. She ran her hand down his arm.

He relished the possessive gesture. "Nothing." Bending, he took her small face between his hands and kissed her. "Just missing you."

She kissed his chin. "Hurry up, let's go."

He smacked her lightly on the rear, pushing her in the direction of the door. "We've been waiting for you."

"I know, I know. I'm running behind and I'm a Nervous Nellie because I didn't make it over to the auditorium today. How do I know everything's been done right?"

Yeager shook his head. "Because someone would have called you to fix it if it wasn't." He herded her out the door and into the golf cart, but she didn't stop fussing the entire ride to the school.

She managed to "what if" the whole way, even while hailing acquaintances in passing carts and waving at other friends walking to the school.

Yeager sat back and let her go at it. Reasoning with her didn't work. Kissing her silly had some effect, but she pushed him away when they were in other people's company. So instead he enjoyed the ocean-cooled breeze, the anticipation in the air as a community assembled for an annual event, and the manic static

of his own personal radio station, KZGC—
K-Zoe-Going-Crazy.

Not until they made it inside the auditorium
did she shut up. "Oh, my God!" she exclaimed, and then she was silent.

A chill ran through him. "What?"

Zoe just shook her head, still mute.

Lyssa took pity on him. "I think she's a little
upset at the change in the festival theme.
There's a great big sign announcing it over the
stage."

"Is that all?" Yeager smiled. "The Sky's the
Limit! sucked anyhow, Big Zee."

She shook her head again, not even shaken
out of her stupor as he'd hoped by the new
nickname.

He frowned. "So what is it? How bad can it
be? Island Magic? Firetail Fun?"

Zoe found her voice. "It's . . . it's Launching
the Millennium. In your honor, the sign says."

Yeager froze. Launching the Millennium?
For him?

When of course he wouldn't be launching
the Millennium at all.

Zoe's voice was tight. "I smell Jerry. Marlene was right. He wants to squeeze everything he can out of your fame."

Launching the Millennium. Yeager continued bracing himself, waiting for the sharpness
of disappointment and pain to stab him.

Suddenly music filled the room. He knew
that a deejay had been hired as the entertainment, because even Zoe admitted the Island
Band couldn't carry a whole evening. The loud
notes were familiar.

Zoe groaned. "I can't believe it. The music from *Apollo 13*."

Suddenly, a spotlight hit them—his vision was now good enough to detect that—and a voice overrode the music.

"Jerry," Zoe muttered. "I'm going to kill him."

Jerry, from somewhere by the stage, went into a spiel about his decision to change the theme of the festival and then introduced Yeager as the festival's special and honored guest, reciting his honors and accomplishments so glowingly that he ended up sounding like a cross between John Glenn and John F. Kennedy.

That embarrassment was followed by a loud round of applause.

Yeager stood through all of it, even managing to smile, he hoped, painfully aware that all those honors and accomplishments were in the past. The fact struck hard all over again. There would be no launch of the Millennium, not for him.

Like a man who has just stopped sliding after a long fall down a mountain, he mentally catalogued himself to see where it hurt most.

But strangely, it didn't hurt so much.

Finally, the spotlight turned away, and the deejay played a swing tune that seemed to please the entire crowd. Dancers jostled him, and Yeager found himself facing Zoe.

"I'm sorry," she said miserably. "I had no idea. I thought we'd sweep you through the streets tomorrow and that would be it."

"Sh," he said, putting his arms around her

and starting to sway to the music. "It's okay."
Strangely again, it was.

Throughout the dance, people kept brushing against him, thanking him for coming to
the island, welcoming him to the festival. Zoe
had told him before that this night was mostly
for the enjoyment of the residents of the island, and now he met many of them, some
whom Zoe had already spoken of, some
whom he'd run across in his few weeks here.

Yeager was able to mask his impaired vision
well enough, though of course some already
knew of it. But it didn't seem to make much
difference either way. In the circle of Zoe's
arms, in the circle of her community, he felt
acceptance and appreciation.

Maybe it was going to be okay.

Watching Yeager smiling and dancing with Zoe
stunned Deke. Something had happened to his
friend over the last few weeks. Yeager had
come to the island to hide from who he had
been and what had happened to him, but now
he was acknowledging, and yes, accepting.

Deke shook his head.

Lyssa touched his arm. "Is everything all
right?"

Looking down into the oval perfection of
her face, Deke shook his head again. "I guess
it is," he said.

She nodded toward her sister and Yeager.
"They look good together."

Deke followed her gaze. "They look
happy."

"I am too," Lyssa said quietly.

Deke closed his eyes for a moment. He knew she was, but that didn't mean what they'd been doing was right. Despite his intention to give Lyssa that one taste of sex, she'd spent several nights in his bed, and she wasn't the only one with an appetite.

Her fingers touched his cheek. "You're thinking too hard again."

He covered her hand with his. "How's that possible? I think you steal my brain cells when I'm asleep."

Her smile was so beautiful that an ache spread over his chest. "Dance with me," she said.

The soft, slinky material of her dress wrapped her body like a sarong, twisting around her neck to leave her shoulders bare. A gardenia was tucked behind one ear, and she looked as tempting and sweet as a tropical drink. Yet she was so much more than that, because beneath all the sweetness, beneath the slinky dress were scars that he'd discovered in his minute explorations of her body. Scars from things like the catheters that had delivered the chemo treatments to Lyssa's body and delivered her back to life.

Taking a deep breath, he couldn't stop himself from putting his arms around her.

She leaned into him. "There," she said, sounding pleased with herself.

He shuffled his feet in time with the music. He wasn't much of a dancer, but the floor was so crowded there wasn't room for anything beyond swaying anyhow.

He rested his chin on the top of her head

and felt the ends of her long hair brushing against his forearms. Soon enough, he was going to be leaving the island. For now he could afford to surrender to the magic of holding Lyssa.

She turned her cheek against his chest. "I heard the most fascinating thing the other day," she said. "It was about your house."

"Hmm." He barely heard her. There was going to be some price to pay for what he'd shared with her, he knew that. He worried about it too. In the end, she'd be okay, she was a survivor, but he hated the idea of causing her even momentary heartache.

"I heard your uncle built the place for a bride. A bride from the mainland," Lyssa said.

"Yeah." Some day another man, young and hopeful, would find Lyssa. He'd stay on her island with her, forever loving her, forever keeping her safe. That was the right ending for her story.

It was.

But he didn't want their story to end. Her body fit against his, her skin tasted like something he'd known all his life. Face it, from the moment he'd seen her, he'd wanted her forever.

Lyssa looked up at him, her eyes dark blue in the dim lights of the room. "Is it true? Is it true that she then refused to marry him? That she didn't want to live on the isolated island?"

He shook his head, bringing his thoughts back to what Lyssa was saying. "No, she—"

She frowned, pleating the smooth skin of her forehead. "But I heard that your uncle then posted those signs. Those No Women Allowed signs."

Deke stopped moving his feet. Those signs. Those No Women Allowed signs. How had he forgotten?

How could he have forgotten?

The air turned cold around him. The night seemed suddenly darker too. He turned his head toward the door, wanting desperately to be away from this moment, away from this woman.

"Deke?" Lyssa's blond eyebrows came together, and she was frowning deeper. "What's wrong?"

"Everything." He stepped back and pushed her away from him. Hadn't he learned this lesson long ago? "Everything about us is wrong."

The color dropped from Lyssa's face. Even her lips paled. "No," she said.

He took a second step back, bumping into another couple, who obligingly made room for him.

"Don't," she said, the sound barely making it out of her mouth.

He closed his eyes and turned away from her. There were things he had to do.

Lyssa gasped for air as she ran up the dirt path into the hills. Desperation and fear spurring her on, she refused to slow, hitching up her tight skirt instead to take longer strides. Thank God for the moonlight. Without it she'd fall for sure.

For the first time since she'd seen Deke, she thought she might lose him. Where before she'd been frustrated by his resistance, this time she knew that it was more than his reluctance standing between them.

There had been something on his face at the dance, some bleakness that signaled she might not have another chance.

Her heart pounding, she sucked in air and ran faster.

Tears stung her eyes. It wasn't fair! She'd waited all these years, lived through an illness that had killed so many others, pulled herself up and pep-talked herself, only to be defeated, inches from true happiness, by a man who had a stupid hangup about their age difference.

She'd had it with men and their moronic sensibilities. She was going to give Deke one more chance to love her, just one more, and if he screwed this up, then fine!

He didn't deserve her.

With Deke's uncle's house in sight—it had been a snap to guess where he'd taken off to— Lyssa found a last burst of speed. In seconds she reached the clearing around the front porch, her sandals sliding against the damp grass.

She jammed her hands on her hips and stared down the two crudely painted signs, NO WOMEN ALLOWED, one on either side of the porch stairs. She hadn't seen the despicable things since her first visit, so apparently Deke had recently pounded them back into place, where they could guard the house as if they were guarding a man's heart.

Silhouetted by the light of a lone bulb burning in the empty entryway, he didn't even glance at her as he dragged something out the front door.

Lyssa held onto her anger. It was too easy to let her feelings for him soften her. Too easy for the memory of his tender touch on her body to gentle her now, when she needed to fight him with everything she had.

As if she wasn't there, he carried the thing in his arms down the stairs. When he was just feet from her, he turned the item and lifted it high, then jammed it into the dirt and grass with all his might.

The FOR SALE sign gleamed in the moonlight.

She crossed her arms over her chest. "What are you doing?"

"I'm selling," he said. From the dirt, he picked up a mallet and pounded the sign deeper.

Lyssa felt like pounding Deke's puny brain. Hot anger again rose in her breast. "I love you," she said through her teeth.

He paused, then slammed the mallet back into the top of the sign.

There was nothing worse than being ignored. She tossed back her hair and tried again. "I love you."

He dropped the mallet and finally looked at her. "You had the story all wrong."

She frowned. "What are you talking about?"

His face was unreadable, but his silver eyes caught the moonlight, and they glittered coldly. "The story of the signs."

She tucked her fists tighter beneath her arms, ignoring an icy premonition. "Tell me."

He turned his back and looked up at the house. "My uncle did build this house for his bride. But she went ahead and married him and they lived in the house happily for many years. I summered with them here when I was a boy. Later, when they became more frail, they moved back to the mainland." He lapsed into silence.

Another cold finger of premonition trailed down Lyssa's spine. She swallowed. "And then?"

He kept his back to her. "And then it seemed like the perfect honeymoon spot when I married. I was a twenty-year-old airman, with only a little money and a big desire to please my brand-new bride."

"You loved her."

His shoulders moved up and down in a shrug. "I thought I did. But obviously the feeling wasn't mutual, because on her side, it didn't even last the honeymoon. I guess the island isolation gave her a taste of what life as an air force wife might really be like. New places, far from family, forever traipsing after me. Within three days of our vows I was back to bachelor."

Lyssa closed her eyes. "And the signs?" she asked quietly.

"I made those myself on night number three after the ferry left the island with my disillusioned and disappointed wife. Bought myself a bottle of tequila and a gallon of paint, and then I made it clear I wanted to spend the rest of my honeymoon alone."

The rest of your life alone, you mean. But Lyssa didn't say the words.

He suddenly turned around. "What? You have no response to my sad tale?"

Lyssa bit her lip. She needed a strategy, not a response. Because she'd had it all wrong. He wasn't afraid to love her because of their age difference or anything as simple as that.

As a matter of fact, he probably wasn't afraid of loving her at all.

He was afraid she didn't really love him.

She hugged her arms tight to her chest. Who would have ever thought this forty-something, tough-hided man would on the inside be so fragile?

Lyssa blew out a long breath. "What are you trying to tell me, Deke?"

"I'm trying to say I'm leaving."

The words dashed against her like frozen drops of rain. "Deke—"

"I'm taking the first ferry out tomorrow."

Lyssa froze, stunned. Tomorrow! Not tomorrow! She needed time to form a plan! Time to figure out how to fight him—no, not fight him, but fight for him.

Her heart started hammering against her chest. "Deke . . ."

But he ignored her and took the stairs two at a time to turn out the light in the entry and then shut the front door.

While he was busy, she tried to formulate the right words, the right explanation, the right persuasion. But even though her mind whirred away at panic speed, she couldn't think how to change his mind.

She couldn't imagine a way to make him trust her and her love.

At dawn, the town of Haven was quiet and calm. As Deke walked down the steep, narrow streets toward the ferry landing, his footsteps echoed eerily.

Recovering from the night before's dance and gearing up for today's events—the Firetail Festival parade and the welcome bonfire for the fish—must be keeping everyone in bed.

Something rustled overhead, and Deke glanced up, startled. But it was only a raven, perched on one of the festival flagpoles, it's blue-black wings stunning against the bright colors of the flag and the gray wash of the early morning sky.

Shoving his hands in his pockets, Deke continued forward, then his gaze caught on a figure in the distance—a familiar blond figure, who was a block or so ahead of him.

She appeared to be dragging a recalcitrant suitcase behind her, and as he watched, the limp-wheeled thing gave up, tumbling into the gutter to play dead.

It shouldn't have struck him as funny— what the hell was Lyssa doing wandering around with a suitcase at this hour?—but his lips twitched as he watched her give the overstuffed canvas a couple of ineffectual kicks.

She'd resorted to muttering to it by the time he reached her side.

He stood next to her, rubbing his chin, unsure of what to say or do. Somehow, he'd avoided a big scene with her last night. As grateful as he was for it, he'd almost trade that for having to see her again like this, with the morning sun playing in her hair and the flush of some emotion—embarrassment? irritation?—on her cheeks.

Damn, but his bed had seemed too wide and cold without her.

"What are you looking at?" she said crossly.

He blinked. Irritation might be too mild a description. "Well, uh . . ."

She narrowed her eyes at him. "Are you going to help me, or what?"

Deke didn't move. "Help you how, exactly?"

"Help me get my suitcase up, you oaf."

He blinked once more. He had a feeling she was close to losing her cool again, like that day on the hillside when she'd cut her knee. Without saying a word, he reached down and gripped the heavy suitcase, setting it on its wobbly wheels beside her.

Lyssa crossed her arms over her chest and tapped one toe. Impatiently.

Deke, aware the situation was at a dangerous simmer, thought it best to get moving. The first ferry left in fifteen minutes. He started to walk past her.

She put her palm on his chest. "Not so fast."

Deke flinched at the pleasure of her touch, but then steeled himself and sighed. "Let's not do this, Lyssa. I don't have time"

Her eyes widened. "You don't have time. *You* don't have time. Oh, that's rich." She stepped forward and glared at him. "*I'm* the one whose been up all night, terrified I'd miss the first ferry.

"*I'm* the one who sorted through twenty-three years of possessions—you should see my room!—to whittle them down to one suitcase. *I'm* the one who also had to compose a letter to my sister, trying to find the right words to explain what in the world would possess me to run off with a stubborn, stuck-in-the-past ingrate like you!"

"Ingrate?" he echoed faintly.

She squared her shoulders. "That's right. You should be thanking me for going away with you."

"I never asked you to go away with me," he pointed out.

"And that's another thing!" She propped her fists on her hips and she was breathing hard, her lush, young breasts pushing against the cotton of her dress. "I tried thinking up the right words to say to you too. Well, forget it. I don't know how to convince you. I only know I love you. So you're just going to have to live with it and live with me. Where you're going, pal, I'm going too."

Deke swallowed, his mouth suddenly dry. "You're leaving the island?"

She threw up her hands. "Is it time for hearing aids already?" An impatient sigh was blown through her lips. "You're leaving, right?"

He rubbed a hand over his hair. "You're going away from Zoe? From this place?"

"Don't you get it? Haven't you been listening?" Lyssa bent to grab the handle of her suitcase. "I'm not going to waste another minute of our lives. I'm just going to be with you, and you can—"

"Take it or leave it?" Deke's heart slammed against his chest.

She looked at him as if he was a madman. "No. The only choice is taking it. Taking *me*."

A buzzing started in his ears. "Are you saying I have to love you?"

"You already do, don't you?" But there was a flash of uncertainty in the crystal beauty of her eyes. "I'm saying you have to have me."

Deke spoke loudly over the buzz. "I'm forty-three years old."

"Well, I'm sterile."

He reached out and stroked her hair. "I don't care."

She pushed her head against his hand. "I don't care about your age less."

"I'm going back to Houston, and then . . ." He shrugged.

"I've always wanted to see Texas," she said. "And then . . ." She mimicked his shrug. "I've always wanted to see 'and then.' "

Still, he shook his head. "A man my age and a woman like you. People are going to talk about us."

"They're going to talk about how happy we are." Lyssa stepped closer. "Please, Deke, don't throw away our future because of what happened in the past."

She looked so damn certain. He took a breath, and the buzzing instantly ceased. All Deke could hear now was the beat of his heart, and even it had slowed to a pounding quiet and sure. He took another breath. "You'll go with me?"

"Always."

"You'll stay with me?" That was the crux of the matter.

"Always."

He looked down at her suitcase. " 'Til death do us part?" he said, testing her one last time.

She smiled, again so certain. "Death wouldn't dare."

Despite his age, his past, his pain, Deke found he couldn't leave that smile behind or the woman who wore it. His arms came around her, and he kissed her hard, holding her against him. "I love you," he said.

She smiled again. "I knew it."

He thought of the tree house and the initials and that telltale heart. He'd known it then too.

But he'd been so afraid.

"Let's go." He put his arm around her shoulders and turned her in the direction of Haven House. "Let's go tear up that letter. You can explain everything to your sister in person." He leaned down to kiss the soft cheek of the woman he was going to marry. "And didn't you say I should see your room?"

17

Oh, how the mighty had fallen, Yeager thought, adjusting his stance on the parade float for better balance. Yes, as the grand marshal's, his vehicle was slated to lead off the parade—his vehicle being a small tractor pulling a flatbed on wheels piled high with cottony stuff he presumed was supposed to represent clouds—but he had to share the small space with two other "stars."

Two other big stars. Not famous celebrities, mind you, but two Abrigo residents, who flanked him wearing oversized suits that would have put Barney the Dinosaur to shame. One costume was furry and flippered. The other had a scaly, slippery texture and trailing fins, which had a tendency to become frenzy-whipped by the breeze and wrap themselves around Yeager's neck and face like octopus tentacles.

Yes, it was true. The mighty had most assuredly landed on his ass, when the man most recently dubbed Captain America was sharing float space with Sammy the Seal and Flossie the Firetail.

It was too late to back out now, though. The parade was scheduled to start in moments, and the tractor driver told them the crowd was five people deep on the sidewalk lining the ten-block-long parade route. In the distance, over the excited rumble of the crowd, Yeager heard teenagers hawking popcorn and caramel apples. Any second they'd turn out of the school parking lot, into the street, and into the annals of Abrigo Island history.

Behind him, the Island Band struck up—well, it couldn't actually be termed a tune, could it?—and Yeager winced. Somewhere back there, the woman who'd shared his bed the night before was gamely leading just about the worst group of musicians to ever assault innocent ears.

And loving every minute of it.

The least he could do was smile.

But he found that he already was smiling. Even when he was forced to grab for Sammy's flipper to keep on his feet as the float lurched forward and turned a sharp right, following the color guard of Boy Scouts and the diminutive little girls who carried a banner introducing him.

"You okay?" asked the muffled voice of Sammy.

Yeager regained his balance as the float straightened out. "Fine. Sorry about that."

"Mmf," the oversized seal grunted. Yeager knew the man inside the suit was actually Island Grocery Dave, as opposed to Island

Drugstore Dave, one of the two men who nursed a friendly rivalry in their competing Abrigo businesses. According to Zoe, the honor of portraying Sammy in the parade was awarded to the Dave with highest receipts for the year, as verified by the resident CPA, another Dave.

However, this particular Dave didn't seem as thrilled as a man with the superior P&L statement should. As a matter of fact, there were some definitely disapproving vibes coming through the mangy gray fur.

"Well, uh, sorry again," Yeager said, deciding to grab for the fish next time, if need be. Inside that kooky costume was Zoe's good friend Marlene. He bumped his elbow against her glittery scales. "Well, here we go, then," he said to her.

"Umf." She was grunting at him too. Maybe those outfits pinched somewhere strategic.

The wind kicked up, and Yeager pulled one of Flossie's twisting fins out of his mouth. "You all right?" he asked.

But then they approached the first parade-goers. Their vehicle paused, the band let out a loud squeal, and the crowd an even louder cheer. Minutes passed while he and his fellow floaters waved, flipped, and finned, as appropriate. Then they slowly moved forward again, and the noise around them subsided a bit.

"Saw you last night," Sammy suddenly said, even as he turned sideways to acknowledge the crowd.

Yeager's eyebrows raised. "Who, me?"

Sammy grunted again.

"I saw you too," said Flossie.

Yeager wondered if they'd been storing those damn costumes in the deep freeze, because the air surrounding them was decidedly cool. "Yeah, well, so?"

"So we saw you with Zoe," the seal said.

Considering they'd stayed at the dance nearly two hours and he'd had her in his arms almost all of that time, he wasn't surprised. What was surprising was the level of animosity in Grocery Dave's voice. Was this guy interested in Zoe himself?

Some strange sensation burned in Yeager's gut. Was this the man who might replace him when he was gone?

Then Flossie chimed in. "You'd better be careful," she said, her voice sounding like it was coming through her teeth as well as her costume.

In response to a shout from the crowd, Yeager automatically lifted his hand, but he couldn't stop thinking of the fish's warning. "Be careful of what?"

The seal snorted. "Not be careful of what. Be careful of who."

"Be careful with Zoe," the fish clarified.

Yeager frowned. "She's a big girl. She can take care of herself."

The fish's massive head shook. "You just don't get it, do you?"

"We take care of her here," the seal said. "There's things you don't know."

Things he didn't know? Yeager didn't like the sound of that. But he wasn't going to discuss Zoe with a couple of oversized ocean-dwellers. Stepping a bit ahead of them, he concentrated on his grand marshal duties for several blocks, which consisted mainly of waving and trying to not to feel stupid.

Things he didn't know?

Gritting his teeth, he stepped back between Sammy and Flossie. "What things I don't know?"

The fish ignored his question and waved a fin at the crowd. "You think it's an accident we're here on Abrigo, that we stay on the island?"

Yeager frowned. "I'm thinking you enjoy the sun, the ocean, the breeze. Paradise."

"People," the fish corrected, somehow managing to make her big-lipped goofy smile, which he could dimly see, look disgusted. "It's the people. The sense of community we've found here."

"Zoe's one of ours. She makes it special here," Sammy added.

"Zoe would make it special anywhere," Yeager retorted, then realized what he'd said. But she would. What was the big deal about admitting it? Zoe was special.

To him.

"You ever live in a small community like this?" Sammy the Seal asked.

Never. He'd bounced around all over the country and some parts of Europe, and he'd never been in a place like this one, where the setting and the citizens all came together in one unique package. Paradise.

The seal snorted, apparently tired of waiting

on his answer. "Thought so. Well let me be
the first to tell you we take care of our own
here, and we don't like the job being made any
tougher than it already is."

"So watch it," Flossie said. "Don't you dare
break Zoe's heart."

Or they'd break his knuckles? Yeager
thought he might laugh. Who would believe a
man like him was being shaken down over his
relationship with a grown woman?

Over somebody he was just passing the time
with?

During the rest of the slow-moving parade,
Yeager tried to dismiss the entire conversation.
But it kept bugging him, not just their warning, but that somehow he'd given the impression the night before that he might break Zoe's
heart.

Jesus, maybe he should heed their warning.
Maybe it was time to drag out his duffel bag
and pack up.

He liked Zoe, he really did, and the last
thing he intended to do was hurt her. From
behind, the Island Band clattered away, and
while it seemed that she and that band were
the ones likely to do the real damage—to his
eardrums—Yeager made the decision to leave
the island.

Soon.

He was glad when they bumped back into
the school's parking lot. He needed to find
Deke, make a few phone calls, get things moving in directions east. The float finally halted,
and the pre-parade organization immediately
fell apart. The dogs from the Canine Club

barked, Girls Scouts squeaked, he heard shouts as someone tried to locate a missing shoe.

Without saying anything to his costumed cohorts, Yeager waited impatiently for an opportunity to get off the float. He could see well enough to find his way back to Haven House, he hoped.

Sammy lumbered off their cloud, and Yeager made his way to the edge of the billowing cotton, with Flossie ahead of him. He heard Zoe's voice nearby, and he hurried his movements, loath to meet up with her right now. He wanted to finalize his plans first.

In his haste, he bumped against the fish. Her soft-stuffed dorsal fin caught him square in the face, knocking his dark glasses askew.

Caught in the bright glare of the sun, Yeager blinked. The glasses he'd worn for months were made of a special material to protect his sensitive eyes from the light. But now he realized they'd been doing quite a job of obscuring his vision too.

His eyes watering, he blinked again, but couldn't bring himself to readjust the glasses. Because he could *see*.

And directly in his line of sight was Zoe.

It had to be her.

She was bending to listen to one of the tiny Brownies who had carried his banner. The outline and shape were Zoe's, he was familiar with them by touch as much as by sight, but now he could see her features, and the color of her hair and the shade of her eyes.

His mouth dried.

She was blond. Feathery blond hair that didn't go any longer than her ears in the front and was just more feathers in the back. He'd known that, of course. He'd become intimate with every part of her body that he could in the past couple of weeks, sifting his fingers through the silky mass of her hair, tracing her small ears with his tongue, running his thumbs over her cheeks, and kissing her nose.

But what he hadn't been able to see was how all the pieces fitted together. How the wispy bangs set off incredibly dark blue eyes that tilted at the corners. How her small and straight nose complemented her high cheek-bones and pointed chin.

With her short, slender build and gamine features, she looked like a fairy.

An island sprite.

He ran his gaze over all of it again, hair, eyes, cheekbones, nose, mouth—

And then she smiled.

He could never have imagined that smile. He dashed the tears from his irritated eyes and blinked some more. She had full lips that were at the top of his Ten Best to Kiss, but when she smiled . . . When she smiled, her full lips quirked up at the corners, and he glimpsed small, even white teeth and some tiny dimples in her cheeks. Her mouth widened, and magic bounced and floated in the air.

Yeager stared, entranced. Soon? He thought he was going to leave something like what he'd just glimpsed soon?

"Commander Gates!" A demanding shout diverted his attention. Yeager turned his head, registered smooth-talking Jerry, recognizable by the proprietary arm he had around a statuesque woman wearing a twinkly crown, and then three men, one with a video camera, another with a 35mm, and another carrying a notebook.

This last one spoke again, peppering him with questions. "Commander Gates! *Celeb!* magazine here. We've been looking all over for you. How are you feeling? Is it true you're thinking of suing NASA for wrongful termination? And what do you think about Marquez Herst as the new pilot of the Millennium? What's Captain America doing on this dot of rock? Is it true you can't bear to watch someone take your place?" The man smiled, his mouth full of teeth, sharp, like a great white's. "Aren't you man enough to make it to Canaveral?"

Yeager pushed his sunglasses onto his face, the back of his neck starting to burn. God, he hated the press. He opened his mouth to tell the asshole where to stuff his nosy questions and nasty inferences, but suddenly Deke was there, standing between him and the predatory reporter.

"Leave it, buddy," Deke said quietly.

To the whir of the video camera and the click of the 35mm, Yeager scrambled off the float. Deke clapped a baseball cap over Yeager's head and rushed him in the direction of his golf cart.

Though the reporter continued shouting questions and the cameramen trotted after them, Deke managed to cut them off with the golf cart and then whipped the vehicle out of the parking lot.

Yeager looked back, hooking his forefinger to slip down his glasses and squinting against the light. The *Celeb!* people had turned their cameras on the other parade participants. Zoe was standing toe to toe with Jerry. Like Yeager, it looked like she figured he was the one who'd given up the game.

She ran her hands through her short hair and then poked the man in the pigeon-breasted chest. There was no hint of that magical smile.

Yeager turned away from her, the reporter's words repeating in his mind. *Can't bear to watch someone else take your place. Aren't you man enough to make it to Canaveral?* He blew out a long breath of air, but it wasn't enough to push away a deepening, heavy sense of inevitability.

He blew out one more breath. "It's over, Deke," he said. "As much as I hate to admit it, that jerk of a reporter is right. I have to leave the island. I have to be at the Cape for the launch."

Yeager decided to break the news to Zoe as soon as possible. She popped into his cottage after overseeing the parade cleanup, and even with the morning's event behind her, he could tell her nerves were strung tight.

"Twelve hours to go and the firetail will be here," she said.

Yeager opened his mouth to caution her again, but as if she sensed what he was going to say, she launched into a hurried apology about the attack from the reporter and cameramen. He shrugged it off but did tell her he expected them to pound on his door at any moment.

Zoe shook her head and startled him by explaining that the Abrigo citizens had stonewalled the nosy reporter.

Yeager frowned. "But they must all know where I'm staying."

"Heck, yeah," Zoe said, nervously pacing around the room. "But they won't snitch. You're one of us, Mr. Grand Marshal. Even Jerry knows he's gone too far in his quest for publicity. We protect our own."

Guilt zinged him, and he shifted uncomfortably at the echo of the conversation he'd had with Sammy and Flossie on the float. He rubbed at the scar along his cheek. "Zoe . . ."

"Hmm?" She fiddled with the pillows on his bed, fluffing them up, then frowning at them.

He swallowed and approached the bed. "Smile for me, honey."

She turned, and her eyebrows came together. "Wha—"

"Smile for me." He ripped the sunglasses off his face and blinked to accustom himself to the light in the room.

She did smile at that, a smile both delighted and diffident. He appreciated those bewitching and surprising dimples all over again. "Yeager." She took a step toward him, then halted and nervously ran her palms down her thighs. "Can you . . . ?"

He blinked some more and nodded. "Better every hour."

He saw her swallow, then she stepped back and half turned away. She picked up a pillow and held it in front of her. "Well," she said. "Wow. Great."

But there wasn't "wow" and "great" in her voice. She wouldn't look at him. She seemed almost apprehensive.

"Zoe. Honey." He ran a finger down the back of her bare arm, and she shuddered but still didn't turn to face him. And then it clicked. He bit back his smile. "Zoe, are you shy, now that I can see you?"

She just hugged the pillow closer. "Of course not."

But it sounded like a bluff. He grabbed her by the shoulder, turned her toward him, and plucked the pillow from her arms to throw it back on the bed. "You are shy."

She looked at a point to the left of his collarbone. "I'm so . . . ordinary."

His jaw dropped. But then he swallowed, thinking fast. "And you've been hiding it all this time."

She nodded, eyes still avoiding his.

"All these nights in my bed, when I've held you and touched you, and yes, tasted you, all that time you've been keeping this ordinary thing from me."

Her gaze flew up at that. "Don't joke with me."

He took her face between his hands and traced the outline of her lips with his thumbs. "You don't know ordinary from squat. Ordinary isn't this mouth or your laugh or the dozens of times you've made me smile or made me feel less alone."

He gathered her close, and maybe she believed him, because she sighed and snuggled against him. Holding Zoe close, having her warm and fragrant in his arms, he realized all that he said was true, and he thought about everything she'd done for him. Every way that coming to the island had been good for him. God, he'd hate to leave her.

Maybe—His mind whirled. Why not? Why couldn't—

"Zoe," he said urgently, tilting her face toward him. "Come with me."

She smiled. "Where?" she said. "Where do you want to go?"

"The Cape. Cape Canaveral. I'm going there tomorrow, and you can come with me."

Her smile fell away, and the happy light in her eyes died. "What?"

"It's time I went back," he explained. "It's time I figured out what the hell I'm going to do. But first I need to watch the launch. You can come with me. We can make it a vacation or something. A couple of weeks and then"— he shrugged—"and then see what happens."

He didn't know what the hell he meant by "see what happens," but he didn't care. It was only clear that he couldn't just make a clean break from her and walk away.

Not yet.

He chucked her under the chin. "What do you say?"

She swallowed. He could follow the movement with his gaze now, appreciating the lines of her slender neck.

"No," she said.

He chucked her again. "C'mon. Lyssa will cover for you, you know she will."

Zoe stepped back and wrapped her arms around herself. He smiled, distracted for a moment by the glimpse of minor cleavage she gave him. He ran a teasing finger over her shoulder. "Did I tell you you look good enough to eat?"

She trembled and looked away. "I'm glad . . . I'm glad your vision is so much better."

"Then come celebrate with me for a couple of weeks. We'll watch the launch, and then we'll do whatever you want. I bet you'd love Disney World."

She slowly shook her head.

"Zoe," he said, spearing his hands through her blond hair. "C'mon honey. Think of all the fun we could have." He bent his head to take her mouth.

She turned her face away. "No, Yeager."

He narrowed his eyes and let her go. "No, Yeager, what? No kisses? No vacation in Florida? No *what*?"

She looked down at her hands. "No, I don't want to leave the island."

"C'mon, Zoe," he said again. He was losing his patience, and he didn't like that either. But he liked less the idea that he would leave tomorrow and never see her again. "This is stupid. You know you want to go with me."

"It doesn't matter what I want." Her fingers twisted together.

"What do you mean by that? If you want to come with me, you just do it." When she didn't answer, he set his jaw and ran his hands through his own hair.

With a deep breath, he tried again. "This is stupid, Zoe. Just tell me why the hell you won't go."

Her voice was husky and almost a whisper. "I don't leave the island," she said.

He waved his hand. "All the more reason to get away."

She looked up at him, her eyes wide and so damn blue you could use the color to paint the whole sky. "I don't leave the island," she repeated.

Something cold and chilly slithered down Yeager's back. "What do you mean, you don't leave the island?"

The conversation on the parade float came back to him. *There are things you don't know.* "Tell me, Zoe," he said harshly, something like fear driving him to force an answer. "*Tell me.*"

Her voice went to a whisper again, strained and hoarse. "I don't leave the island." She swallowed, but the next words were just as rough. "Since we came here three years ago, I . . . I haven't left the island."

Yeager closed his eyes, but there was nothing wrong with his ears, so he heard the next words anyway.

"I don't think I can," Zoe said, and she rushed past him and out the door.

18

It was party time on the moonlit Haven Beach. Zoe tried to lose herself in the crowd's buzz of anticipation, hailing friends here and there, flashing a forcefully cheery thumbs-up to the guys manning the pile of wood waiting to serve as the firetail's signal bonfire.

Sipping on a latte that TerriJean was selling from a cart trundled beachside, Zoe savored the rush of caffeine. The firetail always showed up about midnight, but that was still a couple of hours away. With the Haven House cottages full of guests who required attention, and then the parade this morning, she'd already put in a full day.

Lyssa suddenly appeared at her side. "I've been looking all over for you."

Guilt pinched Zoe sharply. After her upsetting conversation with Yeager she'd left Haven House, unwilling to be anywhere near him and even more unwilling to even think about what she'd said to him, words she'd never confessed to anyone. "Did you need me for something?" she asked.

Lyssa shook her head. "I thought for once *you* might need *me*."

Zoe watched the steam rising from her cup. "I'm fine."

"I talked to Yeager, Zoe. Or should I say, he shouted at me."

Shouted at her sister? Zoe frowned. "He had no right—"

Lyssa put her hand on Zoe's arm. "He's confused. He said you wouldn't stick around long enough to clear it up for him."

Zoe looked out toward the waves. Soon, she told herself, things would be back to normal. Soon the waves would go silver with the fire-tail finally coming home. Soon Yeager and Deke would be gone, and Abrigo would be as it should, and she and her sister would go back to running Haven House in their comfortable, comforting way. Their lives would return to safe, calm predictability.

"He said you told him you won't leave the island. That you can't leave it."

Zoe gripped her cup of coffee and avoided her sister's gaze. "He asked me to go on a vacation with him," she said, instead of agreeing. "But I don't want to."

"Damn!" Lyssa was silent a moment, then smacked her fist into her open palm. "I'm so mad at myself!"

Zoe started at the uncharacteristic display, her coffee sloshing over her hand. "Mad? Why? What's happened?"

"I've done this to you," Lyssa muttered. "I

knew what you were doing and I let you get away with it. We all did."

Zoe hurriedly turned back to the waves, studying them for signs of the firetail. "I don't know what you're talking about."

Lyssa touched her arm again. "Why deny it now, Zoe? You admitted it to Yeager."

She frowned. "He made me say things I didn't want to."

"He made you say the truth," Lyssa retorted, "the bald-faced truth that you're incapable of leaving the island."

A mix of embarrassment, misery, and humiliation washed over Zoe. "It's not . . ." But looking at her sister, she found she couldn't say it wasn't true. She shrugged. "I haven't thought about it that much."

Lyssa heaved a great sigh. "Well, I have. And Marlene and others of us who really know you. But I was the one who let you get away with it. It was up to me to help, and I failed."

No. Zoe was the big sister, the one who was supposed to make everything safe and right. "You didn't fail me because I don't want to leave Abrigo. It's no big deal."

"It is a big deal, Zoe. It's a big deal when you are so scarred—or so scared—that you can't bring yourself to even step off the island."

Zoe snorted indelicately. "Give me a break. Haven't I heard you say you never want to visit Antarctica?" she pointed out. "That doesn't mean something's wrong with you."

"I'm not saying there's something wrong

with you, exactly, it's just that—" Lyssa broke off and sighed again. "Let's go back to the house and talk, Zoe. Please."

She shook her head. "Are you kidding? And miss my moment of triumph when the firetail come back?" Her stomach tightened, but she pushed away the sickening fear that they might not show.

"Zoe—"

"Everything's going to be better once the firetail show up." Zoe guaranteed Lyssa's silence by linking arms with her sister and dragging her over to Marlene and some other friends who had staked out a prime spot on the sand. Despite a lot of graceless muttering, Lyssa finally ended up sitting beside Zoe and the others on the blanket.

As the night wore on, the laughter and movement quieted, and just before midnight the entire crowd was huddled in blankets on the beach, facing the water. The waves washed in and out, and Zoe stared at them hard, determined she would be the first to spot the fish.

Most of the pleasure boats were anchored around the corner, in Haven Bay, but there were two boats anchored off shore, shining searchlights into the waters around them. The marine biologists. Zoe frowned at them, knowing they'd be taking water samples and kelp samples and samples of God knew what else. As she watched them bob for a while, a sickening feeling grew in her stomach. Sympathy seasickness, she guessed, except that the queasiness didn't subside when she looked away.

And didn't subside as the minutes ticked by and waves washed in, unchanging.

And didn't subside when the first of the visitors to the beach gave up their wait and wandered back toward town.

Zoe clasped her hands together tightly, focusing only on the waves as they reached the shore. She looked for treasure in the white foam, the silver, wiggling bodies of the firetail as they spawned a new generation of fish and brought another year of life to the island.

But even though the foam remained plain foam and the hour became later, Zoe kept her focus, even refusing to acknowledge the soft and sad good nights as more and more people—her friends!—stood up, folded their blankets, and with shaking heads walked in the direction of home.

She didn't acknowledge Lyssa either, but just stared out to sea, remembering every summer she'd sat in this same sand, waiting for the firetail. And then remembering every summer she hadn't.

First, there were the years before their family had come to the island. Stuffy summer nights in cramped apartments, where she and Lyssa shared the living room couch as a bed.

And then there were the summers after their parents died, when Lyssa was battling cancer and Zoe sat up at night in the dark, crying into a pillow to muffle her fears. Summer nights when she'd dreamed of, prayed for, the time when they could return to the safety and security of Abrigo, where everything would be all right.

"Zoe." Lyssa shook her arm. "Zoe, we need to go home."

Zoe blinked, looking around. No blankets, no people, no men standing beside the pile of wood. They were alone on the beach. Even the boats out in the water had returned to the harbor.

Everybody had given up.

Shivers broke out over her skin, and Zoe drew up her knees and wrapped her arms around them. "I'm still waiting," she said stubbornly.

"Zoe." There were tears in Lyssa's eyes. "Please. Let's go home."

Zoe frowned. "Why are you crying? Don't cry." She brushed her sister's hair off her forehead. "Don't you feel well?"

Lyssa closed her eyes, and another fat tear rolled down her cheek. "I'm going to hurt you." She buried her face in her hands. "Forgive me, but I'm going to hurt you."

Zoe's still seasick stomach executed another pitch and roll. "Of course you're not," she said. "You couldn't do anything that would hurt me."

Lyssa took her hands from her face and looked up. "I've fallen in love, Zoe."

Zoe swallowed the little bubble of panic that formed in her throat. "Well. Well. What a surprise. Who is it? One of the Daves? Or . . . um . . ." She desperately searched her mind for another possible candidate.

"It's Deke, Zoe. I've fallen in love with

Deke, and I'm going away with him."

"No."

"Zoe—"

"No." She smiled at Lyssa and brushed her hair off her sister's forehead again, like she used to do when Lyssa was a little girl. Like she used to do when her sister was battling leukemia and there wasn't any hair to brush away. "This is where you're healthy," she said reasonably. "This is where we're safe."

Lyssa closed her eyes. "Zoe, listen to me. I'm healthy and safe wherever I choose to be. Wherever I am. I'm okay. I survived. The past is over, and now it's time for both of us to start living."

That panic rose in Zoe's throat again, and she had to swallow twice to keep it down. "Lyssa—"

Her sister caught her hand and brought it against her damp cheek. "Zoe, listen. I'm happy. So happy. Like Yeager makes you happy, Deke makes me feel that very same way." She kissed Zoe's hand. "Be joyful for me," she whispered.

Tears started in Zoe's eyes, but she blinked them away, just as she forced away Lyssa's silly talk. There wasn't time for either. She shook her head and focused back on the waves. "You're just imagining things. Or maybe you're tired. You'll feel differently in the morning, you'll see," she said. "We'll talk about all this then. But right now we have to watch for the fish. We can't miss the firetail's return."

Lyssa blew out a long breath of air.

Zoe spared her a quick glance. "Do you have any matches? When they come, you and I can light the signal fire ourselves."

Lyssa just looked at her for a moment, opened her mouth, closed it, then finally nodded her head. "I have matches," she said. Another tear rolled down her cheek, but then she put her arm around Zoe's shoulders and scooted closer.

Zoe smiled in relief. "Stick by me, kiddo," she said, curling her own arm around her sister's waist.

Lyssa leaned her head against Zoe's shoulder. "I love you. You know that."

Zoe didn't take her eyes off the waves. "Of course I do. And it's going to be all right," she said, the words rolling off her tongue like they had a thousand times before. "You'll see."

The morning after the firetails' no-show, Yeager was packed and ready to leave the island. But he wasn't going anywhere, not until he'd talked to Zoe one more time.

Never before had he asked a woman to do something twice. He'd never had to. But now that the fish had deserted her, he figured she'd be more than ready for a little vacation. Yeah, sure, there were all those mutterings of hers about not leaving Abrigo, but the way he figured it, she was stalling again.

She'd put off making love with him too, hadn't she? But that hadn't lasted long.

And, damn it, he just plain wanted more time with her. Why go cold turkey on a harmless addiction that both parties continued to

enjoy? he asked himself, walking down the
path from his cottage to Zoe's house. A breeze
stirred the warm air, spiced by the scent of
green things and ocean. He was going to miss
this place too, he realized, surprised. The island had created a place for him, unlike any
of the dozens of spots he'd lived in over the
past thirty-three years.

As he expected, Yeager found Zoe in the
Haven House kitchen. The morning sun filled
the big room, and he looked around it for a
moment, really seeing it for the first time.
Shining tile, gleaming hardwood floors, plants
growing in lush display in the window over
the sink. It was homey, he thought, comfortable, yet unique and so pretty, just like Zoe.

But the room was absent of the usual tantalizing smells of her baking and cooking. And
instead of her energetic bustling around the
room, she was quietly sitting at the kitchen table, hunched over a cup of tea, some kind of
knitted thing wrapped around her.

He squinted through the dark lenses of the
glasses he was still wearing to protect his
light-sensitive eyes. "You look like hell," he
said.

She sipped from the mug. "Funny," she answered, her voice devoid of expression.
"When I feel like a million bucks."

He frowned and pulled out a chair to sit beside her. She shifted away, and a sunbeam
coming through the window caught in her
hair, setting it glowing like a halo.

A weird lump growing in his throat, he just
watched her in silence for a few minutes. This

was why she had to come with him, he
thought, determination renewed. While he
knew her scent, her shape, her voice, he hadn't
yet had his fill of her looks. The disarray of
her short blond hair, her full lower lip, even
the new shadows beneath her eyes fascinated
him.

He hadn't had time to get tired of her face.

Though certainly he would. But it was un-
healthy to cut short a relationship that hadn't
yet begun to wilt.

He cleared his throat. "I heard the fish
didn't come," he said, his voice hoarse.

"Yeah." No emotion flickered behind her
shadowed eyes.

He tried to start the conversation again.
"Are you okay?"

She shrugged. "Just tired. Lyssa and I
waited all night."

Although he was glad to have found her
awake, he knew she must be exhausted. "You
haven't had any sleep?"

"I'll go to bed when Lyssa gets up."

Some new tension entered her body at her
sister's name. He frowned. "Is something
wrong between the two of you?"

"I don't know," she whispered, and for a
moment he thought she might break down.
But then she took a long, steadying breath. "I
need to talk to her when she wakes up." She
wrapped her hands around her tea and stared
into the bottom of the mug.

Yeager blew out his own silent, steadying
breath of air, unsure how to play this, unsure
how to play her, in this unfamiliar mood.

Reaching out, he toyed with a lock of her wavy hair and noticed that, unlike every other woman he'd ever known, she hadn't pierced her ears. "I'm leaving on the next ferry," he said gently. "Come with me, Zoe." Like those intact earlobes, there were countless things about her yet to be discovered.

She froze, then bent her head lower over her tea, her hair slipping out of his fingers. "Don't," she said.

His eyebrows came together. "Don't go?" he asked, puzzled. "But there are things I have to do." He touched her cheek, stroking his knuckles against her baby-soft skin. "Come with me."

That made the third time he'd asked her, but who was counting?

She shook her head, as if he didn't understand. "I wish you wouldn't ask me. I can't leave the island, Yeager."

Was she expecting him to beg? He frowned, irritation suddenly prodding his temper. "Don't be coy," he said sharply. "For God's sake, now that the festival is over and the fish didn't arrive, you need to get away. And I'm asking you to be with me."

"Coy?" She lifted her head and looked at him, something sparking in the depths of her eyes. "You think I'm being coy with you?"

That irritation gave him another jab. "What else would you call it?"

She looked back down at her tea. "How about honest?" she said. "I've been more honest with you than I've been with anyone in my life."

He stilled. Even his heart stopped beating for a moment. "Wait a minute. Are you saying you really won't leave the island?"

"Can't," she corrected. There was a long, tense pause. "I don't expect you to understand—you've explored the galaxy!—but I haven't left the island since we came back three years ago."

"What?" But he couldn't help remembering Marlene telling him there were things about Zoe he didn't know.

"It's not something I've exactly talked about or really acknowledged, even to myself, but I'm . . . comfortable here."

"That's ridiculous! Of course you've left the island. You've had to—to—"

"I've had to do nothing but keep Lyssa healthy and keep more tragedies out of our lives."

He shook his head in disbelief, a long silence stretching between them. "I don't get it," he finally said.

"Is it really so hard?" she asked. "Our parents died on the mainland. And that's where Lyssa battled cancer. But here, here's where we're safe."

"Zoe . . ." How could you counteract such cockeyed logic? It was crazy! "Bad things, illness, death, they happen everywhere."

She just shook her head stubbornly. "The island has taken care of us. The island is where we belong."

Yeager's irritation transformed into impatience. He never liked the idea of losing—an argument or a woman. "So your past has made you afraid. That means you're just going to huddle in this house like an old granny for the rest of your life?"

Unable to sit still a second longer, he stood, the legs of his chair bouncing against the floor with the force of his movement. "You're just going to give up and let your fears win?"

He hated that she didn't even bother answering. "Is that it, Zoe? Because of the past, because you're afraid, you're just going to turn your back on us?"

She looked up at that. "What 'us'? Do you mean the two more weeks of 'us' you were so graciously offering me?" Her eyes narrowed. "Big whoop-dee-doo."

That stung. But he wasn't going to let her get away with it. No way would he accept that she was going to let him walk out of her life. "Dammit, Zoe, you're a coward! Can't you see you're refusing to live because you're afraid of what might happen?"

Her eyes widened, and she stood too. "This is coming from you?"

He recoiled at her disdain. "Well, why not from me? I don't let setbacks stop me." Anger rose inside him, hot and impetuous. "Why do you think I'm going to the Cape? Because I'm not accepting NASA's no. Screw the accident. Screw the doctors. I'm going to pilot a Millennium launch, not this one, but one soon, and so I've got to be there."

She stared at him like he'd just sprouted full astronaut gear. She even went so far as to reach up and knock on the side of his skull.

"Hello? Is there a brain in there, or is it all filled up with ego?"

He whipped off his dark glasses. "What the hell is that supposed to mean?" It wasn't blood flowing through his body but lava, hot and bubbling.

Her blue eyes were bright. "It means you've been hiding away on the island all this time too. Instead of acknowledging and accepting that your astronaut days are in the past, you've been skulking here on Abrigo, probably using sex with me as just another way to dodge the truth."

He crossed his arms over his chest, so angry that he could barely breathe. It took him a long moment to find his voice. "I thought I told you to stay out of my head," he finally said harshly.

Instantly, her whole body appeared to sag. "You did," she said wearily, dropping back into her chair. "And I should have listened." She went back to staring into her tea.

There was nothing left for Yeager to do but stalk out of the kitchen. Stalk up to his cottage and grab his stuff. Stalk out of Zoe's life and sail away from her and her island.

The ferry chugged back toward the mainland, and Yeager slumped deeper in his passenger seat and closed his eyes. Maybe if he dozed off, he could forget the play of emotions on Zoe's face during their conversation.

Their *last* conversation.

But she appeared on the screen of his tightly closed eyelids in unforgettable living color, the woman he'd once termed his cure but who had become so much more.

He saw her face, tired and dejected, mourning the loss of her fish. Maybe he hadn't been sympathetic enough about that. Maybe he should have spent a little more time comforting her. Instead, he'd been hell-bent on bringing up a vacation trip off island.

Her face had turned incredulous then, those blue eyes wide, especially when he made the unfortunate "us" remark. Her response ticked him off just thinking about it, and he shifted his legs restlessly. What had she expected? Two weeks, he'd proposed. He didn't have a lifetime to offer her.

He didn't even want the two weeks any more, dammit. Not with someone who accused him of being stuck in the past and running away from his problems. Not with someone who accused him of using her as a distraction.

She'd been his delight.

She'd been his laughter, his friend, his coach in cathartic mudball, the woman who'd reminded him of how much he loved to fly.

And to her he'd been—what?

He pictured her in the kitchen, her hair mussed, the shadows deep beneath her eyes. Something inside him ached, a bittersweet pain. God, he should have kissed her incredible mouth one last time. He should have demanded her smile one last time. Oh yeah, she'd been his delight.

And then that question reared its ugly head again. To her he'd been what?

At the lowest point of her life—no firetail and something obviously wrong between her and her sister—he'd been nothing for her. Nothing.

And now he'd left her.

He slumped even lower and clunked his head against the back of the plastic seat. What was the point of going over this? The fact was, he had to return to face his demons and he couldn't do anything for a woman who continued to hide from hers.

Forcing himself to breathe slowly and evenly, he tried again to sleep.

And suddenly felt someone's gaze upon him.

Groan. The ferry had been nearly full when he'd come aboard, but he'd found himself an aisle seat at the back. Wearing his dark glasses and a baseball cap, he'd hoped to avoid detection.

But just like six weeks before, on his trip to the island, someone was breathing on him.

"Hey, mister."

Yeager decided that ignoring the kid's voice fell in the category of running away from his problems. Unwilling to give Zoe any more ammunition, even ammunition she'd never know about, Yeager opened his eyes and tipped back the brim of his cap.

"Yeah?" he said.

His latest fan was about three-foot-two, forty pounds, with a wild cap of Zoe-like waves of blond hair. Standing beside her was an older brother, nine maybe, who appeared painfully embarrassed. The little Zoe type elbowed her brother in the ribs.

He grimaced and jabbed in her direction with his thumb. "We went to Disneyland," he said gruffly. "She has Minnie, Belle, and Cinderella."

The girl nodded emphatically, and Yeager noticed she held a pink plastic autograph book. "Yeah?" he said again. An astronaut seemed an odd autograph for her girl-star collection, but he straightened and reached for the book.

The sister clasped the thing close to her tummy and gave her brother a look.

He rolled his eyes. "She wants that Flossie the Fish's autograph, y'know? She remembers you from the parade yesterday and thought maybe you could get her to sign my sister's book."

Yeager stared at the duo, stunned. It had come to this? Being recognized as the friend of an oversized, overstuffed fake fish? It was depressing. It was appalling. It was laughable.

Yet suddenly Yeager felt his face break into a grin. He chuckled, some tension inside him loosening. It *was* laughable. He chuckled again, shaking his head.

Wouldn't Zoe get a smile out of this?

Still laughing, he managed to take a scrap of paper with the little girl's address and promised he'd get Flossie's autograph and send it to her. If worst came to worst, he'd buy some kind of goofy, glittery pen and fake one himself, but first he'd contact Zoe and see what she could do.

She'd get a kick out of it, that's for damn sure.

Settling back in his seat, he laughed again. It was a hell of a way to realize he wasn't an astronaut any more.

Zoe was right about that too. He never would be again. Despite all his idiotic bluster, he knew, gut-deep, that it was over for him. He needed a new life, a new identity.

He grinned to himself again, thinking of that crazy island and all the crazy people living on it. They'd created a community for themselves there. A group of people who looked out for one another and protected one another.

He shook his head. So when it came to finding a new identity, maybe being known as Flossie's friend wasn't such a lousy place for him to begin after all.

The ferry bumped gently against the mainland dock. By the time Yeager collected his duffel bag, the last of the taxis had just pulled away, and he found a shady bench on which to wait for the next one.

The mainland air smelled different from Abrigo's. He inhaled a gulp of it, and while it was salty and fresh, so near to the ocean, it lacked something he couldn't quite put his finger on. Stretching his arms along the back of the bench, he ran his gaze over everything in sight: the rows of dusty-windshielded cars, so surprising after weeks around golf carts and scooters, the uninspiring acres of blacktop, and inland, the wash of smog hanging in the blue sky.

He ran his gaze across the wide expanse above him. His heart surged, remembering his parasail and that taste of flight and freedom. He'd go back up there soon. His palms itched, anxious for the chance to hold the controls. Even a small plane would be a fine key to his favorite playground.

Or was it his second favorite, after Zoe's small, eager body?

He forced his mind away from the question. Now that his vision was so clear, he could almost believe the past few months—the island, Zoe—had never happened. He could almost believe his blindness had been a bad dream.

He sighed. Of course that little fantasy would be smashed to smithereens the moment he saw the Millennium leave the ground without him.

Leave the ground without him.

Yeager sat up and ran his hand over his scarred face. Why the hell was he doing this?

Was he really going back to face those demons, or was he going back because it was easier to chase an old dream to the bitter end instead of finding a new one?

Why wasn't he starting to find his new life immediately?

Easy. Because he didn't know where the hell to look for it.

But was that entirely true? He closed his eyes, and there she was again, starring on the dual screens of his eyelids. Zoe.

Zoe laughing.

Zoe holding him against her.

Zoe needing him.

Him needing Zoe.

He popped up from the bench, unsure what to do. Could he find a life on the island? Could he offer more than two weeks to Zoe?

Because if he went back, she deserved *every-thing* from him.

Inhaling a long breath, he touched the scar on his face. What was the right thing to do?

He rubbed the scar again, pacing back and forth. What was it Lyssa had once said? That destiny had a plan?

"Come on, Destiny," he muttered, grabbing up his duffel bag. "Do your thing." If the ferry was still at the landing, then he was supposed to return to Abrigo. If not, he'd continue to make his way to the Cape.

Breath suddenly coming in short huffs, Yeager started jogging toward the dock. Over the roof of the ticket office, he could see the ferry, bobbing on the waves. His heart pounding in his chest, he ran faster, impatiently weaving around small knots of people.

Ducking inside the office, he glanced out the picture window at the ferry, hoping he could get an outside seat.

And saw that it was pulling away, leaving in its path a very rough and very final wake.

19

Zoe sat on the patio of what had been Yeager's cottage, looking out over the Haven harbor and talking to her new friend, Dolly.

"He left you behind too, huh?" She glanced over at the nude plastic woman, who, besides sunglasses, shell necklace, and thongs, now sported a sailor cap set at a rakish angle. Zoe propped up her feet on the table beside Dolly's, then nudged the doll's shapely ankle with her own Teva sandal. "But you're not sorry, are you?"

Zoe nodded as if the other woman had agreed. "Me neither." She spread her arms to encompass the sunshine, the sparkling water, the pleasure boats dotting the protected bay. "I love it here."

Even though the firetail hadn't returned, Zoe didn't care about the island any less. She didn't know what would happen now, though, whether or not they could survive without the fish. But that ship had already sailed, she thought, smiling grimly at her own word play.

"We'll just have to wait it out," she told Dolly.

"Wait out what?"

Zoe started, then glanced over her shoulder. Lyssa stood in the doorway between Yeager's room and the patio, looking so young and vulnerable that Zoe's stomach clenched. Just behind her was Deke, his cool eyes watchful, but Lyssa's hand held firmly in his.

"Wait out what?" her sister asked again.

Zoe took a long breath and shrugged. After staying awake on the beach until dawn, she and Lyssa had walked slowly back to the house without saying a word to each other. But it was obviously time for words now, though she had no idea which ones to choose.

"How are you feeling?" Lyssa said.

Zoe gave a little smile. "Relieved I haven't heard a dozen I told you sos yet. Can you believe it? Not one person, including Jerry, has called me this morning."

"Everyone wanted the fish to arrive just as much as you did, Zoe." Lyssa was silent a moment, then she walked closer to the table, Deke moving with her. "But I want to know how you're feeling about *me*."

Zoe glanced toward her sister, then glanced back at the ocean, the water that she'd always considered their very own protective moat. "You don't really mean to tell me again that you're leaving the island?" she tried, but only half-heartedly. Even from here she could sense the strong emotional current running between

Lyssa and Deke. How could she have missed it before? Her sister had never looked so happy and Deke seemed ... younger somehow and less wary. Just one more thing to lay at Yeager's door.

"Zoe—" Lyssa started.

She squeezed shut her eyes. "I'm terrified for you, Lyssa. I can't help it, but I am."

Lyssa let go of Deke's hand to cross to her swiftly and grip her shoulder. "I know you are," she said. "I understand. But it's time for me to leave the island and live my life."

"It seems like a lot of people are doing that around here."

"Why don't you go to him, Zoe?"

Zoe shook her head. "This is about you, not me." She covered Lyssa's hand with her own. "Are you sure? Haven't you always been content here?"

Lyssa smiled gently. "I've always been content here. But I've never felt, like you do, that it's the only place I can be safe."

Deke had come up behind her and now ran a possessive yet reverent hand down her sister's hair. "I'll take good care of her," he said.

Lyssa turned to him with a frown. "How many times do we have to talk about this? I'm not a child. I'll take good care of *you*."

He smiled, lifting his hands in immediate surrender. "We'll take good care of each other," he said agreeably.

Looking at the man's sexy and charming smile, Zoe could suddenly see what had attracted her sister. Deke's hardness was an all-male counterpoint to Lyssa's sweet serenity, but his eyes were soft as he gazed at her sister, and Lyssa looked confidently smug, basking in his obvious love. Zoe had to smile herself at the sight, though her heart stung at the thought of losing Lyssa.

She swallowed. "When will you be going?" she said.

A new sparkle entered Lyssa's eyes. "Sometime after the wedding."

"A wedding!" Zoe jumped out of her chair. She hugged Lyssa, bussed Deke on his hard cheek, even squeezed Dolly, who let out a celebratory, though somewhat inappropriate, squeal.

Standing back, she gazed at the engaged couple. As hard as it was going to be to see Lyssa go, she had the strangest feeling that this was meant to be. She remembered the day that Deke came to the island and how sure she'd been that she'd make a match for her new guests. "Dang if this isn't going to qualify me a world-class matchmaker."

Lyssa groaned. "Zoe. You had nothing to do with us."

Zoe frowned at her sister in reprimand. "Throw me a bone, why don't you? If you're going to go, the least you can do is leave me with an improved reputation."

Lyssa sighed. "I'd rather leave you with an improved love life. If you only knew . . ." She leaned back against Deke, her expression dreamy.

Zoe smiled sadly. "I do, Lyssa. That's why I can let you go with Deke."

Her sister's eyes widened. "You do love

him! Then why don't you go after him," she
said urgently. "We'll stay and take care of
things around here for a while."

"No." Zoe shook her head, still smiling. "I
won't go. The island is my home, my haven."

Lyssa bit her lip, then shook her head
slowly. "If you can't leave it," she said softly,
"it's a prison."

If you can't leave it, it's a prison.

The words echoed in Zoe's head long after
Deke and Lyssa left the cottage.

She continued sitting on the porch with only
Dolly for company, watching the movement of
the boats in the harbor, the golf carts on the
Haven streets, the visitors on the sidewalks.

As usual, she was a voyeur of everyone
else's life.

And if she kept this up, she'd never have
one of her own.

Just as the thought entered her head, a
cocky raven swooped down to perch on the
patio railing, and the church bells started
clanging the hour. The bird cocked its head,
regarding her with an intelligent gleam in its
eye. *What else do you need*, it seemed to ask, *a
lightning bolt*?

If you can't leave it, it's a prison.

Bong.

If she kept this up, she'd never have a life
of her own.

Bong. Bong.

Zoe inhaled sharply, the breath hurting as it
entered her lungs, and suddenly, she knew.
Being an observer wasn't good enough any

more. Not if it meant never having Yeager.

She found herself standing, her hands shaking so violently she had to grip the back of the chair to steady them. Across the bay, the *Molly Rose* was chugging to the ferry landing on its return from the mainland, the trip that had taken Yeager from her.

Her gaze followed the slow-moving ferry. Could she do it? Could she go after him?

Of course, having Yeager would mean leaving the island. Her never changing, always safe Abrigo. But it had changed. Or, to be honest, she had. Falling in love with Yeager had made her into a woman who couldn't be satisfied by contentment. She wanted what Lyssa had found—passion, joy, love—but did she have the courage to break away from the past and reach for it too?

"Dolly?" Zoe pleaded, wishing the plastic woman would come to life and provide some answers. And then it struck her again. That she should be wishing *herself* to life.

Her hand still shook badly as she reached out to Dolly and plucked the sailor cap from the doll's painted-on curls. She was going to need it before Dolly did. Zoe shot one more look at the arriving ferry and then clapped the hat on her own head. "Don't wait up," she told the doll, and then forced herself to abandon the view without looking back. As she turned away, the raven, apparently satisfied, spread its blue-black wings and soared over Zoe's head.

If Zoe had counted on her sister or circumstances to get in the way of her rash decision,

she'd counted wrong. With a gleeful exclamation, Lyssa promised to take care of everything for as long as everything took and even
helped Zoe pack. In less time than she'd believed possible, Zoe arrived at the dock of the
Molly Rose clutching a small bag and a list of
phone numbers and contact persons provided
by Deke. She'd track Yeager all the way to
Florida if she had to.

Maybe.

First she had to get herself on the ferry.

With Lyssa holding onto her arm, it was
Deke who braved the ticket office for her.
Then they both gently shoved Zoe in the di-
rection of the *Molly Rose*.

She stumbled at first, then halted, looking
back up the long plank walkway. Had she told
Lyssa where the menu lists were? Was the reservations log in its proper place? Would anyone remember to check on the five sets of
Egyptian cotton sheets she'd ordered that had
yet to arrive?

Was she out of her head to be going after a
man who only wanted her for a two-week vacation?

Lyssa would say it was even crazier to let
what happened in the past make her turn her
back on love.

Gripping her bag tight enough to give her
blisters, Zoe forced one step in front of the
other. She stared at her feet, her breath coming
in panicky gasps as she reached the boat and
one of the crew gripped her elbow and helped
her onto the ferry.

She found a seat inside and kept her head

down, hot and cold shivers running over her skin. With her gaze on her tightly clasped hands, maybe she could avoid watching the ferry's retreat from the island.

It worked for a while. The engines thrummed loudly, and the ferry started moving away, but Zoe counted her fingernails and then her knuckles instead of looking out the window. As the boat gathered speed, she squeezed shut her eyes and listened to the roaring pound of her heart.

But then she couldn't take it any more. She shot up from her seat, her mind whirling. *Get to the captain! Get him to take you back!* a voice screamed in her mind.

She lurched into the aisle, looking about her for a crew member, then her gaze fell on the stairs leading up to the second, outside deck. The captain was up there. He had to be.

Sweaty palms sliding up the metal rails, Zoe ran up the stairs and out the doorway into the fresh air. *The captain. The captain.* She looked about wildly, seeing only more passengers, and then—

She saw the island.

Her panic receded. *Thank God,* she thought. *It's still there.*

She ran a hand over her eyes, then looked again. Still there.

Air stuttered into her starved lungs, and she walked, nearly mesmerized, to the deck railing. Holding on, she stared at her beloved Abrigo. It was still there. From the instant the ferry had left the dock, she'd been terrified it had disappeared in a breath of smoke.

A smile eased the tight muscles of her face. The island was as permanent as always, its blue water and cornmeal sand and green, green cliffs. She could even see Haven House and knew that inside Lyssa was safe and sound in the arms of the man she loved.

Tears filled her eyes, but Zoe let them overflow and spill onto her cheeks as she watched Abrigo slowly recede into the distance. Her heart slowed, and she managed a long, deep breath. From far away her home had a different yet just as special kind of beauty. The place she loved was never going anywhere, even if she did.

She watched the island change from rock to dot to smudge on the horizon, and even though it faded completely from her sight, Zoe believed in her heart that the island was there.

But her panic resurged when the ferry docked at landing. Though the other passengers on the upper deck made their way down the stairs, Zoe suddenly couldn't loosen her grip from the deck's metal railing. She couldn't force her feet to move any closer to the mainland.

"Miss?"

Zoe swung her head in the direction of the stairwell. A teenager stood there, holding a half-full plastic garbage bag. "Are you all right, miss?" He walked onto the deck and bent over to pick up a discarded Styrofoam cup.

Zoe swallowed. "I'm . . ." Frozen? Terrified? *Ready to do anything but set foot on the mainland that brought us so much pain?*

The boy's face reddened and he came closer. "I'm sorry, but unless you have a round trip ticket you'll have to disembark now."

His prodding eased some of her paralysis. "Oh. Okay. Sure." She turned away from him and focused on her fingers, forcing each one to relax its death grip on the railing. Then she commanded her feet to move, three steps, four steps, now seven, then all the way down the stairs.

As she approached the ferry's exit, her heartbeat pounded in her ears and she couldn't catch her breath. But still she went forward, holding dizzily to the notion that she had to, that she must. After all, like the boy said, she didn't have a round-trip ticket.

With one step left to go though, Zoe's knees were watery and her palms damp. She halted, dimly aware of the crewmember ready to help her down. *This is it*, she thought, her heart slamming bam-bam-bam against her chest. *Is Yeager worth taking this chance*?

But from somewhere came a certainty that slowed her heartbeat and eased the tightness in her chest. Returning to the mainland wasn't for Yeager. Whether she found him or not, whether he wanted her love or not, returning here was something she owed to herself.

Taking a deep breath, she ignored the crewmember's hand and accomplished the step on her own, staring down at her feet as they came to rest on the mainland they hadn't touched in three years.

Lightning didn't strike, nor did the angels sing. Instead, somebody murmured "Excuse me," and jostled her as they passed, and the very normalcy of the moment gave Zoe the rest of the courage she needed. Still watching her feet, she slowly continued forward, her heart lightening and her spirit healing with each inch of ground covered. Unbidden, a smile broke over her face, and then a hand wrapped around her arm, startling her, and she was jerked against a hard, wide—and familiar—chest. Blinking, she looked up. "Yeager?"

The sun was behind him, lighting his outline in fire, and when he bent his head and took her mouth, the fire ignited her too.

He lifted his head. "Zoe," he said, then he drew her so tightly against him she couldn't breathe again. "You left. You left the island."

Her heart was pounding once more. There was something scratching her neck, and she pulled away to see a ticket in his hand. The red ticket that meant a departure for Abrigo.

She swallowed. "You were coming back?" she whispered.

He pushed his sunglasses off his face and looked at her, his brown eyes seeing straight into her heart. "I was going to let Destiny make the decision," he admitted, a little smile on his face, "when I was trying to choose. I told myself if I could get on the return ferry, it meant I should go back. If not . . ." He shrugged.

She frowned. "But you weren't on the return ferry."

His smile widened, and this one was without his usual charm or seduction, but just filled with sweetness and something else she couldn't name. "When I didn't like Destiny's answer," he said, running a knuckle down her cheek, "I turned on the pilot override."

She frowned again.

"I just decided to wait for the next ferry." His smile died, and he took Zoe's face in both his hands. "I had to go back. There was something I left behind."

His palms felt cool against her hot cheeks, and Zoe could hardly hear him over the nervous ringing in her ears. "Left behind?" she choked out.

"My heart." He shook his head sheepishly. "I know it sounds as corny as hell, Zoe, but I left my heart there and forgot a few other things too."

"Forgot?" She was getting good at this echo thing.

"To tell you I love you. To ask you to be my wife."

That ringing in her ears transformed into full-on church bells, louder and more joyful than the ones on the island. Her eyes widened. "You're going to marry me?" Apollo was going to take her, Zoe Cash, up on his chariot? For life?

He laughed. "If you'll forget all the bad things you know about me and just say yes."

Zoe didn't know whether to cry or laugh or scream or call every resident of Abrigo Island to impart the news. She was going to be married! She was going to be married to Yeager!

But a strange expression crossed his face,

and he took a step back. "Zoe?" he said uncertainly.

She blinked, and then read the worry on his face. A lump formed in her throat, and her eyes filled with tears. She loved this big, confident, golden god all the more because he wasn't sure of her.

When a woman married a man like this, the upper hand was hard to come by.

But she put him out of his misery by spearing her hands through his shining, gold-shot hair and bringing his head down to hers. "I love you," she said against his mouth. "I say yes."

The cool Abrigo sand crunched beneath Yeager's bare feet. He walked just outside the waves' reach, Zoe beside him and snuggled into the curve of his arm.

Smiling, he looked up at the moon. He was glad he'd talked Zoe into returning to the island right away. When he watched the Millennium launch on television tomorrow, he wanted to be here, at the place where his new life would begin.

She followed his gaze, her fairy sprite face turning up to catch the lunar light. "Maybe—" she started.

"No." He stopped and pulled her in front of him, wrapping his arms around her waist. "I wanted to come back here and get my plans in motion right away."

She leaned her head against his shoulder. "Plans you've been awfully quiet about."

He rubbed his chin against the top of her

head, and her special Zoe scent filled him with satisfaction. "As if you've given me much time to talk at all, Miss Hot in the Sack."

"That's Almost Mrs. Hot in the Sack to you, buster."

He laughed softly. "I like the sound of that. And how do you like the sound of this?" The breath he took was long and careful. "What if ... what if we bought that house that Deke's been working on? You could still run Haven House, but I like the idea of a little more privacy for me and my wife and ... a family when we have one."

She went still in his arms. "Oh, Yeager," she said, and there was happiness and tears in her voice. "But what about you? I'm willing to go—"

"I'm not," he said. "I am damn sick of that ferry ride, though, and I'm sure there's a bunch of other people who feel the same way I do. I was thinking about starting a business, a commuter air service to the island. Maybe if it's a little easier to get here, we can keep this place alive with or without the firetail."

She turned in his arms, and hell, if what he saw on her face didn't make him almost start bawling too. She smiled through her pretty tears. "But we'll travel too. Because everything is more precious with a little perspective," she said sagely.

Yeager kissed her instead of disagreeing, but he could have stood on the moon tomorrow and not cherished Zoe any more than he did at this moment.

Movement over her shoulder suddenly

caught his attention. He lifted his head, rubbed at his eyes, blinked, then rubbed them again.

Zoe frowned. "What is it? Are your eyes okay?"

"I hope they're not playing any tricks on me, honey. Look." He pointed to the water.

She turned, gasped, and so he figured she saw what he did. The white froth of the crashing waves had turned silver and crimson and alive in one of the most incredible sights he'd ever seen.

"The firetail!" Zoe yelled. She jumped in the air, landed in his arms, kissed him silly, and then screamed again triumphantly.

Pumping her arms in the air, she ran down the beach, and Yeager had to put on full speed to catch up with her, ignoring the twinges in his stiff leg. "Where are you going?" he shouted.

"The bonfire!" She stopped in front of a cordoned-off pile of wood and started patting down her pockets. "Matches! We need matches!"

He shoved his fingers in his own jeans. "Astronauts and Boy Scouts, we're always prepared." A skinny book of matches changed hands, and in a few moments flames were climbing the tower of wood to signal that the island was back in business.

As usual, good news traveled fast.

In a very short while, Yeager was sharing what was supposed to be quiet time with his wife-to-be with hundreds of Abrigo residents and visitors.

Nobody seemed surprised he was marrying
Zoe.

Everybody seemed happy to welcome him
to their community. His community now too.

A keg of beer appeared on the sand, and
suddenly it seemed the entire island was toast-
ing their happiness. Lyssa and Deke were
there too, and Yeager thought his friend
seemed positively bewildered and besotted by
the beauty who had come into his life.

"Lyssa loves me," he told Yeager, wearing
a stupid grin.

But Yeager refused to rib him about the
sappy smile, pretty certain he wore its twin on
his own face.

Zoe's smile was stunning, and her hair
glowed in the light of the bonfire. "Are you
sure you're going to be happy here?" she
asked.

He couldn't stop himself from touching her
cheeks, her nose, her mouth, marveling at all
that she was and all that she'd given him.
"*We're* going to be happy ever after," he said.

EPILOGUE

Zoe stood just inside the open French doors of the Haven House dining room. Before her, the September sun shone brightly in the sky, and the rippling Pacific caught the light so that the water's surface appeared scattered with gold doubloons. From here she could also see the town of Haven where the scarlet, blue and silver firetail flags fluttered above the quiet streets.

Quiet because almost everyone in town was gathered in her sloping front yard, waiting to witness a wedding.

She clutched her bouquet of white roses tighter, and squeezed the uniformed arm of the man at her side. He looked down at her, but the usually stern lines of his face were soft. "Are you ready?"

Zoe swallowed. "Ready, BG."

She surprised another smile out of him. Yeager's father, the brigadier general, was a straight-shooting, serious man but he seemed to like her. He certainly enjoyed the nickname she'd given him even before they'd met. Every time she used it he went marshmallow on her.

The brigadier general took a quick step forward to signal the beginning of the ceremony. He and Zoe both winced a little as the Island Band struck up what was supposed to be the wedding march, but after a sour note or two or five, the instruments came to a sort of agreement. With one more deep breath, Zoe gave Yeager's father a nod and they stepped forward.

An aisle was created by swagged garlands of jasmine and roses. On either side, their necks craned to get a look at her, stood Zoe's island family: Marlene, Gunther, Susan, Elizabeth, Desirée, Rae-Ann, and the Daves to name only a few. The crowd was also dotted here and there by the assorted military uniforms of Yeager's friends from the Space Center, and Zoe almost giggled when she noticed that one of them had apparently selected inflatable Dolly as his date. Standing propped against the man's side, she looked almost respectable in a backless dress and a wide-brimmed hat.

But as Zoe walked down the aisle, the guests became a blur, because ahead of her were the people she loved most in the world. There was Deke and Lyssa, the best man and the matron of honor. Five days after the firetail had arrived, the impatient couple had dragged her and Yeager to the mainland to witness their justice-of-the-peace wedding. It had been tempting to follow suit, but it was Yeager that had wanted to see Zoe in her great grandmother's white dress and yards of wedding veil.

Yeager. She finally allowed herself to look at him. He stood straight and somber beside the minister, his dark suit the perfect foil for the golden glow of his hair. Zoe's heart stuttered and the bouquet began trembling in her hands. He must have sensed her sudden nervousness, because he smiled then, and in it was the support and reassurance and love she was going to count on for the rest of her life.

Only a few more steps and she reached him. The brigadier general kissed her cheek and clapped his son on the shoulder then took his seat. As the Island Band wound down, hitting only a few more off-key notes, Yeager laced his fingers with hers and slanted a look at her.

"Thank you," he whispered. "Thank you for being you, for marrying me, for giving me this home."

The sun was warm on Zoe's face and her deep and passionate feelings for Yeager blazed in her heart. She smiled up at her husband-to-be and squeezed his hand. Her love for him had opened up her life. "Thank you," she whispered back, "for giving me the world."

Dear Reader,

What a wonderful group of books are coming your way next month! First, fans of Sabrina Jeffries are going to be thrilled that *The Dangerous Lord*, her latest Regency-set, full-length historical romance, will be in bookstores the first week of March. Sabrina's known for sexy, sweeping love stories. Her heroes are unforgettable, and her heroines are ripe for love. You won't want to miss this exciting love story from one of historical romance's rising stars.

Rachel Gibson has tongues a-waggin'! She is quickly becoming known as one of the authors to watch in the new millennium, and with *It Must Be Love*, Rachel has once again proven she gets better and better with each book. Here, a ruggedly handsome undercover cop must prove to be his latest suspect's boyfriend—but when he begins to wish that this young woman really *was* his very own, complications ensue . . . and romance is in the air.

Suzanne Enoch's spritely dialogue and delicious romantic tension have captured her many fans and *Reforming a Rake*, the first in her "With This Ring" series, is sure to please anyone looking for a wonderful Regency-set romance.

And lovers of westerns will get all the adventure they crave with Kit Dee's powerfully emotional *Brit's Lady*.

Happy Reading!

Lucia Macro

Lucia Macro
Senior Editor

Discover Contemporary Romances
at Their Sizzling Hot Best
from Avon Books

HER MAN FRIDAY *by Elizabeth Bevarly*
80020-9/$5.99 US/$7.99 Can

SECOND STAR TO THE RIGHT *by Mary Alice Kruesi*
79887-5/$5.99 US/$7.99 Can

A CHANCE ON LOVIN' YOU *by Eboni Snoe*
79563-9/$5.99 US/$7.99 Can

ALL NIGHT LONG *by Michelle Jerott*
81066-2/$5.99 US/$7.99 Can

SLEEPLESS IN MONTANA *by Cait London*
80038-1/$5.99 US/$7.99 Can

A KISS TO DREAM ON *by Neesa Hart*
80787-4/$5.99 US/$7.99 Can

CATCHING KELLY *by Sue Civil-Brown*
80061-6/$5.99 US/$7.99 Can

WISH YOU WERE HERE *by Christie Ridgway*
81255-X/$5.99 US/$7.99 Can

Buy these books at your local bookstore or use this coupon for ordering:
Mail to: Avon Books/HarperCollins Publishers, P.O. Box 588, Scranton, PA 18512   H
Please send me the book(s) I have checked above.
❑ My check or money order—no cash or CODs please—for $_____is enclosed (please
add $1.50 per order to cover postage and handling—Canadian residents add 7% GST). U.S.
and Canada residents make checks payable to HarperCollins Publishers Inc.
❑ Charge my VISA/MC Acct#_____Exp Date_____
Minimum credit card order is two books or $7.50 (please add postage and handling
charge of $1.50 per order—Canadian residents add 7% GST). For faster service, call
1-800-331-3761. Prices and numbers are subject to change without notice. Please allow six to
eight weeks for delivery.

Name_____
Address_____
City_____State/Zip_____
Telephone No._____   CRO 1299